Main Attraction

Fantasy World Book 1

Elisha Lark

ISBN 979-8-9933584-0-6

Cover design by **Jaqueline Summer | @jsummerdesign**
Cover Illustrations by **Sofia Ferreira | @fairy_attempts**

For all those who still believe in magic.

Chapter One

Sidney

SOME PLACES DON'T JUST exist on a map.

They live inside you, woven into who you are, long before you ever set foot there. Everyone has a dream like that, a little piece of magic that keeps them moving forward.

For me, that dream was Fantasy World.

I'd spent years picturing it: the parades, the castles, the magic. And now here I was, thirty thousand feet in the air, flying straight toward it. It still didn't feel real. Like if I pinched myself, I'd wake up from this whirlwind dream.

The flight attendant walked by my seat, and I tightened my fingers around my acceptance letter. Part of me expected her to tap me on the shoulder and say there'd been some terrible mistake. This letter was meant for Sidney from Michigan, the straight-A honor student who doesn't spill smoothies on school mascots or cry during math tests.

Calm down, Sidney, I reminded myself. *No one's taking this from you.*

I let out a shaky breath and slipped the letter back into my carry-on, right beside three printed itineraries, a mini first-aid kit, and backup socks. If there's one thing Play-It-Safe Sidney knew how to do, it was over-prepare.

When I filled out the application, I didn't think I'd actually get in. It was a middle-of-the-night, can't-sleep kind of decision, one of those choices you don't expect to go anywhere.

When the letter finally arrived, I tossed it onto the dining room table unopened, like it was just another bill. It sat there for three days until Mom sorted the stack.

The second I saw the return address, my heart nearly flatlined. I tore it open so fast I almost ripped the paper, then had to read the words twice before I let myself believe them.

When I told Mom, she looked surprised and somehow not surprised at all, like she'd been waiting for this moment. She blinked a few extra times, processing, and for a second, I braced myself for a barrage of questions:

"Honey, are you sure?"

"What about your summer job at the library?"

"You're afraid of roller coasters, remember?"

But they never came.

Instead, she smiled and said, "That's great, baby." Then she swallowed hard, her voice cracking. "I'm just sorry I wasn't the one who could take you."

She'd watched me grow up dreaming of that park every single day.

I could still remember when the dream first took root. I was five years old, sugar-dusted fingers pressed to my heart as I watched a Fantasy World commercial. The screen filled with sparkly music, smiling kids, and that castle rising like magic before my eyes.

I'd begged Mom to take me, swearing I'd never ask for anything again, but she'd just given me that soft, wistful smile and said, "Maybe someday."

But someday never came. Not when rent was due and dreams were a luxury. Money was always tight for a single mom doing everything she could to keep us afloat.

But the dream never left me.

It only grew. It became less sugar-dusted wonder and more what some people would call obsession. Personally, I liked to call it dedication.

I collected brochures like souvenirs from a life I hadn't lived yet, memorized maps, binge-watched ride-throughs, and studied castle fireworks like they were a final exam. By sophomore year, I knew Fantasy World by heart, just not what it felt like to be there.

Then there was my boyfriend, Zack. Unlike Mom, he didn't see this as a dream come true. He saw it as a mistake. According to him, Fantasy World was for kids, and I was being ridiculous for moving three states away to "play dress-up."

I swallowed the lump in my throat.

All I wanted was for him to get it, to understand what this place meant to me. I could've explained, begged even, and it still wouldn't have changed anything. Zack never budged once he decided on something.

He expected me to fold, to shrink back into the version of me he liked best: quiet, easy, agreeable. But I wasn't backing down this time. This mattered too much.

When I didn't back down, he ghosted me for three days. No calls. No texts. Not so much as a passive-aggressive "K."

Then this morning:

> **Zack:** I'm sorry, Sid. If Fantasy World is important to you, go. I'll be here when you come back.

All the right words, delivered at exactly the right moment. But something about it didn't sit right, and I couldn't pinpoint why. It was more of a feeling, that low, restless unease you get but pretend isn't there. Like a loose thread on a sweater you know you shouldn't pull, but your fingers keep finding anyway.

And I couldn't help but wonder: if I pulled too hard, would the whole thing unravel?

So, I shoved it into the mental box labeled *Do Not Open* and went back to dreaming.

Castles. Fireworks.

My last summer before senior year. My first real adventure.

The overhead speaker crackled to life: "Attention passengers. In just a few minutes, we will be landing at Orlando International Airport."

My stomach flipped as the plane tilted downward. I tightened my grip on the seatbelt like the strap might anchor me to the sky. I hated this part. The rest of flying I could handle, but landing was too bumpy, too unpredictable.

I scanned the cabin for something, anything, to focus on. My fingers found the hair tie on my wrist, snapping it once, then twice. But the movement did nothing to ground me.

I pulled the hair tie free and swept my light brown hair into a high ponytail, then tapped my fingers against the armrest and closed my eyes until sudden turbulence forced them open, my hands white-knuckling the armrest.

But the landing was smoother than expected. I silently thanked the pilot for not crashing us and slowly unclenched my death grip. I exhaled, realizing I'd been holding my breath like it might change something.

As soon as the nerves faded, excitement took their place. In a few minutes, a whole new chapter of my life would begin.

Ready or not, this was it.

As soon as I stepped off the plane, sensory overload hit. Suitcases zipped across the floor, business travelers rushed toward gates, and families clustered around baggage claim. I even caught sight of a little girl riding on top of a rolling suitcase, her dad wheeling her along like a parade float.

I pulled out my phone and fired off quick texts to Mom and Zack, letting them know I'd landed.

Mom responded almost instantly—*Love you! Have fun!*—followed by a flood of heart emojis that made me smile.

Zack's message just sat there.

Delivered.

Read.

But no response.

I sighed and told myself he was busy. I slid my phone back into my pocket and forced my feet forward, merging into the river of travelers flowing toward baggage claim. I wouldn't let one silent message ruin this moment.

The baggage carousel clanked to life, groaning as it spat out suitcase after suitcase, none of them mine. One by one, travelers stepped up to grab their bags. I waited, and still nothing.

A small surge of panic rippled through me.

What if my suitcase didn't make it? I tightened my grip on my carry-on and shifted from foot to foot. What if this bag was all I had? I hadn't even packed deodorant in my carry-on. I'd become the cautionary tale of the girl no one wanted to sit next to.

Then, as if the baggage carousel took pity on me, my deep green hardshell popped onto the belt. The peeling travel stickers and scuffed surface had never looked so beautiful. I hauled it to the floor, and that's when reality set in.

This wasn't a vacation. I wasn't here for a week before flying home.

This was home now, at least for the summer.

I scanned the bustling airport, searching for the two familiar faces who'd make this whole experience feel less overwhelming: Willow Kistler and Ridley Golden, my summer roommates.

They'd arrived on earlier flights and promised to wait.

The roommate match came months ago via a housing email from Fantasy World. I'd never shared space with anyone besides Mom, and the idea of living in a tiny apartment with two strangers made me nervous, to say the least.

What if we didn't click? What if it was awkward?

I'd read enough roommate horror stories to know how wrong it could go. Within five minutes of housing assignments dropping, Willow had friended me, added Ridley, and created a group chat like it was her calling in life.

We exchanged friendly get-to-know-you messages. Nothing major at first. But I learned that Willow's favorite color was yellow, and Ridley had a cat who liked sitting on her keyboard.

The night Willow sent twenty-seven memes in a row and Ridley responded with a single "tragic," I knew I'd found my people. For someone like me, who usually took months to warm up to anyone, that meant everything.

Between the nonstop voice messages and constant meme wars, it was impossible not to love them. Willow with her bubbly energy, and Ridley with her perfectly timed dry humor. Soon we were counting down the days until we'd finally meet in person.

"Sidney!"

The voice reached me before I spotted her. Willow was vibrating with excitement, waving so wildly she almost smacked an innocent bystander. Ridley stood behind her, arms crossed, expression flat, looking like she was already regretting every decision that had led her to this moment.

I bit back a laugh and started toward them, but Willow reached me first, barreling forward and pulling me into a hug so tight it knocked the breath from my lungs. When she finally pulled back, her blonde bob bounced with the motion, and her eyes sparkled with the same excitement that had practically radiated from her texts.

Up close, I caught details her social media hadn't shown, like the faint dusting of freckles across her cheeks and nose, a detail that somehow made her seem even warmer, even more *Willow*.

Ridley hung back, arms crossed, one brow raised as she watched the scene unfold. Soft auburn waves framed her face, but unlike Willow, she didn't look the least bit interested in bear hugs.

"You survived the flight, then?" Ridley said, her tone dry but her eyes warm with amusement.

"Barely," I laughed, shaking my head. "I still can't believe this. You two are actually real."

Ridley raised an eyebrow. "Did you think we were catfishing you?"

"No, of course not." I laughed. "It's just weird seeing you in person."

Willow looped her arm through mine without missing a beat. "Please. We're way better in person."

"You're more three-dimensional," I said, then immediately winced at my lame attempt at a joke.

But Willow gave no indication she thought it was lame. She just smiled and flipped her hair with dramatic flair that didn't quite work with her short bob.

"I prefer to think of myself as life-sized."

Ridley snorted. "She's been talking about meeting you all morning. Practically vibrating."

"Excuse you," Willow scoffed, pressing a hand to her chest. "I was calmly anticipating our long-awaited in-the-flesh meeting."

Ridley arched a brow. "You literally said, and I quote: 'I might explode when I see her.'"

Willow gasped, pressing a hand to her chest. "Et tu, Ridley?"

"Hey, I'm not complaining. It's nice to be welcomed with such enthusiasm."

Before either could reply, the airport speakers crackled overhead:

"Attention, Fantasy World College Program Interns! Your shuttle is now boarding!"

Willow's eyes went wide, her mouth dropping open with an exaggerated gasp. She grabbed my wrist with both hands and took off toward the exit, nearly dragging me with her.

"Come on, girls," she called over her shoulder. "Our chariot awaits!"

Chapter Two

Cameron

My alarm blared with all the grace of a theme park fire drill, yanking me straight out of REM sleep and into the morning.

I groaned.

6:30 A.M. Too early.

I swiped at my phone, silencing it. The room was still dark, save for the small sliver of gold creeping through the blinds.

With a groan, I tossed an arm over my eyes, refusing to admit that morning had actually arrived.

My eyelids weighed a ton. Calling in and face-planting back into bed didn't sound like the worst idea at the moment.

I could use the day off after too many long shifts on stage. Too many days spent waving to a crowd that would forget me before they reached the next attraction.

It wasn't like they were there for me anyway. They were there for Prince Peter, the charming, polished fairytale heartthrob whose sole mission was to sweep Princess Primrose off her satin-slippered feet and into her happily ever after.

And me? I was just Cameron Scott. Not even fully vertical yet, and already calculating how many cups of coffee it would take to fake today's royal sparkle.

Spoiler: it was more than I had... and way more than any self-respecting doctor would approve of.

I dragged a hand over my face and exhaled. Another day, another eight hours of suffocating magic.

I used to love it. Once upon a time, I got this amazing thrill every time I stepped on stage.

Now? All it gave me was a creeping sense of dread and the nagging question: Why did I sign up for this?

No one warns you that living your dream can turn into just another day job.

Laughter drifted in from the other side of my closed bedroom door.

By the sound of it, my roommates were already up and at it. Bright-eyed, bushy-tailed, and probably thrilled about another day in Fantasy World. Part of me wanted to walk in there and burst their over-priced balloon-like hopes and dreams.

I could tell them it's not all it's cracked up to be. That the magic fades faster than you think. But I would let them figure that out in their own time.

The scent of coffee hung in the air. It floated in under the door, warm, rich, and full of promise, like morning's way of bribing me to get up.

I rolled out of bed and tugged on a T-shirt and cargo shorts, standard peasant wear. The Prince Peter costume stayed locked up at the castle. Management didn't trust us mere mortals with royal threads.

Not that I was dying to strut through the park in full costume, anyway. One wrong turn and I'd be mobbed by a pack of sugar-charged five-year-olds screaming for selfies.

I gazed at my reflection in the mirror. If I were ten years older and carrying a stroller, I could definitely pass as a theme park dad. I gave myself a thumbs up and headed for the door.

The moment I stepped into the living room, I spotted them. The roommates.

Porter was drumming on his mug like he'd had coffee for breakfast *and lunch*. Westley hummed a Fantasy World theme song under his breath, feet swinging like a kid waiting for rope drop.

I was starting to question whether renting them the spare room was brilliant... or a slow descent into madness. But it was only for the summer, and I needed the cash.

"Morning, Cameron!" Porter stood, raising his mug in greeting. A few strands of dark red hair flopped into his face as he grinned. "Guess what I dreamed about."

"Let me guess," I said, deadpan. "Magic? Wonder? Unlimited refills?"

"Wrong!" He let out an obnoxious honking noise like a game show buzzer, then he waggled his eyebrows. "I dreamed about Princess Primrose."

"Is that so?" I asked, not even bothering to act interested as I crossed the room to the coffeepot.

"Yep," he said. "Except she was riding a roller coaster and wearing jeans. It was kind of hot."

Westley, tall, lean, and always one grin away from trouble, nodded like this made perfect sense. "I dreamed I got transferred to the castle stage show with Cameron, except when it was time for me to go on stage, I realized I lost my costume and had to perform in swim trunks."

"Did you do... *swimmingly* well?" Porter asked with a grin.

Westley groaned. "You're fired."

I shook my head. They'd only been here a few days and were already tearing through the park like kids on a sugar high, snacking nonstop, chasing magic like it was air. Today wouldn't be any different. Just another churro-fueled quest with zero adult supervision.

"Dude, I read that if you tap on the Raven's Eye Gargoyle three times, it opens a hidden tunnel," Porter said, already moving on to a different topic.

"That's not real," Westley said, shaking his head.

Porter just shrugged and took another big swig of his coffee. "It's on all the forums, man."

I let out a quiet sigh and turned my full attention to the coffeemaker. The pot was still half-full, which meant the universe hadn't completely turned against me yet. I poured a cup and watched as the dark liquid swirled with a generous pour of creamer.

I could've told them the "hidden tunnel" was just an emergency exit behind a prop door. Cleverly disguised, sure, but more likely to lead to a mop closet than a secret lair. Most of the park's so-called secrets were urban legends, passed around like candy by guests desperate to believe in the conspiracy behind the magic.

But I kept my mouth shut.

Let them keep the wonder a little longer.

"Where should we go first?" Porter asked, turning toward Westley like they were plotting a heist.

"We have to ride *Haunted Tower*," he insisted.

"Nah, man. Enchanted Kingdom has to be first," Porter said. "I want to ride the *River Adventure Cruise*. Gotta start with the classics."

"I cannot handle dad jokes this early in the morning," Westley groaned. "Do we have to start with the most boring ride in the entire park?"

"If you want to do it right," Porter said, crossing his arms. "Then yeah. We've got to start with the best. And it's not boring, Westley."

I sipped my coffee, only half tuned in as they debated ride order, snack priorities, and which stage shows were actually worth sitting through.

Their voices trailed behind me, still mid-argument, as I grabbed my keys and slipped out the door.

Outside, the heat had already taken over, making everything a little more miserable. I climbed into my car and shut the door, sealing myself inside the sauna. The AC wheezed to life after a few seconds of stubborn resistance, coughing out the weakest stream of cool air I'd ever experienced.

I put the car in drive and eased onto the road, merging into the usual current of rental vans and over-caffeinated vacationers. The ones with matching family shirts that said things like The Smith Fantasy Adventure-Est. 2025, like they were founding a country instead of chasing overpriced churros.

My worn employee pass dangled from the rearview mirror, swaying with each bump in the road. Just beyond the windshield, the familiar billboards blurred past, but I didn't need to read them. I knew their slogans by heart.

WHERE DREAMS COME TRUE. A WORLD OF WONDER AWAITS.

Those words used to spark something in me. Now they just faded into the background, like everything else.

Maybe I was a little burned out. Even getting bumped up to full-time, Prince Peter didn't feel like a win.

I was no Rico Ramirez, after all.

Rico didn't just *play* Prince Peter, he *was* Prince Peter. People still showed up hoping to catch a glimpse of him, not realizing he'd swapped castle walls for cruise decks and greener paychecks.

And now? They got me. Just a guy trying not to trip over a velvet cape.

As I came to a stop at the next red light, I leaned back and looked up just as a plane cut through the morning clouds. I imagined the people inside, wide-eyed interns clutching park maps and dreams, hearts pounding with first-day adrenaline.

Someone up there still believed in the magic.

Still dreamed about fireworks and fairytales, about becoming someone special. They haven't learned how fast wonder wears thin when it's on a schedule. When you're paid to pretend.

The light blinked green. I stepped on the gas, adjusted the rearview mirror, and gave myself a nod.

"Time to put on the crown."

Chapter Three

Sidney

THE SHUTTLE LET OUT a heavy sigh as it rolled to a stop.

A second later, the doors hissed open. As soon as I stepped off the bus, the air wrapped around me, eager to undo every second I'd spent in the safety of the air conditioning.

Rows of pastel apartment buildings rose like oversized toy blocks, framed by palm trees swaying lazily in the breeze.

Willow bounced on her toes. "Oh, my gosh! It looks like a postcard!"

Ridley snorted. "Yeah... a very budget-friendly postcard."

Chipped paint clung to pastel walls, and the welcome mat in front of the office had seen better days, but the hedges were trimmed, and someone had taken the time to hang tiny flower baskets from the balconies.

"Come on," Willow said, cheerfully linking arms with me and Ridley. "Let's go see our castle for the summer."

We lugged our suitcases up the stairs, breathless and sweating by the time we hit the second floor. One door after another blurred past until we finally stopped in front of apartment 219.

Willow grinned as she pulled a keycard from her bag.

"Here we are," she said, swiping it through the reader. The lock gave a reluctant beep before clicking open. "Prepare yourselves."

She threw the door open. The interior of the apartment stretched before us as we all three poked our heads in.

The apartment was small but practical, with white walls, beige tile floors, and furniture that looked like it had been assembled with an Allen wrench and a prayer. A compact kitchenette hugged one wall, a cramped living area sat opposite, and the two closed doors likely led to the bedrooms.

Willow stepped in first, giving an enthusiastic twirl in the middle of the living room. "Okay, it's not exactly a castle, but it's cute, right?"

Ridley let out a dramatic gasp. "Wait. We don't get princess suites? Outrageous!"

I chuckled, rolling my bag over the threshold. But before I took another step forward, my gaze landed on something I hadn't seen from outside the doorway.

Or rather, *someone*.

A girl perched at the kitchen bar, iced coffee in hand, golden-blonde waves cascading like she'd walked out of a shampoo ad. She leaned in, exuding the kind of confidence reserved for movie stars and girls who never got mosquito bites.

Her smile hovered somewhere between polite welcome, and *I run this place now*.

"Oh, hello," she said, her voice smooth and casual. "You three must be my new roommates."

Ridley and Willow froze, just noticing that we weren't alone.

"Excuse me? Roommate?" Ridley narrowed her eyes. "There must be some mistake. Your name wasn't on the list."

She waved a hand like Ridley had just pointed out an unfortunate weather forecast. "Yeah, last-minute switch. My off-campus housing fell through. Total mess." She raised her cup like she was making a toast. "I'm Renee, by the way."

"Are you an intern too?" Willow asked.

"Nope. Full-time employee," Renee said, shaking her head. Then she smiled. "So, are you guys excited? I remember my first summer internship. It was so much fun."

Willow's eyes sparkled. "You're full-time? That's awesome. You must know everything about this place, then."

"Totally. Let me know if you need help with anything." She flashed Willow a smile.

"So, what department do you work in?" I asked.

"Oh, I'm Princess Primrose in the castle stage show. You should come see one. They are at nine, one, and five. Just a heads-up: the crowds are intense, so get there early."

A ball of unease formed in the pit of my stomach.

Renee wasn't a newbie like the three of us, but a seasoned employee. Suddenly, I felt hyper-aware of how little I knew. Like I'd shown up to a final exam, having only skimmed the syllabus.

Willow let out a gasp so loud I'm pretty sure it registered on the Richter scale. "*You're* Princess Primrose? Oh my gosh, this is like meeting a celebrity! She's the most popular princess in the entire park!"

Renee let out a soft laugh. "Well... one of them, yes. There are a few Primroses. Some do meet-and-greets, some do parades. But I'm the one in the stage show."

"That's the best one," Willow gushed.

"Fantasy World's big on consistency. Only one Princess Primrose can be seen at a time. You can't have her singing in the castle and then popping up on a parade float five minutes later. Gotta keep the magic alive."

But Willow wasn't listening anymore. She was too busy sighing and clasping her hands like she might actually swoon onto the laminate floor.

"My favorite part is when Princess Primrose runs into Prince Peter's arms and he spins her around. It's just so *romantic*."

"Oh, it *is*," Renee said, her smile flickering. "At least when it's done right."

"Wait," I said. "Why wouldn't it be done right? Is something wrong with the show now?"

"Well, we've got a *new* Prince Peter this year." She didn't roll her eyes, but it was close. "Rico, the guy who played Prince Peter last year, left us. Took a cruise ship contract. Now I'm stuck with the understudy who just got promoted."

"Oh," Willow said, her sunny smile returning. "Maybe he'll surprise you! Maybe he's secretly amazing."

Renee scrunched her nose and took a thoughtful sip of her coffee. "Mmm. Doubt it."

"Anyway," she said, waving the moment off with a flick of her hand, "enough of my backstage drama. Let's talk rooming. There are two bedrooms, so we'll need to pair up. Hope it's okay. I already claimed the one on the right."

After a quick round of roommate negotiations, the arrangements were set: Ridley and Willow would share a room, which meant—lucky me—I'd be bunking with Princess Primrose.

Renee grinned. "Hope you like glitter. I shed it like a princess should."

I huffed out a laugh, hoping she was kidding.

I followed her into our room. It was simple, like the rest of the apartment. It had the same white walls and decor that practically whispered *temporary housing unit, don't get too comfortable.*

The bed closest to the door was already made neatly with a pink comforter with tiny pink roses all over it. Renee's luggage sat in a neat stack beside it, with a makeup case open on the nightstand, packed with enough cosmetics to rival a department store counter.

"Welcome to the royal chambers." She swept her hand around the bland space. "Try not to be too overwhelmed by the luxury."

I smiled. "I'll try to keep it together."

The afternoon slipped by in a blur of unpacking and settling in. I straightened the comforter, gave my favorite pillow a fluff, and placed it just right.

Then I set about tucking clothes into drawers and hanging the rest in the closet. My hand brushed something familiar at the bottom of my bag.

My stack of Fantasy World brochures.

My hand stilled above the stack.

I stole a glance at Renee's side of the room, glittery, polished...intimidating.

Maybe it was better to just leave them buried at the bottom of my bag, out of sight, out of judgment. I could already picture Renee's look: polite smile, patronizing eyes, like I was a kid clinging to a fairytale.

I let out a slow breath and pulled them out anyway, flipping through the glossy pages one by one.

I'd memorized it all years ago.

But now... now I was here.

And tomorrow, I wouldn't just be looking at the pictures. I'd be *in* them.

Maybe I'd even ride a roller coaster.

Carefully, I pinned the brochures to the wall above my bed, layering them like a patchwork quilt of color and magic.

My eyes caught on photo from the latest brochure. It was a full-page shot of the castle stage show: Princess Primrose and Prince Peter, frozen mid-performance like they'd wandered straight out of a storybook.

I'd seen this picture so many times. Never separating the fairytale from reality. But now that I was sharing a room with the star of the show, it was glaringly obvious.

She stood center stage, eyes lifted to his in pure wide-eyed adoration. And Prince Peter looked at her like she was the sun, the stars, and every wish ever tossed into a fountain. The chemistry was obvious even in 2d.

My finger traced along the glossy page, something twisting in my chest.

"That's Rico," Renee said quietly behind me.

I glanced over my shoulder. She was a few feet away, arms crossed, gaze fixed on the image.

"He was the best. Born to play Prince Peter."

I looked back at the picture.

Yeah, he looked the part. Tall, confident, with that kind of storybook smile that made kids believe magic was real. Heck, he made *me* believe it.

"Why did he leave?" I asked.

Renee sighed and stepped a little closer.

"I guess he found something better." She tucked a strand of hair behind her ear. "He gave everything to that role. He put his heart and soul into everything he did. And I guess someone noticed. He was offered a spot on the Fantasy World cruise line. And he took it. He left and never looked back."

I paused. "Do you miss him?"

For a moment, I thought she wouldn't respond.

But then her tight expression gave way, turning into something softer. Her tone was low and careful when she finally spoke.

"Yeah. I miss him."

A beat of silence passed between us. Renee looked like she was trying to decide whether she wanted to tell me more or if she had already said too much.

"Do you think that's why you're being so hard on the new Prince Peter?" I asked, regretting the words as she turned her narrowed gaze on me.

"What are you getting at, Sidney?" she said, crossing her arms. But then her lips curled into a smile and I relaxed a little. "Is this your *polite* way of telling me to cut the new guy some slack?"

I let out an uncomfortable laugh. "Couldn't hurt. Right?"

She held my gaze until something unreadable crossed her features. Then she gave a small nod.

"Alright. I'll try it your way. Prince Peter gets a fair shot."

"Do you have any advice for me?" I asked.

Renee glanced back at the picture and sighed. "Just don't fall for the fairytale and you'll be fine. It may seem like a dream, but this is real."

The rest of the evening passed in a blur of unpacking, ordering takeout, swapping stories about past jobs and life, and dissecting every detail of our upcoming orientation schedule. It felt strange, in the best way, to sit there in my new apartment with people who had been names on a screen just a few days ago.

By the time the exhaustion of the day finally caught up to me, I changed into pajamas and collapsed onto the unfamiliar mattress with a heavy sigh.

My body was ready to shut down.

My brain? Not so much.

I reached for my phone, thumb hovering over Zack's name.

I typed. Deleted. Typed again. Backspaced everything.

Finally, I sent the one word that felt safe.

Goodnight.

With a soft sigh, I set the phone on the nightstand and rolled onto my side, pulling the blanket up to my chin.

Tomorrow, the real adventure would begin.

**

"Good morning, everyone," Willow chirped, bright and horrifyingly chipper.

Across the kitchen, Ridley stood in front of the Keurig, wrapped in a blanket like a cryptid that had been rudely awakened from centuries of slumber. She mumbled something that might've been human language before jabbing the brew button with a groan.

I blinked at her, then turned to find Willow practically pirouetting across the kitchen floor, humming something.

"Why are you so awake?" I croaked.

"I'm a morning person," she said, like it was a personality trait worth bragging about.

"That's disgusting," Ridley muttered.

"Oh, come on, guys. It's orientation day! The day. Our grand entrance into Fantasy World." She swept her arm through the air like she was revealing a magical kingdom, never mind the sad little kitchen with a semi-functional Keurig and three empty cereal boxes.

She was already living in the fairytale. I was still trying to crawl out of the prologue.

Ridley squinted at her. "Did you... did you just monologue?"

Willow shrugged. "Maybe."

She turned that radiant beam of optimism on me. "Aren't you excited, Sidney?"

"I—I-uh—" My brain stalled, unprepared for this level of enthusiasm before caffeine.

Was it too early in the summer to fake an allergy to glitter and disappear for three months?

Her smile faltered. "Aww, come on. It's the first day of our summer jobs. New beginnings. Free uniforms. Unlimited access to overpriced churros. What's not to love?"

"Don't forget the soul-crushing exhaustion," Ridley mumbled.

I leaned against the counter, watching her jab button after button on the coffee machine like it was enemy number one.

"Do you even know how to use that?" I asked.

"I was hoping for divine intervention," she said solemnly.

Willow broke into a laugh. "That's a lot of faith to put in a coffee machine."

With a sigh, I stepped in, grabbed a mug, and pressed the correct combination of buttons. The machine sputtered to life and dispensed the dark liquid straight into my cup.

Ridley blinked and turned to me with wide eyes. "Witchcraft."

I handed her the coffee. "It's called knowing where the power button is."

She cradled the mug and blinked back at me. "Teach me your ways, oh Coffee Whisperer."

Small victories. I couldn't control anything else about today, but I could at least caffeinate the people around me.

I grinned. "So, what's the plan for today? We never actually figured out logistics."

Willow lit up like a light switch had been flipped. "Check-ins start at eleven! That's when we get our job assignments, ID badges, lanyards. Basically, the whole magical starter pack."

Okay. That sounded manageable.

Before any of us could reply, Renee swept into the kitchen, already looking like she belonged on a recruitment poster. Not a hair out of place. Makeup flawless. Regal without even trying.

"Morning," she said smoothly. "Don't you all have orientation today?"

Renee's gaze slid to Ridley, who had retreated, once again, into the safety of her blanket. "Shouldn't you be getting dressed?"

Ridley narrowed her eyes and let out a low growl. "Not everyone's programmed for seven a.m. productivity, Your Highness."

Renee blinked. "It's nine-thirty."

"That's basically the same thing." Ridley waved her hand.

Renee slung her bag over one shoulder. "Well, unlike you three, I have to be at work by ten. You're welcome to walk with me."

"Walk?" Ridley echoed, like Renee had suggested a forced march through Mordor.

"Relax. There's a crew shuttle," Renee added. "I just prefer the exercise."

Ridley sighed in relief. "Praise be to the shuttle gods."

Renee turned to me. "So, Sidney. What's it gonna be? Walk with me or ride with the mortals?"

I hesitated. A ten-minute walk didn't sound terrible, but the idea of showing up to orientation as a sweaty mess definitely did.

"I'll take the bus," I said before adding a quick, "Sorry."

"No biggie. Maybe next time." Renee gave me a tight smile, already halfway out the door. "Try not to get fired on your first day."

She swept out like she had a wind machine following her.

Ridley slurped her coffee. "Well, this is it. Caffeine-fueled capitalism with a side of theme park sparkle."

Willow raised her mug. "To magical exploitation!"

Ridley clinked her mug against Willow's. "Catchy. We should put it on a T-shirt."

Willow turned to me. "You in, Sidney?"

Feeling only mildly silly, I raised my granola bar like it was a champagne flute.

Willow grinned. "Now that's the spirit."

We grabbed our bags, stepped into the thick Florida air, and headed toward the bus stop. Ready or not for whatever came next.

Chapter Four

Cameron

THE MIRROR REFLECTED PRINCE Peter. Every hair in place, every seam exact. But under the gold trim and storybook smile, I still felt like a stand-in. A backup plan wrapped in nice clothes.

No one could see the guy underneath. The one who second-guessed whether he belonged here. At least that's what I told myself and hoped to hell it was true.

The pale blue fabric of my costume caught the vanity lights, giving off a subtle sheen. Gold trim lined every seam, detailed and precise, like someone had measured it down to the last thread. The boots were stiff and spotless and polished to perfection.

I am Prince Peter.

I *am* Prince Peter.

I said it like a mantra. But the longer I stared at the guy in the mirror, the more the illusion unraveled.

Sure, I looked like him. But the boots still pinched at the heel. Like they were molded to someone else's stride, though I was the only one to ever wear them.

And I was just a kid playing dress-up in someone else's happily ever after.

I let out a breath and forced myself to look away.

Today was going to be a long one, and I didn't have time to stare down my reflection, willing it to be what it wasn't. Between shows, I'd be switching gears to help with the new summer interns. Safety rundowns, the usual forced-smile.

I drummed my fingers on the smooth wooden surface of the vanity table.

Then a voice came from behind me.

"Looking regal there, Your Highness."

I turned to see Beckett Brooks standing in the doorway, light brown hair slightly tousled, a smirk tugging at the corners of his mouth as he gave me a once-over.

I exhaled through my nose and adjusted my cuffs. "You lost, Beckett?"

"Nah." He leaned casually against the doorframe, arms crossed. "Had to fix a hinge on Primrose's dressing room. Thought I'd swing by and check on our shiny new Prince Peter."

Beckett and I weren't exactly friends, but we weren't strangers either. More like familiar faces in each other's orbit. We passed in hallways, exchanged the occasional nod, maybe the rare sarcastic comment. He was always around, tool belt slung low, repairing something or other.

There was *always* something broken at Fantasy World.

But I had a feeling it wasn't just loose hinges that kept him hovering near the castle. No, I was pretty sure his real reason had golden-blonde hair, flawless posture, and went by the name Princess Primrose.

I let out a long breath. "Just another day."

Beckett snorted. "Not anymore. You're *the* guy now. Right?"

"Yeah," I said as an awkward silence settled over us.

"Well, good luck, man," he said, pushing away from the doorframe. He disappeared down the hallway before I said another word.

My gaze shifted to the glint of gold sitting on the vanity table. The crown rested on the polished surface, almost like it was mocking me. Daring me to pick it up. To put it on.

I stared at it for a long moment, then gave in to the unspoken dare. Lifting the crown, I lowered it over my sandy brown hair and let out a quiet scoff. I looked like a reluctant prince at his own coronation.

"Here goes nothing," I muttered, rising from the dressing room chair.

I crossed the room and stepped into the bustle of the green room. Cast members rushed by, tweaking costumes, adjusting wigs, and running over lines one last time.

The chaos behind the magic.

I drifted to the stage door, already imagining the crowd that awaited. A sea of faces. Hundreds of eyes, ready for the story to begin.

Chris, the stage manager, walked past with his clipboard tucked under one arm, headset in place, eyes scanning the room.

"We're on in five," he called out without slowing down.

And exactly five minutes later, the door swung open, and I stepped onto the sunlit stage.

The music swelled. The crowd cheered. And just like that, I wasn't Cameron anymore.

My eyes raked over the eager crowd.

Cheers, applause, the gleeful shrieks of children waving so hard their arms might fly off. Parents smiled. Phones rose. Eyes locked on me like I had just stepped out of a dream.

For them, this wasn't just a show. This was a fairytale come to life. Funny how a costume can make strangers believe in you more than you believe in yourself.

I curled my lips into the smile they wanted. The one etched onto merch and posters.

"Fear not, fair citizens!" My voice echoed across Kingdom Square, boosted by the mic pack and a sound system worth more than my car. "I have returned, and no darkness shall ever dim the light of our great kingdom!"

Applause rang out again.

It still caught me off guard. That sound of strangers believing the version of me I didn't quite believe in myself. The way a line I'd said a hundred times could still spark that kind of reaction.

I was the star of the show.

That is, until *she* appeared.

Renee—no, Princess Primrose—glided toward me, her gown shimmering where the sunlight hit it just right. Someone had calculated every angle, timing, fabric, and positioning, all to create a moment that looked like pure magic.

It took a lot of effort to make everything look effortless.

I held out my hand to her, and she took it.

"Prince Peter!" She gasped. "You've come to save me!"

I caught her hand, pulling her toward me.

"My princess," I said, quiet enough to sound intimate, loud enough for the mic. "I would cross a thousand realms to be at your side."

We moved through the rest of the scene as if on autopilot, hitting our marks, delivering lines, moving through the carefully choreographed fantasy.

I barely had to think. I could do this in my sleep.

Then came the final scene. The fight with the villain. The dramatic reunion.

The music soared for maximum emotional impact. Then came the moment everyone was waiting for. The iconic lift and spin. The grand finale immortalized on posters, in commercials, and the living rooms of kids twirling in pillowcases and plastic tiaras.

I braced myself.

A beat passed, then Renee ran toward me. I caught her a heartbeat too soon. Not enough for the audience to notice.

But I noticed. *She* noticed.

It was like a missed chord in a melody I thought I knew by heart. Just a half-second hitch, a breath drawn too sharply, her hand gripping my shoulder with just a fraction too much pressure.

But she recovered like a pro.

Her smile stayed steady, her head tilting just enough. Her hand found my chest, setting us back on track.

The crowd erupted.

And then the music came to its final swell, carrying us into the perfect ending: Primrose and Peter, hand in hand, smiling like dreams had just come true.

Exactly what the audience came for.

I bowed, and I smiled.

I smiled like it was easy. Like the gold on my head didn't weigh a thousand pounds. Like I wasn't counting down every second left until I could disappear backstage and breathe again.

Renee dropped my hand the second we crossed the threshold. The castle doors shut behind us, sealing off the cheers like a curtain falling.

Behind the scenes, the cast slipped into routine. Wigs came off, makeup was wiped away, cloaks folded and stashed without a second thought.

The magic unraveled thread by thread.

Chris looked up from his clipboard. "Solid run," he said, flipping to the next note without looking up. "Cameron, work on the spin."

Renee swept by, tugging pins from her hair without slowing. But then she stopped and turned to me.

"I agree with Chris," she said, dropping her tiara onto the nearest table like it was just another prop.

I blew out a slow breath, running a hand through my hair. "Yeah. I know."

She hesitated just long enough to make me think a real comment might be coming. I braced myself.

Then her gaze flicked to mine. Assessing. Not harsh, not warm. Controlled. Like she was still deciding who I was.

"But overall?" She said at last, her lips curving into a faint smile. "Not bad. You've got this."

Then she turned and walked away.

I blinked.

That wasn't what I expected. Renee was never exactly cold, but she wasn't warm either. Most days, she looked at me with a kind of polite detachment. But that? That almost sounded like encouragement.

A castmate, I couldn't even tell who, gave me a quick clap on the back as they passed. "You crushed it, man."

"Thanks," I said, defaulting to Prince Peter's polished, camera-ready smile.

The thing about playing a prince?

No one ever looks closely enough to see if the smile is real.

***

I stood off to the side as the room filled with wave after wave of wide-eyed, over-caffeinated, hopelessly unprepared interns.

Helping with orientation had become part of my yearly routine. I couldn't even remember how I'd gotten roped into it.

I only half-paid attention as the manager, pretty sure his name was Morty, kicked off with the usual pep talk. It was supposed to be motivational, but mostly, it just helped keep the illusion going a little longer.

It wasn't exactly my favorite way to spend a morning, but I knew the drill. Give a quick welcome speech, answer a few eager questions, and let reality do the rest.

The interns trickled in by the dozen. Some clutched folders and notebooks like they were about to be handed the keys to the kingdom. Others whispered to their friends while taking in the larger-than-life Fantasy World posters on the walls: parades frozen mid-twirl, fireworks bursting above the castle, crew members waving like they had no problems beyond the perfectly pressed seams of their uniforms.

I leaned against the side wall, arms crossed, as the lights dimmed. Heads swiveled toward the front just as the screen lit up, playing the usual Fantasy World intro. Dramatic music, sparkles, and all the over-the-top magic they could pack into thirty seconds.

Cue the soaring soundtrack and the polished montage of grinning crew members, cheerful kids, and fireworks timed down to the millisecond. Same voiceover as always. Smooth, cheerful, and dripping with just enough nostalgia to make you forget it was all scripted.

"Here at Fantasy World, we create memories that last a lifetime. From the moment a guest walks through our gates, we bring stories to life—"

I tuned most of it out.

I'd heard it before.

I glanced around the room, taking in the interns' reactions. Some whispered with wide-eyed wonder, fully enchanted. Others looked like they were barely keeping it together, clutching their training packets like a life jacket. A few were already jotting down notes, probably bracing for a pop quiz on the proper way to wave like royalty.

The video faded to black, its triumphant music trailing off into silence. Manager Morty stepped up like he was about to hand out prizes on a game show.

"And now," he said, gesturing to me, "let's hear from someone who's been through it all. Mr. Scott, want to share a few words?"

I pushed off the wall and stepped forward, slipping on the easygoing smile I kept handy for moments like this.

"Alright," I said, settling in at the podium. "Raise your hand if you're excited."

A few hands shot up, some more confident than others.

"Nice," I nodded. "Now raise your hand if you're overwhelmed."

That got a few laughs and a lot more hands.

"Yeah," I said, grinning. "You're definitely not alone."

I let it hang there for a beat before moving on.

I slipped into the usual orientation spiel. The whole bit about how magic is a performance, how even the popcorn carts play a role in the story, and how smiling through exhaustion is basically part of the uniform. They laughed where they were supposed to, nodded on cue, and maybe, if I was lucky, some actually bought into some of it.

"You're going to have days when it feels incredible. When a little kid calls you their favorite crew member. When a family thanks you for making their trip special. When you see the fireworks from just the right angle, and for a second, you remember exactly why you wanted to be here."

As I scanned the room, I noticed some of them leaning in now, caught up in the moment, maybe picturing those little golden moments for themselves.

"And then," I said, lowering my voice just slightly, "you're going to have days where it *sucks*. Days when you're running on four hours of sleep, it's ninety-eight degrees outside, and someone is screaming at you because they think their kid *deserves* to cut in line. Days when you have to smile through a meltdown. Not just from a kid, but from an entire family. And you'll start to wonder... *Why am I doing this?*"

I let the words hang in the air for a moment before continuing.

"And that's the moment you remember, it's not about you. It's about the guest who's been saving for years just to be here. The kid who believes in magic with their whole heart. The family making memories they'll talk about for the rest of their lives. You might not remember every moment of your time here, but they will."

A few quiet nods followed. Some were wide-eyed, some unsure, and a few looked like they were really thinking it over.

"If you remember nothing else, remember this: you are the magic. You make it real for those guests."

Cheesy, but they ate it up. Around the room, faces melted into smiles.

I stepped back from the podium, letting the silence settle. I scanned the room. That's when I saw her. Near the back of the room, one intern hadn't looked away. Her green locked on mine. Her gaze was sharp and steady, like she saw straight through the polished smile and fairytale lines.

I wasn't the type to get caught up in looks, but there was something about her. The quiet confidence. The way she didn't seem impressed, just... curious. And just like that, every line I'd rehearsed vanished from my head.

"Alright," Morty said, stepping forward with his ever-present smile. "Thank you, Mr. Scott. That's advice every crew member would do well to remember."

Morty's voice echoed through the room, but it barely registered. Something about a break and picking things back up after.

As the interns swarmed Morty with questions, I slipped toward the back.

No applause. No fanfare. Just the prince, fading back into the wings.

Chapter Five

Sidney

THE PRESENTATION ENDED, AND the lights returned to full brightness, shattering the last traces of the illusion they'd carefully built over the past two hours.

"Okay, what'd you guys get?" Willow asked, waving her assignment sheet like it was a golden ticket. "Let's all open them together. One, two, three!"

I carefully unfolded mine while Willow and Ridley tore into theirs like kids on Christmas morning.

Sidney Webber–Enchanted Boulevard Gift Shop.

The words stared up at me, sharp black ink on cream cardstock.

Willow let out a squeal that would probably scare small woodland creatures and children. "I'm a character attendant!"

Ridley looked at her card like it had betrayed her. "Carousel operator. I've been promoted to guardian of gently spinning horses."

"That's an important job too," I offered.

"Yeah. Life-changing." Ridley tossed her card onto a nearby table and slumped into a chair.

Willow flashed a grin. "You're basically a hero, Ridley."

"Please never say that again." Ridley rubbed her temples in slow, exasperated circles.

"Sidney, you're in the gift shop?" Willow glanced over my shoulder. "This is *perfect* for you! **Enchanted Boulevard?** That's like the heartbeat of the whole park. You're going to see the parades *every day*! And the fireworks! You'll be *right there* when people walk in for the first time and see the castle. *Ugh*, I'm jealous."

My lips twitched before I could stop them. "Okay... yeah. That actually sounds kind of amazing." I shook my head, grinning. "Okay, but before I have any more emotional breakthroughs, I *need* coffee. *Immediately*."

Willow perked up. "Ooh...grab me one, too."

"Do I look like your personal barista?" I raised an eyebrow and crossed my arms.

"Oh, come on, Sid. You made coffee for Ridley."

I scoffed. "Yes, but that was an emergency. She clearly had no idea how a coffee machine worked. No offense, Ridley."

"None taken," Ridley said without glancing up.

"Please, Sidney." Willow turned to me, clasping her hands together in dramatic supplication. "You're the best roommate ever. Have I told you that today? You *radiate* generosity."

I sighed, already turning in the direction of the refreshment table. "Fine. One lukewarm, complimentary cup of caffeine coming right up."

I laughed and rounded the corner. And of course, because the universe has a sense of humor, I slammed straight into someone.

A very solid someone.

He was tall and radiated confident male energy, but in all honesty, most of my attention was on the cup teetering in his hand. The liquid sloshed perilously close to the rim, and I stumbled back just in time to dodge a near-death experience by caffeine.

A hand caught my arm. "Whoa. Easy there."

His voice curled in my ear, warm and slow like syrup over pancakes, and I hated that my heartbeat noticed before I did.

I looked up—and wow. Hazel eyes, framed by long lashes, and a smile already tugging at the corners like he was *very* used to people bumping into him and making fools of themselves.

He tilted his head, an amused smirk playing on his lips. "You good, Carolina?"

"C-Carolina?" I echoed, still reeling from my brush with caffeinated doom, and the fact that my heart was now drumming loud enough to join the marching band.

He nodded toward my name tag. "Your hair's covering it. All I saw was 'Car olina.'"

I pushed my hair out of the way and pointed to the missing letters. "Oh. Sidney. From North Carolina."

"Carolina, Sidney. Both solid names."

"Right," I said, crossing my arms. "But only one of them is *my* name."

"Oh, is that so?" His mouth curved into a smirk that was a blend of amusement and challenge.

"Do you assign nicknames to every stranger you nearly drown in coffee?"

"Only the ones who look like walking safety hazards."

"Excuse me, sir. It was *your* coffee."

He tapped his chin. "Mmm... I'd call it a shared near-tragedy then." Before I could argue, he extended a hand. "I'm Cameron, by the way."

I hesitated for half a heartbeat, then slipped my hand into his. His grip was steady, warm, and sent a tiny electric jolt up my arm that I pretended not to notice.

But the tiny, flappy things in my stomach were harder to ignore.

He held my gaze for a beat longer than necessary. Like he was waiting for me to say something else. Or maybe *daring* me to.

I pulled my hand free and reached for safer ground.

"I liked your speech. It was—it was..." I searched my brain for the right word. "Magical."

Cameron raised a brow, and I felt my cheeks go hot.

Magical? Was that really the only thing my brain could conjure?

Then his smirk returned. "Magical, huh?"

I nodded. "Yeah. It was... I don't know. Honest. In a good way."

"Careful, Carolina. That almost sounded like a compliment."

I tucked a loose strand of hair behind my ear and looked away. "Don't get used to it."

Something about the way his eyes shifted told me he intended to do just that.

"So," I said, shifting gears, "you're full-time here?"

"Yep. They like to keep us around to make sure you newbies don't run screaming on the first day."

He knocked back the rest of his coffee in one fluid motion, then made his way back to the coffee bar. Without missing a beat, he grabbed two cups from the stack and filled them both with fresh, steaming coffee. He kept one for himself and handed the other to me.

I considered asking for a cup for Willow, but I couldn't find the words. So, I closed my mouth and accepted the cup with a grateful nod.

"Do you do this every year?" I asked before I could talk myself out of it, because nothing says *charming* like awkward small talk with a guy who smells like clean laundry and self-confidence.

He nodded and took a sip of his coffee. "This is my third year in a row. Someone has to protect you newbies from yourselves."

"So basically, you're the unsung hero of the internship program."

"Because I made you coffee, or because I keep interns from walking into oncoming traffic?"

"Both," I said, tearing open a packet of suspiciously chalky powdered creamer. I stirred it in and looked back up at him. "But mostly the intern-wrangling part. The coffee just earned you bonus points."

"I take my role as intern-crisis manager very seriously." He placed a hand over his heart like he was swearing an oath. "Basically, my life's calling."

"So, you're the crisis manager? Good to know. I'll be sure to find you if I have one."

"I'll be looking forward to it, Carolina," he said, tapping his paper cup against mine in a mock toast.

"*Sidney*," I corrected, not trying to hide the edge of irritation in my voice.

A slow smile spread across his face, and he nodded. "Right. *Sidney*. That's what I said."

"That's *not* what you said."

But he was already backing away, that maddening smirk falling into place. "Well, Carolina, best of luck in the gift shop. Try not to knock over any displays." He tossed in a wink for good measure. "And remember, you *are* the magic."

He turned and walked off, leaving me standing there with a coffee cup, a racing heart, and an overwhelming urge to throw something at his retreating back.

What just happened?

I forced myself to take a step forward and then another, heading back to my seat.

I didn't know if I'd see Cameron again or if I even wanted to. All I knew was Willow could get her own damn coffee.

The rest of the orientation passed in a blur, but my mind was stuck in one place.

Or rather, on one *person*.

Cameron.

Would he be in the parade? Working near the castle? I pictured him handing out balloons, laughing like nothing ever rattled him.

Did I want to see him again?

And then, like a bucket of cold water, reality poured over me.

I have a boyfriend. One who hadn't texted me back.

Again.

But I'm sure there was a totally reasonable explanation. Like, he forgot I exist.

I turned my attention back to the speakers, but their words floated past, meaningless. Like my brain had hit mute.

So, I went through the motions. Nodded when everyone else nodded. Laughed when it seemed appropriate.

Once orientation finally wrapped, Willow, Ridley, and I bailed on the shuttle, opting to walk back to the apartment instead.

Willow pulled ahead of us and stretched her arms over her head. "Ugh, that was amazing. I feel like I've been waiting my whole life for this day."

Ridley gave her a skeptical side-eye. "You've been waiting your whole life for a ninety-minute slideshow about princesses and overpriced pretzels?"

Willow clasped her hands behind her back like she was about to deliver a TED Talk. "No, my dear, disillusioned Ridley. I've been waiting for the *beginning* of something magical."

"Magical," Ridley repeated. "Is that your word for 'telling grown adults in wigs where to stand'?"

Willow lifted her chin regally. "I wouldn't call it telling. More like gracefully guiding with poise and purpose."

"You do realize every six-year-old is going to think you control the princesses now, right?" Ridley said with a mischievous grin.

Willow paused mid-stride, her eyes lighting up with something close to villain-level glee. "Oh, my gosh. You're right."

Ridley snorted. "Go ahead. Let the power go to your head. Start making ridiculous demands."

"You should ask for a crown," I offered.

Willow gasped and clutched her chest. "Genius. From this moment on, I'll only respond to *Your Majesty*."

Ridley shook her head and turned her attention to me. "What have you done, Sidney? There will be no living with her now."

"Good thing *I* don't have to share a room with her," I said with a laugh.

Willow flipped her short blonde hair, her voice taking on a haughty tone. "It's fine. I'll graciously allow you commoners to bask in my presence."

"Nope. That's it," Ridley said, picking up her pace and pulling ahead of us. "We're leaving her to melt in the sun."

Willow grinned, unfazed by her abandonment. Their banter carried on the whole walk back.

My phone vibrated, and I pulled it out of my pocket. It was probably Zack. He wouldn't let this day pass without checking in.

But when I glanced at the screen, it was a text from my mom. At least she cared to know how my day had gone.

Tears pricked my eyes, but I refused to let them fall. Not until I was alone. Until then, they had to stay put.

I tried to push thoughts of him away, but it was no use. Every time I tried to think of something else, my thoughts circled right back.

By the time we reached the apartment, my thoughts were in a full spiral.

As soon as we stepped inside, Ridley threw me a concerned look.

"You're quiet," she said, toeing off her shoes.

"I'm just tired," I managed a smile, but the look on Ridley's face said she wasn't buying it.

"Yeah. Same," she said, thankfully not pushing the issue.

But Willow wasn't as easily deterred. She stepped closer, resting a gentle hand on my shoulder. "This is about Zack, isn't it?"

I let out a breath, already knowing there was no point in denying it. "I'm gonna try calling him."

She nodded, her gaze locking with mine. There was no judgment, no advice, just quiet understanding, and somehow, that hit harder than anything she could've said.

Ridley, meanwhile, had already collapsed onto the couch, melting into the cushions like she had physically given up on the day. She waved a lazy hand in the air. "Tell him I said hi. r don't. He probably doesn't care."

The words landed wrong.

I knew she wasn't trying to be mean. It was just classic Ridley, blunt and unfiltered. But I still bristled at the comment.

They both knew about Zack and, let's just say, neither was exactly in his fan club.

Willow thought I deserved better. Ridley had once offered to book a flight to North Carolina and set his house on fire. She was joking...I think.

But they didn't know the *whole* Zack.

Not the way I did.

The version of him who sent me playlists and kissed my forehead when I over-thought everything. The guy who held my hand when life got too hard. The one who held me steady.

I wanted to defend him. To tell Ridley she was mistaken. That Zack *cared*.

But the words died on my lips. He knew how important today was to me. And still, nothing but radio silence.

I knew Zack wasn't a bad guy. I knew he loved me. But that didn't stop the hollow feeling that crept in when he didn't pick up. It was the silence, the absence, that was so loud. The things left unsaid that made me wonder if he felt just as out of place in this relationship as I did.

I turned toward my bedroom door, phone clutched in my hand, and closed it behind me with a soft *click*.

The mattress dipped beneath me as I climbed onto the bed. I curled my fingers tighter around my phone, like it might offer the answers I was looking for.

After a few minutes of staring at my dark phone screen, I shook my head. This was ridiculous. I wasn't going to get answers this way. If I wanted answers then I needed to ask for them.

It takes two to make a relationship work. This was Zack for crying out loud. Not a stranger. He loved me.

I drew in a steadying breath and pressed the call button.

The phone rang.

And rang.

And rang.

And went to voicemail.

I stared at the screen, blinking hard. I swallowed back a lump of emotion.

Okay, maybe he was just busy.

But I knew that wasn't the case. Wednesdays were his days off, and Zack wasn't exactly the type to go out. He was more of the quiet night at home type of guy.

Before I could spiral further, the screen lit up with Zack's name flashing across the screen.

Relief surged through me so fast I nearly dropped the phone in my attempt to answer.

"Hey!"

"Hey, babe." He sounded breathless.

"You sound out of breath. Did you run to the phone?" I let out an uncomfort-able laugh.

"Just working out." His clipped tone made me bristle.

"Really?" I asked. "When did that start? I thought you hated working out."

"What's with the interrogation?" He snapped.

"No, I didn't mean to—" I said softly. I leaned back, watching the ceiling fan spin in lazy circles. "Is everything okay?" I asked, choosing my words carefully.

"Yeah, of course," he said too fast. "Just... missing you. This isn't easy, you know."

"I know." My throat tightened. I picked at the edge of my thumbnail as silence stretched between us. "How are things at home?"

"Hey, I gotta go," he said quickly and the call dropped.

I stared at the dark screen, wishing I hadn't tried to call him. If I hadn't, maybe I could pretend a little while longer.

Because pretending is the easy part. It's the truth that hurts.

Chapter Six

Cameron

THE DOOR STUCK HARD, like even it had second thoughts about letting me in. I gave it a firm shove, and it relented with a soft groan.

I stepped inside, nudging the door shut with my foot. The apartment looked lived in, which was a generous way of saying it was one takeout box shy of a health code violation. The smell of cold pizza and sugary soda hung in the air.

Porter and Westley were planted on the battered couch, surrounded by the explosion of pizza boxes and soda cans. Westley was half-lounging upside down, feet hooked over the back cushions, while Porter gestured wildly with greasy fingers as he talked.

Porter glanced up and flashed me a grin. "Dude, you missed it. Some kid dropped their ice cream right in front of Princess Rosepetal, and she went full tragic heroine."

Westley rolled forward, flipping upright and nearly knocking over a pile of napkins. "I'm talking, 'Oh, dearest traveler, thy dessert hath fallen prey to the cruel hand of fate!'"

Porter lost it, doubling over with laughter, slapping the arm of the couch so hard an empty soda can toppled off the coffee table and clinked onto the tile. "She knelt, dude. Like, full dramatic mourning pose. Straight-up Shakespeare in the middle of Enchanted Boulevard."

I smirked and picked my way through the clutter toward the coffee table. I nudged aside a pizza box with my knuckles and grabbed a lukewarm slice. "Honestly? That's dedication. I respect it."

Westley gave a solemn nod. "We should all aim for that kind of professional-ism."

Porter raised his soda can in a toast. "To fallen ice creams and the unsung heroes who keep the magic alive."

I shook my head. They laughed like life was their own private sitcom, every spill and screwup just another punchline.

That kind of energy was infectious, even if it was a little annoying at times.

I rolled my shoulders, trying to work the tension from my muscles.

Westley swallowed a mouthful of pizza so fast he nearly choked, then thumped his chest and wheezed out, "Hey, Cam. Who was the girl you were talking to at orientation?"

I shrugged, licking grease off my thumb and reaching for another slice, like the name Sidney Webber hadn't been echoing in my head all damn day. "No idea."

They exchanged one of those silent best-friend telepathic looks before turning back to me with matching smirks.

Porter leaned forward, elbows propped on his knees, eyes glittering with mis-chief. "Oh, sure. No clue whatsoever."

Westley grinned mid-bite. "Yeah, 'cause you're always handing out flirty nick-names to random interns, right?"

Great. So they'd heard that.

I exhaled sharply and folded my arms across my chest. "You two wanna say something, or just keep circling like vultures?"

"Depends on if you're ready to pour your heart out," Westley said, still smiling.

"Nope," I shot back.

"Not yet," Porter said, his smirk stretching wider. "But give it a day. Maybe two. You'll fold."

I sighed, already drifting away. The damage was done. They knew. And now they'd milk it for everything it was worth.

"Night, guys," I muttered. "I'm going to bed."

I didn't wait for a reply, just tossed a lazy wave and disappeared into my room, shutting the door behind me with a soft click.

Everything in my room was exactly how I'd left it that morning: the neatly made bed, the half-folded laundry I kept promising myself I'd finish, and the guitar case tucked in the corner, gathering dust.

My eyes lingered there. I used to play all the time. We used to play all the time.

My dad taught me. Summers on the back porch, his foot tapping out a steady rhythm while I fumbled through chord progressions.

"It's not about getting it right, kid. It's about feeling it." That was his motto. Music, cooking, weekends, it didn't matter. If your heart wasn't in it, it wasn't worth doing.

What would he think of me now?

I was eleven when he died. A heart attack. No warning. One day, he was flipping pancakes in the kitchen, humming some old Eagles tune, and the next—just... gone.

After that, it was like my mom unplugged.

She did everything right, worked, paid the bills, made dinner, but she wasn't there. Not really. Whatever made her *her* got buried with my dad.

Somewhere along the way, I stopped playing the guitar as much. At first, because it hurt. Later, because there was no one around to remind me why I'd picked it up in the first place.

Now it just leaned there in the corner, quiet, waiting, like it belonged to someone I barely remembered.

Before I could talk myself out of it, I crossed the room and wrapped my hand around the neck. The wood was cool beneath my fingers, the fretboard dusty under my thumb. I lifted it off the stand and sank down onto the edge of the bed, settling it across my lap as muscle memory took over.

My fingers hovered above the strings. I brushed them lightly across the frets, drawing out a faint whisper of sound. I twisted a few tuning pegs, wincing at the tinny twang when one string rang sharper than I remembered. Eventually, I strummed a chord—G major. Then D.

The motions came back quicker than I expected. But the sound felt off. Warm. Even. Steady.

But empty.

The guitar still worked. The strings still hummed. My fingers still knew what to do.

The problem was me. I'd forgotten how to mean it.

I let the last chord fade into silence, then gently leaned the guitar back on its stand, careful not to bump the wall.

I sank onto the edge of my bed and pulled out my phone.

I scrolled through my social media feed, but nothing jumped out. Checked my messages. Just a few group chats I didn't have the energy to answer. And a text from my mom, asking how work was going.

I stared at it for a long moment before setting the phone down.

She never used to ask. Never used to check in. For years, it was always me reaching out, keeping the conversation alive, pretending a forwarded meme or an "everything's fine" meant we were okay.

Lately, she'd started texting again. Just little things. Am I eating? Still playing guitar? Still alive, maybe? Like she was trying to stitch something back together, something she hadn't even realized had come undone.

And I didn't know what to do with that.

I'd gotten used to silence. To figuring things out on my own.

Was I just going through the motions?

Existing isn't the same as living, and I was starting to think I'd forgotten the difference.

Maybe it was the monotony. Wake up. Go to work. Come home. Repeat. Day in, day out.

But when had it all started to feel so... flat?

When did I stop living and start just playing a part?

I flopped back onto the bed, head sinking into the pillow as I stared at the ceiling.

Exhaustion dragged at my limbs, but my mind refused to quiet. It kept spinning, looping the same thought I couldn't shake:

Something was off. Something was missing.

I just wanted to feel something again. Anything.

Chapter Seven

Sidney

THE NEXT MORNING I got dressed on autopilot, tugging on the stiff uniform: a scratchy white button-up, a bubblegum-pink vest, and navy pants that did my legs absolutely no favors. I pulled my hair into a high ponytail and clipped my nametag in place.

I glanced in the mirror as my reflection stared back at me.

"You can do this."

Even as I said the words, I wasn't sure I believed them. But it was too late to back out. I was officially committed to a summer of sensible shoes and forced smiles.

I pulled away from the mirror and made my way through the apartment.

The moment I stepped outside, I understood why everyone compared Florida to the surface of the sun. I was already sweating through my shirt by the time I boarded the crew shuttle. The air conditioning wheezed half-heartedly, but at least it was better than walking.

When I reached the crew entrance, I tapped my shiny new employee badge against the scanner. The turnstile clicked its quiet welcome as I stepped through.

My feet seemed to move on their own as they led me down a path I knew by heart.

But as many videos I'd seen, maps I'd memorized, pictures I'd seen, none of them could have prepared me for what I was about to see.

I turned the corner, and my breath caught in my throat.

Enchanted Boulevard stretched out before me, bathed in sunlight and music. And at the far end stood the Enchanted Castle, its spires gleaming like the tips of a golden crown. The air shimmered with the scent of sugar and popcorn.

Somewhere, someone let out a shriek of pure joy, and I wasn't completely sure the sound didn't come from me.

For years, I'd imagined this exact moment. Over and over, in a thousand daydreams. And somehow, impossibly, the real thing outshone every one of them.

For a long moment, all I could do was stare, lost in complete silence.

My hands shook as I pulled my phone from my pocket. This was a moment I never wanted to forget. Now, I just needed to capture it in picture form.

I flipped to my camera app and framed the castle dead center and snapped a picture.

But on the screen, the magic vanished. The castle looked flat. Dull. Like a background extra in its own fairytale.

I flipped the camera to selfie mode and held the phone out, trying to squeeze both me and the castle's spires into the frame. But my smile was too stiff, and my face looked washed out.

I relaxed my shoulders and tried again, snapping another photo. But this time, I just looked exhausted.

I shifted the phone higher. Tilted my chin. Scooted a step to the side.

I let out a long sigh.

Why was this so impossible?

This was *the* moment. The one I'd imagined for years. And yet, no matter how many times I tried, I couldn't capture the magic of the moment.

I lowered my phone in defeat.

Maybe I'd hunt down one of the park photographers later. Someone who actually knew what they were doing.

"Want me to take it for you?"

The voice floated over my shoulder. It was light, teasing, and oddly familiar.

I whipped around, ready to thank some cheerful park guest offering to snap my photo.

Instead, my breath hitched as I found myself staring into a familiar pair of eyes and a smirk that could've lit up the whole park.

For a moment, I just blinked, every word tangled somewhere between my brain and my mouth.

He was dressed simply. Just a plain T-shirt and khaki shorts, but somehow he made it look like a casual magazine spread for "Effortlessly Attractive Theme Park Employees Monthly." His hair was artfully messy, that perfect mix of tousled and intentional, like he'd rolled out of bed looking annoyingly good.

I opened my mouth to say something clever, or at least coherent, but nothing useful came out. So, I just snapped my mouth shut.

For a moment, I considered declining his offer.

I didn't really need a picture of myself in front of the castle I'd spent the better part of my life dreaming about. Right?

Instead, I found myself nodding and handing over my phone.

Cameron took it as a smirk slid into place.

He stepped back a few paces and lifted the phone to eye level. I tried to smile, but it felt stiff, like my face hadn't gotten the memo that it was time to be happy.

He studied me for a second, then lifted an eyebrow. "Come on, Carolina. Give me some excitement. Right now you look like you're posing for a passport photo."

"My name is Sidney," I said through clenched teeth, careful not to let my forced smile slip.

He lowered the phone and gave me a quizzical look. "Sidney?" Then he shook his head. "No, I'd remember that name. I'm pretty sure you said your name was—"

"Just take the picture, *Cameron*," I snapped. "Before I start calling you *Florida Man*."

He let out a short laugh, and I hated the way it made my stomach dip.

"Not until you look like someone who actually *wants* to be here," he said, crossing his arms. "Right now, I'm getting 'mildly concerned mall shopper.' Maybe 'underwhelmed DMV employee' if I squint."

I gritted my teeth, my forced smile stretching tighter. "Just take the picture. Please."

I swear, if this ended with me discovering a bunny-ear filter on my face...

"Well, since you said it so *nicely*," he winked.

Then, before I could argue, or tackle him, he snapped the photo. *When I wasn't ready.*

"Seriously?"

He stepped closer and handed me back my phone. I snatched it and swiped opened the photo app, bracing myself for whatever smug, off-center masterpiece he'd managed to capture.

But there was nothing. Just the same castle shots I'd already taken.

"Did you even take it?" My brows knit together and I turned the screen toward him. "There's nothing here."

Cameron leaned in, squinting at my phone.

"Hmm. That *is* strange." But his expression looked the exact opposite of confused. Then he snapped his fingers, eyes lighting up as if he'd cracked the case. "Oh. I know what happened. I must've taken it on *my phone*."

"Then let's redo it." I stared at him, frustration prickling under my skin.

"Nah. Just give me your number. I'll text it to you."

"Are you seriously holding my first castle photo hostage just to get my number?"

"Is it working?"

I bit my lip.

It was a move. A bold one.

And unfortunately for me, it was kind of working. I *really* wanted that picture.

With a sigh, I rattled off my number. I didn't have time to stand here arguing with him.

I had a shift waiting. Customers to greet. Smiles to fake. Souvenirs to sell.

This was strictly about the photo. Definitely not because his smile was doing things to my brain.

Cameron punched in the number, looking far too smug for his own good. A second later, my phone buzzed in my hand.

The photo popped onto my screen. It was perfect. Somehow Cameron had managed to capture the magic, and I looked halfway decent with an actual smile on my face.

"That was sneaky," I said, but I couldn't stop the smile that tugged at my lips.

His grin spread wider. "I prefer *smooth*."

"Yeah, so would I, but here we are."

"Ouch." He clutched his chest. "Wow, Carolina. I didn't know you had that kind of cruelty in you."

I laughed and shook my head.

"Well, I should get going," I said, letting out a short laugh. "Kind of frowned upon to be late on day one."

Cameron nodded, sliding his hands into his pockets like he had nowhere else to be. "I'll walk you. I'm heading that way, anyway."

He angled his head toward the path ahead, that infuriatingly handsome smile snapping back into place. "Come on. You're in good hands, Carolina."

I rolled my eyes but didn't bother correcting him.

He pulled slightly ahead of me, leading the way. He wove through the crowd with ease. Meanwhile, I felt like I'd been dropped into a video game on Level One, set to *Extreme Difficulty*.

While Cameron glided forward like he'd unlocked a secret cheat code, I narrowly dodged a stroller, side-stepped a balloon-chasing toddler, and nearly crashed into a tour group that stopped without warning, as if conspiring to test my reflexes.

By the time we reached the gift shop entrance, I was winded. The storefront loomed ahead, painted in cheerful colors and practically overflowing with souvenirs destined to become future clutter in someone's junk drawer.

"Here we are," Cameron said, flashing me a grin.

I drew in a deep breath, trying to steady my nerves.

"Well. Here goes nothing."

"You'll be fine, Carolina." He tipped an imaginary hat, eyes twinkling. "Try not to let the magic eat you alive."

And with that, he melted into the crowd, leaving me standing alone.

I took another deep breath, trying to steady my nerves, and I took a step forward.

Here goes nothing.

The moment I stepped inside, I was hit with a full-force sensory assault.

Oh wow. This is a lot...

If I thought Enchanted Boulevard was chaotic, this was that on steroids.

The overhead music was all sparkles and bounce, stuck on a loop that never died. I was pretty sure it'd be playing in my head for the rest of my life after today.

The surrounding shelves were stuffed to the brim with stuffed animals, glittering princess wands, and overpriced t-shirts. Each one was a carefully curated trap for tired parents with wallets already stretched to their limits.

Somewhere near the register, a toddler let out a wail so high-pitched it probably cracked glass somewhere, while a sad little puddle of melted ice cream pooled at his feet. His dad, who looked like he hadn't known peace since breakfast, frantically waved a stuffed dragon in front of him like a white flag.

I stepped out of the way as a frazzled mom swept past me, muttering under her breath, "This place is a nightmare."

Welcome to the magic.

Then, someone stepped into my line of sight. She was my height, dressed in the same uniform, with the calm, battle-hardened look of someone who'd survived countless toddler tantrums. Her blonde hair was pulled into a no-nonsense ponytail, her expression equal parts stern and friendly.

"First day?" she asked, offering me a sympathetic smile.

"Yeah," I managed breathlessly.

"You must be Sidney," She extended a hand. "Becca. I'm your supervisor."

I shook it, trying not to let my nerves show. "Nice to meet you."

Becca glanced toward the swirling mass of parents, kids, and overpriced souvenirs, her smile never wavering. "It's gonna feel like chaos, because it is. But don't panic. Just remember: smiles, patience, and, most importantly, never let them see you sweat."

I nodded like that made sense, like I wasn't already mentally running for the nearest exit.

I could do this. Probably.

Five minutes later, I stepped behind the register, doing my best not to panic while Becca flew through transactions like the register was part of her DNA. Scan, bag, smile, repeat. She was basically a customer service ninja.

And then it was my turn.

The first few transactions were smooth sailing. I was ringing up T-shirts, keychains, and enough stuffed animals to start my own plush empire. Scan, bag, smile, repeat. I was actually getting the hang of this.

That is until I pressed the wrong button.

The screen blinked.

Flashed red.

Then completely froze.

And so did my brain.

The guest in front of me—wearing a *Making Magic Happen* shirt, which felt wildly ironic at the moment—let out a sharp sigh and tapped his foot. "Are you serious? It's just a keychain."

I offered him an apologetic smile.

Don't panic. Don't cry. Don't punch him.

I fumbled with the screen, desperately trying to fix it. My fingers suddenly became useless, and my face grew hotter by the second.

And then—

CRASH.

I turned just in time to watch a mountain of teddy bears turn into a plush avalanche in slow motion.

I froze, torn between rescuing the avalanche of plushies or staying with the customer, who looked one second away from plotting my demise.

Then, Becca appeared like some retail fairy godmother, calm, and clearly used to saving baby interns from imminent meltdown. She tapped a few buttons, reset the screen, and gave me a small, reassuring nod.

Crisis averted.

Except for the great Teddy Bear Topple of the Century, which was still very much a thing.

I moved toward the fallen mountain and dropped to my knees, frantically re-stacking the plushies before they could trigger another avalanche. Becca dropped beside me and shoved a unicorn back onto the shelf like this was just another Tuesday.

I sighed. "I'm sorry I'm so bad at this."

"It's fine, Sidney. This is your first day." She turned her attention to me and smiled. "Let's just say... you're doing better than some. Last season, one girl cried in the stockroom for half an hour. Another tried to quit three separate times before lunch."

I blinked. "Did they actually quit?"

Becca grinned. "Nope. They both work here full-time now. One of them is even in charge of the front window display."

Okay. So survival was... possible.

I stood, brushing off my pants like that would somehow restore my dignity.

"Relax, Sidney," she said, giving me a reassuring pat on the shoulder. "This isn't life or death. It's just a gift shop."

As she walked away, I narrowed my eyes at the plushies on the bottom shelf.

Tell that to the teddy bears.

They stared back at me with their beady eyes.

I turned back to the register.

Okay, *I've got this.*

Probably.

Maybe.

Hopefully.

The rest of my shift was more of the same but, thankfully, went a little smoother. Becca kept a close watch and stepped in when things got too intense.

Just before my lunch break, a kid stopped in front of the register and announced, "My legs don't work anymore," and face-planted onto the floor. His dad barely blinked, stepping over him like it was just another Tuesday.

I slipped out the door before I was tempted to join him in his meltdown.

I stepped out onto the sidewalk and inhaled the humid air. Faint parade music drifted in from somewhere nearby.

I pulled out my phone and scrolled through a handful of app notifications. Nothing urgent. Just the usual chaos: a few Florida men making headlines with their latest antics.

A chat bubble popped up from the group thread I shared with Ridley and Willow. I tapped it, surprised to see Renee had been added.

Fine, Renee seemed alright, though I didn't know her that well yet.

A few messages between her and Willow filled the screen. I skimmed until one caught my eye—Renee had asked if anyone wanted to walk back with her after her shift.

Understandably, both Ridley and Willow had passed. They got off work at two. Renee wasn't done until six.

I started typing out a reply.

> **Sidney:** *I'm off at five. I can wait around!*

The typing dots appeared almost instantly.

> **Renee:** *Perfect! Come watch the castle show. I'll be on-stage. It starts at 5:30.*

> **Sidney:** *Excited to see it! Where should I go after?*

Renee: *Watch from the left side of the stage—better view. After the finale, head toward the rose trellis on the right side of the castle. There's a backstage entrance hidden behind it.*

Sidney: *Got it. See you soon :)*

Renee: *Can't wait! You're going to love it.*

I headed back into the gift shop to finish out my shift.

Thankfully, the rest of my shift was mostly uneventful.

After clocking out, I stepped onto Enchanted Boulevard.

The scent of waffle cones and buttered popcorn wafted through the air, blending with the floral sweetness of the manicured flower beds lining the walkway. Soft music floated from hidden speakers—light, lilting, almost familiar. The kind of melody that made you pause without realizing why.

I slowed my steps, letting the weight of the day melt off as the crowd ahead began to thicken. The crowd grew more dense the further I walked.

People gathered near the castle stage, their faces turned toward the wide stone platform. I followed their gaze.

The music swelled, brighter now, laced with trumpets and fanfare. I drifted to the edge of the crowd, standing on tiptoe to get a better view.

A figure stepped into the sunlight.

And my breath caught.

It was Cameron.

Except... not Cameron.

Not the guy who teased me over a castle selfie or called me Carolina with that infuriating smirk.

This version stood taller. Straighter. He wore a powder blue coat trimmed in gold, a sword at his side, and a cape that fluttered behind him with every step.

He looked like he belonged on the stage. Like he'd been drawn into the pages of a fairytale.

Suddenly, everything clicked. The effortless charm. The quiet confidence. Of course, he was the star. The prince everyone came to see.

He was royalty. And I was just... me. A girl on Enchanted Boulevard. A gift shop employee. One tiny drop in the ocean compared to him.

I started to turn away, figuring I could wait for Renee somewhere else.

But then his voice rang out across the square.

"Fear not, fair citizens! For I have returned, and no darkness shall ever dim the light of our great kingdom!"

The crowd erupted in cheers.

But I just stood there, frozen. Something twisted in my chest, part wonder, part... something I couldn't quite name.

Renee, radiant in soft pink, twirled onto the stage as Princess Primrose. She reached for Cameron's hand, and he caught hers effortlessly, guiding her into a waltz that looked like something out of a dream.

Every movement was smooth. Polished. Rehearsed to perfection.

And yet... something felt off.

I watched more closely now. Watched *him*. His smile never slipped. His gestures were flawless. But there was something missing in his eyes. A distance. Like his mind wasn't there with the rest of him.

Like he didn't believe in the magic he was selling. He was just going through the motions.

The performance ended with a dramatic spin. Renee dipped. The music swelled to its final note, and the crowd went wild.

Cameron—no, Prince Peter—bowed with practiced grace. His smile stretched wider, brighter.

But for a split second, I saw Cameron. Something flickered behind his eyes. A flash of something real. Something raw. A crack in the illusion.

Then, it was gone. He turned, took Renee's hand, and the two of them vanished through the castle doors.

The show was over. But deep down, I knew something else was just beginning.

I came to see a fairytale.

Instead, I saw the cracks beneath the crown.

And for some reason, I couldn't look away.

Chapter Eight

Cameron

ONCE AGAIN, I WAS in a silent standoff with the guy in the mirror.

The greenroom was still. No conversation, no stage music, just me and my reflection. Just the way I liked it.

I'd stayed late to run lines, figuring the empty space might help me focus. Instead, I'd spent twenty straight minutes doing nothing but watching myself. Waiting for... something.

"You good?" Renee said, appearing in the doorway.

I flinched. I hadn't even heard her come in.

I blinked, dragging myself back to the present. I hadn't realized I had zoned out.

But it was no surprise. I hadn't been able to focus all day. Not since this morning. Not since Sidney.

I hadn't expected to see her when I walked onto Enchanted Boulevard. One minute I was taking a walk to clear my head, the next I was watching her.

She was facing the castle, completely still, like she didn't want to blink and miss a single detail. Like she was trying to memorize it brick by brick, spire by spire.

And somehow, I was doing the same with her.

I couldn't look away.

I recognized the look on her face instantly. Classic castle awe. I'd seen it a hundred times before. Kids, parents, couples... that wide-eyed, breathless moment when the magic hits.

But it was different this time. Just watching her stirred something deep in my chest. Hell, it felt like I was having my own moment of awe, and it sure as hell wasn't from the castle.

Everything about Fantasy World felt *predictable.* I knew every shortcut, every backstage tunnel, every perfectly choreographed moment meant to keep the illusion alive.

But this was all new to her. It was magical. A moment she would remember for the rest of her life.

Maybe that's why I offered to take her picture.

Sure, I was probably pushing my luck by asking for her number. I wasn't exactly a master in the art of subtlety.

But she'd given it to me. I could still hardly believe it. Both that I'd asked for it that way and that it actually worked.

She probably should have told me to get lost and flagged down one of the many park employees who would be happy to take her picture. But she'd said yes. The look on her face was half flustered and half amused. I think even she was surprised when she started rattling off her number.

A smile tugged at my lips.

"Earth to Cameron."

I shook my head. Right. Renee.

"Yeah, sorry." I sighed and raked a hand through my hair. "My mind's kind of all over the place."

I turned my head to look at her. She was still in full Princess Primrose costume, gown cinched perfectly at the waist, layers of soft pink tulle cascading around her like something out of a storybook.

Luckily, Renee was easy to be around, steady, no drama. If it had been Gwen, our ever-charming understudy and resident nightmare, standing in the doorway instead, I'd have been halfway out the back exit by now, looking for an excuse to disappear.

"I could tell," she said. There was something in her tone that gave me pause. Almost like she was trying to be understanding, but wasn't sure where to start. "You've been staring at your reflection like it owes you money."

I huffed a dry laugh. "What do you want me to say? That I'm spiraling over the metaphysical burden of playing a fake prince?"

"Only if it helps," she quipped cheerfully. Then, her voice shifted into something softer. "You're good at this, Cameron. You've got the whole prince thing down."

I rubbed the back of my neck. "Yeah, but am I *his* level of good?"

The words were out of my mouth before I could stop them.

"Who?" she asked. Her brows knitted together. "Rico?"

I didn't answer.

"Is that what's been eating at you?" she asked, shaking her head. "Look, Rico was good. People still talk about him like he was the gold standard. He had it all. The charm, timing, that flawless storybook smile. He made it all look effortless."

I raised an eyebrow. "Great pep talk. Thanks. Really uplifting."

"Rico was great," she continued. "But you're not his copy. This is your role now. It's your chance to shine. Show everyone that you are just as good as him."

"Right. I'll get right on that."

"Cameron," she said, her voice gentler now. "You're not here to be his replacement. You're here to make the role your own. And honestly? You've got something he never did."

I shot her a doubtful look.

"Oh yeah? What's that?"

"Heart," she said, without missing a beat. "The real kind. The kind people notice. Even when you're too deep in your own head to see it."

I wanted to believe her. But the doubts stuck, like the finale spin I still couldn't quite land, or the way crew members sometimes paused before saying my name, like they were still waiting for someone else to walk through the door.

A beat passed before she offered a small smile.

"Chris wanted us to run the spin, but if it's okay with you, I'm gonna head out. It was my roommate's first day as an intern, and I promised I'd walk her back."

I couldn't help the laugh that slipped out. "You've got your own baby intern?"

"Three," she said with a dramatic sigh. "It's like herding caffeinated puppies with matching name tags."

"Oof, that's rough," I said with a grin. "I've only got two, and they're already a handful."

We sounded like two parents swapping stories about their kids.

A few moments later, she smiled and turned back to the doorway.

"Well, I'm going to head out." She started toward the doorway, but I turned to her just before she disappeared.

"Hey, Renee."

She glanced over her shoulder.

"Thanks."

She nodded and gave me a small smile before disappearing down the hallway.

I considered calling it a day, just walking out, but my feet had other plans. Before I knew it, I was crossing the room to the prop wall. Grabbing a practice sword, a turned toward the mirror.

I couldn't practice the spin without Renee, but I could at least run through my favorite part of the show, the moment Prince Peter addresses the crowd, just before the final sword fight with the evil wizard.

I faced the mirror like it was the audience. I planted my feet and raised the sword.

"A true king leads with honor, not fear."

The words echoed through the empty room. They were steady but hollow, like they were missing the part that mattered.

"A throne isn't a prize. It's a duty."

I huffed a breath of frustration. Something was still off.

The words were there. But the belief behind them was missing.

Where was the heart Renee was talking about?

I closed my eyes and pictured the stage, the hush of the crowd, the moment Princess Primrose entered—

Except this time, it wasn't Renee.

It was someone else entirely. Someone I hadn't expected.

She moved toward me, her silky light brown hair hung in waves around her shoulders. Her eyes sparkled as she looked up at me.

It was Sidney.

And suddenly the line took shape, spilling from my lips before I could process what was happening.

"Come with me, fair princess."

Emotion bubbled just beneath the surface. I didn't just say the line, I felt it.

I was him again.

But the second I tried to grasp it, to hold it, it began to slip away.

I growled in frustration and threw the sword to the ground. The clatter echoed through the room.

Then I saw it. A flicker of movement out of the corner of my eye.

I lifted my gaze.

Sidney stood in the doorway, lips slightly parted, fingers curled tight around the strap of her backpack. She averted her gaze. Guilt lingered in her eyes, like she wasn't sure she was supposed to witness what she'd just seen.

For a moment, we just stood there, locked in each other's gaze.

I couldn't help but wonder what she was doing here, of all places. Her job was at the gift shop, clear on the other end of Enchanted Boulevard.

And yet, here she was, staring at me with those eyes like she had no idea what she was doing to me.

"You lost, Carolina?" I asked, my voice coming out lower and rougher than I meant it to.

"I—no," she blurted. "I was just looking for Renee. I mean, Princess Renee. Not her real title, obviously, but... she's kind of perfect at it, so..."

Her eyes flitted to the floor.

A smile tugged at my lips.

"Is it the sword that's making you nervous? Or the costume?" I teased. "I know it's a little intimidating, but it's still me under here."

She blinked. "Right. But I don't really know you that well. Do I?"

I laughed. "Fair enough."

Though it was a fact, I intended to change.

She shifted from one foot to the other and crossed her arms. "So, um, Renee?"

I reached for my water bottle. "No clue where she went. Best I can offer is a clumsy prince with no sense of boundaries and a slightly inflated ego."

That pulled a tiny smile from her.

My eyes traced the curves of her face, the color of her lips, and how her cheeks were tinged with just the slightest trace of pink.

My eyes lingered on her lips for a moment longer than I intended. I averted my gaze and hoped she hadn't noticed. When she laughed, her entire face lit up. It was captivating.

And I wanted more of it.

Her eyes sparkled as they met mine, and I couldn't help but wonder, what did she see?

The polished fairytale prince... or the fractured guy behind the costume, still trying to believe he belonged there?

I swallowed hard, heart thudding as I stepped toward her, reducing the space between us to mere inches.

"Sidney," I said, her name catching slightly in my throat.

I felt like I was in a trance, and my legs were moving without my consent.

And she didn't look like she was in any hurry to back away from me either.

She looked up at me, eyes wide. "You said my name..."

"Yeah," I said softly, lifting my hand to tuck a stray lock of hair behind her ear.

And then, like the reigning queen of bad timing, Renee stepped out of her dressing room, shattering whatever enchantment had sparked between us.

Chapter Nine

Sidney

AFTER A SHORT WALK from the park, Renee and I reached our apartment. Even before we opened the door, we could hear laughter spilling out.

Ridley and Willow were curled up on the couch, mid-giggle, completely immersed in some ridiculous story.

Willow perked up as soon as we walked in. "Oh my gosh, you guys missed it. You'll never guess what happened—"

"A dad in cargo shorts hit on her," Ridley cut in.

Willow whirled on her. "Ridley! You *ruined* my story."

Ridley raised her hands. "You said to guess. I was guessing."

"You *knew* the story," Willow said, crossing her arms. "You don't get to guess."

I laughed. "Please tell me he opened with something cheesy."

Willow gave a dramatic nod. "He had a toddler on his shoulders and asked if I wanted to share his churro."

Renee dropped her bag by the door, arching a brow. "Okay, but was he at least cute?"

Willow grimaced. "He was wearing socks with sandals, Renee."

Ridley snorted. "This story just keeps getting better."

"Obviously, I'm in serious need of a distraction." Willow said as she leaned back against the couch. She turned to Renee with a grin. "Alright, local expert, what do people do around here for fun that doesn't involve theme park food or foot pain?"

Renee tapped a finger against her chin. Then she smiled. "I actually do know a place you guys will love. It's called The Dive. It's a crew-only bar for Fantasy

World employees only." She leaned back. "It's meant to help 'keep the magic alive.' And also to avoid... complications. Like, say, a park guest walking into a club downtown and catching Princess Primrose making out with the maintenance guy."

"The *maintenance guy*?" Willow gasped, one hand over her heart. "Shouldn't you be locking lips with Prince Peter?"

"It could be worse. It could be a dad in cargo shorts." Renee laughed at the glare Willow shot her. Then she shrugged. "Besides, the new guy doesn't do it for me."

"Well then, maybe *I'll* ask him out," Willow said, eyes gleaming. "I've never dated a prince."

My stomach dropped. Willow was gorgeous. Would Cameron say yes if she asked him out? He would be crazy not to.

Renee shot a glance in my direction. "Be my guest. But I've got a feeling his attention's already...otherwise occupied."

Willow followed Renee's gaze, and I suddenly wished the floor would swallow me whole.

"Oh, really?" She smiled and clapped her hands, eyes lighting up. "Perfect. We're going. Tonight."

I stepped back, already shaking my head. "Yeah... I think I'll pass."

Willow's smile faltered. "What? Why? Aren't you even a little curious?"

"It's not really my thing," I admitted. "Plus, I have things to do. I can't just drop them and go out."

Ridley tilted her head, eyes sharp. "You mean waiting around for a boyfriend who's dropped off the face of the earth?"

Ouch.

"That's not—"

"Sidney, babe." Renee cut in, her smile deceptively sweet. "No chance. You're not staying here to spiral in sweatpants while we're out dancing with hot crew guys and drinking overpriced theme park cocktails."

"I really—"

"You're coming," she said, leaving no room for argument. "Fifteen minutes."

"Make it twenty," Willow added with a wink. "There will be hot guys."

"I have a boyfriend," I reminded them, though it felt less and less true every day.

Willow grinned. "You can still enjoy the view. Having a boyfriend doesn't make you blind. You can still browse the menu."

"Fine," I said, rising to my feet. "I'll go get changed."

I had to admit, the idea was oddly appealing. This was the first time I'd ever truly been out on my own. This was the last summer before my senior year. And wasn't the whole reason for coming here to live a little? It didn't mean I had to throw all my inhibitions out the window. Going out didn't mean I had to make questionable choices.

It was just one night. A harmless distraction. Something to stop me from counting the minutes between texts.

I changed quickly, swapping my work uniform for a yellow tank top and a pair of worn-in cutoffs. I gazed at myself in the mirror wondering if I was dressed correctly for the occasion. Is this what people wore to bars?

I sighed. It wasn't perfect, but it would have to do. I didn't have time to try on my entire closet like some over-the-top teen movie montage.

I slipped the elastic from my ponytail, letting my light brown hair fall around my shoulders. The humidity had given it a slight wave and I had to admit, I actually liked how it looked.

You've got this, Sidney.

***

After a short drive, we pulled up at our destination.

The bar was wedged between a string of neon-lit storefronts, practically invisible unless you knew exactly where to look.

The Dive.

The moment I stepped inside, the atmosphere hit me all at once, dim lights, pulsing music, and air heavy with beer and bad decisions.

I fidgeted with the hem of my top as a flicker of nerves crept up my spine.

It felt like I'd stepped into a secret club where everyone already knew the rules and I was just hoping not to break any.

Ridley and I hovered near the entrance while Renee and Willow moved ahead like the noise and neon were second nature to them.

"Come on, you two," Renee said, waving us forward.

I took a reluctant step forward as she took the lead. She led the three of us through the crowd with an ease that told me she had done this dozens of times before.

We kept following until Renee stopped at a circular booth tucked into a quieter corner, just beyond the main crowd.

"Hey, guys," she said, addressing the table. "Mind if we join you?"

In the low light, I could make out three guys, drinks in hand. They looked up as Renee spoke, their attention shifting to us.

I didn't recognize the first two, but when the third lifted his head, my breath caught.

Cameron.

My heart jolted like it had forgotten how to beat properly. He looked relaxed, like he belonged here.

The low light above him traced the sharp angles of his jaw, catching in the tousled waves of his brown hair. His T-shirt hugged his shoulders just enough to make my thoughts scatter.

Then his eyes found mine.

An easy smile tugged at his lips, and my traitorous heart skipped a beat. He greeted me with a subtle tilt of his head.

Heat rose to my cheeks, and I looked away fast, forcing my eyes anywhere but in his direction.

"Ladies, I'd like you to meet some of my fellow stage show performers." She motioned toward Cameron. "This is our ever-charming Prince Peter, played by our very own Cameron Scott."

Cameron tilted his head in a subtle nod, but he didn't take his eyes off me.

"Next," Renee continued, "the ever-loyal knight number two, Porter James."

Tall and lean, with a mess of red hair and freckles dusting his cheeks, Porter gave us a crooked grin and tipped an invisible hat.

"At your service, miladies."

"And last but not least," Renee said, "the rogue with a heart of gold, Westley Haynes."

Westley gave a relaxed wave, all confidence and charm. His dark brown hair was perfectly tousled, and he had that polished, all-American look like the guy who'd ruled every high school hallway without even trying. He flashed a grin, revealing a mouth full of perfect white teeth.

"Nice to meet you, ladies," he said, tossing a wink in Willow's direction.

She crossed her arms and rolled her eyes, unimpressed.

Interesting. It was the first time I'd seen Willow greet anyone without her usual spark of enthusiasm. Something about Westley rubbed her the wrong way, and it made me wonder if she knew him. I would have to ask her later.

"Cameron, Westley, and Porter are roommates like us," Renee said. "Somehow they all three ending up in the stage show together."

Westley grinned. "Yeah, we were originally assigned to different positions, but somehow the universe rerouted us."

"Remind me again how that happened," Cameron said, peering at Westley over the rim of his glass.

Porter grinned and gave him a friendly slap on the back. "Fate, my friend, and now you're stuck with us all summer."

"Oh, *lucky me*," Cameron muttered under his breath.

"Well, don't just stand there," Porter said, sliding closer to Westley at the back of the circular booth. "Sit down. We won't bite...much."

Renee laughed and slid into the booth beside him, with Ridley following right after. I waited, expecting them to scoot over so I could squeeze in next to Ridley.

They didn't.

Which left me with one option.

I glanced at Cameron. The only open spot was next to him.

He shifted over, patting the seat beside him. "Plenty of room over here, Carolina."

I turned toward Willow, silently begging her to take one for the team. But she just smirked and gave me a not-so-subtle nudge.

"Go on, Sidney. Sit with Prince Charming."

Of course. Betrayed by my own roommate.

I pasted on a smile, ignoring the tiny swarm of butterflies tap-dancing in my stomach, and slid into the seat beside him.

He was close. Way too close.

And of course, he smelled amazing. Clean and fresh, with a hint of something warm and woodsy that made my brain go fuzzy.

Willow slid in beside me, not-so-accidentally nudging me even closer to him.

He casually draped his arm across the back of the booth like it meant nothing.

Unfortunately, my heart didn't agree. It thudded frantically against my ribs like a tiny alarm bell, letting me know that a boy was near.

"Okay," Renee said, resting her elbows on the table. "Who's buying the first round?"

Porter placed a hand over his heart. "Ladies, as true gentlemen, we would never let you pay for your own drinks."

Westley scoffed. "Speak for yourself. I make minimum wage."

Laughter rolled through the group, and just like that, the night found its rhythm. Drinks made the rounds, conversations overlapped and intertwined, and the steady pulse of music in the background became our backdrop.

Westley and Porter were genuinely fun to be around. Their banter was nonstop, and their jokes had the entire table cracking up.

Well, almost everyone.

Willow chuckled now and then at Porter's comments, but the moment Westley chimed in with one of his admittedly excellent one-liners, she'd just take a slow sip of her drink like she couldn't be less impressed.

For a second, it looked like Willow might crack a smile at one of Westley's jokes, but instead, she stood up and brushed imaginary lint from her jeans.

"Well, I don't know about you losers," she said, "but I'm going to dance."

"You're on your own," Ridley laughed. "I haven't had nearly enough liquid courage for that."

"Oh, yeah?" Porter's grin lit up, eyes gleaming with mischief. "Let's fix that. Think you can out-drink me?"

Ridley arched a brow, clearly amused. "Trust me, you don't want to go there. I once had our high school quarterback crying for his mom before I even felt a buzz."

Porter leaned in, his smile widening. "Now *that* sounds like a challenge."

We watched them head off toward the bar, already arguing about who could hold their liquor better.

"Well, I'm sure *that's* going to end well," Willow said, shaking her head.

Westley smirked. "For who? Porter or Ridley?"

"Porter, obviously," she said, narrowing her eyes at him. "Poor guy has no idea what he's up against."

"Really?" Westley leaned back, still grinning. "I think my guy can hold his own."

Willow crossed her arms, fixing him with a glare. "Yeah, I don't think so."

His grin widened as he leaned forward. "Wanna bet?"

Willow rolled her eyes and turned her attention back to me. "Sid, come dance with me? I don't want to go alone. What if some creep hits on me?"

"I'll dance with you," Westley offered without missing a beat.

Willow shot me a wide-eyed look. "See? It's *already* happening."

Cameron nearly choked on his drink as Westley's jaw dropped open.

"Come on, Sidney," Willow said, pressing her hands together in an exaggerated plea.

"Okay, fine." Before I got the words out, Willow was already dragging me behind her toward the crowded dance floor.

We ducked past a couple who were way too cozy for public decency, then landed in a semi-empty spot between a guy with a blue mohawk and a girl rocking a cheetah-print leotard.

Willow was a great dancer, effortlessly moving with the rhythm like she belonged on that dance floor.

I felt completely out of place and stood there awkwardly, silently praying Cameron wasn't watching.

"Dance!" Willow shouted over the music, her voice barely audible.

Before I could protest, she grabbed my hands and started moving, pulling me into the beat whether I liked it or not.

I didn't have much experience in the dancing department. I hadn't even attended my high school prom.

Zack didn't see the point in what he called a "glorified party." Instead, he planned a romantic dinner on the balcony of his apartment.

It was sweet. Thoughtful, even. But still... sometimes I wished I'd gone.

Back then, it felt like something I could skip. But looking back, it was one of those rites of passage I wish I hadn't brushed off.

Willow's laugh snapped me back to the chaos of the dance floor.

She tried to spin—emphasis on *tried*—and ended up bumping into a guy with annoyingly perfect hair. She flashed him a dazzling smile and tucked a loose strand of blonde hair behind her ear like it was part of the choreography.

That was all it took. I was officially dancing alone.

Every so often, a guy would wander my way, but none of them stayed long. Probably didn't take them too long to pick up on the awkward vibes.

After a while, Willow popped up beside me, breathless and beaming. "You should ask one of the guys to dance. They seemed pretty nice."

My gaze flicked toward the booth where Cameron had been sitting, but it was empty. I scanned the room, searching.

No sign of him.

"Looking for someone?" Willow asked, giving me a look that was way too knowing.

I put on my best innocent face. "Just... looking around."

Her grin widened. "You should ask *him* to dance. I'm pretty sure he likes you back. Did you see the way he—"

"Willow, drop it," I said, sharper than I meant to. "Pretty sure my boyfriend wouldn't love the idea of me dancing with someone else."

She didn't flinch. Just gave me a gentle smile and said, "You've been dancing with guys all night, Sid. What makes *him* different?"

But the look on her face said she already knew, and that only made it worse.

I was on edge waiting for Zack to call, and here I was, basically broadcasting my silly crush on the fairytale prince.

Willow leaned in, voice low and conspiratorial. "It's just dancing, Sid. Doesn't have to mean anything."

I raised an eyebrow. "Aren't you supposed to be discouraging this kind of behavior?"

She shrugged, squeezing my hand. "If he treated you the way you deserve, I would."

I opened my mouth to respond, but then my phone buzzed in my pocket.

I pulled it out and stared at the screen.

Zack Neal.

I looked up at Willow, apologetic.

She gave me a soft, understanding smile. "Go ahead."

I glanced back at the phone in my hand.

What would Zack think if he knew I was here?

There was no hiding the noise behind me. No pretending this was anything other than what it was.

He'd hate it. I already knew that.

Suddenly, the entire room felt too loud. Too bright. Too much.

The music blurred into static, humming in my ears.

And the phone in my hand just kept buzzing.

Chapter Ten

Cameron

I STEPPED ONTO THE terrace and let the door swing shut behind me. The music and chatter dulled instantly, like someone had turned the volume down on the world.

Out here, everything felt slower. Quieter. No flashing lights. No forced smiles. Just me and the distant glow of the city.

It should've helped. And for a moment, it did until my thoughts spiraled, and *she* slipped in.

I tried not to watch her. I really did. But she was impossible to miss on the dance floor, confident, completely in her element. Guys kept drifting toward her, one after another, and I couldn't take it. The way their eyes lingered where they shouldn't. The way they danced with her, like they had any right—

I ran a hand through my hair, jaw clenched so tight it ached.

By the time I pushed up from the booth, it didn't even feel like a choice anymore. Either ask Sidney to dance... or get the hell out of there. Sitting still wasn't an option. Not with my chest caving in like that.

I'd made up my mind, I was going to ask Sidney to dance, and I wasn't going to take no for an answer. But halfway to the dance floor, the truth hit me like a brick: Sidney wasn't mine.

What was I even planning to do? March up like some caveman, throw her over my shoulder, and carry her to the dance floor?

I wasn't any different from the other guys hovering around her. Who Sidney danced with was her choice. Pretending otherwise wasn't just arrogant, it was disrespectful.

She was allowed to laugh, to dance, to let guys drift closer without me acting like some jealous idiot.

And yet... part of me still wanted to close the distance. To be the one she smiled at like that.

So, I left before I could do something I'd regret.

I leaned against the railing and tipped my head back. A few faint stars fought to be seen through the city glow.

I tried to let the quiet settle over me. Tried not to wonder if she'd even noticed I was gone.

My eyes drifted toward the door.

Still, I couldn't shake the thought: what would it feel like to dance with her?

Her hand slipping into mine. Her head resting gently against my chest. The music softening around us like it understood something we didn't know how to say.

For a moment, I let myself want it.

Really want it.

My grip on the railing tightened until my knuckles went white, like I could hold the want back with sheer force. But it stayed. Unshakable.

The terrace door creaked open behind me, and Sidney stepped outside.

My breath caught.

She hadn't seen me yet. Her head was bowed, focused on something in her hand. She lingered in the building's shadow, and I couldn't make out what she was holding.

"Hey," she breathed.

I started to respond, but she spoke again before I could get a word out and I realized she wasn't talking to me.

"Sorry, I was out with my friends and—"

I closed my mouth, confused, until I noticed the phone pressed to her ear.

She wasn't talking to me. She was on a call.

I turned back to the railing, trying to give her some privacy.

But I couldn't ignore the tone of her voice. Every word sounded like a defense.

"I—what? I'm not being irresponsible, Zack. I'm just—"

She cut herself off with a sharp breath, her hand curling into a tight, trembling fist at her side.

Zack.

Her boyfriend probably. I hadn't even bothered to ask.

But a girl like Sidney didn't stay single for long.

"So what if I was drinking? I'm twenty-one."

Something shifted in me.

The confident, radiant version of her I'd seen on the dance floor was gone. Now, she looked small. Like she was trying to shrink under the weight of having to explain herself for doing nothing wrong.

That's when I really started paying attention.

I knew that tone, steady on the surface but unraveling at the edges. The kind of voice you use when you're done being talked over. When you're finally standing your ground, even if your hands are shaking.

She wasn't just arguing.

She was reclaiming her voice. Reclaiming space that should've always been hers.

"I'm going to get off here and enjoy the rest of my night. Goodnight, Zack."

She ended the call.

She stood still for a moment, fingers wrapped tightly around the railing like she needed a second just to breathe.

Then she looked up and saw me.

Her eyes widened, surprise flickering into embarrassment. "You heard that, didn't you?"

"I did," I said gently. "I wasn't trying to eavesdrop."

She let out a breath that was part laugh, part apology. "Don't worry about it. Just... boyfriend stuff."

"Long-distance is hard," I said. "Especially when one person starts to feel disconnected."

She nodded, arms crossing over her chest like she was trying to keep the world out. "It's been rough on him. He doesn't say it outright, but I can tell he hates that I'm here. That I'm doing this without him."

I paused before asking, "Is it always like that?"

She hesitated. "He gets jealous sometimes. Not in a scary way or anything, he just worries. A lot. Says it's because he cares."

"But caring shouldn't feel like you're being watched," I said. "And you shouldn't have to explain your every move to prove your loyalty."

She looked away. "He's not a bad person. He just... doesn't know how to handle this. Me being out here, around all these new people. It freaks him out."

"I get that," I said. "I had a girlfriend when I started here. She told me she trusted me, but every time I mentioned a coworker or made plans, she shut down. Said it was the job, not me. But it still felt like I was doing something wrong just by living my life."

Sidney turned toward me, really listening now. "What happened?"

"I stayed longer than I should have. Kept thinking if I just reassured her enough, it would get better. But it didn't. I was losing myself trying to hold the relationship together. And the truth is, trust doesn't need that much maintenance. If it does, it's not trust."

She didn't say anything, but I could see it in her eyes, the quiet unraveling of something she'd been holding onto.

"I'm not saying what you should do," I continued. "But if you ever feel like you have to change who you are to make someone else feel secure... that's not love."

She went still, the tension in her shoulders shifting, like she was trying to rearrange the pieces in her head to see what picture they made now.

"I've been telling myself he's just having a hard time," she said after a long pause. "That if I'm patient enough, he'll come around."

"Maybe he will," I said honestly. "But that shouldn't come at a cost to you. You shouldn't have to make yourself smaller so someone else can feel big enough."

Her eyes glistened, just slightly, but she didn't look away.

"Thanks," she said softly. "For saying that. For listening."

She took a small step back, already starting to retreat.

I almost stopped her. Almost said what I'd been holding back all night.

Instead, I gave her a faint smile. "See you around, Carolina."

She paused in the doorway, just long enough to make me hope she might turn back.

But then the door clicked shut behind her.

And I stood there in the stillness, staring at the space she left behind, hoping the silence might finally tell me something I didn't already know.

Chapter Eleven

Sidney

THE BASS HIT ME like a wave the second I stepped into The Dive. The air buzzed with music and movement as I wove through the crowd, slipping between dancers and sidestepping a couple swaying together in perfect rhythm.

My thoughts were still tangled from the conversation with Zack and the following one with Cameron.

Was Cameron right? Was this relationship already broken beyond repair?

No, I didn't want to believe that. I couldn't. But one question rose above the noise, louder than the music, more pressing than anything else: Did I even want to save it?

Tears stung at the corners of my eyes. For the first time, I didn't have the answer.

I didn't want to think about it. Not tonight. I just wanted to let go. To feel something else. To have fun.

I scanned the room, searching for Willow. I finally spotted her at the bar. She was leaning across the bar, smiling up at the bartender.

I made a beeline toward her, not stopping until I sank into the seat beside her.

She turned to me with grin. "Hey, Sid! I was just telling Gavin he's officially my favorite bartender now."

I glanced up at the bartender and gave him a friendly nod.

Gavin shot me a friendly smile. "Nice to meet you. Can I get you anything? A drink, a shot, a listening ear to tell all your troubles to?"

"Sidney's not drinking tonight," Willow said confidently, then took a long sip of something bright, fruity, and almost definitely stronger than it looked.

I glanced at her, then smiled. "Actually... yeah. I think I will."

"What? Really?" Willow lit up. "That's the spirit! What sounds good?"

I laughed, shaking my head. "No clue. This is my first time at a bar."

Without missing a beat, she turned back to Gavin. "Bring her one of these. Best strawberry margarita I've ever had."

Renee slid into the seat on my other side just as Gavin set a bright pink drink in front of me.

Her eyebrows shot up. "What's this? Sidney making bold choices?"

I reached for the straw and took a long sip. The first taste was pure syrup. The sticky sweetness lingered on my tongue.

Not bad.

I went in for another sip. This one burned all the way down. I fought to keep my face neutral.

"Yep," I said, clearing my throat. "I'll probably be in full regret mode by tomorrow, but right now, I don't care." I took another long sip for emphasis.

Willow raised her glass and tapped it against mine. "Love that for you. But you've got work tomorrow, so I'm only allowing *half*-regret mode."

I laughed, shaking my head. "Deal."

By the time I hit the bottom of the drink, the music had started to seep into my bloodstream. I caught myself swaying a little in my seat.

The lights overhead shimmered in soft, shifting colors, and for a moment, they looked... kind of magical. Like twinkle lights at the end of a really good dream.

Or maybe that was just the margarita. Hard to say.

"Hey, what are you ladies up to?" Westley squeezed in between me and Willow to rest his elbows on the bar.

He aimed a lazy smile at Willow, who didn't so much as glance in his direction.

"Oh, hi, Westley," Renee offered a polite smile.

He leaned in a little closer, eyes still on Willow. "Any of you feel like dancing?"

Renee shook her head. "I've been on the dance floor for the past hour. Taking a breather."

Willow didn't even try to fake a smile. "No thanks," she said, pushing away from the bar and walking off without a backward glance.

The three of us watched her go, the silence stretching just long enough to feel uncomfortable.

Westley shifted. "Well... that was something."

"I'll dance with you," I said, surprising even myself as I slid off the barstool.

Westley's eyebrows shot up, the surprise quickly melting into a slow, pleased grin. "Seriously?"

A few hours ago, I wouldn't have even considered it. Not because Westley wasn't attractive. He absolutely was. Tall, charming, all easy smiles and golden boy confidence. The kind of guy who probably never had to ask twice.

But tonight felt different.

Maybe it was the alcohol still buzzing in my veins, or the way the music kept tugging at me like a dare. Maybe it was just that I was tired of overthinking everything. Tired of being the quiet girl with a plan and sensible shoes.

I wanted to move. To laugh. To feel a little reckless, even if only for the length of one song.

So I smiled. "Yeah, if that's okay."

A broad grin stretched across his face. "Of course it is."

The moment we stepped onto the dance floor, one thing became painfully clear: rhythm was *not* Westley's strong suit.

He started with a simple sway, which wasn't terrible until he decided to get *creative.*

He grabbed my hand and pulled me closer, then released me and stepped back like he was clearing a stage.

And then... he launched into a solo routine that I couldn't have kept up with if I wanted to.

I wasn't sure whether to be impressed or mildly alarmed, but I rolled with it, moving to the beat while he dove headfirst into a mess of pure, chaotic improvisation. No rhythm. No plan. Just unfiltered enthusiasm.

And then came the arms.

Wild flailing movements that brought to mind one of those inflatable tube men outside car dealerships.

I slapped a hand over my mouth, trying, and failing, to smother the laugh bubbling up.

He caught me mid-snort. He slowed a bit and pinned me with his gaze. "What's wrong?"

"Nothing," I said, shaking my head, still grinning. "You're just... very enthusiastic."

He flashed a proud smile. "If you're gonna dance, might as well give it everything you've got."

Hard to argue with that.

With an overly dramatic flourish, he attempted a full spin, like we were suddenly starring in a ballroom montage.

One second he was twirling, the next he was barreling straight toward an unsuspecting bystander.

I lunged forward, grabbed his arm, and yanked him back just in time. He stumbled, regained his balance, then flashed a grin like he'd just nailed a gold-medal routine.

"Bold move," I said, grinning.

Westley beamed, unbothered. "What can I say? I like to keep things interesting."

"Well, mission accomplished."

He smirked. "I'm just getting warmed up."

Westley's grin stretched wide as he spun me into a twirl. I felt lighter than I had in forever, even when he nearly stepped on my foot. Even when his attempt at a dramatic dip almost sent us both crashing to the floor.

We probably looked completely ridiculous. And I kind of loved it.

But then something at the edge of the dance floor caught my gaze. Or should I say, *someone?*

Cameron.

He was watching me with an unreadable expression. Then, the corner of his mouth lifted into a smirk.

The buzz I'd been riding faltered. Suddenly, I was all too aware of how wild my hair must look, how flushed my cheeks felt, and just how ridiculous I appeared twirling around with Westley.

"Hey." Westley's voice cut through the haze, breathless and laced with concern. "You okay?"

I blinked, pulling my attention back to him and forcing a smile. "Yeah. I'm good."

But then the music changed, easing into a slower, more intimate rhythm. I hesitated.

Slow dancing was different. It wasn't just fun or silly. It was closer. More intimate. And I wasn't sure I was ready for that with Westley.

But he'd been an amazing dance partner. I'd had more fun with him tonight than I had in ages. If he wanted to keep dancing... didn't I kind of owe him that?

"Do you want to..." I started, the words slipping out before I figured out how to finish them.

Westley gave me a soft smile. "Normally, I'd be all in. But I think someone else is waiting to cut in."

I blinked. "Who?"

He nodded over my shoulder.

I turned.

Cameron stood just a few feet away, hands in his pockets, eyes locked on me with a look that balanced somewhere between hope and hesitation.

"Hey, Carolina," he said, his voice low and just a little tight around the edges. "Want to dance?"

He held out his hand. I stared at it for half a second longer than I should have. Then, slowly, I placed mine in his.

His fingers curled around mine, and he pulled me closer to him until I was pressed against his chest.

The noise of the bar dulled. The music blurred into the background. Everything else faded.

I tried to stay calm. To breathe normally. To ignore the way my head was spinning.

It had to be the drink.

Just the drink.

Not the way he was holding me like it meant something.

Not the way the world felt like it had come to a stop.

We moved together, slow and steady. No words. Just the quiet rhythm between us, as if we were the only two people in the room.

Then Cameron smiled, a flicker of amusement breaking through.

"So," he said, "did you enjoy your dance with Westley?"

I huffed a laugh. "It was nice."

Cameron snorted. "That's one way to put it."

"At least he had fun," I said, grinning as we both started to laugh.

I liked this feeling.

I liked this version of myself. The one who wasn't checking her phone. Who wasn't holding her breath or second-guessing every move.

Just... present.

Here.

With him.

"So," he said, his voice just above a whisper, "first bar, first real drink, first ridiculous dance partner. You're checking a lot of boxes tonight."

"Aww, come on," I teased. "You're not that ridiculous."

He breathed a laugh and shook his head.

I let out a short laugh. "Not bad for day one, right?"

"Pretty impressive, actually," he said, the corners of his mouth lifting. "If I didn't know better, I'd think you were trying to make some memories."

I tilted my head, studying him through the dim light. "Maybe I am."

His gaze held mine for a second too long, and suddenly the space between us felt smaller.

Cameron's thumb brushed the fabric at my waist, barely there, like he didn't even realize he was doing it. "You surprise me, Sidney."

"How so?"

"I don't know," he said quietly. "You seem so sure of yourself one second, then completely out of your depth the next. But either way, you hold your ground."

"I'm not always as sure as I look," I admitted.

He smiled, but it was softer this time. "Yeah. Me either."

I rested my head on his shoulder, and we stayed like that, just swaying to the music. When the song ended, neither of us pulled back.

I lifted my eyes to his. He had a look in his eyes like he was warring with something in his head.

"Sidney..." he said, low and careful, his eyes searching mine.

He leaned closer until his face was mere inches from mine.

"Hey!" Then, a voice shattered the moment. We sprang apart as Westley came rushing up to us.

Cameron froze, blinking hard, like he'd just snapped awake from a dream. He ran a hand through his hair and let out a long exhale.

"Sorry to interrupt, but we've got a situation," Westley said.

"What kind of situation?" Cameron asked.

"We need to get Porter out of here."

Both our gazes drifted to the booth where we had last seen him.

Porter was slumped sideways across the table, utterly wrecked. His red hair clung to his forehead in damp curls. Across from him, Ridley sat cool as ever, sipping her drink like the queen at midday tea.

Westley sighed. "He and Ridley decided to see who could do the most shots. Spoiler alert: it wasn't Porter."

I winced. "Oh no. That doesn't seem like the best idea."

Westley nodded, dead serious. "Oh, it was. But I wasn't about to stop them. It was also wildly entertaining."

"I guess we have the answer of who can out-drink whom." Cameron sighed, though a flicker of amusement tugged at his mouth. "Come on. Let's go retrieve our lightweight."

When we reached the booth, Porter blinked up at us.

"Heyyyyy," he slurred, grinning far too wide. "Have you guys... ever *really* looked at your hands?"

"Oh no," Ridley muttered flatly. "We've entered the philosophical phase."

"Which means he's about two minutes from hitting the floor," Westley said.

Ridley didn't even glance up from her drink. "I'm not carrying him."

"You're the one who challenged him," I pointed out.

"I didn't think he'd actually go through with it," she said, finally setting her glass down. "He was talking big. I figured he was bluffing."

"I never bluff," Porter mumbled proudly. Then he tried to sit up straighter and nearly face-planted into the table.

Cameron caught him by the shoulders.

"Okay," Westley said, clapping his hands once. "Let's get him out of here before he adds 'banned from The Dive' to his resume."

Cameron hooked one of Porter's arms over his shoulder and hauled him upright. Westley stepped in without a word, slipping under the other side to help steady him.

"Think you can grab the door?" Westley asked me.

I nodded and turned toward the exit. I held the door open while the three of them stumbled into the parking lot.

Porter mumbled something unintelligible, head bobbing between Cameron and Westley as they half-carried him toward the curb. Ridley trailed behind with zero urgency, scrolling her phone like none of this involved her.

Cameron and Westley lowered him to a sitting position on the curb.

"I'll go get the car," Cameron said and disappeared into the parking lot.

Ridley pulled out her phone and snapped a photo. "Nice look, champ. Real strong finish."

Porter let out a dramatic groan and flopped his head against Westley's shoulder. "If you wanted a picture, you could have asked."

"No thanks," Ridley said with a sweet smile. "It's more fun this way."

"Do you think they'd let me sleep in the castle?" he slurred. "I want to be a princess."

Westley rolled his eyes. "You'd get kicked out before you hit the drawbridge."

"Worth a shot," Porter mumbled.

A pair of headlights swung into view as Cameron pulled up.

He jumped out of the driver's seat and circled around to help Westley wrangle Porter into the back.

Porter collapsed onto the seat with a groan, and Westley leaned in to buckle him up like a very drunk, very uncooperative toddler.

Cameron turned to me, brushing a hand through his hair, a little breathless, a little amused. "Well...that was something."

"Definitely something," I said, smiling despite myself.

We stood there for a beat too long, the sounds of the bar fading behind us, the streetlights casting a soft glow over everything.

It wasn't a perfect night.

But somehow, it was still kind of magical.

"Thanks for the dance."

I nodded. "Thanks for asking."

He circled around to the driver's side and slid behind the wheel.

I watched as the taillights faded into the dark.

Chapter Twelve

Cameron

"SHOULD WE CHECK HIS pulse, or just assume the snoring means he's alive?"

Westley didn't even look at me as he said it, arm hanging out the open window, wind tugging at his already-messy hair.

Porter was dead to the world in the backseat, snoring like a chainsaw, cheek smashed against the glass.

I reached for the AC dial and cranked it up, hoping the cold air might shock some life back into him. No luck. He just burrowed deeper into the door like a particularly stubborn hibernating bear.

I didn't answer right away.

Because while Porter's snoring filled the car, all I could hear was her laugh.

"You're awfully quiet over there," Westley said, nudging my hand. "Thinking about Carolina?"

I shot Westley a look. "Her name is Sidney."

He smirked. "So that's a yes."

I let out a slow exhale and tightened my grip on the steering wheel.

Behind us, Porter snorted awake just long enough to mumble something about pancakes and world peace before slumping back into unconsciousness.

Westley chuckled. "He's going to hate himself in the morning."

Silence settled over the car.

Then Westley, as casual as ever, said, "You know the whole boyfriend thing isn't really a thing, right?"

That made me glance over. "What are you talking about?"

He raised one shoulder in a casual shrug.

"Even while we were dancing," Westley said, "she kept doing that thing, you know, pretending not to look for you. Which, by rom-com logic, means she was absolutely looking for you."

"This isn't a movie, Westley," I muttered. "And she has a boyfriend."

"Yeah, and I have a cactus at home that's definitely dead because I forgot to water it."

I gave him a look. "What's your point?"

He sighed like *I* was the slow one. "My point is, things die when they're neglected. If something isn't cared for, if it's ignored long enough, it doesn't survive. Relationships included. And from my point of view, Sidney doesn't look like she's been watered in quite sometime."

I let out an exasperated sigh, "Sidney's not a cactus."

Westley waved a hand. "Fine. She can be a flower or a fern. Whatever you want her to be."

"That's not—" I let out a long sigh. There was no point in arguing, and actually Westley was starting to make sense.

I'd heard part of that phone call. I'd heard the way her voice cracked. The way she tried to sound fine when she clearly wasn't.

Sidney wasn't acting like someone in love. She sounded stressed. Hurt. Like she was trying to hold something together that had already started to fall apart.

"She's all yours," Westley said. "Even if neither of you's ready to admit it."

I kept my eyes on the road. "You don't know that."

He shrugged. "Maybe. But the way she looked at you on that dance floor? Yeah, I'd bet on it."

Something shifted in my chest.

I hadn't let myself think too far ahead. Hadn't let myself *hope.*

But now?

Now I wasn't so sure it was all in my head.

And that one reckless thought, that *maybe* she felt it too, was enough to knock everything off balance.

***

The next morning, I stepped into the green room and instantly regretted it.

How had I forgotten it was a Gwen day?

She was already in full Princess Primrose mode. Her gown was flawless, her crown perfectly in place, arms crossed like she had been practicing royal judgment since kindergarten.

She looked up and smiled. Not the friendly kind. The kind she wore right before slicing someone apart with a glitter-dipped knife.

"Well, well. If it isn't Fantasy World's favorite prince," she said in a voice dripping with sugar laced venom. "You look tired. Rough night saving the kingdom?"

"Morning to you too, Gwen," I said, forcing a smile and resisting the urge to roll my eyes.

She fluttered her lashes. "I love when you bring that moody, brooding energy to the fairytale. Really keeps the dream alive."

I resisted the urge to bang my head against the nearest wall.

Gwen days were always long. Full of sarcasm, passive-aggressive digs, and a running commentary on every mistake I made, helpfully pointed out, of course.

The first hour passed in a blur, and for the most part, she kept her distance, turning her attention to some other poor soul. But that peace ended when we lined up backstage, waiting to take our places.

She gave me a slow once-over, like I was something unpleasant she'd just stepped in.

"What do you want, Gwen?"

She gasped softly, all wide eyes and fake innocence. "What do you mean, Cameron? I'm just going to my mark. Believe it or not, the show doesn't revolve around you."

I bit my tongue. She was trying to get into my head. We both knew it.

I wasn't about to give her the satisfaction.

"You know," she said, flashing a sugary smile, "your crown's crooked. But it kind of works. Gives Prince Peter that rugged, slightly unhinged vibe. Very you."

I adjusted it without looking at her. "Gwen, your passive aggression is showing."

She let out a bright, fake laugh. "But, Cameron, I'm just trying to help."

The music swelled, and Chris gave me the signal. I was grateful for the excuse to step away.

I walked out onto the sunlit stage. The crowd spread across the courtyard. Parents clustered in the shade, kids bouncing with excitement, phones already raised to capture the moment.

I launched into my opening lines, voice steady and confident. The kids in the front row lit up, shouting my name like I was someone real. Someone they *knew*. For a moment, everything else fell away. Just me, the story, and the magic of it all, exactly how it was supposed to feel.

The first act moved like clockwork.

Then Gwen appeared.

She hit her mark with that too-bright smile, her crown catching the sunlight at the perfect angle. The audience adored her. They always did. But the second she spoke, I knew she was going to make me work for it.

Her timing was just barely off, but it was enough to throw off the rhythm. Her cue came. She hesitated, like she'd forgotten it, then delivered the line with so much forced enthusiasm the kids in the front row squealed.

Cute.

She grinned at me. That was no mistake. She messed that up on purpose.

I shifted slightly to recover, gave my next line with a bit more energy.

I tried to refocus. Tried not to let her get under my skin.

When I offered my hand for our usual turn, she took it, then switched at the last second, reaching with the wrong one.

My fingers closed around air.

I recovered quickly, grabbing her elbow like that had been the plan all along. She smoothed over the stumble with a graceful twirl and tossed a playful wink to the crowd. The front row giggled, enchanted.

They didn't see the mistake.

But I did.

From there, she nailed every line. Hit every mark. Picture perfect.

Until the final spin.

I turned, ready for her cue, but she was already sprinting toward me, faster than rehearsed.

I barely had time to react. My hands fumbled to find her waist, but the sudden momentum threw me off. My heel scraped against the stage as I staggered back.

For a breathless second, my grip slipped.

She tilted in my arms, just enough to send panic crashing through my chest. I was going to drop her. Right here. Onstage. In front of a packed courtyard filled with kids, parents, and phone cameras.

I locked my arms and shifted fast, muscles straining to catch her weight and steady myself.

We landed the move technically, but it was awkward and slightly off-balance. I set her down harder than I meant to, and the moment passed like nothing had happened.

Except my heart was still pounding with a mess of adrenaline and barely suppressed anger.

The applause rose around us.

Gwen beamed at the audience, dipping into a picture-perfect curtsy like nothing had gone wrong.

She was the star of the show. And she made damn sure everyone knew it.

Chapter Thirteen

Sidney

THE NEXT MORNING, I woke with a dull throb in my temples.

It wasn't a hangover, but my body felt like I'd run a marathon in stilettos.

I stayed in bed for a while, staring at the ceiling. When I finally glanced at Renee's side of the room, her bed was already empty. Perfectly made, of course, as if she'd never slept there at all.

I reached for my phone. One unread message.

Zack: *Call me when you're done ignoring me.*

That was it.

No *Sorry about last night.*

No *I shouldn't have snapped.*

Not even a lazy *I miss you.*

Just a command. Like checking in with him was some task I'd failed.

My jaw tightened as I swiped to the next message.

> **Renee:** *Day off. Headed into town to run errands. Hope your regrets are minimal.*

A small smile tugged at my lips.

That was the thing, I didn't regret it.

Flashes from last night played through my mind like a music video on loop, the bass thumping against my chest, lights spinning in soft blurs, the rush of movement as I danced blindly, without holding back.

I had spent so much time shrinking myself to fit inside the lines, saying the right things, being the right kind of girl. The one who kept the peace. The one who didn't make waves.

But here, no one knew me. No one had expectations or history or versions of me to compare against. And for the first time in a long time, I felt free to just be me.

Then came the phone call.

Zack's voice, sharp and impatient, had dragged me right back to earth. Back to the version of me he preferred. Predictable. Polished. Easy to manage. He liked girls who smiled at the right times, who didn't ask too many questions, who didn't surprise him.

He liked predictable.

They say absence makes the heart grow fonder. If that was true, then what did that say about us?

It hadn't even been a full week since I last saw him. I thought I'd be counting down the hours. I thought I'd still feel that pull, like something was missing.

But the only thing I felt was the space I had stepped into and how much lighter it felt without him in it.

I tossed my phone onto the nightstand and swung my legs over the edge. The floor was cool beneath my feet.

I dressed quickly, pulling on my work uniform and fastening my nametag in place. Another day, another attempt at pretending I knew what I was doing.

Hopefully, this shift would go better than the last one.

The odds had to be in my favor. I had experience now.

Okay... just one day of it. But still. That had to count for something. Right?

I grabbed my bag, slipped on my sneakers, and left the apartment before I could second-guess myself.

Fifteen minutes later, I stepped off the shuttle and walked toward the gates of Fantasy World.

The sun was already scorching and bearing down on me as I headed down Enchanted Boulevard. I could practically feel the heat rising from the pavement.

The sun was already blistering, beating down on the brick path as I made my way along Enchanted Boulevard. Heat shimmered off the pavement, rising through the soles of my shoes. The crowd was already thickening. Parents with strollers, kids buzzing with excitement, everyone sweating before the real fun even started. I didn't envy them. At least I got to spend part of the day in air conditioning.

Upbeat park music drifted through hidden speakers, too cheerful for how loud my thoughts were this morning. I paused for a moment, letting the atmosphere settle around me, sunlight, color, the smell of sugar and sunscreen.

And without thinking, my eyes scanned the crowd for him.

Cameron.

I caught myself and looked away, scolding the flutter in my chest. I had no business looking for him. Not with my relationship already dangling by a thread. The last thing I needed was to pour gasoline on the dumpster fire that was my love life.

But I couldn't stop replaying what he'd said to me on the terrace last night.

My first instinct was to push back, to tell him he was mistaken. That Zack and I had a history. That relationships take work, and you don't just walk away when things get hard. But every argument I came up with felt thin. Weak. Like ash dissolving on my tongue.

And the way Cameron had looked at me, there was no challenge in his eyes. No judgment.

Just quiet understanding.

Like he knew exactly how I felt.

And when we danced, it had felt effortless. Natural. Like every twist and turn of my past had somehow led me to that one moment. To *him*.

The thought hit too hard, and guilt surged in its wake. I shoved it down.

Focus.

The gift shop came into view, and I forced myself into work mode. Straight spine, neutral expression, thoughts tucked safely away.

Becca was already behind the counter when I walked in, tying her apron with military precision.

She gave me a quick once-over. "Rough night?"

I stretched and offered a weak smile. "Let's just say sleep and I weren't on speaking terms."

"Yikes." She handed me the morning task list. "Well, caffeine's in the break-room and the chaos starts in about twenty minutes."

I groaned.

Becca smirked. "You up for it?"

I nodded, even though part of me wanted to crawl back into bed and stay there until the end of summer.

The morning rush didn't hit quite as hard today.

Somehow, I'd found the rhythm. The steady pulse of customers, the chatter, the whir of the register. I moved through it all with ease.

I could answer questions without second-guessing. I could bag glittery wands and plush dragons without fumbling or dropping anything.

So when a guy in a neon Hawaiian shirt sighed like I was personally ruining his vacation over a keychain, I didn't even blink.

I just smiled. "Almost done, sir."

Becca passed behind me, smirking as she flashed a thumbs-up like she was proud of me for not committing retail-based homicide.

I slipped the receipt into his bag, still smiling.

Maybe I was actually getting the hang of this.

Between customers, I took a step back, pressing my palms to the counter and drawing in a quiet breath.

The front of the shop was a wall of glass, offering a wide, uninterrupted view of Enchanted Boulevard.

It looked like a postcard brought to life, all motion and music and magic.

A little girl twirled near the entrance, no more than six or seven, her pink princess dress spinning around her in a cloud of tulle and glitter. She threw her arms out as she turned, completely lost in her own fairytale. Her parents stood a few steps back, phones raised, trying to freeze the magic in time before it slipped through their fingers.

Something in my chest tugged.

I was once that little girl, spinning in front of a digital castle on my TV screen.

From inside the gift shop, I could hear the faint notes of the parade drifting through the air. Outside, people were already gathering along the sidewalks, waiting for the first float to appear.

It was magic.

Not the kind found in glitter or costumes or even the music itself.

It was the kind that lived in the little things. The way a child's eyes widened over something as simple as a stuffed dragon. The way a family's laughter tangled with the music. The way a place like this could make you forget everything else and feel weightless, if only for a moment.

And standing there behind the counter, I felt it too.

That quiet certainty.

I was exactly where I was meant to be.

It didn't matter if anyone else understood. Not Zack. Not anyone.

For the first time in a long time, I didn't need anyone's permission to feel happy.

I just *was*.

Then Becca appeared beside me, clipboard in hand.

"You've been on your feet all day," she said, her tone casual but kind. "Why don't you go ahead and clock out a little early?"

I blinked. "Are you sure? I still have—"

She waved me off. "We've got it covered. Go enjoy the park for a bit. You've earned it."

For a second, I just stood there, surprised by the offer.

"Thanks," I said, already feeling the weight start to lift.

She gave me a nod and turned back toward the register.

A few minutes later, I stepped outside, the warm glow of early evening washing over me. The air buzzed with music and laughter, and for the first time all day, I wasn't thinking about what came next.

My eyes drifted toward the castle.

On a normal day, I'd be heading that way to meet up with Renee after our shift. But today was her day off.

I could go home. Call it early. Change into pajamas, curl up with popcorn, and put on some feel-good rom-com. A quiet end to a long day.

But Becca had told me to leave early and actually enjoy the park. The idea had its appeal. When was the last time I did anything here that wasn't work-related?

Before I could talk myself out of it, I turned left down Enchanted Boulevard, heading toward the castle.

The parade was in full swing now. Dancers in sequined costumes twirled along the path, their outfits catching the sunlight like stardust. Music filled the air, lively, sparkling, a soundtrack for magic.

Behind them rolled the lead float: a golden carriage draped in velvet banners and woven with ivy. Standing tall atop it were Princess Rosepetal and Prince Callum, waving like royalty to the crowd below.

I didn't stop to watch. I just kept walking, letting the music and movement wash over me.

I wandered through Kingdom Square, the buzz of the parade still humming in the distance, until I spotted a small coffee stand tucked beneath the shade of a sprawling tree. It was half-hidden, like a secret waiting to be discovered.

The scent hit me first. Warm, rich espresso with a hint of vanilla. Suddenly, coffee felt less like a want and more like a *need*.

There was no line. Just the quiet hiss of the espresso machine and the rustle of leaves above.

The menu was nailed to a crooked wooden post, written in a storybook font that curled like vines. Even the simple task of ordering coffee felt enchanted. Every drink had a whimsical name, like "Royal Wake-Up" or "Dragon's Brew."

I ordered an iced mocha latte with oat milk. My favorite.

The barista handed it over with a smile, the cup wrapped in a sleeve that read: *A little cup of magic.*

I took a slow sip.

The cold hit first, followed by the sweet, chocolatey comfort I'd been craving. I closed my eyes for just a second, letting it ground me.

For the first time all day, I wasn't working. I wasn't rushing.

I was just... here.

A sharp voice cut through the air, yanking me out of the moment like nails dragging across a chalkboard.

I turned instinctively, the harshness setting me on edge. My eyes locked onto the source and I froze.

Renee?

"You have to do it *right!*" the woman snapped, spinning around in frustration.

But it wasn't Renee.

She wore the same pink and gold Princess Primrose gown, her crown glinting in the sun, but the posture was different. Stiffer. Harsher. This had to be the understudy, Gwen.

I looked away.

I didn't know who she was yelling at, and I didn't want to find out. Tension flared all the time behind the scenes at Fantasy World. Long hours, heavy costumes, blazing heat, it wore people down.

This wasn't the first argument I'd overheard, and it probably wouldn't be the last.

But then Gwen shifted, and I saw who she was talking to.

Cameron.

I took an instinctive step forward before I could stop myself.

He stood with his arms crossed, his expression somewhere between unimpressed and completely over it. Whatever patience he had left was hanging by a thread.

"It's really not that complicated," Gwen said, flipping her hair. "Maybe if you can't handle a simple spin, they should just bring Rico back."

He didn't react, not outwardly, but something in his eyes went cold.

"Maybe," he said, voice low and steady, "you should remember that performers in full costume aren't supposed to be arguing in front of guests."

Her lips twitched, like she wanted to fire back, but didn't.

Cameron stepped aside and nodded toward the nearby crew-only gate. "Unless you'd rather explain it to management. Again."

I stood frozen, fingers tightening around my drink, caught between the urge to disappear quietly... or start slow-clapping like I was watching live theater.

Gwen shot him a glare before spinning on her heel and sauntering off.

Cameron exhaled hard, muttering something under his breath I couldn't quite catch. He dragged a hand across the back of his neck, then turned and made a beeline for the coffee stand.

I lifted my cup and took a slow sip, eyes following him as he approached the counter.

He leaned in, bracing both hands on the edge of the stand. His shoulders were tense, jaw locked tight.

The barista greeted him with a bright smile, but Cameron didn't even glance up.

"Large black coffee," he said, voice low and clipped.

"$4.25," the barista replied with an easy nod.

Cameron slid his card across the counter, barely blinking. A moment later, the barista passed him a plain white cup.

He took it without a word.

"Girl trouble?" I asked, lifting my cup.

He blinked, like he hadn't noticed me standing there. His eyes met mine, something flickering behind them, surprise, maybe. Recognition. Then came the smirk.

Slow. Effortless. Dangerous.

It should've come with a warning label, because the second it hit me, my stomach did a traitorous little flip.

He nodded toward the small seating area beside the stand, raising a brow. "You got a few minutes? I could use company from someone who *doesn't* think I'm the villain in this story."

"Bold of you to assume that's not exactly what I think," I said, taking a slow sip, letting my gaze linger just long enough to make my point.

His smile deepened. He leaned in, voice dropping low. "If you *do* think I'm the villain, then I'll let you in on a little secret. We make much better company."

He waggled his eyebrows and a smile tugged at my lips before I could stop it.

I nodded. "Alright then. Let's see what kind of villain you are."

A few minutes later, we were sitting across from each other at a small table tucked beneath the shade of a striped umbrella. It was quieter here, just far enough from the crowds that it felt like our own little pocket of Fantasy World.

Cameron leaned back in his chair with a sigh, stretching his legs out in front of him. "That was Gwen," he said. "Renee's understudy."

I raised an eyebrow. "Let me guess. Pure sunshine?"

He gave a dry laugh. "Sure, if your idea of sunshine includes passive-aggression and weaponized compliments."

"Sounds... delightful."

"She has this gift for making everything seem like it's your fault, even when it's not," he said, shaking his head. "Today's performance was just the latest example."

"What happened?"

He rubbed the back of his neck, his expression slipping into something between frustration and exhaustion. "She's been riding me about the lift and spin in the final number. Some days I nail it. Other days... yeah, not so much."

"The lift and spin?" I asked, leaning in a little.

"It's this big dramatic moment at the end," he said, gesturing with one hand. "I'm supposed to catch her mid-run, spin her once, and set her down like we just saved the world with love and choreography."

I laughed. "So basically: drop the princess, doom the kingdom?"

"Exactly," he said with a groan. "And if Gwen so much as stumbles or, God forbid, ends up with a wrinkle in her dress, I'm suddenly Fantasy World's most wanted."

Something clicked in my brain, and before I could stop myself, the words were already out.

"I might be able to help."

Cameron looked up, eyebrows raised. "Yeah? How?"

I hesitated for half a second.

Back in high school, the drama club had been my second home. I wasn't the lead actress type, I liked being behind the scenes. Blocking scenes, fixing timing issues, jumping in to demo choreography when someone bailed last minute. I'd spent more afternoons than I could count scribbling notes in a script binder and trying to coax reluctant freshmen into nailing their cues.

It had felt good, being needed like that. Being trusted to see what others missed.

I shrugged, trying to keep it light. "I assistant-directed a bunch of our school plays. Took dance for years too. I'm no pro, but maybe another pair of eyes could help."

He studied me for a beat, then shook his head. "I can't ask you to do that."

"You're not," I said with a shrug. "I offered."

Something softened in his expression, like he wasn't used to people offering without strings. "Still—"

"It's only a burden if I don't want to," I said, meeting his eyes.

Something flickered across his face, and for a moment I thought he was going to decline, but then he exhaled and gave me a crooked smile.

"Alright, Carolina. If you're sure."

I lifted my cup with a grin. "Absolutely."

He shook his head, still looking half amused, half unconvinced. "I'll see you tomorrow then."

"It's a date," I said and instantly regretted my choice of words.

Too late.

A smirk was already spreading across Cameron's face.

There was no way he was going to let this go.

"Oh?" he said, drawing it out. "A date, huh?"

I waved my hands like maybe I could erase the last five seconds from reality.

"No! I mean—no, not a *date* date. I just meant—ugh." I trailed off, helpless.

He was already grinning like a fool, savoring every second of my panic.

"Whatever you say, Carolina." He said, pushing away from the table and bringing himself to a standing position. "I'll see you tomorrow... for our not-date."

With one last wink, he turned and headed toward the castle.

I groaned and dropped my head into my hands.

Yep, I was *definitely* in trouble.

Chapter Fourteen

Cameron

I WAS IN TROUBLE.

The kind you can see coming from a mile away and still don't bother avoiding.

Because ever since Sidney blurted, *"It's a date,"* I hadn't been able to think about anything else.

She'd tried to backpedal, hands flying, cheeks pink, stumbling over her words. But the damage was done. The words were mine now, and I wasn't letting them go.

Gwen had done her best to get under my skin today, calling me a liability in front of half of Kingdom Square. Normally, that would've worked. But right now? She was just background noise.

My head was somewhere else entirely.

On Sidney.

She had this spark to her, something that drew me in. It was like she knew how to flirt but hadn't quite figured out what to do if someone flirted back.

It left me wanting to flirt more just to see her get flustered.

Tomorrow, she'd be helping me with the lift and spin. Technically, it was for the show.

But I wasn't fooling myself.

I just wanted a reason to see her again.

When I walked into the apartment, it looked like the aftermath of a frat party crime scene. Porter was draped across the couch like he'd lost a fight with gravity, one arm over his eyes, groaning as if the ceiling lights had personally wronged him. Still paying for last night.

At the kitchen counter, Westley sat with a box of cereal, eating straight from it, looking way too pleased with himself.

"Prince Pity returns," he called. "How was your day? More royal theatrics?"

"Prince Pity?" I raised an eyebrow.

He shrugged. "It sounded better in my head. You look wrecked. Rough day?"

"Same circus, different princess," I muttered, dropping my bag to the floor.

From the couch, Porter groaned. "Don't say too many words at once. My brain can't handle it."

Westley snorted. "You did that to yourself. You're the one who thought you could out-drink Ridley."

Porter made a sound that landed somewhere between a laugh and a death rattle. "Worst decision of my life."

"She *obliterated* him," Westley said, swiveling toward me with way too much enthusiasm. "Didn't even blink. Meanwhile, this guy starts quoting *SpongeBob* in a British accent and challenges her to a churro duel."

"I still say I had a shot," Porter mumbled into a throw pillow.

Westley popped another handful of cereal into his mouth and leaned back in his chair. "Next time, aim for someone less intense. Like Sidney. Right, Prince Pete?"

He threw me a wink.

My whole body went still for half a second.

"She has a boyfriend," I said through gritted teeth.

Westley raised an eyebrow. "Already? Man, you work fast."

"You know it's not me."

He grinned. "Keep telling yourself that."

Porter let out a dramatic groan. "Truly a tale of heartbreak and churros."

I wasn't sure if he was talking about me and Sidney or him and Ridley and honestly, I wasn't brave enough to ask.

I took a slow sip of water, leaning against the counter like I had all the time in the world. "Well, good news, Porter. If you ever want a rematch, I'm sure Ridley's already training for round two."

"Nope," Porter said without hesitation. "I've seen death. I'm good."

Westley snorted, then turned toward me, his grin sharpening. "Alright, Cam. What about you? Tell us about the emotional damage you endured."

"Yeah, how was Gwen?" Porter chimed in.

"Gwen was her usual ray of sunshine," I said, unsure if I should tell them about the next part. I ran a hand through my hair and didn't bother trying to hide the smile tugging at my lips. "But... there was one good part."

Porter cracked one eye open, instantly suspicious. "With Gwen?"

I didn't miss the flicker of amusement in Westley's eyes.

"I don't think he's talking about Gwen." He leaned forward and rested his elbows on the counter. "Did you see Sidney?"

Porter perked up a bit and looked at me. "This I've got to hear."

So, I told them about running into Sidney in Kingdom Square.

About how I'd spotted her near the coffee stand. How she didn't look away when she saw me. Didn't do that polite, awkward smile most people give before moving on. Instead, she actually *listened* while I vented just enough to take the edge off.

"She didn't even try to change the subject," I said, a little more quietly than I meant to. "Just... let me get it out. No judgment."

Westley and Porter listened in silence. It was rare to find either of them at a loss for words.

"She's going to help me with the lift and spin," I added.

Westley grinned. "She's helping with your choreography now? Careful. That's dangerously close to rom-com montage territory."

I shot him a look. "Why are you so obsessed with rom-coms? Besides, it's not like that. She offered."

He gave me a slow once-over, like he was reading every word I wasn't saying. "And you accepted. Without hesitation."

"She knows dance stuff," I said quickly. "She's done theater, took lessons. It's practical."

Westley waggled his eyebrows. "So is brushing your teeth, but I don't invite people to help me with that."

I groaned and lobbed a potholder at his head. He ducked, laughing.

"You're so obvious, dude," he said, grinning.

"I'm not—" I started, then grimaced as the next words left my mouth. "She has a boyfriend."

"Yeah," Westley said, his tone softening a notch. "You keep reminding us."

"I'm not trying to mess with that," I said. "It's just... easy to talk to her. I haven't had that in a long time."

Porter cracked one eye open. "Whoa. Genuine emotion from Prince Peter. Didn't have that on my bingo card."

I rolled my eyes and dropped into the chair across from them.

"Deny it all you want, we see you," Westley said. "You like her."

"I barely know her."

"But you want to," Westley countered. Then he smirked, almost to himself. "And if you ask me, that boyfriend of hers doesn't sound like he's gonna be around much longer."

I hadn't planned for this. Hadn't expected someone like her to show up and knock me off my rhythm.

I liked her. No question. She was beautiful, sharp-witted, and the kind of person who made time feel lighter when you were around her.

Yeah, I wanted it to be something.

Just... not while she was with someone else. I wasn't going to be the reason they broke up, and I sure as hell wasn't interested in being a temporary summer distraction.

Porter yawned, sinking deeper into the couch cushions. "Wake me up when we stop pretending you're not falling for her."

Westley laughed. "You'll be the first to know."

I rolled my eyes, but the smile tugging at my mouth gave me away. "Idiots."

The apartment eventually went quiet. Porter crashed early, sprawled face-down on the couch with one arm dangling like he'd been dropped from a great height.

Westley disappeared into his room, claiming he needed to "mentally prepare" for another day of "Fantasy World madness."

I slipped into my room, shut the door, and finally exhaled. The first real quiet I'd had all day.

Dropping onto the edge of the bed, I stretched my arms overhead before letting them fall limp at my sides. I pulled out my phone, scrolling through notifications until my eyes landed on an unread message from Sidney.

> **Sidney:** Let me know what time tomorrow works for practice. I get off at five, so anytime after that works for me.

I stared at it longer than I should have before typing a reply.

> **Cameron:** Come to the castle after your shift.

I set the phone on my nightstand and leaned back against the pillows, dragging a hand across my jaw. My eyes were heavy, but sleep felt miles away.

Sidney was helping me with a scene. A few spins. Some choreography.

That was all it was supposed to be.

But the thing was... she was different. She didn't just listen when I spoke. She actually heard me. She laughed like she meant it, not like she was humoring me. And she had this way of looking at me, just for a second, like maybe she saw past the costume, past the crown, to the person underneath.

She was beautiful, sure. But it was more than that. She made me feel lighter. Like maybe I wasn't just going through the motions every day.

I shut my eyes, telling myself not to overthink it. But my brain had other plans, replaying her smile, her voice, the way she'd stood there in Kingdom Square like I was worth her time.

Sleep came slowly, but just before it pulled me under, one thought slipped through.

If she wasn't taken, would I already be falling for her?

I ignored the small voice in the back of my head that told me I already was.

Chapter Fifteen

Sidney

I SMOOTHED THE EDGES of a folded t-shirt, just to give my hands something to do. It was the first calm moment all day, and I didn't realize how much I needed it until a soft sniffle pulled me out of it.

I glanced up, spotting a little girl standing just a few feet from me, gripping her father's hand like he was her lifeline. She couldn't have been older than five. Her tear-streaked cheeks were blotchy, her tiny chest rising and falling with every hiccuped breath.

Her father crouched beside her, his hand resting gently on her shoulder, but whatever comfort he whispered wasn't reaching her. Her wide, tear-filled eyes scanned the shop, then locked onto mine.

I offered a small smile and crouched down so we were eye to eye.

"Hey there, sweetheart," I said softly. "What's got you upset?"

Her lower lip quivered, but she stayed silent.

Her father sighed, tired and a little helpless, dragging a hand through his hair.

"She lost her favorite stuffed animal on one of the rides," he said, gently rubbing her back. "Pretty sure it slipped off during the carousel."

A familiar spark stirred in my chest, and something Cameron had said during orientation came back to me.

Magic wasn't just in the rides or the shows, it lived in the small, unexpected moments. The ones that could turn an ordinary day into something unforgettable.

I also remembered something Becca had told me once during a quiet lull between customers: every now and then, we were given the chance to create something special. She called them *Magic Dust Moments.*

If there was ever a time for one... it was now.

I leaned in and lowered my voice to a whisper. "Can you tell me about your missing friend?"

She hiccupped, then nodded, wiping her nose with the back of her sleeve. She lifted her head and looked at her father, who gave her a small smile and a nod.

"She's a bunny," she whispered as she looked at me with her watery eyes. "With a pink dress."

"That sounds like a very special bunny," I said. I tapped my chin a few times as if I were deep in thought. "And you said she was last seen at the carousel?"

She sniffled again and glanced up at her dad, as if to confirm. When he gave a small nod, she turned back to me and nodded too.

"You know what? I've got a friend who works near the carousel," I said. "How about I ask her to start a special search just for your bunny?"

"Really?" she said breathlessly, like the word itself might shatter if she believed in it too much.

I nodded, then stood and offered her a small, reassuring smile. "Wait right here. I think I have something that might help."

Crossing over to the register, I crouched down and rummaged through the storage shelves beneath it, searching for what I'd spotted earlier. A moment later, I straightened with a small plush Princess Primrose doll in hand.

"In the meantime," I said, holding it out to her, "I have a very special friend who could really use the love of a little girl."

Her eyes went wide. She gasped, bouncing on her toes. "Princess Primrose!"

She took the doll without hesitation, hugging it so tightly it looked like she never planned to let go.

"Thank you!" she squeaked, her smile bright enough to light the entire castle.

Out of the corner of my eye, I saw her father's shoulders drop, tension melting away like he'd been holding his breath for miles. He let out a quiet sigh before reaching for his wallet.

"How much?" He asked softly, already pulling out his card.

I shook my head. "It's on us."

He paused, surprise etched on his face. "Wow. That's... really kind of you." After a moment, he added, "We're staying at the Evermore Resort. I can leave my number just in case the bunny turns up."

I nodded and jotted it down on a slip of paper while his daughter clung to her new doll, every trace of her earlier tears replaced by pure joy.

Her father thanked me more than once as they made their way toward the exit, the little girl bouncing on her toes with every step, hugging Princess Primrose like a treasure she'd never let go.

Even after they were gone, I couldn't stop smiling.

This. This was why I wanted to work here.

Pulling out my phone, I sent a quick message to Ridley, asking her to keep an eye out for the missing bunny.

I was just turning to put the doll bin back when a flicker of movement caught my eye—

And I froze.

"Well, look at you, Carolina," he said, that familiar smirk tugging at his lips. "You just made that little girl's whole day."

But his gaze didn't move on. There was something in his eyes, something softer, warmer.

Something I had no business wanting.

"I came to walk you to the castle," he said, like it was the most casual thing in the world.

I arched a brow. "You didn't have to come all the way down here just to walk me."

"I didn't," he said, giving a lazy shrug. "I was already in the area."

I narrowed my eyes. "Really? You just happened to be lurking by the gift shop?"

"'Lurking' is a strong word," he countered. "I prefer... casually observing."

I crossed my arms, but my smile gave me away. "Right."

"You coming? Or are you just going to interrogate me the whole way?"

I rolled my eyes and fell into step beside him anyway, because despite everything, I kind of liked that he came to find me.

The path to the castle was bathed in golden light, the last of the sun catching on the spires ahead. Around us, the park was beginning to shift, day guests lingering for one last photo, the faint strains of music drifting from somewhere in the distance. Cameron's stride was easy, unhurried, like he had all the time in the world, and for once, I didn't feel the need to fill the silence.

Every so often, our shoulders brushed, a tiny spark that kept pulling my focus away from the fairytale skyline and back to him.

When we reached the castle, he held the side door open for me with a mock formality that made me roll my eyes again. But I stepped through anyway.

The moment we stepped into the green room, everything shifted. The quiet, after-hours calm I'd seen before was gone, replaced by a whirlwind of activity. Performers wove past in half-finished costumes, adjusting wigs, running lines, and warming up their voices.

I was still taking it all in when Renee spotted us. Her gaze flicked from Cameron to me, and a knowing smirk spread across her face. Arms crossed, she cut a direct path toward us like a woman on a mission.

"Since when are you two a thing?" She asked, one eyebrow arching. "Did I miss the part where you started hanging out with Prince Charming?"

"It's not like that," I said quickly.

Cameron pressed a hand to his chest, feigning injury. "Wow. Thanks, Carolina. Really feeling the love here."

It was the way he said it, low, easy, dripping with playful charm, that sent a flutter straight through my stomach.

Before I could overthink it, he gave a theatrical sigh and stepped back. "Guess I should get into costume," he said, holding my gaze just a beat too long. "Try not to miss me too much."

"I'll do my best," I shot back, matching his smirk.

I watched him go, maybe a second longer than I should have, before turning to find Renee grinning like she'd just caught me red-handed.

"So," she drawled, eyes flicking between me and where Cameron had disappeared, "since when is my favorite intern so invested in our little show?"

"It's not for me. It's for Cameron."

That earned me a more curious look. "What about him?"

I hesitated, then told her about yesterday, how Gwen had blindsided him, tossing Rico's name around like a weapon until Cameron was questioning whether he even belonged up there.

Renee groaned. "Ugh, she's the worst. Nobody likes her, but she sucks up to the stage manager, so we're stuck with her."

"Well, it got to him," I said. "She had him second-guessing himself."

"That's ridiculous. Cameron's a great Prince Peter."

I arched a brow. "Funny. I recall a very recent conversation where you were saying something similar?"

"Okay, fine," she admitted, arms crossing. "He's a little stiff on the final lift and spin. But that's just nerves. He'll loosen up."

"That's exactly why he asked me to watch today," I said. "I told him I did drama club and dance back in high school, and he figured maybe I could help figure out what's throwing him off."

"Sid," Renee said, amusement curling in her voice, "this isn't high school drama club."

Ouch.

Her expression faltered the second the words left her mouth. "Wait—no, that's not what I meant." She sighed, shaking her head. "Sorry. If Cameron thinks you can help, who am I to argue?"

"Only the star of the show." I teased, letting out a short laugh before shaking my head. "You might be right. This is your turf. Say the word, and I'll step back."

Renee squeezed my hand. "Please. Stay. It'll be way more fun with you here. Besides, it might be beneficial to have you here. It might give Cameron some incentive to show off."

I opened my mouth to protest, but before I could utter a word, Cameron reappeared.

I tried not to stare, but I couldn't ignore the tiny flip my stomach did at the sight of him dressed in his full Prince Peter costume.

I swallowed. Hard.

A minute ago, he'd just been Cameron: the guy who smirked too much, made up ridiculous nicknames, and always had a snarky comeback ready.

Now, he looked like he'd stepped straight out of a fairytale, wearing confidence like it was tailored to him.

And I had a serious weakness for princes.

Amusement flickered across his face like he knew exactly what effect he was having on me.

"Ready to start?" he asked, his gaze holding me in place.

"Yeah," I managed, the word barely finding its way past the sudden dryness in my throat.

Cameron and Renee moved to the center of the now-empty greenroom, slipping into character like flipping a switch.

The pacing, the dialogue, the blocking. Everything clicked.

And yet, every time Cameron called her *princess*, something sharp and unwelcome stirred in my chest.

I told myself it was nothing. Just a passing thought. But the longer I watched him smile at her like she was the only one onstage, the tighter that knot pulled.

I shoved the feeling down, locking it behind a mask of indifference. This wasn't about me or whatever jealous mess my emotions were trying to turn this into.

Then came the final lift and spin.

Cameron stepped into it, and there it was, a hesitation so quick most people would miss it. But I didn't.

They landed the move, and Cameron stepped back, turning to me with an exhale that sounded like bracing for bad news. "Well? How bad was it?"

"It wasn't bad," I said.

One eyebrow arched. "Carolina, I didn't bring you here for platitudes. I need a fix, not flattery."

Of course, he wouldn't let it slide. That was the thing about Cameron, he wanted honesty, even if it stung. I hesitated, choosing my words carefully. "You're doing almost everything right. But... you're thinking about it too much."

He tilted his head, like he was testing the weight of my answer. "So I should... what? Blackout and hope for the best?"

The corner of my mouth tugged up despite myself. He was standing close enough that I could catch the faint scent of his cologne. Warm, clean, and entirely unfair when he was already wearing that ridiculous prince costume. My chest gave an unhelpful flutter.

"Not exactly," I said, keeping my voice steady. "I'm saying you need to feel it, not overthink it."

He groaned, running a hand through his hair in mock frustration. "Right. Super helpful. I'll just go hunt down 'the feeling' and get back to you."

I thought for a second, then pushed to my feet, brushing off my hands. "Alright, hang on. Try the lift with me."

Cameron blinked, caught off guard. "Wait. What?"

Renee lit up like it was opening night on Broadway and she had front-row seats. She stepped back, grinning. "Oh, I am *definitely* watching this."

"It's the easiest way to show you," I said, adjusting my stance. "Okay, before we actually do it, bend your knees a little before the lift. It'll give you more control, especially once the spin starts. And your timing's a hair off, you're hitting it like a straight 1-2-3, but it's really a quick 1-and-2. That's what keeps throwing you off."

He arched a brow. "You got all that from seeing it twice?"

I hesitated, then shrugged. "Not exactly. I may have... watched the castle show on YouTube. A lot."

His smirk deepened. "Of course you did, fangirl."

"Alright then, Carolina," he said, that glint in his hazel eyes daring me, "show me what you've got."

My throat went dry. Cool. Totally fine. I could handle this.

Probably.

He slipped into character so effortlessly it was unfair. Regular Cameron was already enough to throw me off balance, but Cameron in full-on Prince Mode? That was a whole different level of dangerous.

I hesitated, just for a second, before he glanced over his shoulder. "Renee, you wanna grab her a copy of the script?"

"I don't need it," I blurted, stepping forward before I could second-guess myself.

They both looked at me.

Cameron's eyebrow lifted, the corner of his mouth curving like he was trying not to laugh. "Right. Super fan. How could I forget?"

"Don't judge me," I warned.

"Wouldn't dream of it," he said, raising his hands in mock surrender, though the glint in his eyes told me he definitely was.

Cameron extended his hand and gave me a half-smile.

I took it before my brain could interfere. Stepping into the role of Princess Primrose was surprisingly easy as my theater experience came back to me.

Word for word, move for move, I mirrored him through the opening beats of the castle dance.

A flicker of surprise crossed his face, like he hadn't expected me to keep up.

Then, his hands found my waist.

Air. Breathing. Right.

Those were things I used to know how to do. Now, standing in the middle of the greenroom in the middle of *his* scene, they felt impossible.

What exactly had I just signed myself up for?

His eyes locked with mine, and for a moment something flickered there. Something I was afraid to decipher.

He held me in his gaze for a moment, and I didn't dare look away.

Then he cleared his throat and took a step back, his hand slipping from my waist.

"Maybe this isn't the best idea," he said, rubbing the back of his neck.

I couldn't help the disappointment that surged through me. He was looking me like I was a puzzle he wasn't sure he *wanted* to solve.

But I wasn't about to let him back away that easily.

I rose onto the balls of my feet, a grin tugging at my lips. "What's the matter? Worried I'll outshine you?"

From the sidelines, Renee let out a low whistle, arms folded as she leaned back like she'd just scored front-row seats to the drama. All she needed was a bucket of popcorn and maybe a program.

"Oh, come on, Cameron," she said with a knowing smirk. "You *have* to follow through now."

His jaw tightened, but the faint curve at the corner of his mouth gave him away. He was enjoying this far more than he'd admit.

"Alright," he said, voice dropping into a teasing drawl. "But if I drop you, that's on you, not me."

I arched a brow and crossed my arms. "If you drop me, I'm haunting your dressing room. Hope you enjoy jump scares in the mirror."

He let out a soft laugh, but then straightened. Prince Mode: reactivated.

I took a few quick steps back, drawing in a steadying breath as he gave me a small nod.

Okay. Here goes nothing.

I exhaled, pushed off, and ran toward him, copying the move I'd watched Renee perform more times than I could count.

But the second Cameron caught me, I knew—something was off.

His stance was too stiff. My timing was a hair late. And he hesitated just enough to throw the whole thing.

"Nope, nope, nope—!" I yelped as gravity took over.

We tipped sideways, but before the floor could knock the air out of me, Cameron twisted, taking the brunt of the fall so we landed in a tangled heap, his back to the ground, me sprawled across his chest.

For a second, I just lay there, breathless, trying to process the fact that I hadn't been flattened.

But now I was very aware of how close we were.

Neither of us moved.

Then Cameron let out a low groan. "Okay... maybe I *do* suck at this."

Laughter burst out of me before I could stop it, bubbling up until I could barely breathe. The absurdity of the fall, the tangle of limbs, we were a mess.

And I was still half-draped over him, suspended somewhere between mortified and... something else entirely.

Cameron lifted his head, a grin playing at his lips. Then he was laughing too.

Then his fingers grazed my cheek, tucking a stray strand of hair behind my ear.

Laughter died in my throat.

It wasn't dramatic. Just an easy, thoughtless gesture. But it knocked the air from my lungs all the same.

I was acutely aware of everything: the press of his arm still looped around my waist, the solid warmth of his body beneath mine, the faint scent of *him*.

His eyes caught mine, hazel threaded with gold, and for one suspended heart-beat I couldn't look away.

"Should I give you two a minute?" Renee's voice sounded above us.

The spell shattered. Heat rushed to my face as I scrambled off Cameron, nearly tripping over my own feet in my hurry to put actual air between us.

"Nope! All good! Totally fine!" I blurted, brushing at my clothes like I could wipe away the embarrassment.

"Well," Renee said in a mock-bright tone, "that was... graceful."

Cameron stayed on the floor a beat longer, eyes on the ceiling until a low, amused breath slipped out.

"Oh yeah," he said, sitting up with a slow shake of his head. "We crushed it."

Chapter Sixteen

Cameron

ONE SECOND WE WERE mid-spin, the next gravity had staged a full rebellion.

Sidney yelped, I twisted to keep her from hitting the floor, and we ended up in a heap. Me flat on my back, her sprawled across my chest. For one dizzy heartbeat, neither of us moved. Then Renee's voice cut in, all smug amusement, and the moment shattered.

Now, a minute later, I was still trying to piece together what had just happened. "Well, that was something."

I exhaled, scrubbing a hand over my face, trying to make sense of the last sixty seconds of my life.

It didn't take Sidney long before she was back into serious mode. I wasn't nearly as quick on the recovery.

Every coherent thought I tried to summon scattered before it could take shape, dissolving the second I looked at her.

"Also, another thing I noticed, you're tensing up before you lift," she said, her tone all business. "You need to let the motion carry itself."

I blinked at her. "Cool. That cleared up exactly nothing."

"It means you're trying to do the whole lift yourself," she explained. "Renee doesn't just stand there, she jumps into it to help. You have to match her momentum instead of muscling through it."

I crossed my arms. "So, you're telling me this entire time, I've just been... trying too hard?"

Renee, never one to let an opportunity slide, smirked. "Wow. Shocker."

I blew out a breath, rolled my shoulders, and locked eyes with Sidney.

"Alright, Carolina," I said, letting a smirk creep in. "I'm ready to give it another shot if you are. Think you're brave enough?"

"Okay, but try not to launch me into the next kingdom," she teased.

"Where's the fun in that?" I murmured.

She gave me a look. "Just do it the way I showed you. It'll work, I promise."

I arched a brow at her. "Fine, Carolina. We'll do it your way."

She ran toward me.

My hands caught her waist, the warmth of her sinking into my palms. Instinct told me to lift right then, but I forced myself to follow her lead, to match the timing in her stride.

And then momentum took over. We were spinning. The world reduced to a blur of color and motion. Her fingers tightened on my shoulders as mine held her steady.

It was seamless.

I lowered her slowly, my hands reluctant to let go. My pulse thundered in my ears. Whether from the spin or from the fact that it had actually worked, I wasn't sure.

But my eyes lingered on hers a heartbeat too long, and I realized it might not have been the lift stealing my breath at all.

"Okay, seriously," I said, my hands still resting at her waist. "How did that actually work?"

Sidney looked up at me, grinning like she'd known all along. "Told you."

"I guess I just needed the right partner."

Her eyes met mine, and something unspoken passed between us. A slow smile tugged at her lips like she felt it too.

That's when Renee swooped in, practically glowing with mischief.

"Well, unfortunately, you're stuck with me," she said, "but, Sidney, you could be our new understudy. Ever thought about acting?"

"Nope," Sidney said with a grin. "Hung up my acting shoes the moment I got my diploma."

Renee tilted her head, eyes sparkling. "What? I'm just saying... if Gwen happened to get fired, and you just happened to take her spot, I wouldn't be mad."

Sidney laughed, shaking her head. "Yeah, I'm sure they're just dying to replace Gwen with someone who has zero experience."

Renee shrugged. "I mean, you two looked adorable. And the chemistry? Off the charts. That's gotta be worth something."

"You're in too deep now, Carolina," I said.

Sidney gave me a warning look. "Seriously, if you don't drop that nickname—"

I tilted my head, grinning. "What? Want something fancier? I could start calling you *Princess*."

That landed.

Her eyes widened just a fraction, a faint flush coloring her cheeks. She shook her head slowly. "Don't you dare."

But her eyes told on her. They were bright, sparking with the same electric thrill still running through me. She might never admit it out loud, but she loved the banter. We both did.

"Either way," I said, "I owe you one. For once, I actually feel like I can pull this off."

Renee clapped once, grinning like Christmas came early. "Wow. A humble moment from Cameron Scott? Didn't think those existed."

Sidney's smile softened, the teasing still there but warmer now. "Don't worry. I'm sure it's temporary."

Her phone buzzed, pulling her attention. She glanced down, brow knitting in focus, then her expression shifted. Subtle, but enough to catch me. Her lips curved into a smile. Not the polished one she gave guests, but something real. Unfiltered. The kind that lit up her entire face.

And just like that, my thoughts scattered.

She took a small step away, still reading whatever was on her screen, the space between us feeling bigger than it should have.

Beside me, Renee let out a knowing hum.

"Careful, Cam," she murmured, her tone dripping with amusement. "Keep looking at her like that, and people are gonna start talking."

I rolled my eyes. "Right. And you wouldn't be the first one starting the rumor?"

Renee's shrug was pure innocence. "Not my fault if the story writes itself."

I didn't bother answering, but my jaw tightened as my gaze found Sidney again.

"Hey, good news," she said, closing the distance between us.

I blinked, dragging my focus back to reality. "What's up?"

She turned her phone toward me. "Bunny's safe and sound."

Ridley, pink bunny in hand, grinned from the screen. My brain took a second to catch up—oh. Right. The bunny, the kid, and Sidney, casually fixing everyone's problems like it was just part of her day.

I nudged her arm. "Look at you. Saving the day twice in one day."

She shrugged like it was nothing, but that small, unguarded smile stayed put.

Renee arched her back in a long, exaggerated stretch. "Alright, Sid. We should probably clear out before the fireworks. Castle's off-limits once the show starts."

I smirked. "Wouldn't want guests figuring out the fairy tale has an upstairs break room."

Sidney was already glowing, bright and breathless, like her own personal firework show had kicked off early.

She turned to Renee, eyes wide with hope. "Wait—the fireworks?! I've never seen them. Can we stay?"

Renee groaned. "Sid, I'd stay for you, I swear, but I've been here since 7:30, I've suffered in the heat, and I'm one sweaty monologue away from a full breakdown. I'm going home."

Sidney's smile faltered, and the tiny drop in her expression hit me harder than I wanted to admit.

I glanced at Renee, forcing a grin to mask the fact that I cared more than I should. "You're not seriously gonna play the villain on her first fireworks night, are you?"

"Yes, I absolutely am." She leveled me with a flat stare. "I've been awake since the ass crack of dawn. Maybe you should stay with her, *Prince Charming.*"

Sidney's voice dipped, softer now, the spark from a moment ago already dimming. "It's fine. I'll see them another time."

Maybe it was the way her voice lost that brightness. Or maybe I just couldn't stand seeing it go, but the words were out before I could stop them. "You could stay. Watch them with me."

She looked at me, startled at first, and for half a heartbeat there was something in her eyes. Hope. But then it flickered, replaced by something more guarded.

She hesitated, and I could almost see the war going on in her head.

"No, seriously," she said quickly, shaking her head. "It's okay. I don't want to be in the way."

I laughed under my breath. "Carolina, you *have* to see the fireworks. The soundtrack, the projections, the castle glowing like it's alive. It's unreal. And the finale..."

My grin faltered. "It's—"

The rest didn't come.

Because right then, mid-thought, it hit me.

When was the last time I'd actually felt that kind of excitement here?

Not the on-cue, for-the-crowd kind. Real excitement.

It was barely more than a flicker, but it was there. And it was because of her.

I glanced at Sidney, wondering what on earth this girl was doing to me.

Renee's knowing smile said she'd noticed the shift. Her gaze flicked between us before she gave an easy shrug. "I think you should stay."

Sidney's eyes found mine, uncertainty flickering there. "You're sure? Haven't you been here all day too?"

"Nah," I said with an easy grin. "I came in late."

Lie. I'd been here since 6:30, but she didn't need to know that.

Renee didn't call me on it. She just gave Sidney a parting smile. "Have fun, you two."

The door clicked shut behind her, and suddenly it was just us.

A short while later, we were tucked off to the side of Kingdom Square. The sky had deepened into twilight, a rich blue bleeding toward black. The crowd shifted with quiet anticipation, voices dropping as the soft swell of instrumental music floated through the air.

The fireworks were only moments away.

Sidney's lips curved into a gentle smile. The kind of smile that made you want to stand still long enough to memorize it. I caught myself watching her instead of the darkening sky, the glow from the lamplight brushing gold over her hair.

Then the music shifted. The first note of the soundtrack rolled through the park.

She looked up, eyes wide with wonder, just as the castle erupted in a blaze of color. Fireworks streaked into the sky, leaving trails of gold and sapphire that glimmered against the night. Their light flickered in her eyes like stardust in motion.

I lasted maybe three seconds looking at the fireworks before deciding the view beside me was far better.

Every burst painted her face in a different hue. Amber, gold, deep sapphire, then the soft blush of pink that traced along her cheekbones. She didn't blink, caught in that quiet awe I'd seen a hundred times in kids seeing magic for the first time.

And just like that, something shifted. That faint spark I'd felt earlier burned steadily now, warming places in me I thought this job had worn down to nothing. I saw the park the way I used to. Before the burnout.

Because I was seeing it through her.

In the way her fingers curled together, like she was holding on to the night before it slipped away. In the way her breath caught, quiet and reverent, as if she was afraid to disturb the magic around her. In the certainty shining in her eyes. Like she still believed in all of it with every fiber of her being.

"This is... unreal," she murmured.

I swallowed, forcing my voice to sound casual. "Yeah. Not bad."

But inside, I finally understood.

This is why people spent thousands to be here. Why parents carried sleeping kids out the gates. Why crew members endured the heat, the exhaustion, the endless lines, the impossible guests.

It was for this.

For a moment like this.

For the chance to believe in magic again.

Chapter Seventeen

Sidney

My shift passed in a blur of folded t-shirts, restocked shelves, and pointing wide-eyed tourists toward the nearest bathroom.

I had the gift shop rhythm down: answer questions, ring up souvenirs, smile, repeat.

It was a slow morning, which meant more time to straighten displays and tackle the little tasks that always got pushed aside. But quiet shifts had a way of letting your mind wander until the thoughts looped so many times you couldn't reel them back in.

Mine kept circling the same question:

What was I still doing here?

The gift shop had its perks, free cotton candy, swapping stories with Becca between customers, but my heart was somewhere else entirely.

I'd been stopping by the castle for a while, just hanging around, pitching in when it made sense. But then it shifted. I started dropping in *before* my shift, sneaking back during lunch, lingering long after I should've gone home.

For the past three weeks, the castle magic had slowly drawn me in.

At this point, I might as well have been working two jobs. One that paid, and one fueled entirely by caffeine and this strange, impossible-to-shake sense of belonging.

I didn't hate the gift shop; it was a perfectly nice place to work. But it was still just that: work.

Stocking plushies. Answering the same five questions on loop. Smiling through complaints about popcorn prices.

The castle crew? That never felt like work.

Even when it was loud, messy, and exhausting.

Even when Gwen was involved.

There was a rhythm there too, just a different kind. Renee cracking jokes while stretching. Porter turning every stage note into a comedy routine. Westley shouting Shakespeare with a juice pouch in hand. Chris moving through the green room like a one-man hurricane of costume fabric and last-minute fixes.

And then there was Cameron.

Since the night we watched the fireworks, Cameron had kept his distance. Still friendly, still himself—but there was a space between us now, an unspoken line he wouldn't cross. I couldn't blame him. I still technically had a boyfriend... at least on paper.

I had plans. A whole life mapped out waiting back home. Falling for the guy in the prince costume was never part of it.

But then Cameron would flash that crooked smile, say my name in that low, teasing voice, and watch me like I was something he didn't quite understand but wanted to figure out.

And suddenly, Zack felt worlds away.

Not that he seemed to notice. He'd stopped making time for my calls and, if I was honest, I'd stopped making much effort to call him. The relationship was fizzling, and we both knew it.

But instead of saying it out loud, we kept ignoring the obvious, as if silence might somehow fix what was already broken.

I knew the right thing would be to call Zack and end it. It wasn't fair to him, or to Cameron, to keep holding on to both. Right now, it felt like I was only halfway in with either of them.

I was halfway through refolding the same t-shirt for the third time when two familiar voices cut through my spiral.

"There she is!"

I sighed and looked up.

Porter stood like he was unveiling royalty, arms stretched wide. Westley was beside him, grinning like my existence had just made his day.

"What are you doing here?" I asked, crossing my arms.

Porter clutched his chest in mock offense. "You wound me. We came to admire your retail excellence."

His gaze drifted toward the cotton candy machine. "And, uh... for snacks."

"Snacks first, shenanigans second," Porter added with a sage little nod.

"There are three snack carts between here and the castle," I said. "Go harass one of them."

Westley grinned and ignored me completely. "Excellent point, Porter. Candy now, chaos later. We're professionals, after all."

I rolled my eyes, marched to the machine, and spun up two cloud-sized servings big enough to block sunlight. Then, I handed them over like the world's most reluctant sugar dealer.

"So, what brings you to this fine establishment?" Porter asked, already halfway through his first bite. His words came out muffled through a mouthful of pink fluff.

"I literally work here," I said flatly, not even pretending to hide my eye roll.

Westley folded his arms, smirk firmly in place. "Nah. She's avoiding us."

Porter clicked his tongue in mock disappointment. "You thought you could escape us? Foolish, Carolina. We are everywhere."

Westley swatted him on the arm. "Dude. You can't call her Carolina. That's Cam's thing."

Porter's grin sharpened like he'd been waiting for this all day. "Whoops. Must've slipped."

I gave him a look that said I wasn't buying it, but Westley just nodded toward my gift shop uniform like it was a stain I'd eventually wash off. "I'm just trying to figure out what you see in this place. Why haven't you transferred yet?"

I scoffed. "You act like it's inevitable."

Porter gasped, pressing a hand to his chest. "Act like? Sweetheart, it's already happening. You've got one foot out the door and into the castle."

"You just haven't admitted it yet," Westley added.

I barely got a word out before Porter steamrolled right over me.

"Anyway," he said, as if it were nothing, "stage manager was asking if you're coming by later."

I blinked. "Wait—what?"

Westley smirked. "Yeah, apparently someone noticed you actually know what you're doing back there. Weird, right?"

Porter grinned. "Almost like you belong."

I stared at them, words refusing to cooperate.

Porter nudged Westley with his elbow. "See? She hasn't even noticed she's been recruited."

I shook my head. "No—no. I never signed up for anything—"

"And yet," he said, slinging an arm over my shoulder, "you keep showing up like you've got a room in the castle."

Westley crossed his arms, smirking like he already had the verdict. "Just admit it, Sid."

I narrowed my eyes. "Admit what?"

Porter's grin widened to something downright dangerous. "That you love us."

I groaned, ducking out from under his arm. "Keep dreaming."

Westley shrugged. "Didn't hear a no."

Porter cut him a sly glance. "Think she'll fight this right up to the bitter end?"

Westley nodded with mock solemnity. "Absolutely. Classic denial case."

"I am not in denial!" I shot back.

They didn't even bother responding, just stared at me, smug as cats who'd already caught the canary.

I crossed my arms, trying to stare them down.

"So..." Westley drawled, "see you after your shift?"

I hesitated.

I could say no, stand my ground. Go back to my perfectly safe gift shop routine and pretend this whole castle detour hadn't been quietly pulling me in for weeks.

But the word wouldn't come. And from the way their smirks widened, they knew it.

I sighed, shutting my eyes for a beat. "Fine. I'll be there."

Porter gasped like I'd just agreed to sign my life away. Westley grinned like he'd won a bet.

And I wasn't so sure they hadn't.

Chapter Eighteen

Cameron

TIME AT FANTASY WORLD didn't move in days. It moved in moments.

Somewhere between that first day in the greenroom and now, Sidney had stopped being the intern who helped Prince Peter get his act together and started becoming something else entirely.

She was a constant. Something we had all come to rely on.

She wasn't on the schedule. Wasn't being paid. But she showed up anyway. Every day after her shift, sometimes before it, sometimes on her breaks. She'd claim she was "just passing through," even as she picked up clipboards, straightened costume racks, and made herself indispensable without even trying.

No one questioned it.

Not Chris. Not Renee. Not the rest of the cast or crew.

And definitely not me.

If anything, I found myself waiting for it, the soft click of the backstage door, her slipping in with a half-drunk iced coffee and that quiet determination in her eyes that said she wasn't here to kill time. She was here to be part of it.

And she was.

She learned the rhythm faster than most people on payroll. Knew which props were always misplaced, which quick changes cut it close, which cues made Westley turn into a one-man improv show.

It was hard to remember what the place felt like before she started coming around.

And if I were being honest, I wasn't sure I wanted to.

She crossed the room toward the water cooler, the kind of unhurried walk of someone who already belonged here. I found myself trailing after her and leaning against the wall like I'd just happened to end up there.

"You know, Carolina," I said as she took a slow sip from her paper cup, "most people don't just accidentally end up working the castle show."

Her gaze lifted over the rim before she set the cup down. "I'm not working. I'm just... around. Pitching in where I can."

I let a smirk tug at my mouth. "Right. And I wear this costume every day for fun."

She laughed. "It's not the same."

"Isn't it?" I tilted my head, studying her. "Because from where I'm standing, it kinda feels like you're one of us."

That pulled a small smile from her lips. She was too far in now to pretend she was just a bystander. We both knew it.

My gaze dipped to the clipboard in her hands, pages covered in cues and call times she read like they actually meant something to her. I couldn't pinpoint when she'd first started carrying it around, but the fact that Chris trusted her with it said everything.

I nodded at the clipboard. "You're holding that like you're running the show."

She glanced over, one brow lifting. "Chris asked me to cover while he's on break."

"Ah," I said, grinning. "So you've been promoted to unofficial assistant stage manager?"

Her mock glare didn't last long. She looked down at it, lips curving. "Pretty sure someone handed this to me once, and now I can't get rid of it."

I chuckled. "Yep. That's how they rope you in. One clipboard and suddenly you're part of the furniture."

"If anyone tries to sit on me, I draw the line," she said with a laugh.

Her gaze flicked toward Westley and Porter, who were huddled together snickering like they were plotting world domination. "I should probably go see what those two are up to before Chris comes back and thinks it's my fault."

"Good luck with that," I said, leaning against the wall. "You're gonna need it."

She rolled her eyes, but there was a grin tugging at her mouth as she headed their way.

I leaned back against the wall, watching as she crossed the room toward Westley and Porter. Whatever they'd been whispering about vanished the second she joined them. Porter straightened up like he'd been caught, and Westley grinned like he'd just found a new co-conspirator.

Within seconds, they had her holding one of their scripts, reading lines with exaggerated accents while they argued over who was more "emotionally authentic."

And she somehow kept them on track.

No one stormed off. No one threw anything. They actually got through the scene without anyone dying of frustration.

That was the part that got to me. Not just how quickly she'd slipped into the rhythm here, but how different everything felt when she was around.

Rehearsals ran smoother. The greenroom felt lighter. Even Porter and Westley seemed to like her enough to behave.

She could keep denying it all she wanted, but from where I was standing, it was obvious.

She was one of us now.

The idea of her leaving at the end of summer wasn't just some far-off date anymore, it was starting to feel like a clock I could hear ticking in the background.

Somewhere along the way, the castle stopped being just a job, just a set of walls I walked through every day. It had become the place where I felt something I hadn't in a long time.

And more often than not, she was right in the middle of it.

At some point she drifted across the room, chatting with one of the costume ladies. She laughed, head tipped back, eyes bright, and something about it made me pause.

Then she glanced over, met my gaze, and smiled like it was the most casual thing in the world.

It knocked the air out of me before I even realized it.

She lifted a hand in a quick wave, completely unaware she'd just upended my focus for the rest of the day.

"Dude."

I turned and found Porter at my shoulder, wearing that smug, I-know-something-you-don't grin. Westley flanked him with a matching smirk, which told me whatever this was, it wasn't going to end in my favor.

Fantastic.

"What?" I asked, trying to sound bored, even though my brain was already scanning for what they might've seen.

Porter tilted his head toward where Sidney stood across the room. "You and Sidney have been looking pretty cozy lately."

I groaned. "You've got to be kidding me."

Westley grinned. "We're just making an observation. You're around each other *a lot.*"

"She's just helping out," I said, sharper than I meant to. "That's it."

Porter gave a slow, disbelieving nod. "Right. Just the intern who somehow learned everyone's cues, half the stage manager's job, and exactly how to make you smile like a sap."

I kept my expression flat, but my chest tightened.

"No deeper meaning at all," Westley added with mock sincerity. "Just your friendly neighborhood intern. Saving the day, one prince at a time."

"Exactly," I muttered.

Porter bumped my arm. "Which totally explains why you look at her like she's the last churro in the park."

Westley leaned in, dead serious. "And this man loves churros."

I rolled my eyes and didn't answer. Because the truth? They weren't wrong, and that was the part I didn't feel like explaining.

"I do not look at her like that."

Westley smirked like he'd been waiting all day for this. "Hate to break it to you, man, but... yeah. You really do."

"Absolutely," Porter said, nodding sagely. "I've literally seen you watching her while trying to act like you're not watching her."

I gave them both a deadpan stare. "You two need hobbies."

"Maybe," Porter said with a shrug. "Still doesn't make us wrong."

"I'm not staring," I shot back. "It's called facing a direction."

They traded a look, equal parts smug and delighted, that made me want to throw something.

"All I'm saying," Westley drawled, "is you're different around her. Softer. Almost... pleasant."

Porter tapped his chin in exaggerated thought. "And that started what... three weeks ago? Can't imagine what might've caused it."

I narrowed my eyes. "Don't say it."

They grinned in unison. "Sidney."

I threw up my hands. "You're both ridiculous."

But my mouth betrayed me, curving into a smile I couldn't quite kill. I was still wearing it when the door swung open and Gwen swept in like a royal decree no one wanted.

Her heels clicked across the tile with the kind of sharp, deliberate precision that made the whole greenroom tense a fraction. Gwen didn't walk so much as advance, eyes already locked on the costume rack like it had personally offended her.

She reached it in three strides, nose wrinkling as though the air itself had betrayed her.

"Ugh." The sound dripped with disgust. She flicked through the hangers with jerky, impatient snaps. "Why do these always look like they've been through a wind tunnel?"

From across the room, Porter caught my eye. His look said, *Good luck with that.* I gave the slightest shake of my head. Don't engage.

But Gwen wasn't the type to let a room breathe without her voice filling it.

"Cameron." My name cracked like a whip, and before I could even process, she was pivoting toward me with one of the prince jackets slung over her arm. "What does this smell like to you?"

I blinked at her, already regretting being in her line of sight.

She closed the distance and thrust the sleeve toward me like she was presenting Exhibit A in a courtroom drama. "Smell it. Right here."

Every instinct screamed *absolutely not*, but I leaned in anyway and sniffed. My brows pulled together. "Fabric softener?"

Her eyes narrowed. Wrong answer.

I wasn't in the mood for this. I turned on my heel and retreated toward the opposite end of the greenroom.

Behind me, her voice rose. "These smell like hairspray! And clearly, they haven't been laundered properly. I swear, if I have to wear something that smells like high school show choir again—"

The rest dissolved under the sound of conversation and the growing distance between us.

I exhaled, tension bleeding off my shoulders one knot at a time.

I tried to summon to mind all the reasons I liked this job.

Chapter Nineteen

Sidney

"Ugh. One more clueless stagehand and I'm going to lose it—" Gwen's voice sliced through the room, each click of her heels against the tile like a warning shot.

Beside me, Porter muttered under his breath, "And so it begins."

I straightened before I could stop myself, muscles going tight. It wasn't just her volume, it was the way the air seemed to bend around her. Heads tilted. Conversations stalled. People found excuses to be anywhere else.

She tossed her hair over one shoulder, scanning the room like a queen surveying her court for signs of rebellion. Her eyes passed over racks of costumes, crew members, and finally—me.

"Oh." The word landed with a faint, amused lilt. Her lips curved, but it wasn't a smile. Her gaze swept over me from head to toe, slow enough to sting. "You're still here."

I forced my expression into something flat, unreadable. But inside, something twisted hard and cold. It was one thing to wonder if you belonged here, it was another to have someone point it out for the entire room to hear.

I wasn't going to give her the satisfaction of seeing me flinch.

"Yeah," I said evenly. "Looks like it."

Her brows lifted. "Seriously, though. What do you even do here?"

The question lingered like smoke, wrapping itself around the insecurities I'd been trying to keep locked down since day one.

She huffed, a quick exhale of dismissal, and spun away without waiting for an answer like I wasn't worth the follow up.

"Places, everyone," Chris called, his voice brisk enough to cut through the tension but not enough to clear it.

Around me, the greenroom shifted back into motion, but I stayed tucked in my usual spot at the observation window. From here, I could see almost everything onstage without being in the way. I curled my fingers into my palms, willing my heartbeat to slow.

Gwen could think whatever she wanted. She could make her digs, try to edge me out.

But I wasn't going anywhere.

Westley passed close behind me, leaning in just enough to murmur, "Buckle up. This one's gonna be rough."

I didn't answer. My focus stayed on the stage. Cameron stepped out first, his posture steady, every movement deliberate. Gwen followed a while later, gliding into her mark with perfect poise.

From my vantage point, the opening beats looked fine. Lines landed. Blocking worked. I let my shoulders ease just a fraction, daring to think maybe this wouldn't implode after all.

Then came the cue for the finale lift.

Cameron's timing was flawless, turning toward her, hands ready.

But Gwen didn't leap. Didn't even try to meet him halfway. She stopped short, like she'd changed her mind at the last possible second.

From the window, I saw Cameron adjust, twisting to keep them both upright. It saved them from disaster, but the lift still landed wrong. It was crooked, heavy, stripped of all the effortless grace it was supposed to have.

The magic drained from the scene in an instant.

I stayed frozen at the glass, my stomach twisting. Even from here, I could see the sharp line of Cameron's shoulders as he set her down. This wasn't just a missed cue. It was the weight of the whole show slipping, and there was no covering it.

Gwen started in the second her heels hit the greenroom floor, spinning on Cameron like she'd been rehearsing the speech all afternoon.

"See? This is exactly what I've been saying. You're still doing it wrong."

Cameron's reply was flat, drained of anything resembling emotion. "Yep. All my fault."

He stood there breathing hard, hands curled into tight fists at his sides. He didn't look at her. Didn't look at anyone. But from where I stood, I caught the quick twitch in his jaw. The kind that said he was two seconds away from saying something he'd regret.

I braced for him to snap.

Instead, Gwen pivoted and locked onto me.

The change was so fast it was like watching a hawk shift its sights mid-flight.

"You." Her manicured finger cut through the air, sharp as a dagger. "You're always lurking around. What do you think?"

My stomach knotted instantly. This wasn't curiosity. It was bait.

If I said nothing, I'd look like I was afraid of her. If I said the wrong thing, she'd make a sport out of it.

Beside me, Porter and Westley exchanged the kind of look that translated to *good luck surviving this one.*

I drew in a slow breath, forcing my voice to stay even. "I think lifts work best when both people are... actually helping each other."

Her brows shot up, a predator scenting weakness. "Oh, so now you're an expert?"

"No," I said carefully, holding her gaze. "But I've seen Cameron pull it off just fine when his partner actually—"

"Ah." Her interruption was sugar-laced poison. "Let me guess, you think Renee's so much better?"

Silence stretched, and that was all the confirmation she needed.

Her eyes lit with satisfaction as she folded her arms. "Of course. Everyone loves Renee."

She didn't wait for a reply. Instead, she pivoted on her heel and zeroed in on Chris at the far side of the greenroom.

The stage manager barely had time to glance up before Gwen was standing in front of him, arms crossed, lips set in a perfectly rehearsed pout.

"This just isn't working," she declared, projecting like the audience was ten rows deep. "Cameron can't get the lift right, and frankly? I don't feel safe trying it with him."

From across the room, I caught Cameron's sharp scoff. "Oh, come on—"

"Gwen..." Chris's sigh carried a warning.

She ignored it entirely, steamrolling ahead. "And now we've got all these random people loitering around rehearsal, pretending they know everything." Her gaze flicked over me, quick and dismissive, before she turned away as if I didn't even exist.

Chris exhaled through his nose, fingers pinching the bridge of it like he was holding back a headache. "Cameron, if the lift isn't working, maybe it's time to scrap it. Gwen's got a point."

Cameron's jaw tightened, his voice flat but sharp enough to cut. "The lift works when my partner actually puts in the effort."

Chris looked like a man regretting every decision that brought him to this exact moment. "Okay, let's put a pin in this. Cameron, keep running it. Gwen, dial it back. And Sidney..." He hesitated just long enough for me to brace. "...maybe give the cast a little breathing room."

My cheeks burned. I glanced at Cameron, still rigid, still holding it in, but he didn't take the bait.

Gwen, of course, was all smiles. "Thanks, Chris. I knew you'd be reasonable."

Then she turned that same syrupy grin on me before strutting off like the crown was already hers.

Chapter Twenty

Cameron

By THE TIME REHEARSAL wrapped, the air in the greenroom still felt tense with Gwen's theatrics and my patience was shot.

Sidney didn't look much better. Arms crossed tight, jaw set, she paced a short loop near the wall like a storm cloud trying to decide where to strike. She wasn't just annoyed, she looked wound tight enough to snap.

I crossed the room and tapped her elbow lightly, careful not to spook the hurricane. "Come on," I said. "Let's grab some food. You look about two seconds from throwing something, and I'd really rather not be the target."

Her eyes flicked to mine, irritation softening just enough for a quick flash of amusement. Then she exhaled, the fight in her dropping by half a degree.

"Fine," she said, though her tone carried a warning. "But I'm not making any promises. I might still throw my fries at you."

I shrugged, falling into step beside her. "I'll take my chances. Fries are worth it."

We ended up at Baxter's, a quick-service cafe tucked right where Enchanted Boulevard spilled into Kingdom Square. The place looked like it had stepped out of a watercolor painting: painted wood trim, hand-lettered signs in looping script, and the air thick with the mouthwatering pull of garlic fries and grilled hot dogs.

I steered us to a table outside beneath a yellow-striped umbrella. From here, the castle's spires rose perfectly against the sky, like the park itself was trying to remind us that Fantasy World was supposed to be fun.

Sidney settled into the chair beside me, her knee brushing mine for just a second before she tucked herself in. I pulled up the menu on my phone, tilting the screen toward her, and she leaned in to see—close enough that I caught the faint scent of her shampoo, something bright and citrusy.

We scrolled together, lingering over a few options, trading quiet comments until we'd made our choices. My thumb tapped the final confirmation, and the app flashed our order number.

Now, all we had to do was wait.

I set the phone on the table, but she stayed angled slightly away, arms folded tight, her gaze fixed on some point across the square.

"You don't have to let her get to you," I said gently.

She exhaled slowly as if she was trying to steady her nerves. "I know. But she's just so—"

"Oh, I know," I cut in with a short laugh.

Silence stretched between us, not uncomfortable, just... heavy.

The sounds of the theme park filled the silence. The clink of cutlery, chairs scraping over pavement, the hum of conversation from the next table. Somewhere, a faint melody drifted through the air. It was Fantasy World in full swing. The happiest place to spend a Saturday afternoon.

But Sidney wasn't happy. She was frustrated.

I was used to Gwen, but she wasn't. This was all new to her.

She picked at the napkin in front of her, tearing off small pieces that she stacked in a neat little pile.

"I hate that Chris just lets her walk all over him," she said at last, her voice low but edged.

I shrugged. "Chris treats conflict like it's contagious. Gwen makes herself his problem, so he just takes the quickest way out."

"That's so unfair."

"Yep." I leaned back in my chair. "Welcome to theater."

She didn't answer, and I didn't push. Her gaze stayed fixed somewhere past the edge of the table. The breeze tugged at a loose strand of her hair, but she didn't seem to notice.

My phone buzzed with the pickup alert, pulling me out of the moment. I got to my feet and headed for the counter, the smell of fries and grilled onions growing stronger with every step.

When I came back, Sidney hadn't moved. She sat exactly as I'd left her, arms folded tight, shoulders tense, eyes still clouded with frustration.

I slid the fries toward her. "Eat. It'll do more good than silently threatening the shrubbery."

A smirk flickered across her face. She took a fry, bit into it, and spoke around the bite. "So basically, whoever yells the loudest wins?"

"That's her superpower," I said with a shrug. "She's relentless. Eventually, people give in just to make her go away."

Sidney leaned back against the bench, exhaling sharply. "That's disgusting."

Before I could think twice, I reached across the table and tapped her wrist, my voice quieter now. "Hey. As much as I want you to stay... you don't have to. If it ever gets to be too much, Gwen, the show, any of it, you're allowed to walk away."

She looked up, and for a long moment, there was no sarcasm, no shield, just the weight of her gaze holding mine. Like she was letting the words settle in.

Then she shook her head. "I'm staying. This matters to me."

I felt a smile creep in before I could stop it.

Her eyes narrowed. "I hate that look."

I laughed. "Then you're in trouble, Carolina, because it's not going anywhere."

She rolled her eyes, but the smile tugging at her lips betrayed her. The knot in my chest loosened enough to let me breathe easier.

"What?" she asked, her voice softer now, catching something in the way I was watching her.

I tilted my head. "So... what do you want to be when you grow up?"

Sidney let out a half-scoff, half-laugh. "Are you serious right now?"

"Dead serious," I said, leaning back with a shrug. "Unless your dream job really is 'gift shop intern slash part-time actor wrangler.'"

She raised an eyebrow at me, but there was amusement tucked at the corners of her mouth. "Wow. Haven't heard that question since high school."

I grinned. "Guess I'm bringing it back. So, what's the current answer?"

"Well, I'm going into my senior year. My major is hospitality management."

I shook my head. "I didn't ask what your major was. I asked, what you want to be when you grow up."

She hesitated then, chewing her fry more slowly, eyes shifting like she was weighing whether to answer. When she finally set the fry down and wiped her hands on her napkin, it felt like a deliberate move, like she needed a clear runway to say it out loud.

"I had a plan," she said finally, her voice quieter now, like the words weren't meant for the whole world to hear. "Still kind of do. Get my degree. Work at a hotel while I save up…"

I leaned in a little, elbows on the table. "But what's the real dream?"

Her gaze flicked to mine, and she gave a short, almost embarrassed laugh. "I don't even know anymore. I used to think I wanted to start my own small event company. Birthdays, weddings, community festivals. It sounded… respectable. Like the kind of thing someone like me was supposed to do."

"Someone like you?" I asked.

She hesitated, then shrugged one shoulder. "A straight-A student. A good girl. The one who always follows the rules, says yes to everyone, never makes waves." Her mouth curved into something that wasn't quite a smile. "I've never really had any adventures. I've been so busy doing the right thing that I never stopped to ask if it was what I actually wanted."

Her gaze drifted toward the castle in the distance, the sunlight catching on its towers. "That's why I came here. This internship was supposed to be my last big adventure before I went home and got serious. But…" She trailed off, her fingers picking at the corner of her napkin. "Now I'm starting to think maybe it shouldn't be my last."

I didn't say it, but I could already see it. Sidney stepping outside the life she'd always been expected to live, chasing something unknown, something hers. From the look in her eyes, maybe she could see it too, even if she wasn't ready to admit it yet.

"Makes sense," I said, nodding slowly. "Sounds like you've got it all mapped out."

Her lips quirked, almost shy. "I made a five-year plan my senior year of high school. Color-coded tabs, bullet points... the whole thing."

I couldn't help but smile. "And you've stuck with it?"

"For the most part." She toyed with the edge of her napkin, eyes distant. "It's safe. Practical. It lets me be creative without... you know... ending up broke in a shoebox apartment, living off instant ramen."

I tilted my head. "Not a fan of shoeboxes?"

"I like knowing where I'm going," she said, softer now. "Even if it's not perfect."

Something in the way she said it, the quiet, almost like she was trying to convince herself, made me lean forward.

"So what happens," I asked, "if you end up somewhere better than the plan?"

Her gaze snapped to mine, brow furrowing. "Better?"

"Yeah." I gestured faintly around us. "Like... this. All of it. You didn't plan to be here, but you're good at it. People notice you. You matter here."

She looked down. "Sometimes it doesn't even feel real. Like I accidentally wandered into someone else's story."

I waited until she glanced up again. "Maybe you did," I said. "And maybe that someone is the person you're becoming. The one you were meant to be all along."

Sidney looked up at me again, and for a moment, there was nothing guarded in her expression. No deflection. Just... soft wonder, like she was really considering what I was saying.

"Stop doing that," she said at last, her voice lower now, almost wary.

"Doing what?"

"Saying things like that. It makes it really hard not to like you."

The corner of my mouth lifted. "Then I guess I'll just have to keep saying them."

She reached for another fry but didn't eat it, just rolled it between her fingers like she needed the motion to keep steady.

I watched her for a beat, then let my tone go casual. "So... where does Zack fit into the five-year plan?"

Her hand stilled.

"I used to think he was part of it. The plan, I mean. I really did." She brushed at an invisible crumb. "But now... I'm not so sure."

I didn't rush to fill the silence. Just let it stretch, leaving space for her to find the words.

When she finally looked over, her gaze lingered, like she was trying to read something in me, maybe even give herself permission to say it.

"I don't know what we are anymore," she said at last. "We barely talk. And when we do, it's like we're both acting in some bad play, pretending everything's fine because neither of us wants to be the one to admit it's not."

I nodded slowly. "That sounds... exhausting."

"It is."

"Do you want to fix it?" My voice stayed soft, but the question hung heavy between us.

She met my eyes again, lips parting like the answer was there but tangled. "I used to think I did," she said finally. "But lately... I'm not sure. I feel like I'm changing, and he's not even paying enough attention to notice."

"He'd be an idiot not to," I murmured.

Her gaze flickered away. She reached into the basket, plucked a fry, and this time actually ate it.

A small, crooked smile tugged at her lips. "Thanks... for listening."

"Anytime, Carolina."

She held my eyes for a beat longer than necessary, the air between us tightening like a pulled thread. Her smile softened, almost shy, before she looked down at the table. Like she wasn't quite ready to let me see everything in her expression.

I could've said something else. I almost did. But instead, I leaned back, letting the moment linger, both of us knowing it didn't need words to mean something.

***

The next day, Renee was back, and thank God for that.

Everything just ran smoother with her onstage. The cues hit sharper. The energy stayed steady. Even Chris looked less like he was seconds from throwing himself off the turret tower.

Two shows in, and we'd finally found our rhythm. Backstage was a quiet hum of movement and focus, the kind of flow where everyone knew their marks without thinking.

Until a sudden, sharp gasp cut through the air like a dropped cue.

I turned toward the sound just in time to see Renee's heel slide out from under her. Her face twisted in surprise, pain, and something almost raw flashing across features that, until that moment, had been pure Princess Primrose.

Her hand shot out, fingers curling around the edge of the prop table like she could will herself upright.

The room froze. Even Porter, who could crack jokes in his sleep, went silent.

"You okay?" someone called, though the answer was written in the strain around her eyes.

"Fine," Renee said, but her voice betrayed her.

She tried to shift her weight, testing it, and her entire face pinched with pain. Her other hand grabbed for the table again, as if letting go would send her toppling.

Nope. Definitely not fine.

A stagehand darted forward, catching her elbow and steadying her before she could tip.

Across the room, Sidney shot upright from her seat. She didn't rush forward, but her eyes never left Renee. I could read the question in her eyes: *What do we do?*

Then Chris appeared, hair wilder than usual, eyes wide. The man looked like he'd just sprinted across three lands and through a parade to get here.

"What happened?" he demanded, scanning the room in quick, jerky sweeps. His gaze landed on Renee, still braced against the prop table, and his shoulders sagged. "Call the understudy. Cancelling isn't an option."

Of course it wasn't. Fantasy World didn't do cancellations. You could go onstage in a cast, a boot, or a neck brace, and they'd still expect you to wave like royalty and hit every mark.

From somewhere near the sound booth, a muttered, "Calling Gwen," slipped into the air, said with the grim resignation of someone lighting a match in a fireworks factory.

My stomach sank. This was going to go well.

A stagehand pulled out her phone, fingers moving fast but tense, like she already knew this wasn't going to end well. She tapped the screen, lifted it slightly, and hit speaker.

"What?" Gwen's voice snapped through the line.

Chris's posture shifted instantly. His shoulders squared, his voice took on that brittle customer-service tone he reserved for guests who believed their fast pass was a golden ticket to the kingdom. "Hi, Gwen. Renee's hurt. We're gonna need you to cover—"

"Not my problem."

The words hit like a slap.

Then the call disconnected.

For a beat, no one moved.

The stagehand lowered the phone slowly, her frantic gaze darting to Chris. "She hung up."

Chris's jaw tightened until I thought I heard something crack. For a second, I thought he might actually implode.

"Okay," he muttered to no one in particular. "Alright. Plan B. We—"

But Gwen was Plan B. She was the only understudy we had.

There was no other plan. Not with Gwen out, Renee hurt, and a full crowd waiting outside.

Around us, people shifted, exchanging quick glances, the unmistakable energy of *not it* spreading like static.

I scanned the space, pulse picking up. My mind ran through options, every one of them bad, until my gaze landed on the only person who could make this work.

She was still standing there. Watching. Waiting.

I felt the decision lock into place before I could second-guess it. I just hoped she wouldn't hate me for it.

"Sidney," I said, my voice cutting through the tension. "She can do it."

Chapter Twenty-One

Sidney

I choked. "I'm sorry...what?"

Every head in the room turned toward me in perfect, horrifying unison, like I'd just been named tribute in some Fantasy World–themed Hunger Games.

And Cameron? He didn't flinch. Didn't so much as blink. He looked infuriatingly calm.

"Sidney knows the whole routine," he said, giving me a reassuring nod.

"No, I do not," I hissed at him. "I work in the gift shop, remember?"

"Come on, Carolina," he said, that infuriating smirk curling at the edges. "Be a hero."

Every rational part of me was already halfway to the exit, mentally waving a white flag and shouting, *Turn around. Go back to folding T-shirts. Pretend none of this is happening.*

Before I could bolt, Cameron's hand landed lightly on my arm. He tugged me a few steps out of earshot, lowering his voice so only I could hear.

"Sidney, listen to me," he said, and it wasn't cocky now. It was calm, steady, like he was trying to anchor me. "You know the show. You've seen it a hundred times. You can do this."

My chest tightened. "No, I *can't*. I'll mess it up. I'll—" I shook my head, glancing toward the stage door. "I'm not you. I'm not Renee. I don't belong out there."

His expression softened, but there wasn't a shred of doubt in his eyes.

"You belong here more than you think. You've got the timing, the presence." His hands settled gently but firmly on my shoulders, his gaze holding mine. "Sidney... you can do this."

"Cameron," I said, my voice barely more than a whisper. "I can't—"

"Yes, you can," he said gently but firmly. "We've done this before. And we can do it again. Together. Trust me."

A shaky laugh slipped out. "Please don't make me."

"I'm not making you," he said quietly, leaning in until I could feel the warmth of his breath. "This is your choice."

My pulse was thundering, my brain screaming *absolutely not*. And yet, the way he was looking at me made it impossible to move toward the door.

I swallowed hard, gave the smallest of nods. His grin spread, and with a single glance toward Chris, he said, "She's in."

Chris blinked, still processing. "She hasn't even rehearsed—"

Then Cameron's gaze slid back to me, and that smirk sharpened just enough to make me briefly consider lobbing the nearest prop straight at his head.

"Trust me," he said, like it was the most obvious thing in the world. "She's got this."

Cameron Scott was insane. Actually insane.

I folded T-shirts. I lined up plushies in perfect color gradients. I directed panicked parents to the nearest bathroom like my life depended on it.

I was *not* a performer.

Even in high school, I was the kid dressed in black, whispering cues into a headset from the wings, not the one in the spotlight. And definitely not the one about to be shoved into it.

From there, it was a blur.

One second I was still clinging to the "I can't do this" panic, and the next I was being herded into the dressing room. A small army of crew members closed in with the speed and precision of a pit crew.

Hands worked through my hair, twisting and pinning until every strand vanished beneath a halo of soft blonde curls of the Primrose wig. Someone dusted shimmer across my cheeks, the scent of powder and hairspray mixing in the air. A sudden puff of glitter caught the light as it settled over me.

I barely had time to breathe before they spun me toward the mirror.

I blinked once. Then again.

Because the girl staring back wasn't me. She was... someone else entirely. Someone with bright eyes and a crown that caught the light. Someone who looked like she belonged in the castle.

Like a princess.

My heart stuttered, then kicked into overdrive, racing to keep pace with what was happening.

Ready or not... I was Princess Primrose.

The moment I stepped out onto the stage, the world seemed to tilt.

Sunlight poured across the stone courtyard, sharp and golden, painting everything in a storybook glow. Every head turned toward me. Kids balanced on their parents' shoulders, clutching autograph books. Cameras lifted. Guests stared with wide-eyed, expectant smiles.

And I froze.

My heart slammed against my ribs, the sound so loud it drowned out the triumphant swell of the music. My feet might as well have been cemented to the stage.

Cameron was wrong. I couldn't do this. I wasn't a princess.

I needed to turn around. Slip back inside the castle before anyone realized the mistake. Pretend this had never happened.

But before I could retreat, Cameron stepped forward.

He didn't say a word. He didn't need to. His eyes found mine, steady and sure. And somehow, that was enough.

The cue came.

I pulled in a shaky breath, praying I wouldn't faint in front of two hundred strangers. One step forward.

Then, miraculously, the words left my mouth, sounding far more confident than I felt.

"Oh, my dear friends! I have returned just in time for the festival!"

The voice didn't sound like mine. It rang out bright and certain, threaded with a confidence I didn't recognize, like it belonged to someone who knew exactly who she was and why she belonged here.

No stammer. No hesitation.

Just... a princess.

The crowd reacted in a heartbeat, cheers bursting, giggles bubbling, tiny hands clapping against parents' arms. A little girl in a plastic tiara pressed her hands to her mouth and stared at me like I'd stepped straight out of her bedtime story.

And somehow... something clicked.

Every time I moved past Cameron, our eyes caught, holding for just a second too long. The crowd didn't notice. They were wrapped up in the fairytale, oblivious to the quiet current running between the lines.

When the moment came, he extended his hand, timed perfectly with the music. I slipped mine into his.

"Are you ready, Princess?" he asked, low and warm, meant only for me.

I swallowed, the word Princess doing dangerous things to my knees. "Ready," I breathed, though I wasn't sure if I meant for the dance or whatever this was between us.

We moved together. Well, he moved, I did my best not to trip. His hand was steady at my waist, his steps guiding mine as if we'd practiced for weeks.

And then came the finale.

I pulled in a breath, trying to steady the rush in my chest.

Then Cameron's gaze locked with mine.

Sure. Unwavering. Like he could see the part of me that was still terrified... and believed in me, anyway.

I ran.

Each step rang out on the stage, syncing with the pounding of my heart. This wasn't just hitting my mark, it was trust. It was me handing over every ounce of fear, every what-if, and letting him catch it.

And he did.

His hands found my waist, strong and certain, pulling me into the lift like we'd been doing it for years.

The castle spun. The sky spun. My dress fanned out in a cloud of pink tulle.

When my feet came down, I hardly felt them land. I was still caught in him. In the way his eyes held mine, like the rest of the world had gone silent.

For a moment, it wasn't a performance.

It wasn't a role.

It was just us.

The music shifted, bright and final, breaking the moment apart piece by piece.

He stepped back slowly, fingers trailing from my waist like he wasn't ready to let go.

The applause crashed over us, but all I could hear was the echo of my heartbeat and the part of me that wished the music had never changed.

He reached for my hand, fingers curling warm and sure around mine, and together we sank into a final bow.

The moment we slipped through the stage doors, the green room erupted.

Laughter. Applause. Hands clapping my shoulders. Voices tumbling over one another in a blur of praise and disbelief.

Chris pushed through the crush of bodies, a stunned smile tugging at his mouth. "Not bad, Webber. Not bad at all."

Somewhere behind me, Porter's voice cracked through the noise, gleeful and way too loud. "I cannot believe that just happened."

Westley gave me one of his signature slow nods, like he was delivering a royal decree. "Didn't even drop a line."

Then I turned.

Renee sat off to the side, her ankle propped on a pillow. She wasn't clapping like everyone else. Just watching me with a smug little smile, like she'd known exactly how this would end.

"Well, well," she said, her voice warm and smug all at once. "Looks like we've got ourselves a new understudy."

I froze, the word *understudy* snagging in my brain like a loose thread.

Wait. What?

My gaze flicked from her to Chris, half-expecting a camera crew to leap out from behind a curtain and yell, *just kidding*.

"You're already here every day," Chris said, like it was the most obvious thing in the world. "Might as well make it official."

"I... I work in the gift shop," I managed, the words sounding far off, like someone else had said them.

Chris just shrugged. "Then we transfer you. Technically, you'd be Gwen's understudy, though I doubt she's lining up to cover Renee anytime soon." His voice softened, his eyes holding mine. "It's your call, Webber. But it's on the table."

I stood there, still in the wig, glitter dusted across my cheeks, adrenaline bleeding out of my veins until I felt lightheaded.

This was supposed to be a summer internship. A quick, shiny detour before *real life* kicked in. Something for the résumé.

I wasn't supposed to get attached.

I definitely wasn't supposed to want *this*.

But the truth hit me all the same.

It was loud and chaotic and terrifying. It was people who laughed too hard and believed in me more than I believed in myself.

It was glitter and missed cues and running on no sleep.

And somewhere in the middle of all that... it felt like *home*.

I glanced over at Cameron.

He didn't push. Didn't even speak. Just stood there with that patient half-smile, like he'd been waiting for me to catch up to something he'd known all along.

My pulse was still racing, my hands faintly trembling, but my voice, when it came, was steady.

"Okay," I said. "Let's make it official."

His smile deepened, and for some reason, that felt like its own kind of victory.

By the time I clocked out that afternoon, the transfer request was already submitted.

That night, I sat cross-legged on my bed, the quiet of my room pressing in on me. My phone lay in my hand, Zack's name glowing on the screen like it was daring me.

This wasn't sudden. I'd been feeling the cracks for a long time, tiny fissures I'd ignored because it was easier than facing them. But today had pulled it all into focus.

The way Cameron had looked at me told me I could do more than I believed. The way I'd actually stepped up, terrified and shaking, and somehow made it work. For the first time in forever, I'd done something that scared me... and it hadn't broken me.

And now, staring at Zack's name, I knew it wasn't just about a role or a show. It was about the way I'd been living, stuck in place, letting life make the choices for me.

It was time to stop. It was time to let go of what was holding me back.

I took a breath, my thumb hovering for only a heartbeat before I pressed the call button.

It rang once.

Twice.

Then went to voicemail.

I lowered the phone, staring at the screen like I could will it to change. Like if I waited just a few seconds longer, his name would light up and everything would feel normal again.

It didn't.

Not earlier this week. Not last night. Not now.

The truth settled in, I was done waiting for someone who had stopped showing up.

I opened our message thread. The empty screen stared back at me, quiet and unchanging, like it knew this wasn't how our story was supposed to end. But endings don't always ask for permission.

What other choice did I have?

I'd called. I'd waited. I'd hoped.

And he hadn't picked up.

I drew in a steadying breath, my fingers hovering only a moment before I began to type.

> Zack, I've been trying to get in touch, and maybe that silence says enough.

> This summer has changed a lot of things for me, and I think, deep down, we both know we've been growing in different directions for a while now.

> You've been a big part of my life, and I'll always be grateful for that. But I can't keep holding onto something that isn't there anymore.

> I wish you the best.

> –Sidney

I read it once. Then again.

My finger hovered for a beat longer than it should have, then I hit send.

The second the message vanished, the guilt came.

Not because I didn't mean it. I did.

But because I'd wanted our ending to look nothing like this. Because he hadn't answered, and part of me still hated that it came down to a few typed lines instead of a real conversation.

I set the phone face down on the bed, sinking back into the pillows as if the air had gone out of me.

Letting go hurt.

But for the first time, it didn't feel like loss.

It felt like space.

And maybe... space could turn into freedom.

***

The next morning, I got to the park before the gates even opened.

The walk to work felt different. The air smelled sweeter. My steps didn't drag. My heart felt steady in a way it hadn't in months.

Today was for changes. My transfer request had gone through faster than I'd hoped. I could start as Princess Primrose's understudy right away.

But I couldn't just vanish from the gift shop. Not without talking to Becca. After everything she'd done for me, she deserved to hear it from me, not second-hand.

I passed the cotton candy stand, the sugar scented air followed me as I stepped into the gift shop.

Becca stood behind the register, lining up a row of stuffed bunnies in tiny promotional sunglasses. Her head popped up the second she spotted me. "You're early," she said, one eyebrow lifting. "Finally caught the retail bug?"

My stomach twisted. Maybe she didn't know yet. Maybe I'd have to actually say the words.

She smirked. "Relax, Webber. You look like you're about to confess to a crime. We're going to miss you around here."

I let out a breathless laugh. "You heard about the transfer?"

Her expression softened into something warm. "I heard. And yeah, I'm sad to see you go. But more than that? I'm proud of you. Fantasy World's all about believing in something bigger. And if this is part of your something bigger—go."

That lump in my throat formed fast. "Thanks. I'll miss this place."

"Well, if you ever get homesick for folding T-shirts and cleaning up cotton candy disasters, you know where to find me."

"And if you ever need me," I grinned. "I'll be over at the castle. I'm Princess Primrose's new understudy. Or... actually, the understudy's understudy."

Becca's eyes went wide. "Oh wow. Should I curtsy or something?"

"Please don't."

"Too late." She dropped into the most dramatic curtsy imaginable, one arm extended like we were in the middle of a Broadway finale.

A laugh slipped out.

"Really, Becca," I said, my voice catching just a little. "Thank you. For everything."

Her smile was all warmth and unshakable confidence. "Go sparkle, Webber. You've got this."

And just like that, she set me free.

One chapter closed. Another cracked open, waiting.

When I stepped into the green room, Renee was already there, perched on the edge of a chair like she'd been counting the seconds.

She'd been to the doctor that morning. Luckily, her ankle was fine. Just a strain, nothing serious. One night's rest and she was already back on her feet.

Which meant yesterday's performance had been a onetime thing.

And honestly? That suited me just fine. I wasn't in any rush to go chasing the spotlight again.

"Hope you're ready to be royal," Renee said brightly, practically buzzing with energy. "Because your princess training starts now."

I blinked. "My what?"

She nodded solemnly, as if delivering a royal decree. "Every Primrose goes through it. It's tradition. And guess what? You're up."

Before I could even process that, a low, familiar chuckle sounded behind me. I turned to see Cameron leaning in the doorway, arms crossed, grin unapologetically smug.

"Well, well," he drawled, pretending to be impressed. "How's our newest royal recruit?"

"Can we not make this a thing?" I said, already bracing for the teasing.

He pushed off the doorframe, strolling closer with that infuriating glint in his eyes. "Oh, Carolina," he said, voice low and teasing, "it's already a thing."

Turns out, "princess training" was not the gentle, fairy-godmother-style mentoring I'd been picturing.

Renee took charge like a woman on a mission. One book balanced on my head, and two minutes later, she was circling me with the precision of a sparkly drill sergeant determined to correct my posture and possibly my entire personality.

"Back straight. Shoulders down. Chin up," she barked, her gaze laser-focused on my every move.

Across the room, Cameron had found a spot against a prop table, arms crossed, watching like this was his new favorite show.

"You know, Carolina," he said, all mock sincerity, "if the princess gig doesn't work out, you'd make an excellent end table."

Next up: the royal wave.

I stood beside Renee, trying to mimic her smooth, graceful wrist flick, elbow poised, hand lifted like I was blessing the masses, not awkwardly swatting invisible gnats.

I frowned, adjusted, tried again.

From across the room came a suspiciously choked sound. Cameron, of course, was failing miserably at hiding his grin.

"A little more grace," he said, barely keeping a straight face. "And a little less... windshield wiper."

Next on the agenda: line delivery.

Because apparently today's theme was *public humiliation with a side of sparkle*.

I did my best to channel the soft, sweet, storybook warmth of Princess Primrose. I was holding it together... until Cameron decided to be Cameron.

"Let's hear it, Carolina," he called, lounging like a man who lived to cause trouble. "Give me your best 'Welcome, noble guests.' Sell it like your tiara depends on it."

I narrowed my eyes, lifted my chin, and summoned every scrap of my dormant theater kid energy.

"Oh, noble Cameron," I said with an exaggerated flourish, "how thoroughly I loathe your presence."

He doubled over, laughing. "Majestic."

By the time break rolled around, I was exhausted. But it was a good kind of exhaustion. The kind that came with aching cheeks from too much laughter.

Outside, the breeze rushed over my flushed skin, tugging at stray strands of hair. I leaned against the railing, just breathing it in.

Footsteps sounded behind me until Cameron appeared at my side with his hands shoved into his pockets.

"So," he said, flashing that crooked smile. "First day as royalty. How's it feel?"

I let out a breathless laugh. "Honestly?" My gaze drifted back to the castle, its spires cutting sharp against the sky. "Kind of incredible."

His smirk softened.

"You know," he said, voice dropping just enough to make it feel like he was telling me a secret, "I think you were made for this."

I arched a brow. "What? Getting bossed around by Renee and endlessly harassed by you?"

He grinned. "Exactly."

I shook my head, fighting a smile I didn't want him to see.

He turned toward the door, pausing just long enough to throw over his shoulder, "I'm heading back in. Try not to miss me too much."

"I'll survive," I said, but my voice came out warmer than I meant it to. "I'll be there in a minute. Just want to... soak it all in first."

He nodded like he understood, then disappeared inside, leaving me with the wind, the castle, and a heartbeat that wasn't quite ready to settle.

I wandered over to a bench and sank into it, letting the afternoon heat settle over me. The air shimmered, carrying the faint scent of popcorn and the distant hum of laughter. Sunlight spilled across the square—still bright, but softening at the edges like the day itself was exhaling.

A few minutes passed before an older man eased down beside me with a quiet groan.

"How's the park treating you?" he asked.

I smiled, tapping my name tag. "I actually work here."

He chuckled, adjusting his glasses. "Sidney from North Carolina," he read. "Nice to meet you. I'm Andrew."

"Pleasure to meet you too," I said.

The strap of his sun-faded backpack slid down his shoulder as he settled in. A "First Visit!" button gleamed proudly on his shirt.

"First time at Fantasy World?" I asked.

"Yep. Seventy-six years old, and I finally made it." His grin crinkled the corners of his eyes.

"What made you come now?"

He looked toward the castle, and something in his smile softened. "Always wanted to. Just... never got around to it. Work, kids, life. Then my granddaughter told me, 'There's no expiration date on dreams.'" His gaze lingered on the spires. "So here I am."

I followed his line of sight, my chest tightening.

"You're never too old for Fantasy World," he added.

"You're right about that," I said.

We talked for the rest of my break, about his grandkids, about the mischievous parrot who could mimic his laugh, about how walking through the gates felt like stepping into another world. His voice was full of quiet wonder, like every sight and sound was a long-awaited gift.

Then, without warning, his tone shifted, dipping into something softer.

"My wife always wanted to come," he said, eyes fixed on the castle. "We kept saying 'someday.'" He paused, and I could hear the years tucked inside the silence. "But someday passed. And so did she."

The words landed heavy, settling in my chest.

"I feel like I let her down," he murmured.

I looked at him for a moment, then back at the castle. The place she'd dreamed of, the place he was finally standing in. "Something tells me," I said gently, "that she just wanted to be with you. And that mattered more than anything else."

For a long moment, he didn't speak. Then he smiled faintly, though his eyes carried a sheen of unshed emotion. "You're a wise young woman. Thank you for sitting with me," he said as he pushed himself to his feet.

"And thank you for sharing your story," I replied.

"I think I'm going to ride a roller coaster." His gaze lingered on the sign for Adventure Cove, a small smile tugging at his lips. "Time to see what I've been missing. Life's too short for regrets."

The words landed like a pebble in still water, sending ripples through me that kept spreading long after he'd stood and walked away.

I stepped back into the green room, the cool air wrapping around me after the heat outside. Laughter and scattered chatter filled the space, but Andrew's words were still the loudest thing in my head. *Life's too short for regrets.*

I'd barely made it two steps before Cameron appeared in my path, leaning casually against a prop table like he'd been waiting for me.

"So, rumor has it," he said, his smile slow and knowing, "you still haven't had a proper park day."

I tilted my head. "Who told you that?"

"Westley told Porter. Porter told me. And now I'm personally offended."

I folded my arms, fighting the twitch of a smile. "I've been busy. And I've done plenty around the park."

"Uh-huh. Then tell me. Have you done any of these?" He closed in, stepping toward me as he ticked things off on his fingers. "Iconic rides? Fireworks from the *best* spot? Eating your weight in overpriced, totally unnecessary snacks?"

"I watched fireworks with you," I said, placing my hands on my hips.

"Doesn't count," he said with a shake of his head. "Have you watched them since then?"

I opened my mouth to argue, but the words stuck. "...No."

He sighed, shaking his head like I'd just broken his heart. "Tragic. Absolutely tragic. Clear your schedule, Princess. We're both off tomorrow, and I'm taking you to the park."

"Bossy," I said, but the word came out softer than I meant it to.

"See you tomorrow, Princess." Something flickered in his eyes. "It's a date."

Chapter Twenty-Two

WILLOW ANSWERED THE DOOR with a small, knowing grin, like she'd been expecting me.

"She's still asleep," she said, leaning against the frame. "You're about to become her least favorite person."

She stepped aside and ushered me inside.

I smiled and stepped past her. Willow pointed me toward Sidney's door and wished me luck.

I hesitated for a moment before knocking lightly. No answer.

I turned the knob and eased it open.

Sidney was curled in a fortress of blankets, only a tumble of messy hair and one bare arm in sight. She looked so warm and content that, for a split second, I almost felt guilty.

Almost.

"Rise and shine, Carolina," I said in my brightest, most obnoxiously cheerful voice. "Big, magical day ahead."

A muffled groan floated up from somewhere inside the blanket fortress.

"If you're not early, you're late," I added, stepping closer until I was right beside her bed.

One bleary eye cracked open just enough to give me a sleepy glare. "What are you? A walking motivational calendar?"

"Wrong," I said, grinning down at her. "I'm your official Fantasy World tour guide, sworn to give you the perfect day you didn't even know you needed."

"It's six in the morning," she mumbled, burrowing deeper into the covers like she could disappear entirely. "What about the *sleep* I need?"

"Sleep," I said, hooking my fingers under the edge of her blanket and giving it a teasing tug, "is for people who don't have rope-drop bragging rights to earn."

Before she could protest, I grabbed the edge of her blanket and gave it a dramatic yank, and stopped cold.

Pink tank top. Glittery letters spelling out *Resting Princess Face*. Matching shorts dotted with tiny gold crowns.

It was ridiculous. Adorable. And for some reason, my brain short-circuited for half a second, storing the image away like I'd need it later.

A grin tugged at my mouth before I could stop it. "Nice jammies."

She sat up and shot me a bleary-eyed glare. "Do not judge me."

"Oh, I'd never judge," I said, though my tone was already betraying me. "I just wasn't emotionally ready for this level of royalty."

The pillow came flying at my head. I caught it and gave her a triumphant grin.

"You're the worst," she muttered.

"Yep. And you're stuck with me all day."

She huffed, a tiny smile threatening to slip through. "Fine. Give me ten minutes."

I didn't move right away.

She crossed her arms, breaking the moment. "That's your cue to leave, Your Highness."

"Right." I laughed, backing toward the door as she shooed me out, already wondering how many more smiles I could get out of her today.

True to her word, ten minutes later she stepped into the hall dressed in a light blue tank, matching shorts, hair swept into a loose ponytail that looked like it had taken no effort at all.

I was simple. Casual. And somehow better than any Primrose gown she'd ever worn onstage.

"You ready?" I asked.

"If you're expecting full hair and makeup at this hour, you might want to schedule a wellness check," she said dryly.

"Oh, I wouldn't dare interfere with your signature *just rolled out of bed* aesthetic. Very... authentic."

She crossed her arms, but not before I caught the flicker of self-consciousness in her eyes.

"Carolina," I said, the teasing dropping out of my voice. "You look great. Honestly... I've never seen you like this before. I like it."

Her smile came slowly, like she was deciding whether to believe me. "Alright, fine. That just got you a coffee. My treat."

"Not a chance. Today's on me."

We fell into step toward the park, the early air still cool on our skin, the sound of distant music drifting in from the gates. Neither of us spoke for a while. We didn't need to.

There was silence between us, but it didn't feel empty. It felt comfortable.

Instead of heading straight for the gates, I angled us toward the little coffee stand tucked just outside the entrance. The air smelled faintly of espresso and caramel, and the early morning chatter from the crowd softened into background noise.

"Two iced mochas with oat milk," I told the barista without hesitation.

Sidney blinked at me. "How on earth did you know my favorite drink?"

I shrugged like it was nothing. "You ordered it the day we met, in Kingdom Square. Right after Gwen ambushed me."

Her expression shifted, softened in a way that made me almost forget to grab the cups when they were placed on the counter.

What I didn't tell her was that I remembered the exact way the light had caught her hair that day, and how her laugh had felt like the only thing keeping me grounded. I needed her more than she realized that day.

I handed her the cup instead. "Better drink up. You'll need the energy for the race to our first ride."

Her brows lifted. "The what now?"

"The race," I said, grinning over the rim of my coffee. "We're going to be first in line for whatever ride you pick."

A spark of mischief lit her eyes. "Alright. Fine. But we're starting with the River Adventure Cruise. Endless dad jokes. No mercy. Basically, Porter times fifty."

I grinned. "Game on."

We joined the crowd at the rope, the energy thrumming like a starting line before a marathon. The crew member gave the nod, and the mass surged forward. Someone bumped Sidney hard enough to throw her off balance, and my hand shot out to steady her.

Then, my hand found hers, and we were off.

We ran, dodging strollers and weaving between groups. The world narrowed to the sound of our feet on the pavement, the rush of the race, and the warmth of her hand in mine.

By the time the River Adventure Cruise sign came into view, my chest burned, but not from the sprint.

"Victory," I panted, still holding her hand. "Has never tasted sweeter."

And it was because *she* was by my side.

Chapter Twenty-Three

Sidney

I GLANCED DOWN AT our still-joined hands, my pulse tripping over itself.

Did he even realize he hadn't let go?

His hold wasn't tight. Just steady, like he was making sure I didn't get swept away in the shuffle of the queue. And maybe it meant nothing. Maybe this was just Cameron, being Cameron: thoughtful without even realizing it. But the quiet warmth of his palm against mine made it feel like something.

It wasn't until a crew member waved us forward that he finally let go, and the sudden absence left a strange, weightless ache in my fingers.

We stepped into a weather-worn boat with a sun-faded canopy. Sliding into the front row, I found my legs brushing his, the bench seat feeling narrower than it probably was.

At the bow, our tour guide was waiting. He was dressed in a khaki shirt, wide-brimmed hat just a little too big, and a grin that said this was the greatest job on earth.

"Welcome aboard the River Adventure Cruise!" he announced. "I'll be your fearless leader. Unless we hit a snag. Then it's every tourist for themselves."

Cameron leaned in, close enough that I caught the faint scent of his cologne. A grin tugged at his lips.

"Brace yourself, Carolina," Cameron murmured. "Things are about to get real."

The boat groaned as it slid forward into the manufactured twilight of the jungle. Overhead, thick vines draped low, swaying in the faint breeze from hidden fans. From the brush came a deep mechanical growl. It was clearly fake, yet still enough to make my shoulders tense.

"If you look to your left," the guide announced in his best nature documentary voice, "you'll spot one of the rarest creatures in the jungle... a tourist who isn't taking pictures. Quick, make a wish."

Cameron tilted his head toward me.

I pressed my lips together, trying to keep a straight face. The worst thing I could do was laugh too early. Cameron would never let me live it down.

We drifted past a family of animatronic elephants spraying arcs of mist into the air. One trumpeted with a tinny squeal that sounded like it had been recorded in a mall parking lot before smartphones existed.

"And here we have our resident elephant herd enjoying a refreshing spa day," the guide said. "Don't worry, they're all wearing trunks... except Carl. Carl's a free-spirit."

I caught Cameron watching me from the corner of his eye, clearly waiting for a reaction. His mouth was curved in that way that made him look both smug and unfairly attractive.

"If I start laughing at these," I muttered, "push me overboard."

"It would be my honor," he said, eyes glinting.

We rounded a bend, revealing an explorer camp in shambles, tents collapsed, crates spilled across the mud, and a few unlucky adventurers clinging to tree branches while a rhino pawed the ground below.

"Ah yes," the guide said. "Our brave explorers, demonstrating the number one rule of the jungle: if you can't outrun the rhino, at least outrun your friends."

The image of Cameron shoving someone out of the way to save himself popped into my head, and I had to bite back a snort. "Should we send them snacks or thoughts and prayers?" I asked under my breath.

Cameron pressed a hand to his mouth to hide a laugh. "Both. Just to be safe."

Another bend revealed a roaring waterfall, sheets of white crashing into the river. The boat veered behind it, cool mist brushing my cheeks. For a second, I let my eyes close, letting the sound and spray soak into me.

"And now, folks," the guide said with the gravitas of a movie trailer voiceover, "nature's original shower. Refreshing, invigorating, and with better water pressure than most city apartments."

A few people chuckled.

"Not quite as luxurious as your uncle's koi pond," he added, "but it's got fewer koi judging you."

Cameron leaned in toward me. "Man's got material."

I shook my head, grinning despite myself.

The boat slowed, the hum of the motor softening as the jungle faded into painted rockwork and neatly trimmed hedges. Sunlight spilled back over the water, breaking the spell of the ride. Guests shifted in their seats, gathering bags and phones, that subtle, collective signal that the adventure was over.

"Thank you," the guide said with a theatrical bow. "I'll be here all week. Tips accepted in the form of applause or granola bars."

Cameron kept hold of my hand as he helped me step onto the dock.

"Totally worth dragging you out of bed for, right?" he said.

"Maybe," I murmured, though the smile tugging at my mouth probably gave me away.

We stepped into the sunlight, which felt harsh after the twenty minutes of shaded bliss.

Cameron's hand closed around my arm. "We should ride that next. No park day is complete without riding Prince Peter's horse."

I gave him a look. "Prince Peter's... horse?"

A flush crept into his cheeks. "I mean, the carousel. Have you ever ridden it *here*?"

I laughed. "I've ridden a carousel before. How different can it be?"

"That's not the point," he said, already guiding me in that direction, his hand lingering just a second too long. "You have to ride the one here."

The music grew louder as we neared, that slightly off-key calliope tune somehow both cheerful and tinged with nostalgia. Sunlight caught on the mirrored panels above the ride, scattering warm flecks of gold across the pavement.

Up in the operator's booth, Ridley leaned casually against the controls, her Fantasy World vest a little rumpled, nametag flashing in the light. She spotted us instantly and gave us a small wave.

We queued up behind a family with two little girls in matching pigtails. The line moved quickly, but as we neared the gate, I noticed nearly every horse was already taken. The carousel spun in a blur of color and music, riders laughing as they bobbed up and down.

"Looks like we might have to wait for the next one," I murmured, though part of me wasn't sure if that was disappointment or relief.

Cameron only grinned, his gaze fixed on the ride like he had a plan.

The carousel slowed, the music fading just enough for Ridley's voice to carry from the operator's booth. "Well, well," she called. "Didn't take you long to make it to the romantic rides."

"It's not romantic," I said quickly, heat creeping into my cheeks.

"Are you sure?" Ridley's eyes cut to Cameron, her grin turning sly. "Because Prince Charming here looks like, he knew exactly what he was doing bringing you over. Or are you going to deny this was all his idea?"

My eyes widened, flicking between her and Cameron.

He didn't bother denying it, just shot her a slow, smug smile. "Think you can squeeze us in, Ridley?"

Her brows lifted. "For you two? Always." She hit the switch, and the gate swung open with a creak. "Pick your steeds, lovebirds."

I groaned under my breath, but Cameron was already steering me toward the largest horse on the outer ring. Of course he would pick the most dramatic one, its mane carved in sweeping curls, the gold-painted saddle catching the light like it was designed to demand attention.

He rested one hand on the pole and swept the other out with mock chivalry. "Your chariot awaits, Princess."

I rolled my eyes, but the corner of my mouth betrayed me with the start of a smile. "Do you practice these lines, or do they just come naturally?"

"Natural talent," he said without missing a beat, then leaned in, his breath warm against my ear. "I am a prince, after all."

I climbed onto the horse, the brass pole cool beneath my fingers, forcing myself not to think about how his gaze followed me the whole time.

Cameron swung onto the horse beside mine in one fluid motion.

The ride jolted to life, the horses rising and falling in a steady, unhurried rhythm. Music swelled around us, and the world blurred into a whirl of color.

I realized I was smiling before I could stop myself. Maybe it was the music, maybe the sunlight, but more likely, it was the way Cameron's smile felt so easy.

The carousel began to slow, the horses dipping lower with each turn until the music softened into a final, lilting note. The world came back into focus.

Cameron swung a leg over his horse and stepped down first, then turned toward me, hand extended. "Your royal dismount, Princess."

I took it, meaning to just let him steady me, but the second my foot hit the platform, the horse shifted with a soft creak. My balance tipped, and before I could stop myself, I stumbled forward, straight into him.

His arm looped around my waist, holding me close. For a heartbeat, neither of us moved. I could feel the steady beat of his heart against my shoulder, the faint scent of his cologne mixing with the warm air.

"Careful there, Carolina," he murmured, voice lower than usual.

"Yeah," I said softly, forcing myself to step back even though every part of me noticed the way his hand lingered a fraction too long before letting go.

Ridley met us at the exit gate. "Hope you enjoyed your magical moment," she said with exaggerated sincerity. "I expect wedding invitations when the time comes."

Chapter Twenty-Four

Cameron

THE AIR WAS THICK with popcorn, cotton candy, and deep-fried temptation. Basically, the scent of delicious regret. My stomach rumbled in approval.

I was about to suggest grabbing lunch when I saw it. A row of carnival booths stretched ahead, pulsing with neon lights and the kind of shameless optimism that dared you to throw away your money.

And there, wedged between balloon darts and a basketball hoop with a rim clearly designed for heartbreak, was the ring toss.

"I'm doing this," I said, already pulling out my wallet.

Sidney laughed beside me, the kind of laugh that said she was already convinced I'd fail.

"Oh no," she said, her tone light but dripping with mock judgment. "You're *that guy*."

I turned to her. "Excuse me. What guy?"

She folded her arms, one brow lifting in exaggerated pity. "The guy who spends twenty bucks trying to win a plush dinosaur that costs $4.99 in the gift shop."

I scoffed. "It's not about the plush. It's about the principle."

"Ah, yes," she said solemnly. "The sacred honor of the ring toss."

"Exactly." I pointed at the booth. "Watch and learn, Princess. You're about to witness greatness."

Choosing to ignore her complete lack of faith, I stepped up to the ring toss booth and handed over some cash. The kid running it was maybe sixteen, visor slightly crooked. He looked like he'd rather be anywhere else. He took my money and slid me a stack of plastic rings without a word.

How hard could this be?

Simple geometry. Basic physics. Just a well-angled toss.

I squared my shoulders, lined up my shot, took a slow breath—

And missed. Completely.

Sidney snorted.

"I don't know what's funnier," she said, eyes gleaming, "that you missed or that you looked so *confident* doing it."

"Beginner's miscalculation," I muttered, shaking off the betrayal of my own coordination.

I handed over more cash, lined up my shot, took my time...

Missed. Again.

"The sun was in my eyes," I grumbled.

She tilted her head, lips curving. "It's literally behind you."

"...Physics is rigged."

Five attempts later, my dignity was dangling by a single frayed thread. I sighed, turned toward her, and gestured to the booth. "Alright, Carolina. If you think you're so great, let's see you prove it."

Her grin was pure confidence, like she'd been waiting her entire life for this challenge.

Without a word, she strolled up, handed the attendant a single bill, and, without even bothering to aim, tossed a ring.

It landed with a perfect little *clink*. First try.

I blinked and turned to her with an incredulous look. She gave me a small, triumphant grin in return.

The game attendant froze for a beat, blinking like he wasn't sure what just happened. "Wow. That was... really fast. Uh, pick your prize, miss."

The game attendant blinked, genuinely stunned. "Wow. That was... really fast. Uh, pick your prize, miss."

Sidney gave the shelf a quick once-over, then lifted a finger and pointed to the most obnoxious thing there: a fluorescent pink unicorn roughly the size of a small child.

The attendant cracked a smile as he handed over the prize, his gaze lingering a beat too long. My hand found Sidney's elbow, and I steered her away before he could get any ideas.

She hugged the absurdly large unicorn to her chest, laughing softly, eyes alight with victory.

I nodded toward the plush. "Should I be jealous of that thing?"

"You should," she said with a grin. "It understands me."

And with that, she strutted off like she'd just been crowned Miss Fantasy World, the unicorn tucked proudly in her arms as if it were a trophy.

I watched her walk ahead, that victorious bounce in her step pulling a smile out of me before I could stop it.

"Nice work, Princess," I murmured under my breath.

She smiled over her shoulder. "Come on, I'll make it up to you with a churro."

Right on cue, my stomach growled in agreement.

The scent hit first, fried dough, cinnamon, and sugar, rolling over us like a delicious ambush.

Without thinking, I veered off course, drawn in like a moth to a deep-fried flame.

Sidney followed, clearly unaware she was being led to *the* cart. The golden standard of churros. If there were a Hall of Fame, these would be first-ballot inductees.

"You're about to witness greatness," I told her. "This cart is elite. Churros so good they'll ruin all others for you."

The crew member handed over my prize, a warm, golden churro, dusted in cinnamon sugar and glinting in the Florida sun like snack gods had handcrafted it.

I turned to Sidney, holding it up with mock ceremony. "Behold! The crown jewel of theme park cuisine."

She glanced at me. Then at the churro. Then back again.

Before I could even sense the danger—*snap*.

Half was gone, and she popped her share into her mouth.

My jaw dropped. "Did you just—?"

"I thought we were sharing," she said, completely unfazed.

"I paid seven bucks for that churro," I said, deadpan. "And you split it like we had a court-approved snack agreement."

She shrugged, licking cinnamon sugar from her fingertips. "You said it was the best in the park. I wanted to experience greatness."

I narrowed my eyes. "Unbelievable."

She grinned, already angling for another bite. "Delicious, too."

"This feels toxic," I muttered.

Sidney didn't even blink. "Then do what's best for you," she said sweetly. "And surrender the churro on your way out."

I stared at her. "You already took half."

She nodded toward what remained in my hand. "Yeah, and now I want half of *that*."

"Not a chance," I said, clutching it like it was a priceless artifact. Then, I took a massive bite, never breaking eye contact, while cinnamon sugar rained down like petty confetti.

She burst out laughing.

This wasn't over.

No, this was war.

We drifted onto a quieter path, the noise of the crowd fading until it was just the faint hum of music and the crunch of gravel under our shoes.

Sidney slowed, letting her fingers trail along the edge of a planter. Her smile was still there, but softer now, like it had turned inward.

"This place," she murmured, almost to herself, "it's everything I dreamed it would be. But also... not."

I glanced over. "Not in a bad way, I hope."

She shook her head. "No. Just... different. I spent so long imagining it, building it up in my head. And now that I'm here, it's like..." Her brow knit slightly. "Like I'm afraid to enjoy it too much. Like if I do, the magic might slip away."

I let that hang between us for a moment before answering. "Maybe that's the trick. Stop chasing the version you pictured and start paying attention to the one that's right here. Fairytales and reality don't always align, but that doesn't make them any less magical."

Her gaze lifted to mine, curiosity and something softer flickering there. "You actually believe that?"

"I didn't," I admitted. "Not for a long time. But then someone showed up, started stealing my snacks and getting under my skin, and... somehow, things started feeling magical again."

Her smile came slowly this time, deliberate, like she knew exactly what she was doing. "Sounds like you might actually like having her around."

I smirked. "Oh, she's the absolute worst."

She laughed, bumping her shoulder against mine, and we kept walking.

Sidney trailed her fingers along the wooden railing as we crossed the arched bridge into the Fairy Gardens, a tucked-away corner of the park draped in ivy-covered trellises and glowing lanterns. The soft trickle of a nearby stream threading through the quiet.

Then, softly, like she wasn't sure if she meant to say it aloud, she murmured, "I broke up with Zack."

I stopped mid-step. So did she.

She didn't look at me right away, just kept her gaze on the fountain ahead, where sunlight flickered across the water like scattered gold.

"You okay?" I asked, carefully.

She gave a small shrug, her eyes still fixed on that distant point.

"I don't know. Maybe. It wasn't some huge, messy thing. No fight, no dramatic goodbye. I just... realized I didn't want to keep pretending everything was fine."

Something in my chest tightened.

She went on, her voice low but steady.

"Do you regret it?" I asked.

She shook her head without even pausing. "No. I think I regret how long I stayed. But not leaving."

I nodded, letting the weight of that settle between us.

We kept walking, our pace naturally slowing. The sounds of the park faded until it felt like we'd slipped into our own quiet corner, a space that belonged only to us.

I didn't press her for more. Didn't try to fill the silence.

I just stayed beside her, step for step, hoping she knew I wasn't going anywhere.

The next few hours unfolded one ride at a time. Sidney gravitated toward the slower ones. Boat rides, storybook spinners, anything that stayed safely on the ground. No towering coasters. No heart-stopping drops.

One of these days, I was determined to get her on a roller coaster. I could already picture it, her hand gripping mine, knuckles white, her laughter breaking free somewhere between the climb and the plunge. The wind tearing through her hair, her eyes wide with that mix of fear and exhilaration. And me, stealing every second I could to watch her instead of the track ahead.

For now, though, I kept the thought to myself. Let her have her gentle rides, her slow turns, her fairy tale scenes. There'd be time for the big drops later.

By the time we looped back toward Adventure Cove, the sun was sinking low, bathing everything in that soft, golden glow that made even the scuffed pavement shimmer like it belonged on a postcard.

Without warning, Sidney gasped and grabbed my arm like she'd just spotted a celebrity.

"Cameron!" She was practically bouncing. "Pineapple swirl. We *have* to get one."

I followed her gaze to the snack cart and grinned. She wasn't wrong. Pineapple soft serve at Fantasy World wasn't just dessert, it was a rite of passage.

We made our way over, and when the cast member handed her the cup, it was a towering swirl of golden perfection.

Sidney took a slow, reverent bite, her eyes fluttering shut like she'd just unlocked the universe.

"Light, creamy, tart," she murmured, each word dripping with bliss. "This might be the best part of my day."

I couldn't help smiling. She looked so genuinely happy in that moment it almost felt wrong to interrupt it.

Almost.

My eyes drifted to a passing crew member wrangling a massive bouquet of colorful balloons.

Game on.

"Hey, Princess," I said, nodding toward the balloons. "We should get your picture holding those."

Sidney's eyes lit up. "Oh, absolutely."

She handed me her ice cream without hesitation and made a beeline for the balloon vendor.

Here's a fun little behind-the-scenes fact: they don't actually let you hold the balloon bouquet. Something about safety, logistics, and *not losing an entire bouquet of helium-filled expenses to the sky.*

But they do let you hold the strings while they step out of frame to make it *look* like you're holding them.

Sidney was deep in cheerful conversation with the vendor when I made my move.

One quick, stealthy swipe of the spoon, and I scored a generous bite of her pineapple soft serve.

Cold. Tart. Light. Basically, summer in a spoon. And absolutely worth it.

I was halfway through a second bite when she turned around, catching me mid-crime. Her eyes went wide in exaggerated horror. *"Cameron."*

I looked up innocently, spoon still in my mouth. "Yes?"

She pointed at me like I'd just committed a felony. "You did *not* just do that."

I casually lifted the cup for another spoonful. "Oh, but I absolutely did."

Her mouth dropped open. "You are officially the worst human alive."

"Yeah, yeah. A real tragedy." I took another slow, deliberate bite, locking eyes with her as her glare sharpened. "Possession is nine-tenths of the law, Princess."

"That doesn't apply to ice cream, you criminal." She marched back over and reached for the cup, but I twisted away just in time, holding it high like a trophy. "Sleep with one eye open."

Still grinning, I scooped up another spoonful and held it out to her. "Come on," I said, like I wasn't still savoring my victory. "Truce?"

She crossed her arms, eyeing the spoon as if it were laced with TNT. "This feels like a trap."

"Not a trap," I said smoothly. "A very generous peace offering."

Her eyes narrowed, but she didn't turn away. Didn't swat my hand. Just stared a fraction too long.

Which meant I was *winning*.

Until she leaned in.

The moment her lips closed around the spoon, I knew I'd lost.

She pulled back with maddening calm, but something shifted in the air. Her gaze lifted to mine, steady and unreadable, and for a heartbeat the world went still.

My attention dropped to her mouth, and suddenly I forgot how to breathe.

I swallowed hard.

Get it together, Cameron.

She tossed her hair and flashed me a grin.

"I still want that photo," she said, strolling toward the balloon vendor like she hadn't just knocked my entire world off its axis.

"Yeah, Princess," I murmured under my breath. "Anything you want."

I snapped a few shots while she posed, the bright balloons bobbing over her head. A minute later, she skipped back, scrolling through the photos with a satisfied hum.

She glanced up, smirking. "What, no clever scheme to hold *these* hostage for my number?"

"And why would I need to do that?" I smirked right back and tossed in a wink. "I already have it."

She rolled her eyes but didn't argue, her attention sliding back to the screen. Once she'd deemed a few photos acceptable, she lowered the phone and looked at me with a softer smile.

"We should probably start scoping out a spot for the fireworks."

I was already on my feet. "I've got one in mind."

Her brow arched in mock suspicion. "Oh yeah? And where's that?"

I turned, holding out my hand. "Do you trust me?"

She hesitated for just a beat, eyes narrowing like she was calculating the risk. Then, without a word, she slid her hand into mine.

Chapter Twenty-Five

Sidney

I STARTED QUESTIONING MY life choices the second Cameron steered us into the line for *Water Mountain*.

I stopped short, folding my arms. "Wait. This is a water ride, isn't it?"

"Sort of," he said, far too casually. "It's mostly mist. Barely a splash. You'll be fine. Trust me."

I shot him a glare sharp enough to cut rope and slipped my hand from his. "That's exactly what people say right before you end up soaked and miserable."

He clutched his chest like I'd wounded him. "Carolina, how could you doubt me?"

I raised a brow.

"I know the exact seat to keep us dry. And if anything tries to splash you, I'll try to save you."

I wasn't buying it. Not even close.

And yet, somehow, I still let him reclaim my hand and lead me forward, my better judgment dragging its feet a few paces behind.

By the time we were settled into the log-shaped boat, I was still unconvinced. But then we began drifting, the river ahead shimmering like it had been poured straight from a storybook.

Lanterns swayed above us, their golden light scattering across the water in ripples and dancing like slow-motion fireflies. The air smelled of damp earth and something faintly floral, like wildflowers after rain. Somewhere ahead, soft, whimsical music threaded through the croak of hidden frogs and the gentle rustle of leaves overhead.

It was the kind of quiet magic that slipped under your skin and made you wonder if maybe the stories were real after all.

I turned my head, ready to make a half-sarcastic comment.

But Cameron wasn't watching the river. Or the lights. Or the path ahead.

He was watching me with a smirk locked in place.

"I don't like that look," I said, narrowing my eyes. "It screams you're up to something."

He leaned back against the bench and gave me a little shake of his head. "Just making sure you're enjoying the ride, Princess."

His eyes met mine, and for a heartbeat I was caught, lost in the warm pull of his hazel gaze. The rest of the world blurred at the edges until there was nothing but him and me.

I looked away first, feigning interest in the lanterns drifting above as my pulse kicked up.

The boat drifted deeper into the dark, and the music shifted to something bouncy and playful.

Cypress trees loomed on either side, their roots curling into the water. Animatronic animals peered from the reeds, crafted with such care they could almost pass for real. Reflections shimmered like scattered stardust, fireflies traced lazy paths through the air, and even the ripples trailing our boat seemed brushed with light. Somewhere in the distance, laughter floated on the breeze.

For a moment, the park didn't feel manufactured at all.

It felt enchanted.

"Okay, okay," I said at last, shooting him a reluctant smile. "I get it now. This is... nice."

His eyes lit up as if I had just crowned him champion.

"Are you," he said, hand pressed to his chest in mock shock, "admitting I was right?"

"Let's not get carried away," I said, rolling my eyes.

He only smirked and brought his arm to rest on the seat behind me.

The boat rounded a bend, and the music softened into a gentle lull. Then—

Click. Click. Click.

My stomach dropped in sync with my jaw as we began to climb.

Oh no. No, no, no.

I whipped my head toward Cameron, who now wore the most smug, self-satisfied grin I'd seen all day.

"What is this?" I demanded, clutching the safety bar like it might save my life.

He glanced over, perfectly calm. "Huh. Did I forget to mention the drop at the end?"

How had I forgotten about the drop? I'd seen the videos. I'd watched people scream like their souls were leaving their bodies on this exact ride. It was firmly cemented on my *absolutely not* list.

My jaw tightened. "You—"

"—are the best tour guide you've ever had?" Cameron cut in.

"Cameron Scott, I swear to all things magical, I hate you right now."

He laughed, completely unfazed, like we weren't seconds from plunging off a cliff. "No, you don't, Princess."

I gripped the safety bar harder, knuckles white, eyes clamped shut. Bracing for the inevitable.

Then I felt it.

A light brush of his fingers against mine. He pried them gently from the bar and threaded his fingers through mine.

The fear didn't vanish, but it shifted. Enough to let me breathe. Enough to hold on.

"Open your eyes," he said, voice low and coaxing. "Trust me."

And for some reason, I listened. I cracked one eye open, then the other.

The sight hit me like a rush of air, stealing whatever breath I had left. Fantasy World stretched out in every direction, a dream made real beneath us. I could see everything: the castle, Enchanted Boulevard, every ride lit in its own glow.

Twinkling lights laced the winding paths, the river shimmered like a ribbon of silver weaving through the trees, and the Enchanted Castle stood at the heart of it all, glowing as if it had been lifted straight from the pages of a storybook.

Then the sky erupted. Fireworks bloomed above the spires in dazzling bursts of gold and sapphire, each one cracking the night open and scattering light across the world below.

"...Wow," I breathed.

"Told you," he murmured, his voice softer than usual, threaded with something I couldn't quite name. "You haven't really done Fantasy World until you've seen the fireworks from up here."

"It's beautiful," I whispered before I could stop myself.

"Yeah," he said quietly. "It is."

But he wasn't looking at the view. He was looking at me.

Our eyes met, and for one suspended moment the rest of the world slipped away. His smile curved, small and crooked, and something in my chest tightened. I held my breath, wondering if he was about to say something that would change everything.

"And now," he said, still holding my gaze, "we drop."

Huh?

That was not what I expected him to say.

Then the boat tilted forward, bringing me back to reality.

"No—"

Cameron's grin widened, mischief sparking in his eyes. "Too late."

And then we dropped.

I screamed.

His laughter burst beside me as the world tilted and spun. Lights smeared into streaks, wind tore past my ears, and everything dissolved into a chaotic, breathless blur.

SPLASH.

A wall of water crashed over us, drenching me in seconds. I gasped, blinking through droplets as they slid down my face. My clothes clung like shrink-wrap, every inch of me soaked, and for a few stunned heartbeats I just sat there trying to remember how to breathe.

And Cameron?

He was bone dry.

I turned toward him in slow motion, water dripping from my lashes, betrayal radiating off me like steam from my soaked clothes.

"You—" I sputtered.

He attempted a concerned look and failed miserably. "You good, Princess?"

I dragged my hand over my face. "You said you'd shield me."

"I said I'd *try*," he replied, looking far too pleased with himself.

My mouth dropped open as another droplet trailed down my nose.

"Oh, Princess," he managed between laughs, "you look like you just survived a hurricane."

Before I could fire back, his hands came up, brushing the dripping water from my face with surprising gentleness. His thumbs swept over my cheeks, chasing away the stray droplets clinging to my lashes.

"You're a menace," I muttered, though my voice had softened. "A fully sanctioned, theme-park-certified menace."

He chuckled, the sound low and warm. "And yet, you voluntarily spent the day with me. Curious."

I narrowed my eyes.

His grin only widened.

I let out a dramatic, half-hearted sigh. "I'm clearly not great at making smart decisions."

He nudged my shoulder, his eyes lit with mischief. "Yeah, but admit it, I'm the best bad decision you've made all summer."

I turned toward him, comeback ready, but the words stalled.

The look on his face stopped me cold.

No smirk. No sarcasm. Just open, quiet joy, like this day had meant something to him.

A smile tugged at my lips before I could stop it. "Yeah," I said, softer than I intended. "That's true."

***

The park had finally quieted.

Night had fully claimed the sky, the last streaks of sunset long gone. Across the way, the castle still glowed, soft and golden, like a memory reluctant to fade. Its reflection rippled on the damp pavement, still slick from water rides and the nightly cleanup.

Most of the crowd had thinned. A few families wandered toward the gates, kids slumped in strollers, parents moving at an easy, unhurried pace. Cast members waved them off with tired smiles. Even the music had changed, no longer bright and bouncy, but gentle and lilting, like the park itself was winding down.

I tilted my head back as we walked. "Okay," I said, my voice quieter now. "You were right."

Cameron didn't hesitate. A low, smug hum rumbled from beside me. "I always am."

I glanced over at him, shaking my head but smiling. "How are you real?"

His brow lifted, amused. He let out a laugh. "What do you mean?"

"You didn't even scream on the drop."

His smirk curved back into place. "Are you impressed?"

"Suspicious," I muttered.

He bumped my shoulder with his. "Let me guess, you're hoping I screamed so you don't have to admit you were the only one who did."

"Please," I scoffed. "I was completely composed."

"You shrieked like a baby goat."

I gave him a look. "I did not."

We walked in silence after that. It was easy. Comfortable. The kind of quiet that let me replay the day in my head. The laughter, the rides, the moments that felt like they belonged in their own little bubble. I hadn't expected to have this much fun. I hadn't expected him to be such a big part of the reason why.

Somewhere along the path, our hands brushed. Once, then again. And then his fingers curled around mine.

He didn't let go. Neither did I.

Holding his hand felt like the most natural thing in the world. I never wanted to let go.

By the time we reached the employee apartments, the sounds of the park had faded behind us. The walk had gone by too fast, and I caught myself wishing for just a few more minutes. Just a little more of this.

Of him.

He slowed to a stop at the edge of the walkway. He hesitated for a moment, like there was something he wanted to say.

His voice was soft when he finally spoke. "You smiled a lot today."

"I'm pretty sure you did too. Might've even laughed."

It had been the kind of day you wish you could freeze in place. Warm sun, easy laughter, too much sugar, and just enough wonder to make the outside world feel miles away.

But reality has a way of kicking the door in without knocking. Showing up in the most unexpected ways.

"Sidney?"

I stopped mid-step.

That voice. I knew it instantly.

My stomach dropped, my pulse stuttered as I turned.

He stepped toward me, and for a split second, the world seemed to narrow until it was only him. Zack.

The late-night lamps along the path caught on the edge of his duffel bag, the canvas worn and sagging against his shoulder. His shirt was wrinkled from travel, his hair wind-tossed like he'd just stepped off a bus or out of a car after hours on the road. And then there was that smile, easy, familiar, and completely at odds with the thud of disbelief in my chest.

He looked exactly the same, and yet seeing him here felt wrong, like a puzzle piece forced into the wrong spot. Like he had simply walked out of one world and into mine.

"Zack?"

He stood only a few feet away, like nothing about this was strange. Like crossing state lines and showing up uninvited after your girlfriend ended things was perfectly normal.

"What are you doing here?" My voice came out tighter than I meant, the confusion winding itself into every syllable.

"I wanted to surprise you," he said, stepping forward before I could react. His arms went around me, pulling me into a hug I didn't return. "Thought I'd come down for the weekend to see my girlfriend."

The word cracked through me. "Girlfriend?" My voice was sharper now. "Zack... did you get my texts?"

He shook his head like it was nothing. "Yeah, about that. I lost my phone. Had to get a new one."

"You didn't think to mention that?" I blinked at him, disbelief prickling under my skin. "You could've texted me."

"Didn't have your number," he said with a shrug. "Didn't have it memorized. You don't have mine memorized, do you?"

"Well, no," I admitted. "But you could've messaged me. Instagram, email, literally anything—"

"Sid," he cut in, his tone already edging toward frustration. "I lost everything. My phone, my logins. It was a mess, okay? I came all this way because I wanted to see you. I thought you'd be happy."

His arm slipped around me, and he kissed my forehead. It should have felt sweet, but something in the timing, especially the way his eyes flicked to Cameron right after, made it feel like a warning instead of affection.

"And who's this?" Zack asked. His voice was casual, but there was a hard edge underneath.

Cameron didn't flinch. "Cameron," he said with a short nod. "We work together."

"You work together. Right." His eyes lingered on Cameron a beat too long before cutting to me, as if he could read something between us if he stared hard enough.

Cameron's gaze found mine, steady and unblinking. His eyes searched my face like he was taking inventory of every flicker in my expression, making sure I was okay.

I forced a small nod. It was barely there, but it was enough.

His mouth curved, not into a smile, but into something more guarded, like he was swallowing whatever he really wanted to say. "I'll see you around, Sidney."

No teasing nickname. No trace of the easy warmth I'd grown used to.

I don't know why, but it stung.

He turned and walked away.

Zack glanced back at me. "So... who is he, really?"

I paused. "We work together. He's a friend."

He studied my face like he was piecing together a puzzle and didn't like the image forming. "Right."

My instinct was to fill the silence, to smooth over whatever edge had just crept in.

I let out a breath. Changing the subject was far safer. "Where are you staying?"

"The Island Hotel."

Close enough to walk. But Zack wasn't the walking type.

"Wait," I said, my brows pulling in. "How did you even know where I live?"

He sighed, as if I'd just accused him of something absurd. "Your mom told me. Don't worry, I'm not stalking you."

"I didn't say that," I replied, sharper than I meant. His eyebrow lifted in that subtle warning way I knew too well.

"Whatever," he said, brushing it aside. "I'm tired. We'll hang out tomorrow."

"Zack, I have to work."

"Then call in."

"I can't. I already used my day off."

He stepped closer, his voice tightening. "So what, you can't make time for me? I flew here for *you*."

My chest tightened, that old reflex tugging me toward the easiest route. Just agree, just make it easier, just keep the peace. I forced my voice to stay even. "I can't give you the whole day. But... we could grab lunch. You could hang out at the park, and I'll meet you after my shift."

The words left a sour taste in my mouth. What was I doing? I'd broken up with him. And still, I was offering him something.

"Fine," he muttered, like the word cost him. "Lunch."

Then he turned and walked away, no goodbye, leaving the air between us colder than before.

Chapter Twenty-Six

Cameron

I SHOWED UP TO work early the next morning, though I couldn't have said why. It wasn't like I was getting anything done. My head had been spinning since before I stepped inside the castle.

When I'd gone to bed last night, I told myself I was fine. Sure, seeing Zack had knocked me sideways, but I'd convinced myself not to overthink it. She'd looked at me like she wanted me there—like the day we'd spent together still meant something, even with him standing right beside her. I thought I could sleep on it and let it go.

Except I didn't sleep.

I lay there, staring at the ceiling, replaying the same moment over and over. The way his arm slid around her like it belonged there. The way she didn't move away. The way "girlfriend" rolled off his tongue like it was fact.

And the way she didn't correct him.

At first, I told myself maybe she'd tried to end things, and he just showed up before it stuck. That made sense. But the longer I lay there, the more a colder thought started to sink in.

Maybe it never ended at all.

By the time I stepped into the green room, that thought had settled in my chest like ice. I kept to the edges, fake-scrolling my phone, fake-checking the prop list, anything to keep from looking at her too long.

Didn't matter. I still knew exactly where she was. I could track her by the sound of her laugh, the shift in her voice, like some part of me was wired to notice.

And yeah, neither of us had promised anything. I had no claim on her. But that didn't stop it from stinging. It didn't stop me from feeling like I'd been played. And it sure as hell didn't stop it from mattering more than it should.

By the time lunch rolled around, I was ready to disappear.

Gwen, who had been tolerable for most of the morning, was now yelling at someone in the corner.

It didn't matter.

I had my target: the door. Step one was to leave.

Step two was not look back.

Then I heard Sidney's voice.

I turned, and there she was, right in front of Gwen, looking like she was two seconds from crying or sinking into the floor.

I should have kept walking and let her handle it. But something hot and protective flared in my chest, and my feet were moving before I had time to think.

I reached them just in time to see Sidney frozen, shoulders locked tight, while Gwen went in for the kill, her voice low but cutting clean.

"*I* was hired as Renee's understudy," Gwen said, stepping closer. "Me. Not you. You don't go on unless I'm dead, hospitalized, or, God forbid, have laryngitis."

I slid in beside Sidney, shoulder to shoulder, and met Gwen's gaze with a steady calm I did not feel.

"What's the issue, Gwen?"

Gwen gave a tight, unimpressed smile. "Perfect. Maybe *you* can help explain to Webber how things work around here. She seems a little unclear about her role."

I glanced at Sidney.

"Sid," I murmured, keeping my tone steady. "You okay?"

She gave the smallest nod, but her eyes shimmered with emotion.

"I want this fixed," Gwen snapped, jabbing a finger at the corkboard.

That's when I noticed it. The schedule.

And right there, plain as day, was Sidney's name. Not as a backup. Not buried in fine print. She was listed to play Primrose on Renee's day off, a slot that normally went to Gwen.

"Did you talk to Chris?" I asked, keeping my voice calm but clipped.

Gwen blinked, caught off guard. "Not yet. But obviously I'm going to. This *has* to be some kind of mistake."

"Then go talk to him," I said. "But don't take it out on Sidney."

She drew back like I'd just slapped her, then quickly recovered. Tossing her hair, muttering something under her breath, she turned and stormed off down the hallway, her heels clicking with every step.

I exhaled and stepped closer to Sidney.

"You okay?" I asked again, softer this time.

She gave a small nod, but her fists stayed clenched.

Questions about Zack burned in the back of my mind, but none of them mattered right then. All I cared about was reminding Sidney Webber exactly who she was.

I reached out and gently unclenched her hands, keeping one in mine just long enough for her to feel it.

"You're stronger than she makes you feel," I said quietly. "Don't forget that."

She let out a breath and glanced at me. Her eyes shimmered before she gave me a single nod of her head. "Thanks... for stepping in."

"Yeah. Of course."

She shifted, twisting the edge of her sleeve between her fingers. "I know things are weird right now. I swear, Cameron, I didn't know Zack was going to show up like that."

"You don't owe me an explanation," I said. "You don't owe me anything."

"But I want to." She stepped closer, close enough for me to see the nerves flicker across her face.

"He never got my text message," she said. "The one where I ended things. He said he lost his phone."

I raised an eyebrow. "You broke up with him over text?"

Her arms crossed, chin lifting in quiet defiance. "I tried calling. Over and over. He wasn't answering or replying to anything. What was I supposed to do, hire a skywriter?"

A low laugh escaped me. "Honestly? I'd pay to see that."

She rolled her eyes, but the corner of her mouth twitched. "It wasn't my first choice. But he made it impossible to talk to him. Every message felt like it was disappearing into a black hole."

I nodded slower now, my voice quieter. "So when he showed up…"

"I froze," she whispered, her voice barely above the hum of the hallway. "He still thinks we're together."

"How did he take it when you told him?" I asked.

She hesitated, gaze sliding away.

My smile slipped. "You didn't tell him."

"I'm going to," she said quickly. "I just—haven't yet."

"Sid," I said, running a hand through my hair. "Tell me, I'm not just imagining this. This thing between us. Tell me you feel it too."

She was silent for a moment, and I thought she wasn't going to answer, but then her eyes met mine, and she nodded. "I feel it too."

I let out a slow breath, watching her twist the edge of her sleeve. "Then you need to tell him before we go any further. I'm not going to be the third wheel, or the side guy, or whatever you want to call it."

Her cheeks flushed, and she shook her head. "That's not what I'm trying to do."

"I know," I said, softening my tone. "I just don't want to be part of something messy. You deserve better than that. So do I."

She met my eyes then, uncertainty flickering across her face. "I will tell him. Soon."

"Good." I gave a small nod. "And for the record, I appreciate you telling me this at all. You didn't have to."

A faint smile tugged at her lips. "You're not judging me, are you?"

"Oh, I'm definitely judging you," I said with a hint of a smirk. "A breakup text? That's brutal."

Her laugh came out shaky but real, a crack in the tension. "Fine. Next time I'll go big. Something dramatic. A haiku. Or maybe I'll train a parrot to deliver the news."

I gave a mock-thoughtful shrug. "Creative. But still no good."

She tilted her head, a spark in her eyes. "Alright, Mr. Perfect. What's your breakup strategy? How would you break up with me?"

I let the question hang for a moment, then smiled. "Unfair question."

Her brows lifted. "Oh yeah? Why's that?"

I met her gaze, holding it a beat longer than I probably should have. "Because I would never break up with you."

Something shifted in her expression. Her lips parted like she had a comeback, but nothing came out. The air between us felt heavier, warmer.

I didn't give her a chance to recover.

Turning away before I could change my mind, I tossed over my shoulder, "See you around, Princess."

Chapter Twenty-Seven

Sidney

I SLID THE PHONE back into my pocket without replying and headed for Baxter's.

Zack was already there, sitting stiff and silent, arms folded like he was holding himself together by sheer force.

"Hey," I said as I slid into the seat across from him.

"Hey," he answered flatly, spearing a fry into ketchup. "I seriously don't get how you deal with this place."

I shrugged with a small smile. "It's not so bad. The stage show's pretty magical. Did you see it?"

Zack rolled his eyes. "Yeah, but... you're not actually in it, right? You're like the understudy's understudy or whatever?"

It was a light jab on the surface, but it landed deeper—dismissive, like it didn't count if I wasn't center stage.

"I fill in wherever they need me," I said, keeping my tone even. "It's more than just waiting around. I help a lot with—"

"Sure," he cut in, shrugging like the whole thing was inconsequential. "Just seems like a lot of work for a role you might never actually get to do."

I shifted gears again, launching into the entire story about Gwen and her unnecessary, over-the-top drama. Zack sat there in silence, unreadable, and I couldn't tell if he was actually tuned in or just letting my words wash over me.

Then he spoke, and I realized he'd caught every syllable.

"Well... she's not entirely wrong. You *are* her understudy."

I bristled. "You're kidding me, right?"

He gave a lazy shrug, like the whole thing was barely worth the effort. "She probably felt threatened or something."

"You think that makes it okay?"

He popped another fry into his mouth, chewing like we were discussing the weather. "I'm just saying, it's not like you were promised anything. Maybe she felt blindsided."

I opened my mouth, ready to fire back, but the words stalled on my tongue.

He had a point. She probably had felt that way. But that didn't excuse her behavior. How she had so carelessly stomped on my self-esteem. And it wasn't even my fault. I hadn't asked for the role. I hadn't asked to be assigned instead of Gwen.

I wanted to say all that to Zack. Make him understand. But what was the point? He wasn't going to get it.

"You don't have to stay all day," I murmured. "I'm sure you have better things to do."

"You're right about that. Better than chasing after someone who will barely look at me," he shot me a steely glare. "If I'd known you didn't plan on making time for me, I wouldn't have bothered coming."

I pulled in a steadying breath. "You knew I had to work, Zack. This isn't a vacation for me."

His jaw tightened. "Yeah, but I didn't expect to feel invisible."

The words struck harder than I wanted to admit. Guilt flared, but I shoved it down before it could take root.

"This is my break," I said, my voice low and frayed at the edges. "We can either spend it fighting... or we can eat."

He leaned back in his chair, arms crossing in that unshakable way that made him look both defensive and immovable. "Fine. Let's eat."

We picked at our food in a silence so thick it felt like another presence at the table. The soft clink of silverware on plates was the only sound, each one landing louder than it should have. When it was time to leave, he muttered a goodbye without meeting my eyes. I didn't stop him.

The rest of my shift blurred into a series of hollow smiles and mechanical movements, my body on autopilot while the weight in my chest pressed heavier with every passing hour.

By the time I got home, Zack was sprawled on the couch, remote in hand, flipping through channels with the kind of restless focus that told me nothing would ever be good enough. He didn't look up.

I slipped into my room, stripped off my work clothes, and pulled on a pair of cut-off shorts and a pink tank top.

When I came back out, he was gone from the couch, the faint sound of cupboard doors opening and closing leading me to the kitchen.

"Got any snacks?" he asked, voice muffled, head deep in the fridge.

"There's probably something in the cabinet," I said, already bracing for him to complain it wasn't what he wanted.

Instead, he tore into the unopened pack of cookies on the counter, snapping the plastic seal like he was starving. I opened my mouth to warn him, but it was already too late.

Ridley materialized in the doorway as if summoned by the sound. Her eyes dropped to the cookies, then lifted to Zack, narrowing into a look sharp enough to cut glass. Without a single word, she strode over, snatched the pack from his hands, and pivoted out of the kitchen like a queen reclaiming stolen treasure. I half-expected her to toss in a hiss or a slow, menacing head turn on the way out.

Zack stared after her. "What the hell was that?"

"That was Ridley," I said, shaking my head. "Rule number one in this apartment: don't touch her snacks."

He gave a disbelieving huff, but before he could fire back, Willow breezed in. She was still in her Fantasy World vest, glitter clinging to her hair and cheeks. Her bag hit the floor with a thud before she perched herself on the arm of the couch.

"Hey, just talked to the guys," she said, glancing between us. "We're heading to—"

"The *guys*?" Zack interrupted, brow lifting in suspicion.

Willow folded her arms, her voice cool but pointed. "Yeah, Zack. Her *friends*. You'd know that if you actually talked to her." Then she turned to me, her expression instantly softening. "You coming, Sid? We're heading to The Dive."

Zack let out a short, humorless laugh. "A bar? Come on. That's not really Sidney's thing."

I arched a brow at him, but he kept going, like my expression hadn't even registered.

"She hates loud bars," Zack said with a smirk. "She'd rather stay in and watch the same rom-com for the hundredth time. Trust me."

Willow turned to me, one brow arched. "And what do *you* want to do, Sidney?"

"I'm going to the bar," I said without hesitation.

His eyebrows shot up. "Wait—what? You can't be serious."

"You're welcome to come," I said, grabbing my bag. "Or you can stay here. Your choice."

By the time we reached The Dive, Zack was still scowling, trailing behind me like he'd been dragged here against his will.

I followed Willow and Ridley through the door, the low thrum of music spilling out onto the street. Zack came in last, his posture tight and bristling.

From across the room, Renee and the guys spotted us and waved us over to a booth. Cameron's gaze found mine almost immediately. The easy curve of his smile stood out in the haze of neon and noise, like it was meant only for me.

I took a step forward, ready to join them when Zack's hand wrapped around my wrist.

"Dance with me," he said. His tone was low, and I wasn't sure if he was asking me or telling me.

I turned to him, my first instinct to say no, to explain, to walk away, but the look in his eyes made me pause. For just a moment, he wasn't the Zack I'd been drifting from. He was someone afraid of being left behind.

I still wanted to say no. But my head dipped into a nod, and I let him lead me onto the dance floor.

The music's bass thumped through the floorboards as his hand settled on my waist, pulling me closer to him.

This wasn't the first time I'd danced with him, but something about the way he was holding me felt wrong.

I drew in a quick breath, my eyes darting around the room. Overhead, the lights smeared into hazy halos, and I blinked hard, refusing to cry in the middle of a bar.

The air pressed in on me until I felt like I was suffocating. Heat radiated from every direction, and the bass pounded in my skull until it drowned out everything else.

Zack's eyes locked on mine, like he could read exactly what was going through my head.

"I need a minute," I said, pressing a hand against his chest.

He blinked, thrown, but I didn't wait for him to respond. I slipped into the crowd, through the sea of bodies.

The lights blurred into streaks. The music pounded from every direction, each bass note vibrating through my ribs. My steps grew heavier, slower, until I finally pushed open the bathroom door with shaking hands.

I gripped the sink like it might anchor me, forcing my breaths into a steady rhythm.

In. Out. In. Out.

I raised my head as my reflection stared back at me.

She didn't even look like me. She looked terrified.

Just someone barely holding it together, hiding behind the thin mask of "I'm fine" when she was anything but.

I couldn't avoid it any longer. He deserved the truth, and stretching this out would only make it worse for both of us.

I don't know how long I stayed in there but at least three songs went by as I gathered my courage to go back out there and do what I needed to.

My phone buzzed in my pocket. I pulled it out, already bracing for a text from Zack asking where I'd gone.

But it wasn't him.

It was the group chat.

> **Willow:** Is Prince Alarming planning to let you hang out with the rest of us tonight?

> **Ridley:** I'm betting he keeps her away.

> **Westley:** Maybe she needs Prince Charming to rescue her from the dark wizard.

> **Cameron:** Just say the word, Princess, and I'll be there.

I shook my head and slid my phone back into my pocket, forcing a breath into my lungs. My hand lingered on the bathroom door for a beat longer than it should have before I pushed it open.

The music slammed into me first—louder now, vibrating up through the floor and into my bones. Lights pulsed in sharp, dizzy bursts, painting the crowd in flashes of red and gold. I stepped into it, my heartbeat still hammering, each inhale a deliberate effort to stay steady.

And then I saw him.

Zack.

He was tucked away in a corner booth, half in shadow, like he didn't want to be noticed.

Only... he wasn't alone.

A girl was draped across his lap, arms hooked lazily around his neck. Their faces were pressed together in a kiss that was far too deep, too certain, to be mistaken for anything casual.

I froze. The music receded to a dull, distant throb, replaced by the hot rush of blood pounding in my ears.

She shifted then, pulling back just enough for her face to catch the light.

And my stomach dropped.

Gwen.

He was kissing Gwen.

The moment Gwen spotted me, her lips curved into a smug, poisonous grin. "Oh, hi, Sidney," she said, her voice dripping with mock surprise.

Zack's head snapped around. "Shit," he muttered, shoving Gwen aside as if that could erase what I'd just seen.

I turned on my heel and walked out. If he had something to say, he could let the wind carry it.

"Sidney!" His voice chased me, footsteps closing in before his hand caught my arm.

I wrenched free. "Don't touch me."

"Just—can we talk?" His voice was strained, breathless.

"There's nothing left to say." I jerked my chin toward the booth. "Whatever that was? It's all yours." Then I motioned between us. "This? We're done."

"You're really walking away from this?" he snapped, bitterness roughening his voice.

"Yes." My reply was flat, final.

His grip tightened, dragging me a fraction closer. "Coming here was a joke. You're not the same girl. That message should've been all I needed. But no, I had to be the fool who thought I could fix it."

I met his eyes, my voice like ice. "You told me you didn't get the message."

He let out a sharp, bitter laugh. "Who the hell ends a relationship over text?"

I tried to yank my arm free, but his grip only tightened.

"Let me go," I said, my voice low and steady.

"I'm not letting you walk away. Not when you're acting like this."

I pulled harder, breaking his hold, stumbling back a step.

Zack lunged after me, reaching again. I turned to dodge him, but he misjudged the distance. His hand missed my arm and clipped my cheek instead.

The sting bloomed instantly. Not enough to knock me back, but enough to freeze me in place.

My hand flew to my cheek on instinct. For a heartbeat, we just stared at each other, the air between us charged and still.

"Sidney—" he started, stepping toward me, his hand half-raised. "I didn't mean to—"

"I know," I said, holding a hand up to stop him. "Just... don't touch me. Please."

His arms fell to his sides.

I had not even realized Cameron had stepped closer until I heard his voice, low and steady, with a dangerous edge that sent a shiver down my spine.

"It's time to go, Zack."

Zack's eyes narrowed. "Back off. You didn't see—"

"I saw enough," Cameron said, his tone tight with restrained fury.

Zack's gaze flicked to me and then locked on Cameron. "Of course. Prince Charming to the rescue. You have been just waiting for your moment, haven't you?"

He wasn't finished.

"You know what?" he snapped. "Maybe *this* started before I even got here. Maybe that is why you broke up with me. Too busy getting close to *him* to say it to my face."

I wanted to fire back, to throw his words right at him, but I couldn't. Because he wasn't completely wrong. I *had* grown closer to Cameron. I hadn't meant for it to happen, but it had, all the same.

"Zack," I said quietly, "I'm not putting all of this on you. We have been drifting for a while. Even before I came here."

He fixed me with a cold stare. "No. Don't do that. You made this choice, Sidney. You ended us the second you took this internship."

His mouth twisted. "You know what hurts the most? That I believed you. That I thought we were still okay while you were out here playing fairytale with him."

The words landed like blows. I opened my mouth, but nothing came out.

He gave a bitter laugh. "Tell me, Sid. Did you even feel guilty the first time you kissed him, or was I already out of sight, out of mind?"

Cameron stepped forward, his eyes blazing. "You're way out of line."

I turned back to Zack, my voice quiet but steady. "I didn't cheat on you."

He let out a sharp laugh, folding his arms across his chest. "Sorry, Sidney, but I don't believe anything you say."

I held my ground. "Before I came here, I was already gone, Zack. You just didn't see it."

That landed. He blinked, thrown for the first time.

"I waited for you, Zack. I called. I texted. I kept trying, and you kept disappearing. It felt like I was in a relationship alone. Even the night I ended things, you wouldn't pick up. What was I supposed to do, just keep waiting forever?"

Zack's eyes flicked between me and Cameron, searching for proof of a betrayal that wasn't there. But the heat in his expression was fading.

He stood frozen, tension etched into every line of him, the truth settling.

Finally, he turned away.

His voice was tight, edged with bitterness. "You'll regret this."

Without another glance, he walked off, disappearing through the doors.

I stayed rooted to the spot, staring at the space he'd just occupied.

"You okay?" Cameron's voice was quiet, careful.

"I've got to get out of here." The words tumbled out before I could stop them. I headed for the door, but he caught my wrist as I passed.

His eyes searched mine, looking for answers I couldn't give. Not now, maybe not ever. I didn't even know what I was feeling beyond the tight, frantic knot in my chest.

"I'll be okay," I said softly, though I wasn't sure I believed it. He gave me a small nod and let go.

I turned toward the exit.

Air. Space. I needed both before I drowned in this room.

I burst through the doors and broke into a sprint.

I didn't know where I was going. I only knew I couldn't stay. Not in there. Not with all those eyes, all that noise pressing against me.

I ran.

Past the bar, past the music spilling into the night, past the smear of neon lights and the swell of voices. My pulse pounded in my ears, drowning out everything else. The lights felt too bright, the air too heavy, every sound pressing in like the world itself was trying to trap me. I just needed space. Somewhere no one could follow.

I didn't stop until the noise thinned and the streets went still. That's when I saw it, a forgotten park crouched in the shadows, half-swallowed by weeds.

A rusted chain-link gate sagged at the edge, a narrow gap just wide enough to slip through.

I ducked inside, drawn toward the promise of quiet. Of being unseen. Of finding a place as empty as I felt.

The walkway was cracked and crowded with weeds, each step crunching over dry leaves. An empty playground emerged from the shadows, its swings swaying in the night breeze as if moved by a hand I couldn't see.

I slowed at the sight of a rusted merry-go-round, its paint flaking away to reveal the dull sheen of bare metal. It looked like it hadn't spun in years. Lowering myself onto it, I felt the low, aching groan of metal beneath my weight.

I let it rock gently, my hands curling around the cool bars.

For several heartbeats, I sat still, staring into the dark. The wind whispered through the trees, carrying the faint blare of a car horn from somewhere far away.

The first drops of rain came soft and slow, tapping against the metal beneath me. I tilted my head back, noticing for the first time the heavy clouds that had gathered while I wasn't paying attention.

I should have gotten up. I should have looked for shelter. But I didn't move.

The rain grew heavier, pressing down on me in a cold, steady sheet until it soaked through my clothes and traced icy paths down my cheeks.

And with it, everything I'd been holding back began to break loose.

The tears slipped free, as if they had been waiting for this exact moment to escape.

All the hurt, the frustration, the quiet ache I'd kept buried these past few months rose to the surface at once, demanding to be felt.

I cried for the girl who kept smiling when she wanted to scream. For the version of me that kept patching over cracks instead of letting myself break.

I cried for the relationship that had chipped away at me piece by piece, leaving me smaller, not stronger. For every time I stayed quiet just to keep the peace, convincing myself that silence was safer than speaking.

Eventually, the tears slowed, but the rain didn't. It sank into everything, my clothes, my hair, my skin. It seeped into my thoughts, washing over memories I didn't want but couldn't forget.

It felt good to cry. To let it all out.

I wasn't healed. Not even close. But something inside me felt different. The weight in my chest had shifted, like I had finally set down a piece of it, leaving just enough space to breathe again.

My hands shook as I dug out my phone. Zack's name sat there in my contacts like a stone I'd been carrying for too long. My thumb hovered for a second, just long enough to feel the pull of hesitation, and then I hit delete.

The name vanished.

Next came the message thread. One swipe, and it was gone too, years of words reduced to nothing in an instant. My mom used to say the best way to move on was to burn old letters. Maybe this was the digital equivalent.

It wasn't the same as a bonfire, but it still gave me something I hadn't expected. Relief. A strange, quiet sense of closure I knew I would never get from Zack himself.

The phone buzzed in my hand, jolting me. I nearly dropped it when Cameron's name lit up the screen.

I swiped to answer. "Hello?"

"Hey," Cameron said, his voice low and uncertain. "I'm sorry. I know you need space. I just wanted to make sure you're okay."

The silence stretched.

How was I supposed to answer that? I wasn't okay. I was a mess, crying in the middle of an abandoned park.

"Are... are you okay?" His voice was barely a whisper now.

I swallowed hard, the words sticking before I forced them out. "Can you come get me?"

"I'm on the way."

Chapter Twenty-Eight

Cameron

I DIDN'T THINK. I just ran.

The rain was coming down in sheets, blurring everything as I yanked open the car door. Cold water hit my face, soaking through my shirt in seconds, but I barely felt it. I dropped into the driver's seat, hands fumbling with the keys. My pulse was so loud it almost drowned out the sound of the ignition catching.

The engine roared to life. I threw the car into gear and backed out of my space. The tires squealed against wet pavement as I shot out onto the road.

The downpour grew heavier, pounding the windshield until the world outside dissolved into streaks of light and water.

The wipers clawed back and forth, but they were barely making a dent in the blur. I leaned forward, squinting into the storm, knuckles locked white around the steering wheel. Every instinct in my body told me to push harder, drive faster.

All I could think about was getting to her.

If she was out in this... No, I couldn't let my mind finish that thought.

Sidney never asked for help. She didn't need saving. She handled things. She held herself together even when everything around her was falling apart.

But she'd called me. She'd asked for help.

Nothing was going to stop me from getting to her. Not the rain, not the storm, not anything.

The GPS led me to a small, overgrown park only a few blocks from The Dive.

I pulled straight into the lot, not bothering with a parking space, and killed the engine. The moment the car stopped, I was out. The rain immediately soaked through my clothes.

I pushed open the mangled chain-link gate and stepped through. Weeds clawed at my legs as I cut across the forgotten park, my eyes scanning the shadows until I saw her.

Sidney.

She was curled in on herself on a rusted merry-go-round, arms locked around her knees, head bent low.

"Sidney!" I called, my voice straining to rise above the rain as I pushed forward.

She didn't move. Didn't even flinch. For a moment, the storm swallowed my words before they could reach her.

I slowed, every step heavier than the last, my heartbeat pounding so hard it ached in my chest. "Sid..." The second time came out quieter, almost fragile, more plea than call.

Her head lifted, and the look in her eyes made my heart drop.

Her hair clung to her cheeks in dark, wet strands, her clothes plastered to her skin. For a heartbeat, I saw her on Water Mountain just days ago, laughing, drenched, light in a way that felt unreachable now. That memory felt like it belonged to a different lifetime.

She held my gaze, but something burned behind her eyes. A question. A need, something she couldn't seem to voice.

So I didn't ask.

I didn't try to gather up the pieces, even though every instinct in me ached to hold them together. This wasn't about fixing anything.

It was about staying. Just being there.

If there was one thing I could give her right now, it was that.

I eased myself onto the merry-go-round beside her.

And we sat.

Long enough for the sound of the storm to become the only way I could measure time passing.

When she finally spoke, her voice was so quiet I almost missed it.

"I didn't even cry when we broke up. When I sent that message." A soft, humorless laugh escaped her. "Isn't that messed up?"

I didn't answer.

Her breath left her in a trembling exhale, more shiver than sigh.

"I don't even know why this is hitting me so hard," Sidney said, her voice low, almost frustrated. "I wanted to end things. I meant it. I was done."

"Feel what you need to," I said softly.

She let out a sharp little scoff and shook her head. "God, I'm a mess."

She drew her knees tighter to her chest, staring past me like she was trying to piece herself together in real time. "I really thought walking away meant I was finally strong. That I'd grown past needing him. Past letting him make me feel invisible."

Her next inhale caught, like the air itself had turned heavier. "But now... it's hitting me. Not because I miss him. Not because I want him back. Just..." Her throat worked as she searched for the words. "I spent so long making myself small to keep him comfortable. And now that he's gone, I don't know how to be anything else."

My throat tightened. I wanted to tell her she was wrong. That she was so much more than what he made her believe. But I stayed quiet.

"He used to say I was too emotional. That I felt everything too much. Eventually... I started to believe him." She shook her head. "All my life I've felt torn between not being enough or being too much."

"You don't have to prove anything, Sid," I said gently, reaching for her hand. She looked down at our hands as I threaded our fingers together. "There's a whole crew back at The Dive who already think you're incredible."

"I'm sorry," she muttered.

"What for?"

Her gaze flicked up to mine, and for a second, I caught the shadow of every doubt she'd just spilled.

"Sid," I said, leaning in just enough that my voice carried over the rain. "I don't care if you're still figuring out who you are. I don't care how long it takes. The only person I want is you. And if you need time to find yourself, then I'll be right here while you do."

Something in her eyes softened as she searched my face. Finally, a slow smile spread across her face.

A quiet laugh slipped from her, lighter than before. "Okay. Deal."

I rose and offered her my hand. "Come on. Let's get you out of the rain."

She didn't hesitate. Her fingers slid into mine, and I pulled her up.

The drive back to my apartment passed in a silence. Sidney rested her head against the window, eyes tracking the smear of gold and white lights outside. I caught myself glancing at her more than once, trying to read the quiet, but I didn't press. She'd speak when she was ready.

When we stepped inside my place, I flicked on the light and immediately caught the state of things, shoes kicked into the corner, a laundry basket abandoned by the bathroom door. Not a disaster, but definitely not guest-ready.

But if she noticed, she didn't say a word.

Westley and Porter still weren't home. They were probably still at the bar.

When I suggested she stay the night and she agreed, relief loosened the knot in my chest. She started to say something about the couch, but I shut that down with a shake of my head before the thought could take shape.

"You're staying in my room," I said, setting my keys on the counter. "Bed's ready. Door locks."

She hesitated. "Cam, I can't—"

"You can," I said, cutting in, gentle, but leaving no room for argument. "And you will. I'll take the couch."

I crossed the small living room in a few strides and paused at my bedroom door, glancing back to make sure she was following. She was quiet and still, but there.

Inside, I pulled open a drawer and found a pair of sweatpants and a T-shirt. They would be too big on her, but it was better than staying in wet clothes.

I held them out.

She hesitated for a moment. Then her eyes met mine, and she opened her mouth in what was sure to be a protest.

"No arguments," I said, raising a hand. "You're soaked and shivering. I'm not letting you sleep in wet jeans just to prove you're stubborn."

She looked at the clothes. "Wait... these are yours."

"Yeah," I said, a faint smile tugging at my mouth. "Good observation, Detective Webber."

The corner of her mouth quirked up.

"I'll give you a few minutes to change," I added, stepping back toward the hall. "I'll make some tea."

I eased the door shut behind me and headed for the kitchen. Chamomile felt like the safest bet. I didn't know how she liked hers, so I added two spoonfuls of sugar to both cups, just in case she needed comfort tonight as much as I did.

I looped my fingers through the mug handles and carried them back to my bedroom door.

I knocked lightly with one knuckle.

"Come in."

When I stepped inside, she was seated on the edge of my bed. As I suspected, she was drowning in the clothes I'd given her. My T-shirt hung loose, slipping off one shoulder to reveal a pale curve of skin. I tried not to let my eyes linger too long on her bare shoulder.

"Hope it's okay," she said softly. "I hung my clothes in your shower to dry."

I nodded and held out one of the mugs. Her fingers brushed mine as she took it, curling around the ceramic like she needed the warmth. Steam drifted toward her face, and she took a slow sip, eyes closing briefly as if the heat was something she could breathe in.

Her gaze drifted around the room, lingering on the uneven stack of books on my nightstand, the hoodie draped over the chair, the posters I'd never bothered to take down. A prickle of awkwardness crept in.

A bedroom was like a biography written without words, made up of the things you left lying around without thinking. Mine revealed more than I'd ever intended, what I valued, what I ignored, what I couldn't seem to let go of.

Would she see it as lived-in or just lazy? Comfortable or cluttered?

Her gaze landed on the guitar propped in the corner.

"Do you play?" she asked, tilting her head toward it.

I leaned back against the wall, trying for casual, even though my pulse had other plans. "Used to."

She crossed the room, her fingertips gliding over the strings and fretboard as if committing them to memory.

"Why did you stop?" She asked.

I paused, not because I was unwilling to answer, but because it came from a part of me I rarely touched.

"My dad taught me," I said softly. "He used to play after dinner most nights. Nothing fancy, just songs that meant something to him. He always said that if you could make someone stop what they were doing and really listen... that was its own kind of magic."

Her gaze lifted to mine, a quiet understanding already there.

"He died when I was twelve," I said, the words catching heavier than I meant them to. "I tried to keep playing after that, but... it never sounded the same."

She held my eyes for a moment, then glanced back at the guitar.

"Can I try it?"

My eyebrows lifted. "You play?"

"Barely." Her smile was small but genuine. "A few lessons in high school. I'm not great."

I tilted my head toward the guitar. "Go for it."

She picked the guitar up with both hands, holding it like it might break if she wasn't careful. I sat on the edge of the bed, and she joined me, close enough that our shoulders brushed. My pulse quickened, but I forced myself to keep my expression neutral.

She tried a few chords, hesitant at first, then settled into a slow, uneven rhythm. And then, almost shyly, she began to play *Peaceful Easy Feeling* by The Eagles.

My throat went dry.

There was no way she could've known how much that song meant to me. How many nights I'd heard it spilling from my dad's own guitar strings or him humming it in the kitchen.

The notes wavered in places, the tempo pulling back, but the way she played held me completely.

I listened until the song ended, and silence settled around us.

"That was my dad's favorite band," I said, my voice quieter than I intended, the words heavy in my chest.

Her head turned, eyebrows lifting. "Really?"

I nodded, a smile tugging at the memory. "He sang this song so often I honestly thought he'd written it."

"Well," she said finally, her voice quieter than before, "your dad had great taste." She glanced up, a hint of curiosity in her eyes. "So... how am I doing?"

"You're getting there," I said, letting the corner of my mouth lift. "But your F major's a little shaky."

She let out a shaky laugh. "I did warn you that I'm not very good."

"Here," I said gently, reaching for her hand. My fingers brushed hers. "Let me show you."

I guided her fingers into place, taking my time. My touch was light, just enough to coax her hand into the curve it needed, my fingertips brushing over hers as I adjusted each one.

"There," I said softly, the word barely above a breath. "Now, try it."

She strummed again, and the sound rang out without a trace of the earlier hesitation.

Her smile was small, but it lit her eyes in a way that caught me off guard.

I never thought I could hear that song again without it hurting. But with her playing it, the ache was gone. It felt right. Like the music still held a piece of my dad, and now, it would hold a piece of her too.

When the final chords faded, she handed me the guitar and eased back against the pillows. She shifted closer to the wall, quietly making space for me.

I took the guitar without a word and sat beside her. It wasn't the best position for playing, but the closeness mattered more than comfort.

She leaned in, resting her head lightly against my arm like it was the most natural thing in the world. I stayed perfectly still, afraid of breaking the moment.

I started to play, fingers finding a few quiet chords.

I was rusty, out of practice, but she didn't seem to care. She just stayed there, curled into my side, while I let the music wander wherever it wanted.

I'm not sure how long we stayed like that, her leaning into me, me playing whatever came to mind, but at some point her breathing slowed into a steady rhythm. I glanced down.

She was asleep.

Carefully, I set the guitar aside and began to ease away.

But her fingers brushed my arm.

"Stay," she murmured, eyes still closed, voice barely more than a breath. "Sidney..."

Her eyes opened, and the look she gave me stopped everything.

She didn't need to say another word. That look could have asked for anything, burn the world, rebuild it from ash, and I would've said yes.

I sank back onto the pillows and drew the blanket around us. She shifted closer, her head finding its place against my chest, and my arm slipped around her like it had always belonged there.

Within moments, she was asleep again.

And somehow, with her beside me, it felt easy.

Familiar like an old Eagles song.

Like the most natural thing in the world.

Chapter Twenty-Nine

Sidney

I woke to sunlight spilling in through unfamiliar curtains.

For a moment, I stayed still, blinking up at a ceiling I didn't recognize.

This wasn't my room.

This wasn't my bed.

And these definitely weren't my clothes.

It took a minute for my brain to catch up, but then I remembered the events of the day before.

The rain. The bar.

Zack. Gwen.

Cameron.

I turned my head, half-expecting to find him still there beside me. But his side of the bed was empty.

I reached out, fingers grazing the space where he'd been.

I sat up slowly, the oversized shirt slipping off one shoulder. My body ached with that heavy, post-breakdown fatigue, like I'd been wrung out and left to dry overnight. With a sigh, I raked my fingers through my tangled hair and reached for my phone on the nightstand.

Three unread messages waited for me. Willow, Ridley, Renee.

I'd texted them the bare minimum last night: something happened with Zack, I'm not coming back to the apartment.

Thankfully, they hadn't pried. I wasn't ready to untangle it for them yet... maybe not even for myself.

Luckily, they hadn't pried.

I tapped into the group chat.

> **Willow:** *Hey, babe, how are you holding up? We love you. Call if you need anything.*

> **Ridley:** *If you need me to set something on fire, just say the word.*

> **Renee:** *On a scale of 1 to full-blown villain origin story, where are we?*

I smiled.

My people. Always there. Ready to either hype me up until I believed in myself again or commit minor arson on my behalf. Both options were equally appreciated.

I tapped out a quick reply: *I'm okay. I'll call you later.*

It wasn't the whole truth, but it was enough for now.

I set the phone down and let out a slow breath.

That's when I saw it. Something on the dresser I hadn't noticed last night.

A picture frame.

I frowned, curiosity tugging me out of bed. The floor was cool beneath my bare feet as I crossed the room.

It was a picture.

Of me.

Alone.

My breath caught. For a moment, I just stared, wondering if I was still half-dreaming. But no, I knew that photo instantly.

Cameron had taken it my first day at Fantasy World, right after that ridiculous fake-phone stunt. He'd worn that infuriating grin, and I'd been caught mid-reaction, half eye roll, half laugh, when the shutter clicked.

It was one of my favorite pictures. There was no fake smile. It was just me. The *real* me.

And he'd kept it. Framed it.

Something shifted low in my stomach. Because this wasn't just a photo. It was a choice.

He'd chosen to keep that moment, to give it a place here.

And I didn't know what to do with the warmth that came with that realization.

I drew in a slow breath, then crossed the room to the door.

Time to face the world. With any luck, I could slip out unnoticed, make a quiet escape before anyone even realized I'd been here.

Two seconds later, I regretted everything.

Porter and Westley were already in the kitchen, mid-breakfast, when I stepped out.

Porter froze, coffee halfway to his lips, eyebrows climbing so high they practically left his face.

Westley glanced up, took one look at me, and choked on a mouthful of Pop-Tart like he'd just witnessed a car crash in slow motion.

Panic shot through me like a jolt of static.

Oh no. Oh no, no, no—

Porter leapt into action, thumping Westley on the back while Westley hacked like he was fighting for his life.

Between gasps, Westley wheezed, "Wait. Did you and Cam hook up?"

Heat climbed my neck, setting my ears on fire.

"What?! No! Oh my gosh." My hands flew up like I could physically smack the words out of the air. "This is not—I mean—we didn't—just no!"

I flailed toward the oversized T-shirt swallowing me whole, like that proved anything.

If anything, it made me look *more* suspicious.

"This is not what it looks like," I croaked helplessly.

Porter crossed his arms, one brow arched, his grin pure smug. "Right. So... what *does* it look like, then?"

I opened my mouth—

Nothing. Not a single coherent word made it past my lips.

Westley, finally catching his breath, gave a solemn nod. "No, no—let her keep going. I want to see just how deep this hole gets."

"This is not what it looks like," I said, folding my arms tight across my chest. "Period. End of story."

Porter and Westley exchanged a look that practically screamed, *Yeah, right.*

I groaned, dragging a hand down my face, wishing I could just melt through the floor and spare myself whatever humiliation was coming next.

Naturally, that's when the universe decided to make things worse.

The door swung open, and in came Cameron, fresh from a run, shirt clinging to him in damp patches that left little to the imagination. My brain told me to look away, to keep my dignity intact. My eyes did not cooperate.

He slowed, gaze flicking between us.

One earbud popped free. "Okay... what did I walk into? Who's being accused of murder?"

"Oh, nothing important," Porter said smoothly. "Just Sidney making her grand exit from your room... in your clothes."

Westley jumped in without missing a beat. "Classic walk of shame. We were honored to witness it, honestly."

Cameron froze, his face twisted in confusion. His eyes slid to me, lingered on the oversized T-shirt, then came back up to my face.

And then—"...Oh."

Heat shot straight up my neck, flooding my face. I groaned, burying it in my hands. If I couldn't see them, maybe they'd stop existing.

"Please. Explain. Now."

When I risked peeking through my fingers, Cameron's mouth was already twitching, that maddening almost-smile threatening to take over. He looked way too pleased for someone who was supposed to be helping me out of this mess.

"What?" he asked, all wide-eyed innocence. "You mean you don't remember?"

My stomach did this weird flip, half from the way he said it, half from knowing exactly where this was going. I shot him my sharpest glare. "I remember *exactly* what happened. We slept. That's it."

"Wait, wait, wait," Porter cut in, holding up a hand like he was cross-examining me. "You went to sleep where exactly?"

I could feel the trap before I even stepped into it. But I answered anyway. "...In Cameron's bed."

Westley's grin spread like a slow fuse catching fire. "Right. And where was Cameron?"

My brain screamed *don't answer*, but my mouth stalled out. "...Uh—"

They both let out a perfectly synchronized *ooh*, the kind that instantly transported me back to the middle school cafeteria, complete with the mortifying spotlight of unwanted attention.

Cameron crossed his arms, looking more irritated than embarrassed. "Seriously? How old are you guys?"

Porter beamed, clearly delighted with himself. "Don't worry. We've already had *the talk*. We know what happens when two people love each other very much."

I groaned again, dragging my hands down my face. If the ground wanted to open up and swallow me whole, I would not object.

"Alright, show's over," Cameron said, lacing his fingers with mine. "Time to whisk the princess away before the embarrassment becomes fatal."

I laughed, letting him tug me toward the door as we made our dramatic exit.

"Make good choices!" Westley called after us.

Cameron rolled his eyes, muttering under his breath, "I'm moving out," as we slipped outside.

His hand stayed wrapped around mine, warm and steady, until we'd put a full block between us and the apartment. I told myself it was just momentum from our escape, but the longer it stayed, the more aware I became of it.

"Well," I said, finally catching my breath, "that was humiliating."

Cameron glanced over, that easy grin tugging at his mouth. "If you live with them long enough, you build immunity."

"I feel like I need a vaccine."

He chuckled, the sound low and warm. "You did great. Only minimal panic flailing."

"Wait," I said after a few blocks, "don't you have work today?"

He shook his head. "Day off."

"Seriously?"

"Seriously. You too, right?"

I narrowed my eyes. How did he even— "How do you know my schedule?"

He just shrugged. "I know things."

"Okay, stalker," I said, trying to sound more annoyed than curious. "So who's your understudy? I don't think I've ever seen him."

Cameron glanced over, his mouth tugging into that faintly amused smile that always made me feel like I'd walked into the middle of one of his jokes. "That's because I don't have one."

I stopped mid-step. "Wait—what?"

"No understudy," he repeated, pivoting so he could walk backward in front of me, like this conversation was more entertaining than wherever we were headed. "If I'm not there, they run the alternate version. Prince Peter suddenly gets called away on a diplomatic mission to the Kingdom of… I don't know, Whereverland."

I wanted to roll my eyes, but his delivery was so deadpan, I almost believed him for half a second.

Then he stopped right in front of me, grin tilting just enough to look dangerous, leaning in so close I could feel the faint brush of his breath. My heart stuttered like it had forgotten the rhythm.

"Or maybe," he said, voice dropping to a conspiratorial whisper, "he's off chasing after a certain princess, trying to convince her to fall for him."

I blinked at him, caught somewhere between flustered and completely out of words. My brain was still stuck on the way he'd leaned in, so close it had scrambled my thoughts.

I gave his shoulder a light shove. "You are ridiculous."

His grin only widened, like he knew exactly what he was doing. "You say that like it's a bad thing."

I shook my head, trying to steer my brain back on track. "Hold on. You're telling me there's an alternate version of the show?"

"Yep."

"How have I never seen it?"

"Because you're off those days," he replied with an easy shrug.

Fair enough. Still, my curiosity was officially piqued. "So what's it about?"

His eyes lit up, and his tone shifted to mock-dramatic. "Well, instead of Prince Peter and Princess Primrose, the kingdom is left in the capable hands of Princess Rosepetal and Prince Callum."

I gave him a flat look, though I was fighting a smile. "That's not real."

"Of course it's real," he said with such deadpan conviction that I almost believed him until the grin cracked through. "Okay, maybe not. I've got an understudy, you've just never met him because you're never on the schedule when he is."

I shook my head, fighting a smile. "So, does Gwen hate him too?"

"Strangely enough... no," Cameron said, almost like it baffled him. "She actually seems to like him. Which is weird, because I'm pretty sure she hates me."

I laughed under my breath. "Guess he must be really charming."

We turned off the main road, following a narrow side street that wound through a quiet neighborhood. The houses were older, ivy creeping along fences, porches cluttered with mismatched chairs and potted plants. No cars passed, just the soft clang of a wind chime and the crunch of gravel under our shoes.

Cameron walked beside me in silence. As we passed a leaning mailbox and an empty driveway, he reached out, running his fingers along the top of a worn picket fence. The wood looked smooth, weathered from years of sun and storms.

"This neighborhood's nice," I said, aiming for casual, but something about the way he looked at the place made me think this house mattered.

"I used to live here." His gaze lifted toward the second-story windows of the pale-blue house. "We moved after my dad died. My mom couldn't stay. Too many memories."

"I'm sorry," I murmured, reaching out to touch his arm.

He glanced at my hand before looking back at me.

"She kind of shut down after that," he said. "I think she didn't know how to be in the world without him. And I didn't know how to help."

My eyes drifted to the neatly kept lawn, then to the white porch swing swaying gently in the breeze. I tried to picture Cameron as a kid sitting there, legs too short to reach the ground. The image tugged at something in my chest.

"I get that," I said softly, my voice catching before I could stop it. "Where's your mom now?"

He let out a slow breath. "She calls. Birthdays. Holidays. We keep in touch, I guess. But it's not... close. Hasn't been for a long time."

There was no anger in his voice, just the quiet kind of acceptance that comes after years of knowing something won't change.

I nodded, the words settling.

"I was raised by a single mom too," I said. "My dad left before I was born. No big story. No fight. He just... decided we weren't part of his story anymore."

I hesitated, tugging at the edge of my sleeve.

"My mom did everything. Two jobs. Always showed up. But she always seemed... tired. Like she was carrying something heavy I wasn't supposed to ask about. So, I didn't."

Cameron didn't answer right away, but he nodded like he knew that kind of silence, had grown up inside it, too. And somehow, that said more than words ever could.

He reached over, lacing his fingers through mine.

His eyes held mine, and for a moment we just stood there with each other.

We kept walking, turning down a shaded street where tall trees cast long shadows across the pavement. The world around us seemed to dim, as if it knew we needed the quiet.

After a while, he exhaled, like he was about to say something he'd been carrying around for a while.

"My mom's been texting me," he said finally. "Asking if we could meet up. Have dinner."

I glanced over at him. "And?"

"I keep putting it off." His thumb rubbed the back of my hand, almost absently. "I don't know if I should go."

"That's up to you," I said carefully. "But... maybe it would be worth hearing what she has to say."

He nodded slowly, like he was turning the thought over in his mind, then reached into his pocket and pulled out his phone. I watched as his thumb hovered over the screen, hesitating for just a second before he started typing.

My stomach twisted. I already knew what he was doing.

A few moments passed in silence, just the soft tap of his fingers on glass. Then he glanced at the screen, exhaled, and looked at me.

"She wants to meet tonight," he said. His voice was steady, but there was something in his eyes that, like he was bracing for the idea to land. "Would you... come with me?"

The question caught me off guard. "You want me there?"

"I haven't seen her in over a year," he admitted, slipping his phone back into his pocket. "I don't know what she's going to say. But... I think I'd rather not go alone."

I let the words settle between us. It wasn't how I pictured the rest of my day. It felt messy. Personal. Too close. But then I thought about the way Cameron had shown up for me.

I nodded. "Yeah. I'll go."

He searched my face like he was waiting for me to take it back. "You sure?"

"No," I said honestly. "But I want to be there for you. Show up how you did for me."

Something unspoken passed between us, softening the lines of his expression.

"Thank you," he said quietly. "Really."

I shrugged, even as my heart thudded harder. "Just promise you won't abandon me at the table with awkward small talk."

His smile, the first real one since he'd brought it up, was enough to ease the knot in my chest. "Deal."

Chapter Thirty

Cameron

THE DOOR SWUNG OPEN with a cheerful jingle as Sidney and I stepped inside.

The scent of coffee and stale grease filled the air.

Sidney lingered a step behind me as my eyes swept the diner.

It didn't take long to find her. My mom sat in a corner booth, hands clasped tight on the table, posture straight.

She hadn't seen us yet.

I pulled in a sharp breath, trying to steady myself, to find some scrap of courage I wasn't entirely sure existed.

"You okay?" Sidney's voice was soft beside me, a thread of concern woven through it.

I nodded once. "Yeah."

Her hand slipped into mine, fingers curling in a gentle squeeze. It was such a small thing, but it landed hard, quiet reassurance that whatever this turned into, she was on my side.

We crossed the room toward the corner booth. My mom's gaze lifted, locking on us. The moment she noticed Sidney, her expression shifted, polite smile in place, posture a little straighter.

"Hello," she said, her voice balanced neatly between cordial and distant.

"Hey, Mom," I said, sliding into the booth across from her.

Sidney didn't follow. She held a hand out and gave my mom a warm smile. "Hi. I'm Sidney. It's really nice to meet you, Mrs. Scott."

A pleasant smile formed on my mom's face, but I could see the wheels turning. She was wondering who Sidney was to me.

"Call me Nora," she said. "It's nice to meet you too, Sidney."

Sidney slid into the booth beside me. I reached for a laminated menu, not because I cared what was on it, but because I needed something to keep my hands from betraying how restless I felt.

A waitress appeared, took our drink orders, then disappeared again. Silence filled the table once again.

Finally, my mom spoke.

"I didn't realize you'd be bringing someone, Cameron." Her tone was light, wrapped in politeness, but the smile didn't reach her eyes.

My shoulders tightened. "I didn't know that would be an issue."

"It's not," she said quickly. "Just... unexpected."

From the corner of my eye, I saw Sidney glance at me. Her expression was gentle, but there was a flicker of uncertainty there. I wanted to reassure her. The last thing I wanted was for her to feel unwelcome.

"Cam, maybe I should give you two some time alone," she said softly.

"No." The word left my mouth sharper than I intended. I leaned in, lowering my voice so only she could hear. "I want you to stay."

And I did. More than I could put into words. Having her beside me wasn't just comfort, it was the only thing keeping me from feeling like I was twelve years old again, bracing for a conversation I didn't know how to survive.

My mom's expression softened, a flicker of guilt passing across her face. "I'm sorry, Sidney. I didn't mean to make you feel out of place. I'm still learning how to navigate all this."

Our drinks arrived. I took a long sip of Pepsi, letting the cold fizz buy me a few extra seconds before I had to say anything.

Eventually, Mom spoke again. "So, how did you two meet?"

"Sidney's a summer intern," I said.

"Oh." Her gaze shifted to Sidney, polite smile in place. "That's nice. Do you work in entertainment too?"

Sidney nodded. "Yes. Cameron's been great about helping me get settled."

Not exactly true. If anything, I'd been the one leaning on her more than I'd ever admit out loud.

Mom gave me a small smile. "You always did like to stay busy."

I nodded, still unsure if that was meant as praise or a quiet jab about how rarely I called.

Sidney gave me a reassuring smile, like she could sense the conversation drifting into dangerous silence.

"He's basically a local legend," she said. "I saw a kid ask for his autograph the other day."

Mom's eyebrows lifted in surprise, but Sidney wasn't done.

"It was adorable," she went on. "This little boy marched right up to him, shoved a crumpled park map into his hands, and said, 'Are you Prince Patrick? Can you sign this for me?'"

I groaned. "It was Peter. Prince *Peter*. And I told him that...politely."

Sidney grinned, clearly enjoying herself. "Oh, he signed it. But then he bowed like the actual royalty he is. The kid's face lit up like it was the best day of his life."

Mom laughed, and for a brief moment, the stiffness in her shoulders eased.

"Prince Patrick, huh?" she teased, glancing at me.

I shook my head but noticed how her smile lingered a little longer than usual. And yet, there it was. A faint shimmer in her eyes.

"Patrick was Cameron's father's name," she said quietly.

The words caught in my chest. I swallowed against the lump rising in my throat.

Sidney's eyes widened. "Oh. I'm so sorry. I... I didn't know."

I shook my head. "No, his name isn't a bad word, Sidney." I let my gaze settle on my mom, my voice steady but firm. "We shouldn't stop saying it. He deserves to be remembered."

Mom's eyes dropped to the table. "I never intended to do that, Cameron..."

Silence stretched between us again, heavy enough to make the clink of dishes from the kitchen feel loud.

Half an hour later, the food had come and gone, leaving behind scattered plates and the syrupy remains of half-melted ice in our sodas.

Mom pushed the last bite of her salad around her plate, the soft scrape of her fork cutting through the lull.

"You look good," she said finally, her tone softer than before. "You seem... happy."

I wasn't sure what to do with that, so I just nodded. "Thanks."

But something in her posture changed. I noticed the twitch in her shoulders, the way her fingers fussed with the edge of her napkin. She was building up to something.

"I've been doing a lot of thinking," she said, her voice calm, but too calm. "About the past. About you."

My hand froze around my glass.

"I wasn't there for you," she said. "Not really."

Her gaze dropped to the table as her fingers twisted the napkin tight. She blinked rapidly as if holding something back.

"I was drowning in grief, Cam," she whispered. "I couldn't see anything past it. And you—" Her voice caught. "You were just a kid. You needed more than I gave. You deserved more."

The words hit like they'd been years in the making, equal parts apology and confession.

Sidney's hand came to rest on my arm.

"I'll give you two a minute," she said softly, already starting to slide out of the booth.

"Sid—" I reached for her without thinking, fingers brushing hers.

She gave me a small, reassuring smile. "It's okay. I'll be right outside."

I watched her slip away, the booth feeling a little emptier the second she was gone. Then I turned back to my mom.

"I'm sorry," she said softly. "I know it's late, maybe too late, but I need you to hear it. I see what I missed. What I let slip by. What I lost with you."

Her eyes finally lifted to mine, and for once, there was no distance there. No polite detachment. Just something that looked a lot like regret.

"I want a second chance," she said, her voice catching on the last syllable. "If you'll let me. To be your mom again."

Her gaze fell to her plate, as if she couldn't bear to watch my reaction.

I swallowed hard, my throat tight, words fighting to get past the lump there. "Just you being here... it means more than you probably know."

She nodded slowly, her eyes still wet but fixed on mine now, like every word I said mattered.

"It's going to take time," I said. "But... yeah. I'm open to that."

She gave me a fragile smile. Neither of us said anything for a few moments.

"Can I ask you something?" she said at last.

I nodded.

"Who is Sidney?" Mom asked, her tone softer now, almost cautious. "What does she mean to you?"

My hand drifted to the back of my neck, rubbing there as if I could work out the sudden tension. I was suddenly aware of the weight behind the question, of how careful I needed to be.

"She's... a friend."

She studied me for a long moment, like she was sifting through my answer for all the things I didn't say. When I didn't offer more, she let out a quiet breath, leaning back slightly.

"In that case," she said, "I'll start with some classic mom advice."

I arched a brow, equal parts wary and amused. "Oh, yeah?"

She tilted her head toward the door, where Sidney had disappeared. "Don't let her slip away. That girl's in love with you."

I froze. "Wait—what?"

Love? The word landed heavier than I expected, settling somewhere in my chest. Sidney and I cared about each other.

But love?

Surely it was too soon for either of us to know that.

And yet... what I felt for her sat dangerously close to it. Close enough that maybe my mom wasn't entirely wrong.

She smiled then. "You may not see it, Cam, but I've been around long enough to recognize the look of two people doing everything they can not to admit they're falling."

My gaze dropped to my hands, fingers curling around each other. "I'm not sure..."

She reached over, brushing her fingertips against mine in a gesture that felt oddly grounding. "Sweetheart, I haven't seen you this lit up since you had that crush on Miss Jensen in kindergarten."

I groaned, dragging a hand over my face. "Please do not bring up Miss Jensen right now."

"She was lovely," Mom said, completely unfazed. "Blonde, wore little strawberry earrings. You drew her seventeen pictures of dinosaurs in a week."

"Yeah, and Sidney hasn't seen any of my dinosaur artwork, so clearly this is not the same thing."

Mom laughed softly. "All I'm saying is... don't run from something real just because it feels big."

My eyes drifted toward the door, the one Sidney had disappeared through. She was out there. Still waiting.

And maybe Mom was right.

Maybe I was already in deeper than I wanted to admit.

We lingered in a quiet that felt... different now. Not strained. Not heavy. Just still. After a few more minutes, we stood and made our way to the register.

Before I could even reach for my wallet, Mom slid her card to the cashier.

The waitress smiled as she handed back the receipt. "Your friend already covered hers," she said.

Sidney. Of course.

I'd be finding a way to pay her back.

Outside, the fading light painted everything in soft gold. Mom paused just beyond the door, turning to face me.

"Thank you," she said, her voice low. "For being here. For letting me say what I needed to."

I nodded. "Thanks for coming. For... trying."

Her smile this time was unguarded. She stepped forward and wrapped me in a hug. For a long moment, she just held on, her breath catching in quiet, uneven waves.

"I know I can't fix the past," she whispered into my shoulder. "But I promise I'll keep trying. If you'll let me."

I nodded again, unable to trust my voice, caught somewhere between forgiveness and grief.

When she pulled back, her hands lingered on my arms like she wasn't quite ready to let go.

Her eyes were misted, but behind them was something I hadn't seen in years. Hope.

"You've grown into a man I'm proud to know, Cameron," she said softly. "Truly."

Then she stepped away, walking slowly toward her car. At the door, she glanced over her shoulder, offering one last wave before climbing inside.

I stood there until her taillights disappeared down the road.

I turned, letting my gaze sweep the sidewalk, searching.

And there she was.

Sidney sat on a bench just outside the diner, legs crossed, hands folded neatly in her lap. Waiting.

I closed the distance in a few easy strides. My head was still spinning from everything that had just happened inside, but somehow my chest felt lighter. More grounded.

She rose as I reached her. "Hey," she said softly. "How'd it go?"

"It went... great," I said, a quiet laugh slipping out. "Better than I ever expected."

Her smile bloomed, warm enough to thaw the last bit of tension I'd been carrying. "I'm glad."

For a moment, we just stood there, the rest of the world moving around us.

I really looked at her then, the way her eyes searched mine like she already knew what I wasn't saying.

My gaze dipped to her mouth, and for a single suspended heartbeat, I let myself imagine it, closing the space between us, kissing her the way I'd pictured since the moment we met.

But I didn't.

Not because I didn't want to. Not because I was afraid.

I waited because when I kissed her, I wanted her to know exactly what it meant. No confusion, no hesitation, no second-guessing. Just truth.

And now I knew—

It wasn't a matter of *if*.

It was *when*.

Chapter Thirty-One

Sidney

THE NEXT MORNING, CAMERON was already posted at the park gates, two coffees in hand like he'd been waiting for me.

"Pretty sure this is officially our thing," he said, passing me one.

"Could be worse," I said, taking a grateful sip.

He tilted his head toward the castle at the far end of Enchanted Boulevard, its spires gleaming against a cloudless, already-too-bright sky. "Fair warning, the CEO's here. Chris is on meltdown number... I don't know, eight? He wants every line perfect, every cue sharp, every costume steamed like it's about to hit the runway. We're talking DEFCON One."

I raised my cup in mock salute. "Sounds... fun."

"Oh, it gets better," Cameron said, tone bone-dry as we fell into step. We passed pastel storefronts with windows dressed like storybook scenes, the smell of churros drifting from somewhere up ahead. "He's starting with the castle show. So we get to be under a microscope first thing."

"Lucky us," I muttered.

He smirked, matching my pace. "Word of advice? If Chris is in your line of sight, make sure you're doing something useful. *Anything*."

"Noted," I said. "What about Gwen?"

"Circling," he said, jaw tightening just enough for me to catch it. "She's waiting for the perfect moment to make it about her."

"Shocking," I deadpanned. "How's Renee handling it?"

"See for yourself," Cameron said, giving me a pointed look. "Welcome to the storm."

He pushed open the greenroom door.

We'd barely made it three steps inside before Renee swooped in.

"The CEO is already here," she hissed, eyes darting like she expected him to materialize behind me. "And Chris almost passed out because the interns gave him a lukewarm latte. A lukewarm latte, Sidney. Do you understand what that means?"

I blinked. "That the interns are definitely getting fired?"

"No!" Renee all but shrieked, grabbing my shoulders in a mild but desperate shake. "It means the CEO will think *we're* lukewarm!"

Cameron and I exchanged glances.

"Renee," I said, keeping my tone as even as possible, "there is no universe in which the CEO cares how hot Chris's latte was."

She inhaled sharply and let it out. "Okay. Right. You're right. Totally right."

But her expression shifted. She closed her eyes for a long moment, and when she reopened them, I could see the panic flickering there.

"Sidney," she said, her voice dropping to a low, serious note. "I need you to go on for me."

My stomach plummeted. "Wait. What?"

"I can't," she said, shaking her head. "Not today. I'm too in my head. If I screw this up, it won't just fall on me, it'll hit everyone. But you? You're ready. And I trust you."

My mouth opened, but no words came out. Somewhere between *Are you completely insane?* and *I might actually throw up*, my voice just... failed.

Behind Renee, someone shouted, "THE DRAGON PROP IS STUCK IN A DOORFRAME!" A puff of smoke rolled dramatically across the floor, turning the scene into something between a backstage crisis and a low-budget disaster film.

I tightened my grip on Renee's shoulders, forcing her to meet my eyes. "Breathe. You've got this. You're amazing, and unless the CEO's completely blind, he's going to see that too. You can do this."

Her eyes shimmered. "Sid—"

"Seriously, Renee?" a familiar female voice scoffed from behind us.

We turned to find Gwen standing there, arms crossed, head tilted like she was about to deliver bad news she was secretly thrilled about.

"If you can't handle the pressure," she said sweetly, "I'd be more than happy to step in."

Her smile was pure predator.

Renee's jaw flexed, but she didn't break.

Cameron moved in beside me, his tone calm but edged with warning. "Renee's fine. She's going on as planned. Right, Renee?"

Renee straightened, fire sparking back into her eyes. "Absolutely."

"Oh, and Sidney?" She turned a poisoned smirk to me. "Tell Zack I said hi."

The name landed like a blow to the ribs, fast. Heat surged up my neck, my pulse hammering in my ears. She'd aimed for the softest spot and didn't miss.

Before I could react, before I could even think, Cameron was already there.

No raised voice. No flare of temper. Just quiet, unshakable steel.

"Walk away, Gwen," he said, meeting her gaze without a blink. "Now."

She blinked once, then smiled like the whole exchange was beneath her. With a slow, mocking wave, she turned and sauntered away.

Renee let out a sharp breath, her voice low but seething. "She's a snake."

I nodded, though my chest still felt caged, the air stolen by Gwen's barbed words.

Cameron's gaze found mine, his brows knitting in quiet concern. "You okay?"

I gave the smallest nod, but it was a lie, and we both knew it. My eyes dropped to the floor as I blinked hard against the sting. It wasn't just Gwen. It was Zack. The show. Renee fraying right in front of me.

Cameron stepped closer, his hands settling lightly on my shoulders. "Hey," he said, his voice soft but steady. "Look at me."

I kept my eyes down. If I looked at him, I'd splinter. And I'd promised myself, no more tears over Zack.

"I'm fine," I said, my voice cracking.

"No," he said, calm and certain. "You're not. Sidney... look at me."

I lifted my eyes to meet his.

"I don't care what Gwen says," he continued. "And neither should you. She's poking where it hurts on purpose. That's what she does."

My throat burned, but I nodded.

He stepped closer. "Come here."

His arms wrapped around me, and I let myself sink into his warmth.

His hand slid to the back of my neck, fingertips curling gently into my hair, his steady breath ghosting against my temple.

We didn't speak. We didn't have to.

Little by little, like magic I hadn't expected, the sharp edge of the hurt dulled. It was still there, but no longer crushing.

When he finally eased back, it was only enough to find my eyes. His gaze searched mine, and I wondered what was going through his mind.

His thumb swept beneath my eye, catching a tear I hadn't even felt fall. "I've got you," he murmured.

And in that moment, I believed him completely.

When we finally stepped apart, Renee was gone. In her place stood Westley, eyes wide as he glanced between us.

"Okay... what emotional wreckage did I just walk into?"

A shaky laugh slipped out, hovering dangerously close to a sob. "Just Gwen, sprinkling her usual sunshine and rainbows."

Cameron shot him a look. "Sid's about one sarcastic comment away from punching a castle wall."

Westley crossed his arms with a theatrical huff. "Screw that glitter-coated snake. Sid, don't take it out on the walls. If you want to punch something, aim for the throat. That'll take her down."

Renee reappeared at his side, shaking her head with a quiet laugh. "I second that."

From down the hall, Chris's voice snapped us all back to reality. "Everyone in costume now! I want this show perfect!"

He strode past at a near-jog.

"Where's my cue sheet?" he barked into the void. "And will someone fix the fog machine? And if these mic packs screech at me one more time—"

Right on cue, a piercing shriek of feedback split the air. I winced. A prop tree toppled with a pitiful thud.

And that's when *she* struck.

I didn't even see Gwen come in. One second, the chaos was all Chris, and the next, she was gliding toward him like she owned the room. The smile on her face was pure sugar, but it made you want to check your back for knives.

"Chris?" she called, syrup-sweet. "Maybe it's time to rethink who your strongest Primrose is today?"

The room froze. All eyes turned to her.

Chris pivoted slowly, the weariness in his eyes edged with a look that said he was two seconds away from quitting show business entirely.

"And what exactly are you suggesting?" he asked, voice low, frayed at the seams.

Gwen clasped her hands and tilted her head in feigned concern, only making her look even more dangerous.

"I just think," she purred, "with the CEO out there, we shouldn't be taking any chances. Some of us thrive under pressure... and some don't. You wouldn't want the whole thing to fall apart, would you?"

Beside me, Renee went rigid.

Anger simmered beneath my skin.

Chris lifted a hand, his voice slicing through the charged silence. "No last-minute cast swaps. Renee's going on. End of discussion."

For a flicker of a second, Gwen's smile cracked. Then it was back, as if nothing had happened.

"Of course," she said lightly, stepping back with a breezy laugh. "I'm just looking out for the team."

Chapter Thirty-Two

Cameron

TECHS ZIPPED THROUGH THE greenroom, clipboards in hand, panic in their eyes. Costumes were being triple-checked, like someone might've swapped a ballgown for a burlap sack. The fog machine gave a wheeze that sounded a lot like a death rattle.

Somewhere out there, the CEO was already in the crowd, probably deciding whether the show ran on Fantasy World's signature magic or the incompetence of an overworked cast.

Renee paced the floor like she could walk her nerves right out of her system. She adjusted her tiara for the sixth time, smoothed her skirt, then repeated the entire process like she was on a loop. Her lips moved constantly, reciting lines under her breath. Sidney trailed just behind her, offering quiet encouragement.

"You've done this a thousand times," she murmured. "You're ready. You're not going to throw up."

Renee wrinkled her nose. "No promises."

Sidney bumped her shoulder with a half-smile. "Fine, but if you do... aim for Gwen."

That earned a laugh.

Gwen had kept her distance since her little "cast swap" scheme got shot down. But apparently, lurking in the shadows had lost its charm. She swept into the room wearing a broad smile.

And it was aimed squarely at Renee.

"Hey, gorgeous," Gwen chirped, breezing over like they were brunch buddies instead of sworn enemies in matching tiaras. "That blush is working overtime. You look *stunning*."

Renee blinked, clearly caught off guard, and crossed her arms. "What do you want, Gwen?"

Gwen leaned in, fingertips brushing something invisible from Renee's shoulder with all the delicacy of fake concern. "Your bodice clasp is a little loose. Want me to fix it before it turns into a wardrobe moment?"

Sidney's eyes met mine, and I could tell we were thinking the same thing.

Gwen didn't fix things for people.

She sabotaged them.

Usually with sparkle. Always with a smile.

And right now, she was smiling way too much.

"I think it's fine—" Renee began, but Gwen was already circling behind her, fingers busy with the fabric.

I stepped forward, ready to intervene.

"There," Gwen said at last. "Perfect."

She floated off, humming like she'd just done the world a favor.

The moment she was out of earshot, Renee let out a breath like she'd been holding it for three straight minutes. "That was weird, right?" She was already tugging at the edge of her bodice, like she didn't trust it to stay put.

"Weird," I said flatly.

Sidney stepped closer, arms crossed, eyes still on the spot where Gwen had disappeared. "She was being nice. That's how you know something's wrong."

A few minutes later, Gwen reappeared, this time carrying two cups of coffee.

"Here," she said, extending one toward Renee. "Thought you might need it."

I had to fight the urge to sprint over and knock it out of her hand. It was probably poisoned. Or cursed.

Renee accepted it slowly, studying the cup like it might detonate. Then, her gaze lifted, unimpressed. "What are you doing?"

Gwen's smile faltered. "What do you mean? I'm just being nice."

"Why?"

Something flickered across her face before she smoothed it over. "Because we all need this show to go well. If it bombs, we all go down. So maybe for today we drop the rivalry. Work together. Clean slate."

The look Renee gave her screamed *not a chance*, but she still glanced at the coffee like she couldn't decide whether to sip it or dump it in a potted plant.

Then the speakers overhead let out a sudden, ear-splitting screech.

Gwen startled, just enough to conveniently bump into Renee, sending hot liquid across the front of her Primrose gown.

The sound that tore from her throat was half gasp, half growl.

"Oh, no!" Gwen gasped, her voice dripping syrupy concern. "I'm so sorry!"

She lunged for a stack of paper towels and began blotting furiously at the stain, as if a few napkins could undo sabotage.

"Stop," Renee snapped, jerking out of reach. "You're making it worse."

"I didn't mean—really—I'm sorry," Gwen gushed, piling it on thicker with every word.

Fury flared in Renee's eyes. "You did this on purpose."

Gwen reeled back, expression wounded. "What? No, Renee, come on—I didn't! Ugh, I'm just such a klutz sometimes."

She pressed a hand to her chest, the picture of injured innocence.

But no one in the room was buying it.

Least of all, me.

"There's no time to fix this," Renee whispered, turning to me.

She wasn't wrong.

Due to budget cuts, there were no backup dresses. No miracle fix. Just a lead costume soaked in coffee, three minutes on the clock, and the CEO waiting in the front row.

Which left one possibility.

Gwen tapped her chin. "I might have an idea..." she said, drawing it out like she expected a drumroll.

Renee didn't flinch. Her voice was ice. "Let me guess. You're offering to take my place."

Gwen gasped. An actual gasp. "No! Renee, *please.* This is your moment. I wouldn't *dream* of stealing it."

My stomach twisted.

"I was just going to suggest," she said, tone dripping with sugar, "you borrow *my* Primrose dress. It might be a little snug, but you should be able to squeeze into it."

Across the room, Sidney's eyes snapped to mine.

We didn't need words.

We both knew exactly what this was.

And it wasn't help.

Renee went still, like she didn't trust it either. But what choice did she have?

She locked eyes with Gwen, holding the silence like a weapon. One beat. Two. Then she let out a sharp breath. "Fine."

Without another word, she turned and followed Gwen toward the dressing rooms.

Just as I stepped toward the stage, Renee reemerged, now zipped into Gwen's Primrose dress. It fit perfectly, not snug at all, despite Gwen's not-so-subtle dig.

Renee looked radiant. Regal.

And furious.

I stepped onto the stage and hit my first mark, delivering my lines and movements like muscle memory. But my focus was split, counting down to Renee's entrance, heart pounding harder with each beat. Because my gut told me something was off.

Then her cue came, and she came out on stage to a cheering crowd.

She looked perfectly poised. Glowing. Like nothing had happened.

The audience cheered on cue, swept up in the magic.

I scanned past rows of children in sparkly tiaras and light-up wands, past parents balancing popcorn tubs and melting ice cream cones until I saw him.

Front row. Center.

The CEO. *Harrison Conway.*

He was young, maybe late twenties, but with the sharp, no-nonsense air of someone who didn't bother with pleasantries.

He was dressed in a crisp navy suit. Arms folded. Posture straight.

His features were schooled into an expression of cool detachment, like he was already calculating the show's worth in dollars and cents.

Everything onstage was clicking into place. Every cue landed, every step hit right on time. We were in sync, the first act sliding by without a hitch. By the middle of the second dance sequence, that dangerous flicker of hope lit in my chest, maybe we'd actually make it through this.

Then I twirled her.

It was perfect. Cameras snapped. Kids cheered.

And then—*rip.*

Not a dramatic tear. No sharp snap. Just the quiet, treacherous whisper of fabric surrendering.

Renee's eyes flashed wide as she twirled back toward me, the sparkle in them just barely betraying her panic. Her smile stayed locked in place for the audience, but I caught the change, the slightest hitch in her step, the faintest drag of her foot as her skirt swished around her ankles.

I tightened my grip on her hand, redirecting us before the misstep could spread. One fluid shift, and the next turn became a gentle pull. I drew her in close, close enough for her skirt to brush my boots, and let our steps slow into something softer.

From the audience's perspective, it probably looked deliberate, a tender pause in the middle of the choreography, a romantic flourish written into the dance.

Small enough, the crowd wouldn't think twice. Small enough, if we were lucky, that the CEO wouldn't either.

Her eyes found mine, gratitude flickering there as her lips shaped two silent words: *Thank you.*

I gave the faintest nod, just enough for her to catch before we spun apart again.

And then it was time.

The final lift.

Renee hesitated, just for a heartbeat, gathering her skirt in both hands as she drew in a breath. Then she ran toward me—

—but the torn seam had already betrayed her.

The once-smooth satin sagged low on one side, dragging at her ankles. The hem snagged against her shoes, tangling around her like creeping vines, and before I could lunge forward to steady her, her foot caught.

She stumbled.

And went down hard.

Gasps rippled through the square like a wave. A child whimpered. Someone near the front whispered, "Oh no," in the hushed tone of someone watching a fairytale shatter.

I dropped to my knees beside her before the stage crew could even move.

"You okay?" My voice was low, careful.

She gave a small nod, though her breath hitched around the edges. A wince flickered across her face before she forced it into a smile. Her cheeks were flushed, her eyes glassy.

I eased her to her feet, one hand firm at her back, the other gripping hers like I could shoulder the weight of the moment if I just held on tight enough. The crowd erupted in polite applause.

But out of the corner of my eye, I noticed one person who didn't clap.

The CEO stood motionless, arms crossed, his expression carved in stone.

A tight knot formed in my chest, but I kept my posture steady.

"Did he see?" Renee whispered.

"Yeah," I responded, not wanting to lie to her.

With one arm still around her, I guided her offstage.

And just before we slipped through the doorway, I saw *her.*

Gwen.

Lurking in the shadows, arms folded.

She was smiling.

Chapter Thirty-Three

Sidney

"No, no, no…" I breathed, watching Renee hit the stage hard.

From the observation window, I couldn't catch every detail, but I saw enough. The skirt dragging low, fabric slipping loose, and now she was sprawled across the stage. And she wasn't moving.

My stomach dropped. I held my breath, frozen.

Then Cameron dropped to his knees beside her, and she shifted, just barely.

Relief hit like a rush of wind, and I exhaled.

I tore myself from the window and started for the stage entrance, only to nearly collide with Porter rounding the corner.

"Whoa—" he stopped short, eyes locking on mine. "What happened?"

"It's Renee," I said, my voice catching. "She fell. Onstage."

His expression hardened instantly. "Shit."

Without another word, he fell in beside me, our strides in sync as we rushed through the greenroom toward the stage door.

We reached it just as Cameron and Renee were stepping through.

"Renee," I said softly, but she didn't even look my way.

Her fierce gaze was pinned on Gwen.

"You," she hissed, the word slicing through the air. Then louder, her voice trembling with fury, "You did this!"

Renee surged forward like a live wire, fisting a handful of Gwen's hair before anyone could react. Gwen shrieked, stumbling back, arms flailing, but Renee's grip only tightened.

"Renee!" Cameron lunged in, locking both arms around her waist and dragging her back. She fought him every inch, feet scrabbling against the floor, hands reaching like she could tear the truth out of Gwen with her bare fingers.

Westley and Porter jumped into the fray, shoving themselves between the two, arms up in a frantic blockade.

"Let me go!" Renee's voice was ragged now, twisting against Cameron's hold. "She did this. She gave me that dress on purpose! She knew it would rip!"

"You're insane!" Gwen shouted, stumbling into the wall. "I was trying to help!"

Heat surged under my skin. Porter shot me a sidelong look, one brow arched in mock caution. "Do I need to hold you back too?"

My fists clenched, nails biting into my palms, but I shook my head.

By now, a ring of wide-eyed performers and crew had formed, drawn in like moths to a flame.

And then Chris stormed in.

He cut straight through the circle and stopped dead center. "Well," he said, shaking his head, "that was a disaster."

Both Renee and Gwen snapped their attention to him.

"The CEO saw everything," he added, his voice flat. "And let's just say... he didn't look impressed."

Renee stepped forward, urgency sparking in her voice. "Chris, Gwen sabotaged—"

He lifted a hand, slicing her words in half. "I believe the fall wasn't your fault," he said evenly. "But this fight was uncalled for. You're suspended, Renee. Two weeks."

Renee froze, the weight of it hitting her like a blow.

Across the room, Gwen crossed her arms, a satisfied smirk tugging at her lips.

"But Chris," Renee protested. "She sabotaged my dress."

Chris ignored her and turned to the rest of us. "We don't tolerate physical altercations, period. I don't care who did what. This is a professional show, not a high school hallway."

The words landed like a gut punch. "Unless someone has actual proof of sabotage, that's the end of it. Renee, you're out. Gwen, you're stepping in as Primrose."

Gwen's face lit up like she'd just won a crown. She fluttered her lashes and gave a syrupy smile. "Thank you, Chris. I won't let you down."

I glanced at Renee. Her jaw was clenched, eyes glassy with unshed tears, holding herself together like it was taking everything she had not to fall apart.

Chris let out a long breath. "That's it. Everyone, go home. We'll regroup in the morning."

Silence followed. No one argued. No one even moved at first. Then slowly, people began gathering their things, the energy in the room sinking like a deflated balloon.

Morale had officially hit rock bottom.

Renee bolted for the door.

"Renee!" I shouted, already chasing after her.

She didn't slow.

Didn't glance back, but I continued chasing her.

I followed her past the greenroom, weaving through crates and costume racks, until I caught sight of her near the back exit to the employee parking lot.

"Renee, please." My voice came out low, winded. "Just talk to me."

She froze, back still to me, shoulders locked tight like she was holding herself together by sheer force.

For a moment, I thought she'd keep walking, just push through the door and disappear.

But then she stopped.

Not all at once. More like she deflated, breath leaving in a shaky exhale before her shoulders lifted and squared again.

When she turned, her eyes shimmered with unshed tears.

"I'm fine," she said, but the words rang hollow. "Seriously. I just need some space."

"Renee..."

"I'll be okay," she said. "I just... I need a minute to not fall apart in front of everyone."

The words hit like a punch, and before I could stop myself, I blurted, "I'm going to find proof. I swear to you, Renee, I'll figure out what she did, and I'll make sure everyone sees it."

Her eyes lifted to mine, glassy and exhausted. A faint, crooked smile tugged at her lips.

"Thanks. But I can't talk about it right now," she said, her voice low and frayed. "Because if I start... I'll either cry or throw a chair through a window. And I'm pretty sure both are frowned upon in the employee handbook."

I nodded and stepped back.

"Okay," I said quietly. "But if you need me, you call. I mean it."

Her gaze met mine, and she gave me a shaky smile. "I know."

Then she turned, fingers curling around the door handle. She drew in one last breath, squared her shoulders, and stepped through. The door shut behind her with a soft click.

I stood there staring at the door for a minute.

Gwen thought this was over. That the show had gone on and she'd walked away victorious.

She was wrong.

The next act would belong to us.

Chapter Thirty-Four

Cameron

WHAT A MESS.

Renee was gone. She had stormed out without so much as a glance back.

And who could blame her?

Not after everything that had just gone down.

I watched the doorway, still waiting for Sidney to return. She'd taken off without a second thought, chasing after Renee. And I was stuck here, wondering if I should've gone too.

Relief hit me when the door finally cracked open and Sidney stepped back through.

I crossed the room in a few strides.

She gave me a little shake of her head, and I knew Renee wouldn't be coming back. Not today at least.

And Sidney looked like she wasn't far behind her.

Her eyes scanned the room until they landed on Gwen. She took a step forward, and my hand shot out, closing around her arm.

When her eyes met mine, they were lit with fury.

For a moment I thought I might have to hold her back, but that's when Westley leaned toward Porter, whispering loud enough for the room to hear.

"Is it technically illegal to put hair removal cream in someone's shampoo? Asking for a friend."

I watched Sidney's eyes as the fires slowly died down and a ghost of a smile broke through.

The sound set off a ripple of chuckles that turned into a chorus of laughter.

Gwen, of course, didn't join in. She crossed her arms, rolled her eyes, and tossed her hair over one shoulder. She glared at us like we were all children playing a game she'd already won.

I gave Sidney's hand a small squeeze then laced my fingers through hers. My thumb brushed lightly over the back of her hand, a silent promise that I was still here. Still with her.

"Come on," I murmured. "Let's get out of here."

Her fingers curled tighter around mine, like she needed an anchor. She looked up at me, and for the first time since all of this started, a flicker of softness broke through the tension in her face. She nodded.

We made it halfway to the door, her hand still warm in mine, when Gwen's voice drifted after us.

"Oh, Sidney."

Sidney froze, but she didn't turn around. Her whole body went tense.

Damn it, Gwen. You couldn't just let her walk away, could you?

"It seems like you move on pretty fast," Gwen said, her tone honeyed and cruel. "Let's just hope no one steals this one from you too."

Sidney stiffened at my side. Her grip crushed mine, every ounce of her anger and hurt channeling straight into my palm.

I turned, my gaze locking on Gwen with enough heat to scorch. I wanted to tell her exactly what she meant to me, which was nothing. Less than nothing. She couldn't touch Sidney, not where it mattered. The words were on the tip of my tongue.

But before I could open my mouth, Westley beat me to it.

"Gwen," he said smoothly, "you've already nailed the villain role. No need to audition for 'petty side character' while you're at it."

Sidney didn't so much as glance back. She just kept walking, her hand locked tight in mine all the way to Kingdom Square, like if she let go, she'd unravel right there in the hallway.

And that's exactly what happened when we reached the fountain.

She stopped. Shoulders rising with a shaky inhale, then falling in defeat. Her hands clenched at her sides, opened, clenched again.

I hung back a few feet, every instinct telling me to close the distance, but something told me she needed the space first.

So I waited. Watching.

Then she moved. Pacing in a tight loop, shoes scuffing against the stone. She looked like she wanted to scream. Or cry. Or both.

"She's lying," Sidney burst out. "She knew exactly what she was doing. That wasn't a wardrobe malfunction. That was sabotage. She planned it. She—"

Her voice cracked. She turned away, pressing the heel of her hand to her eyes like sheer willpower could stop the tears from falling.

That was it. I couldn't hold back anymore. I stepped forward and pulled her into my arms.

She didn't resist. She leaned into me, her head dropping against my chest as she let go.

"I know," I said quietly, the words heavy in my throat. "I saw it too."

We stayed there in silence, the noise of the park drifting around us. But all of it was muted, like it belonged to another world.

Her shoulders trembled, just enough to make me wonder if she was crying or clinging to the edge of control. Either way, I didn't let go.

My hand traced slow, steady circles along her back. I lowered my chin to the crown of her head, holding her there, willing her to feel it, that she wasn't alone.

"Chris just gave it to her," she whispered, her voice raw and bitter. "Like none of it mattered. Not the sabotage. Not Renee. Not any of it."

Her head shifted against me as she shook it.

"And Gwen just stood there... smiling. Like she'd won." Her voice cracked. "And I just... I let her. I didn't speak up. Didn't stop her. I froze."

My chest tightened. I tilted my head down toward her. "There wasn't anything you could've done. But this isn't over. We didn't lose."

She stilled and pulled back, just enough for her eyes to meet mine. Something fierce flickered there, burning through the doubt.

"No," she said. "We didn't. And we're not going to."

I arched a brow, the corner of my mouth twitching despite everything. "What are you thinking, Princess?"

Her gaze slid past me, steady and faraway, like she was piecing together a puzzle I couldn't see yet. "She's not smart enough to pull this off alone."

I frowned. "Go on."

"Chris didn't say Gwen was innocent," she said, stepping out of my arms. The sudden absence of her hit me hard. "He said there wasn't proof. Like he's just waiting for someone to hand it to him."

"And you think someone helped her?"

"There's no way she pulled this off by herself. The timing, the placement of the tear, it was too exact. Too convenient. She had to have help. If I had to guess, she had help from someone in the wardrobe department."

"Detective Webber returns." I nudged her shoulder lightly, trying to cut through the fire in her expression. "So... when do we start?"

She exhaled, focus sharpening. Her eyes drifted toward the castle, calculating, determined.

"Soon," she said. "But first, we've got a friend to cheer up."

Chapter Thirty-Five

Sidney

BEFORE I STEPPED INTO the apartment, I knew I had my work cut out for me.

Renee was camped on the couch in a blanket burrito, eyes locked on the TV like it held the secrets of the universe. The overacted drama and swelling violins confirmed it, she was deep into a soap opera binge.

Her hair, usually runway-ready, had surrendered to a messy bun with flyaways staging a full escape.

Willow and Ridley lingered in the kitchen, clutching half-empty mugs and trading glances that said they were just as concerned as I was.

All three of us knew it. Renee needed a reset.

A night stitched back together with laughter, even if we had to drag her into it kicking and screaming.

I pulled out my phone and fired off a text to Cameron. After a few quick messages back and forth, the plan was set. The meeting spot was close, just a short walk away at one of the Fantasy World resorts.

Even though Willow and Ridley were within earshot, I still sent them the details. Willow caught my eye and gave an eager bounce. Ridley offered a quick nod of approval.

Perfect.

Now for the hard part: getting Renee on board.

"Renee," I said gently.

No response.

"Renee," I tried again, stepping right into her line of sight, blocking the TV.

Her eyes narrowed.

"Move, Sidney," she said flatly. "I need to see if Ramone's girlfriend wakes up from her six-month coma today. If she doesn't, he's going to be *devastated*."

"I'm sure Ramone will survive without you," I said, grabbing the remote and switching off the TV.

"Sidney," Renee groaned, dragging out my name like it physically pained her. "Just let me sit here and rot."

"Not a chance." I planted my hands on my hips. "Get up and get dressed. We're going out."

"I don't feel like going out." She reached for the remote. I pulled it back just before she lunged for it.

"Nope. Not happening. No roommate of mine is going to sit here wallowing in self-pity."

With a dramatic groan, she buried her face deeper into the couch cushion. "I swear, if you drag me to a bar—"

Willow crossed the room and plopped down beside her. "Who said anything about a bar?"

Renee lifted her head just enough to squint suspiciously. "Then where—?"

I grinned. "Trust me."

It took a little more convincing and a lot of eye-rolling, but twenty minutes later, we were out the door.

The moment we stepped into the glow of Sea Breeze Resort, it felt like the world had decided to throw on its vacation filter. Suddenly, everything was softer, brighter, like we'd checked our real lives at the door and stepped into someone else's daydream.

Golden light washed over the entrance, the palm trees swaying like they'd been given stage directions. The air smelled of saltwater and sunscreen, a mix that whispered summer, vacation, and zero responsibilities.

A wide fountain stretched across the courtyard, its water sparkling as it leapt in rhythm with the string lights overhead.

Renee slowed, eyes flicking around. "I'm confused. Why are we at the Sea Breeze Resort?"

We followed the path past the fountain to a tucked-away restaurant painted in retro pinks and blues, the kind of colors you'd find on an old beach postcard. A neon sign buzzed above the door, throwing a warm glow over the patio crowd spilling outside.

Renee stopped short, her gaze locking on the name. "Scoops? You brought me to an ice cream shop?" She arched one brow, unimpressed. "This is your grand plan?"

I crossed my arms. "Name one problem ice cream can't fix."

"Diabetes," she shot back instantly.

My smile faltered. "Okay, besides that."

Renee let out a reluctant laugh. "Fine. Even if it's not the solution... it's definitely worth trying."

We stepped inside. In the far corner, Cameron, Westley, and Porter were packed into a circular booth tucked against the wall. Porter spotted us first and waved like we were long-lost relatives instead of people he'd seen yesterday.

We made our way over. I slid in next to Cameron, who casually draped his arm along the back of the booth, his fingers brushing my shoulder in that easy way that made my pulse skip. Renee dropped beside me, while Westley and Porter shifted so Willow and Ridley could squeeze in.

Porter tilted his head. "Okay, not that I'm complaining, but why are we here again?"

I nodded toward Renee. "So she can drown her sorrows in ice cream."

Westley leaned back, a smirk tugging at his mouth. "A much classier option than The Dive. No sticky floors. No questionable karaoke."

Ridley snorted. "And no drinking competitions." Her gaze slid to Porter, who immediately groaned.

"Come on," he protested. "That was one time."

"One time you passed out under the table," Ridley shot back.

Porter grinned sheepishly. "Still won the first three rounds, though."

"That's not how I remember it," said Ridley with a scoff.

Renee laughed, shaking her head. "Honestly, I'm impressed Porter remembers any of it."

Before Porter could dig himself deeper, a waitress appeared with menus, moving briskly between us. Cameron flipped his open, a grin spreading as if he'd already spotted trouble.

He tapped his finger under *Legendary Sundaes*, eyes gleaming. "So... who's feeling brave?"

Renee gaped at him. "You're joking, right?"

I leaned in to scan the page. "What exactly is the Ice Cream Mountain?"

Cameron lowered his voice. "Let's just say it makes that Dive competition look like warm-up practice."

Porter grinned. "Am I going to pass out again?"

"It's everything," Cameron went on, eyes gleaming. "Eight scoops—vanilla, chocolate, cookies and cream, strawberry, mint chip, butter pecan, butterscotch, and rocky road. Then they drown it in hot fudge, caramel, peanut butter sauce... top it with brownies, cookies, candy, whipped cream, and cherries. Basically, if it doesn't belong, it's on this thing."

Ridley arched an eyebrow. "That sounds absolutely insane."

A grin tugged at my lips. "Correction, it sounds perfect."

When the waitress came back, we didn't hesitate. "One Ice Cream Mountain," Cameron said with all the gravity of a man signing a peace treaty. "And seven spoons."

She gave us a look that landed somewhere between admiration and deep concern. With a smirk, she scribbled it down and vanished toward the kitchen.

A few minutes later, another server appeared, this one clearly living for the drama. He cleared his throat like he was stepping onto a stage.

"Ladies and gentlemen," he boomed, voice echoing across the restaurant, "we have a table bold enough to face the legendary Ice Cream Mountain. Many have tried. Few have survived."

Laughter rippled through the room. Someone at the next table clapped. A group near the bar whooped like we'd just announced an engagement. Even the hostess craned her neck for a look at the lunatics about to ruin their digestive systems.

Renee groaned and dropped her head onto the table. "What have we done?"

"Made history," Cameron said proudly, leaning back like a king awaiting his crown.

Willow already had her phone out, eyes sparkling. "If we're going down, we're going viral."

I grinned, lifting an imaginary spoon like a sword. "To glory."

The server crossed the floor with great ceremony and set the monstrosity down at the center of the table. The thing practically cast its own shadow. Scoops piled sky high, rivers of hot fudge and caramel dripping down the sides, an avalanche of whipped cream ready to slide off at the first wrong move.

"Best of luck, brave souls," the server intoned, retreating like he was backing away from live explosives.

Westley let out a low whistle. "Sweet holy hell."

Porter gripped his spoon with mock gravity. "So, is this where we yell *charge*?"

All eyes landed on Renee. She hadn't said a word yet, but the reluctant smile tugging at her lips said enough. She lifted her spoon in quiet solidarity.

That was all the permission anyone needed.

Porter struck first, scooping a heroic bite. "This is a sacred moment," he declared, eyes wide as he chewed.

Westley pointed at the towering whipped cream like it was a battleground. "Alright, which heathen is bold enough to claim the first cherry?"

Cameron leaned in, eyes glinting as they met mine. "I wouldn't mind taking that honor."

I smacked his arm, grinning. "Not sure you're ready for that kind of responsibility."

His voice dropped low, teasing. "Wanna bet?"

Before either of us could move, Willow darted in, snatched the cherry, and popped it into her mouth with a victorious smirk.

The table erupted, half laughter, half outrage, but mostly the kind of energy that made me think we'd just declared ice cream war.

"Too slow, lovebirds."

Chaos broke loose.

Spoons clashed like weapons, the clang of metal drowned beneath the laughter tumbling out of our booth. Everyone was shameless, Cameron claimed the cookies and cream, Porter nearly choked on a rogue brownie, and I kept swiping bites off Renee's plate just to see how long it would take before she snapped.

"Sid, are you serious right now?" Renee swatted at me, her glare ruined by the laughter tugging at her mouth.

I grinned around a mouthful of whipped cream. "Every woman for herself."

Porter elbowed Cameron, grinning like the devil. "You saw that, right? Sidney just stole off Renee's spoon."

Cameron's eyes were already on me, his smirk spreading slow and dangerous. "That's basically an indirect kiss."

My pulse tripped. I smacked his arm with my spoon, aiming for casual but missing by a mile. "What's wrong, Prince? Jealous?"

His gaze didn't waver. He leaned in, voice dropping low enough to curl heat down my spine. "Very."

I lifted my spoon to swat him again, but this time he caught my wrist midair.

The laughter around the booth blurred to static. All I felt was his shoulder brushing mine, the warmth of his hand holding me there, my breath catching like I'd forgotten how to do something as simple as inhale.

Then, just when my heart couldn't pound harder, he grinned and swiped a dollop of whipped cream onto the tip of my nose.

I gasped. "You did not—"

"Did," he said smugly, leaning back.

"Okay, enough of that, you two," Ridley groaned. "Before I actually throw up."

I wiped the cream from my nose, cheeks still burning, and risked a sideways glance at Renee—half praying for backup, half bracing for judgment.

She wasn't glaring. She wasn't even smirking.

She was laughing.

Not the polite, reluctant kind she gave when she was humoring me, but real laughter—bright and unrestrained, spilling out of her like she hadn't remembered she could. Her shoulders loosened, her eyes caught the light, and just like that, the heavy edge of the night seemed to melt away, the way the sundae in the middle of the table was slowly collapsing under its own weight.

Renee set her spoon down and shook her head, still smiling despite herself. "Okay, fine. This was a good idea."

Her voice softened as her gaze traveled around the booth, pausing on each of us in turn. "Thank you. Really."

Cameron lifted his spoon like a toast, his mouth curved in that easy smirk. "To Ice Cream Mountain."

Porter clinked his spoon against Cameron's with a laugh. "And to whatever absolute nonsense Sidney drags us into next."

The rest of us joined in, spoons tapping together in a sugar-sticky clatter that sounded more like kids playing than any kind of formal toast.

A comfortable hush settled over the table, the kind that lingers after shared laughter, soft, earned, easy. My gaze drifted across the booth, and when I looked up, Cameron was already watching me.

There was a quiet smile playing at his lips, faint and secretive, like he knew something I didn't. He leaned in just enough that his words belonged only to me.

"Hey, Carolina," he murmured, low and easy. "Feel like sneaking out? I know a spot with the best view of the fireworks."

The booth, the chatter, the sticky spoons, all of it blurred. I nodded before I could overthink, and together we slipped out, murmuring quick goodbyes that no one seemed to notice.

Outside, the night air was warm, but a soft breeze was threading through the air.

"If we head toward the pier," Cameron said, checking his watch, "we'll make it just in time. Fireworks start in five."

We wandered down the path until the pier stretched out before us. I moved to the railing, resting my elbows on the cool wood. Below, the water shimmered with the shifting glow of Fantasy World's lights, each ripple catching a different color. From somewhere in the distance, faint parade music floated through the air.

Cameron stepped up beside me just as the first firework split the sky. Brilliant color burst wide before dissolving into darkness.

Another followed. Then another.

Each hiss, each muted boom, filled the night, leaving a breathless pause between every bloom.

We stood together in that fragile space between explosions, just the two of us, like the rest of the world had quietly agreed to step aside and let this moment belong only to us.

I turned to look at Cameron only to find him already watching me.

His face was painted in firework glow, but it wasn't the color that held me still. It was the look in his eyes.

His expression held something I couldn't quite name.

No, that wasn't true.

I could name it, but I was terrified of being wrong.

My heartbeat thundered, wild and unsteady, like it was trying to break free of my chest.

And then he moved.

No hesitation. No second thoughts. Just the quiet certainty of him leaning in, closing the space between us as if this had always been where we were headed.

His lips brushed mine, soft, hesitant, asking a question I'd been aching to answer.

So I did.

The kiss was fragile at first, just a breath of contact between us. But then a small whimper escaped my lips, and it was like a dam burst.

He answered with a low sound of his own, deep and desperate, pulling me closer until there was no space left to pretend. The kiss deepened, urgent now, hungry, like we'd both been waiting far too long for this moment.

His hand curved around my waist, anchoring me, while the other cupped my cheek, thumb brushing over my skin as if he needed proof I was real. I leaned into him, chasing the warmth of his mouth, the taste of him, the way he kissed like every second mattered.

The world tilted, blurred, vanished. There was only the rush of his lips against mine, the fireworks exploding above us, and the wild rhythm of my heart beating in sync with his.

Every kiss after that was deeper, fiercer, until it felt like the whole night was collapsing into us.

When he finally pulled back, I was breathless.

So was he.

His eyes locked on mine, wide, unsteady, like he'd just jumped without looking to see if I'd follow. And for one impossible moment, I swore I saw it. Everything I wanted to believe. Everything I was terrified to name.

And that was the problem.

Because if I named it, if I admitted it, then it was real.

And real meant messy. Dangerous.

Unforgivable, considering the pieces of my life I hadn't let go of yet. The thought of Zack, of promises I'd made, crashed into me like cold water, dousing the fire we'd just lit.

But then panic slammed into my chest. This wasn't some casual kiss. This was more.

It meant something, maybe everything, and the weight of that realization nearly knocked me off my feet.

Panic clawed up my chest, and I stumbled back a step.

Confusion flickered across his face. "Sid?"

"We shouldn't have done that." As soon as the words were out, I wanted to claw them back.

I didn't even know why I said it. Every inch of me still burned from that kiss. I wanted him. God, I wanted him.

A flicker of hurt cut through his expression.

"Was I wrong?" His voice cracked softly. "About where this was going?"

My stomach twisted painfully, guilt and longing twisting together until I could hardly breathe.

"No," I blurted, too fast, too desperate. "No, you weren't. I just..."

I tore my gaze away, blinking at the glittering hotel windows, at the fading trails of fireworks dissolving into the night sky. Anything to avoid drowning in the truth of what had just happened and how much I wanted it to happen again.

"You know what I mean."

Cameron shook his head once.

"No, Sidney. I don't." His voice was steady, but tight around the edges, like it was costing him to keep it that way. "And if you're waiting for me to say I regret it? I won't. Because I don't. I'd make the same choice again. Every single time."

"Don't say that," I blurted, the words scraping out of me before I could think.

He reached for me.

I flinched. Just barely, but it was enough that he noticed.

His hand froze midair.

"This isn't—" I stumbled over myself, words crashing out in a rush I couldn't hold back. "This isn't the time, Cameron. There's too much happening, too many things we don't even know yet, and maybe, maybe it wasn't what we thought. Maybe we just... needed something. Something to hold on to. Something to make it easier."

"Easier?" Cameron narrowed his eyes in confusion. "Sid, what are you talking about?"

"I don't know. I don't know!" I closed my eyes as the panic I felt my words turn frantic.

Cameron closed the distance and put his hands on each of my shoulders. "Sid, breathe."

I sucked in a few gulps of air that steadied my nerves slightly. But it wasn't enough. I could feel the panic simmering beneath the surface.

"I'm sorry. I don't know what that was. I guess I just needed a distraction." I regretted the words instantly.

I wished I could shove them back down, bury them deep and never let him hear them.

But he already had.

Cameron's expression fractured, and he let his hands drop from my shoulders.

"A distraction," he echoed.

He took a step back, and I knew there was no going back. I had hurt him.

There would be no fixing this.

But still, I had to try.

"Cameron, wait, I didn't mean—" I lunged forward, reaching for him.

I rested my hand on his arm, but when he looked at me, he looked nothing like my Cameron.

His walls were up. That spark in his eyes was gone, replaced by something cold and hard.

Chapter Thirty-Six

Cameron

THE WORD FOLLOWED ME out to the parking lot, echoing louder than the sound of my own footsteps.

Distraction.

By the time I slid behind the wheel, my chest was tight, hands gripping the steering wheel like it might hold me together. The car was quiet, but my head wasn't.

Her face. Her voice. That hesitation.

Streetlights blurred past in streaks of gold, each one pulling me deeper into the mess of it. I replayed every second, the silence, the guilt in her eyes, the way it felt like something cracked open inside me when I forced myself to walk away.

I could've turned the radio on, drowned it all out, but even the thought of music felt wrong.

Silence was punishment, but it felt like what I deserved.

How could she kiss me like that, pull me in so completely, only to tear it all away?

Didn't she know what she meant to me?

Or maybe she did... and just didn't feel the same.

The thought gutted me.

Had I imagined it all? Built something in my head that never really existed? Was I just reading into moments that meant nothing to her?

No.

I couldn't believe that. I *wouldn't*.

You couldn't fake that. Not the way she kissed me. Not the way she looked at me like I was the only person in the world.

Sidney wasn't the kind of girl who gave away pieces of herself carelessly. She guarded them. Held them tight.

And I *felt* it. When she leaned in. When that soft little breath slipped from her lips as they touched mine.

She wasn't just reacting. She was there with me.

But the thought did little to bring me comfort.

I pulled into my parking spot and killed the engine. I sat there for a moment, gripping the steering wheel so tightly that my knuckles turned white. I slammed my palm against the steering wheel.

But it didn't help. Nothing would.

Light spilled from the living room window, which meant Porter and Westley were already home. I'd driven around for at least an hour.

For a second, I considered staying in the car, just sitting there until the night bled into morning.

I threw the door open and climbed out of the car.

I trudged up the stairs toward my apartment door and stuck the key in the lock.

I cracked open the door and stepped inside.

"Finally," Porter said, tossing a handful of popcorn into his mouth. "We were taking bets on whether you'd actually come back or just drive off into the sunset with Sidney."

Westley looked up first, then elbowed Porter in the ribs. "Uh-oh," he muttered. "He's got *the* look."

I narrowed my eyes. "What look?"

"Oh yeah. I see it too." Porter chimed in, all too eager. "The *Sidney pissed me off again,* look."

"What are you talking about?" I snapped. "Sidney has never pissed me off. You have no idea what that would even look like."

Westley grinned like he'd just scored a point. "Okay, maybe *pissed off* isn't the right word," he said. "But there were definitely moments you weren't exactly...

thrilled with her. Like that night at The Dive when you overheard her talking to Zack. Or that time she—"

I held up a hand. "Do you write this stuff down in a little diary or something?"

Porter turned toward me, curious now. "So what happened this time?"

I shot him a look. "Why do you automatically assume it was her?"

Porter raised an eyebrow. I crossed my arms, doubling down.

From the couch, Westley smirked. "Okay, then. What'd *you* do?"

I opened my mouth, ready to snap back with something, but the words caught somewhere between my pride and the truth.

Because the truth was, I wanted to be angry. I wanted to throw out some cutting remark, blame her for pushing me away.

But instead, all I could think about was how much I wanted to defend her. Even now. Even after everything.

I let out a long breath and ran a hand through my hair.

"She..." I started, but the words caught. My jaw tightened. "Nothing. Every-thing. I don't know. It doesn't matter."

Westley stared at me. "Yeah, see, that definitely sounds like it matters."

Porter pushed himself up from the couch, stretching like he had all the time in the world before nodding toward the kitchen.

"Right this way, Cameron," he said, his voice dipping into mock profession-alism. "Let's step into my office."

I knew better than to humor him.

But somehow, against my better judgment, I followed.

He crossed the kitchen in three lazy strides, opened the fridge, and grabbed two sodas. He tossed one to me and cracked open the other.

Leaning on the counter, he raised an eyebrow. "Alright. Spill it."

I stared him down, trying to hold the line. But this was Porter. He could out-stubborn anyone.

Silence stretched. Porter blinked.

It was obvious he wasn't going to let this go.

Finally, I let out a long sigh. "I kissed her."

The second I said it, the weight of it hit me all over again.

"*Finally!*" Westley's voice exploded from the living room.

He came barreling in, looking like he'd won the lottery. "I thought you two were gonna circle each other for *years*."

Porter waggled his brows. "So? She a good kisser?"

I groaned and shoved my stool back, ready to make a run for it. "I don't have time for this."

Porter grabbed my sleeve before I could escape.

"Oh, you have time," he said, grinning. "Because if you didn't, you wouldn't be standing here looking like someone stole your churro."

I dropped back onto the stool with a sigh and cracked open the can. "This is gonna be a long night."

Westley sat beside me, all smug satisfaction. "Wait, so you *wanted* to kiss her? Right?"

"Of course I did," I muttered, watching the bubbles fizz to the top of my soda can before popping.

"Then what's the problem?" Porter asked.

Westley snapped his fingers, his eyes widening like he'd just cracked a code. "Ohhh. You didn't ask permission, did you? You *have* to do that. Some girls don't like it when you just go for it."

I gave him a flat look. "That's not the problem."

"Then tell us," Porter said, waving a hand like he was urging a stubborn witness to keep talking.

I exhaled slowly, already second-guessing saying anything at all. "We were watching the fireworks. It was perfect. I leaned in, kissed her, and she—" I hesitated, the memory flashing too vividly. "She kissed me back. She was into it. I could tell. The way she sighed when—"

"Ahh, gross, man!" Westley groaned, clapping his hands over his ears. "We don't need details. Get a room."

"No good. She won't *go* with him to the room," Porter cut in, deadpan.

A smirk tugged at the corner of my mouth, but it didn't stick.

"She called it a distraction," I finally said, the words rough in my throat after too long a silence.

Westley winced. "Ouch."

Porter froze, his drink stalled halfway to his mouth. "She said what?"

Westley shook his head, already gearing up. "That's a crappy move. She—"

I cut him off with a look sharper than I meant it to be. He clamped his mouth shut.

"Damn, man," Westley muttered instead, leaning back in his chair. "That's rough."

Porter leaned forward, the usual smirk gone from his face. That alone was unsettling. "So what now?"

"Nothing," I said finally. "I'm done chasing her. If she wants to keep running, that's her call."

"Uh-huh. Cool story." Porter raised a brow, sharp and unblinking. "Now tell us what's really going on."

I scowled, bristling under the scrutiny. I hated how easily he saw through me, how obvious it must've been that I was unraveling.

"That is what's going on," I said, the words landing heavier than I wanted them to.

But even as I said it, I knew they didn't believe me.

And I didn't believe myself either.

Porter snorted. "Come on. You're *obviously* in love with her. You really gonna let the summer slip away without telling her?"

"I never said I was in love with her."

Westley shrugged. "You didn't have to. We can *see* it. Hell, we've even got bets on how long it'll take you two to figure it out."

I scoffed, shaking my head. "Hope one of you picked never."

"Not a chance," Porter said, chuckling. "None of us bet on that. You and Sidney belong together. You should see the way she looks at you, man."

"It doesn't matter," I said, my voice flat.

Westley tilted his head, studying me like he was connecting dots I didn't want laid out. "Have you even admitted it to yourself yet?"

I frowned. "Admitted what?"

"That you love her. Pay attention."

The words landed like a punch, even though he said them casually. My first instinct was to deflect, laugh it off, turn it into a joke. But the air stuck in my chest wouldn't let me.

I leaned back in the chair, exhaling slowly, eyes drifting up to the ceiling. The plaster lines blurred while my brain turned over the truth I'd been trying to bury. Because deep down, I knew.

Yeah. I loved her.

Maybe I had for longer than I realized.

But what good was saying it out loud if Sidney didn't feel the same? If all she saw when she looked at me was someone temporary, someone to lean on until the storm passed?

"She doesn't want this," I muttered, barely loud enough for them to hear. It wasn't really meant for them anyway, it was me, admitting it to myself in the smallest way I could.

Out of the corner of my eye, Westley and Porter exchanged a glance, one of those silent conversations they'd perfected. The kind that told me they were already on the same page about me, whether I liked it or not.

Porter leaned forward, his voice steady in a way that made it impossible to brush off.

"Or..." he said carefully, "maybe it's like she said. She's overwhelmed. Yeah, her wording sucked, but she didn't actually say she *didn't* want this. Did she?"

I stiffened.

"Not...exactly." I shook my head. "But I don't want to just be a distraction to her. If she wants this, I need her to be all in. I can't keep chasing her."

"You're right about that," Porter said with a firm nod. "She knows how you feel. She's the one who pulled back. The ball's in her court now."

Westley barked out a laugh. "Terrible advice, man. Girls love to be chased. You ever seen a single romance movie?"

Porter smirked. "Yeah. Like Halloween? Friday the 13th? Chasing doesn't always end well, Wes."

"You know damn well that's not what I meant," Westley shot back.

Porter turned to me, completely unfazed, and dropped his voice into his best Ghostface impression. "We could just call her up. *Hello, Sidney...*"

I groaned, rolling my eyes, but before I could fire back, Westley leaned into it with a grin. "You joke, but I bet she'd be into it. Buy the mask, really commit. Girls love that stuff."

Porter blinked, deadpan. "What kind of girls are you hanging around?"

"The fun kind," Westley said, waggling his eyebrows.

Despite myself, a grin tugged at my mouth. Their ridiculous back-and-forth was working to pull me out of the heaviness.

They were too much sometimes, but right now, they were exactly what I needed.

***

The next day I showed up ten minutes early, like that would somehow fix anything.

Chris was already zipping around, barking orders like he'd downed three espressos before sunrise.

But my eyes went straight past him. Straight to the corner.

Sidney stood with one of the costume girls, their heads bent in what looked like a serious conversation. For a second, I caught myself wondering what it was about, but I shoved the thought aside. I had enough circling in my head without adding that to the list.

I was still wrecked from last night. And judging by the shadows under Sidney's eyes, I wasn't the only one. She didn't look at me. Not once. Like if she avoided me hard enough, none of it had ever happened.

My gaze lingered longer than it should have. Long enough to feel it burn. Then I forced myself to look away. Pretend I didn't care. Pretend it didn't still sting.

Don't be obvious. You're an actor, remember? You can fake this. Pretend she doesn't mean a thing.

Fantastic. Now I was giving myself internal pep talks. Really crushing the whole personal growth thing.

But I could handle this.

Smile. Stay calm. Put on the act.

Pretend I hadn't spent the night staring at the ceiling with her face replaying on a loop in my head.

Chris clapped his hands together like he was about to host a game show. "Alright, listen up! I've got big news," he boomed.

I braced for impact. With Chris, "big news" could mean anything from a minor update to the end of the world. And given how the last one went, I was betting on the latter.

"The CEO is giving us a second chance."

Okay. Not what I was expecting.

The room broke into a low murmur of gasps and frantic whispering.

"He'll be returning in two days for a do-over," Chris continued, his gaze sweeping the room before zeroing in like a laser. "Cameron. Gwen. You two are running scenes nonstop until it's perfect. I want chemistry. I want conviction. And I want no one's costume falling apart this time."

I managed not to groan, but inside I was already diving out of an imaginary window.

Spending that much time with Gwen ranked right up there with unmedicated dental work in terms of pain.

Still, I nodded, because that's what professionals do, even when they're screaming on the inside.

After a few practice runs, I needed a break. I crossed the room to the water cooler, filled a paper cup, and took a long drink.

Movement flickered at the edge of my vision. I froze.

I didn't need to look to know it was Sidney.

Still, I risked a glance before forcing my eyes away. Her face gave nothing away, but her posture did. She was tense, uncertain, vulnerable in a way that made my chest ache.

"Can we talk?" she asked, so quietly I almost missed it.

For a split second, I considered ignoring her. Pretending I hadn't heard. Pretending I was too focused, too busy, too anything. It would've been easier. Safer.

But instead, I sighed and turned fully toward her.

"I think we said everything we needed to last night."

Something flickered across her face, gone almost before I could register it.

"Okay. Fine. We won't talk about that," Sidney said in a clipped tone. "But there's something you need to know."

I hesitated, water cup still in hand. "Kind of busy right now, Sid. Can it wait?"

"Look, I know you're still upset about last night," she said, arms folding, feet planted like she wasn't giving me a choice. "But can we hit pause on that? You're still my friend... right?"

That one hit harder than I wanted it to.

I met her eyes and let out a long, resigned breath. "Yeah. I'm still your friend," I said quietly. "Lead the way."

I followed her down a side hallway, away from the rehearsal chaos and Gwen's voice barking about her lighting.

Lighting. For an outdoor stage show.

Not much anyone could do about the sun, but of course Gwen would be the one to think otherwise.

I didn't know what I was expecting when Sidney stopped at a narrow costume storage room, but it definitely wasn't this.

The girl I'd seen Sidney talking to earlier stood by a rack of dresses, twisting the sleeves of her oversized shirt like they might unravel if she pulled hard enough. Her gaze darted to the door, the moment I stepped through.

For a split second, I wondered if Sidney had dragged her in here against her will.

"Cameron, this is Brooklyn. She's one of the costume directors."

I offered a nod. "Hey. Nice to meet you."

Brooklyn gave a nervous one in return, though her fingers kept twisting at the hem of her oversized sleeves.

"I, um... I work in wardrobe," she said, her voice barely above a whisper. "And right before the show... Gwen—" she faltered, flicking a quick glance at Sidney like she needed strength to keep going "—Gwen told me to loosen the seams on the Primrose dress."

My eyebrows knit tight. "Wait. What? Why?"

"I thought it was for her," she rushed out. "Like maybe she needed a little extra room, just a quick adjustment. I didn't think anything of it. Not until..." Her voice dropped. "Not until I saw the dress rip on stage. That wasn't about fit. It was meant to come apart."

The air stilled. My jaw locked as a slow burn ignited in my chest. I couldn't decide if I felt more sick or furious, but mostly, I hated how unsurprised I was.

"Did you tell Chris?"

Brooklyn shook her head quickly, eyes wide. "No. I can't. Gwen... she knows people. She could get me fired. And this is my first season. I can't lose this job."

Sidney stepped in before I could speak, her voice calm and steady, a quiet anchor. "You're doing the right thing, Brooklyn. We won't let anything happen to you. I promise."

Brooklyn let out a shaky breath and nodded. "Okay," she whispered. With one last nervous glance, she slipped past me and hurried down the hall.

The silence that followed wasn't empty. It pressed in, heavy, charged with everything left unsaid.

I leaned back against a shelf, dragging a hand over my face. "Thanks," I said finally, my voice rough. "For bringing her to me."

Sidney gave a faint nod.

This was a mess. Gwen hadn't just pulled a petty stunt. She'd humiliated someone deliberately. Targeted her. Torn her down. And then let the entire world believe it was an accident.

That wasn't competition. That was calculated.

What little respect I had for Gwen dissipated.

I exhaled, rubbing the back of my neck. "We'll need more than this. Brooklyn's word alone won't hold up. Gwen'll twist it, deny it, make her look like she's lying. We need something concrete, something Chris can't ignore."

Sidney's eyes sharpened, that fire I knew so well sparking to life. "We'll get it."

I gave a humorless laugh. "And how exactly do you suggest we do that? Gwen doesn't leave evidence lying around. She's too careful."

Sidney stepped closer, close enough that the warm vanilla of her shampoo curled into the air between us. "She's careful," she agreed, voice low, "but she's also cocky. When Gwen thinks she's already won, she stops watching her back. That's when we'll get her."

"And you think she'll just... hand us the match to burn her with?" I asked, arching a brow.

Sidney's mouth curved, not into a smile, exactly, but into something sharper. "Not if she knows what she's doing. But if she thinks the fire's already lit? She won't be able to resist fanning the flames."

She outlined her plan for me in detail.

I tried to focus on the strategy, but my gaze kept snagging on details that had nothing to do with sabotage. The way she leaned in when she spoke, the careful precision of her words, the crease in her brow when she thought hard. My throat went dry, and I forced myself to look away, to shove every stray thought back into the box I'd barely managed to seal.

Focus. This isn't about you and her. This is about stopping Gwen.

Still, the more Sidney laid it out, the more I felt something shift inside me. As reckless as it sounded, it might actually work.

I straightened, giving a slow nod. "Alright. Then we don't confront her. Not yet. We wait. Watch. Let her trap herself."

Sidney's gaze met mine, steady. "Exactly."

Gwen wanted the spotlight.

That was fine. She could have it.

She was about to star in the performance of a lifetime.

Chapter Thirty-Seven

Sidney

RIDLEY AND WILLOW WERE already waiting for me by the time I arrived at Baxter's.

I threaded through the patio tables and dropped into the chair across from them, slinging my bag onto the empty seat beside me. "Sorry I'm late," I said, still a little winded. "Castle crowd slowed me down."

Ridley waved me off. "You're fine. We just sat down."

Willow glanced up, grin already in place. "Perfect timing. We were debating fries."

"Definitely order the fries," a voice chimed in from behind me.

I turned, and found Renee sliding into the chair beside me like she was on the lam. Oversized sunglasses. A headscarf pulled low. She looked like she was auditioning for *Celebrity in Hiding*.

I arched a brow. "Going incognito?"

Ridley narrowed her eyes. "Why do you look like you're dodging the FBI?"

Renee adjusted her shades. "I'm suspended, remember. I'm not sure if I'm even supposed to be in the park right now."

Willow popped to her feet, already scanning the menu board. "Okay, I'm grabbing snacks before we get busted."

I watched her weave through the line toward the registers, disappearing for a few minutes into the bustle of orders and clattering trays. When she came back, she was balancing a tray piled high, fries spilling over the edge of their basket, a salted pretzel the size of her head, and enough napkins to survive a natural disaster.

She set it down in the center of the table like a peace offering.

Every hand reached in at once. Salty fries vanished by the handful, the pretzel was torn apart in seconds, and one of the dipping cups nearly tipped over before Ridley caught it with a lightning-fast grab.

Ridley raised her iced coffee in mock salute. "Carbs solve everything."

Even Renee relaxed a little, pushing her sunglasses up just enough to sneak a fry. For a moment, the tension melted, replaced by the simple rhythm of friends tearing into snack food like it was the most important meal of their lives.

"Okay, spill," Willow said. "What did you call us here for?"

I took a breath and laid it all out, the Gwen situation in full. What we knew. What we suspected. What we still needed proof of.

Ridley and Willow leaned in as I spoke, hanging on every word. But when I got to the part about Brooklyn, and what she'd confessed, Renee went very still.

She didn't interrupt. Didn't even blink. Just slid her sunglasses up onto her head and fixed her gaze on the table, lips pressed tight as though she was swallowing it down one piece at a time.

"That snake," Ridley muttered, shaking her head.

"Yeah." My voice came out harder than I intended, bitterness lacing every word. "All of it was her."

Renee's jaw tightened, her tone flat. "Honestly? I'm not surprised. Gwen's always been like this."

Across the table, Willow shredded the edge of a napkin into ribbons, her brows pulled tight. "So... what do we do? I mean, you didn't call us here just to vent."

"You're right." I straightened, feeling the weight of their eyes on me. "I have a plan."

"Good." Ridley leaned forward, iced coffee forgotten. "Let's hear it. Whatever it is, I'm in."

"First thing," I said, turning to Renee, "you have to be there today. Stay in the wings if you want, keep a low profile, but when the moment comes, we're going to need you. Gwen might coast through the first two shows, but the third? That's when the CEO will be watching."

The noise of the patio seemed to fade as the table went still. Three pairs of eyes locked on me, leaning closer as I laid it out, step by step, every angle covered, each of them a piece of the plan.

No one pushed back. Not a single flicker of doubt. Just quiet nods, steady and sure, like they'd already decided to follow me wherever this went. And it hit me, this wasn't just a cast of coworkers. This was family I'd found by accident. Friends willing to run into the fire with me, no questions asked.

"I'm in," Renee said finally. Her head tilted, and when she spoke again, her voice was lower. "But what's going on between you and Cameron? You two have been... weird lately."

I froze, fingers tightening around the edge of my soda cup. Great. Just what I needed, this conversation turning into a spotlight.

Willow perked up instantly, all wide-eyed curiosity. Ridley leaned forward, practically glowing with the thrill of drama.

"I didn't want to bother you with that."

Renee's expression softened in an instant. "Sidney, I don't care what's going on with me. I'm always here for you. I'm not so self-absorbed that I can't listen to someone else's problems."

"Yeah," Willow chimed in quickly. "None of us think that about you."

"Not anymore," Ridley muttered under her breath.

"What was that?" Her gaze swept the table, suspicion narrowing her eyes. "Wait. Hold up. Did you all think I was self-absorbed?"

The silence was brutal. None of us answered. Instead, we all stared at our plates like they'd suddenly become works of art.

Because truthfully, when we'd first met her, we had expected exactly that. A snooty princess type.

"Okay... maybe a little," Willow admitted at last, grimacing like the words tasted sour.

"But that was before we knew you," I rushed in, heart thudding as if I could patch over the sting before it landed. "Now we do. And we love you, Renee."

Renee laughed, shaking her head like she couldn't decide if she should roll her eyes or smack us. "Alright, fair. I can see it. I probably do come off a little unapproachable at first."

"Resting princess face," Ridley muttered.

Every head whipped her way. And then a chorus of laughter sounded around the table.

When the giggles finally ebbed, Renee turned back to me, her smile fading into something softer, steadier. "Alright, Sid. Spill it. What happened with Cameron?"

I groaned, dragging my hands down my face like maybe I could hide behind them. "We kissed," I mumbled through my palms.

Ridley leaned in, one brow cocked. "And that's a problem because...?"

"Because," I muttered, voice muffled, "it was the best kiss of my life...and I told him it only happened because I needed a distraction."

Renee winced, sympathy flickering across her face. "Ouch. Sid..."

"I know, and I don't feel that way at all. I'm an idiot."

"You're not an idiot," Willow whispered.

"No, not an idiot," Renee agreed, choosing her words carefully. "Maybe just a little..." She trailed off, clearly searching for something gentler.

Ridley didn't bother. "I mean... she's kind of an idiot," she said with a shrug.

Willow smacked Ridley's arm. "Not helpful."

But I laughed anyway, the knot in my chest loosening just a little. "No, Ridley's right. It was stupid. That kiss meant everything to me, and I pushed him away. After everything he's done... he didn't deserve that."

Ridley gave a small, approving nod.

"I should tell him," I said, feeling the certainty settle low and solid in my chest. "I should tell him I'm sorry. That I was an idiot. That I'm done running."

Around the table, every head had nodded, sealing the plan with a kind of quiet certainty. And that was when I knew I couldn't keep hiding behind excuses anymore. At some point, I had to tell Cameron how I really felt.

But by the time I reached the castle, I knew my confession would have to wait.

I couldn't tell him now. Not with the castle looming in front of me, music already spilling faintly from the stage speakers. Timing was everything, and the last thing he needed before a show was me dumping more feelings onto his shoulders.

I spotted him near the side entrance, half in costume, shirt open at the collar, cape draped loosely over one arm. He leaned against the wall, phone in hand.

"Hey," I said, slipping up beside him.

His gaze lifted before he slid his phone into his pocket. "Hey. Everything good?"

I nodded. "The girls are in."

Relief flickered across his face, softening the hard line of his jaw. For a moment, some of the weight on his shoulders seemed to lift. "Good. Westley and Porter are on board, too."

I hesitated, searching his expression. "You sure you're ready for this? For your part?"

His smile was small, almost wry, but steady. "I'm a good actor, remember?"

My heart stuttered. Because yes, he was an actor, but what I saw in his eyes wasn't performance. It was weight. Fear. Determination. All of it unspoken, pressing in the silence between us.

I almost reached for his hand. Almost let myself close the distance. But the moment wasn't mine to take, not yet.

So instead, I nodded. "Alright. Let's do this."

Chapter Thirty-Eight

Cameron

I PACED THE LENGTH of the greenroom, restless energy crawling under my skin. The clock seemed determined to drag each minute toward showtime like it was hauling bricks.

Across the room, Gwen, already in full costume, was barking orders at Westley and Porter. They trailed after her like overeager interns, both wearing the same mischievous grin.

Porter held out a water bottle like he was presenting a sacred relic. "Hydrate, queen. Your vocal cords deserve only the finest."

Westley swooped in right behind him, fingers fluffing the back of her gown with exaggerated care. "Stage-ready perfection. Wow. Is that new shimmer spray?"

Gwen blinked at them, her expression tightening until it looked carved from glass.

"Why are you two following me like a pair of designer-handbag Chihuahuas?" she snapped.

Porter only beamed. "Just here to support our leading lady."

Westley elbowed him with a laugh. "She called us designer," he stage-whispered, grinning.

Porter laughed too. "Means she thinks we're fancy."

The corner of Gwen's mouth twitched downward like she'd just bitten into something sour. She muttered something under her breath before spinning on her heel. Her skirt swished dramatically as she disappeared in a flurry of glitter and irritation.

I almost pitied her. Almost.

Westley and Porter were playing their parts a little too well. They were just irritating enough to rattle her without stepping far enough out of line to get themselves caught.

I crossed to the refreshment table, more for something to do than actual thirst. I poured myself a cup of water anyway, letting the motion steady my nerves.

I had barely raised it to my lips when the hairs on my arm prickled. An unwelcome presence settled at my side.

Gwen.

She stepped in close, cutting off my personal space, her expression tight and unreadable.

"Okay, seriously," she snapped. "What's going on?"

I blinked, all innocence. "Good afternoon to you, too, Gwen."

Her eyes flashed. "Why are Westley and Porter following me around? Are you trying to break me? Because it won't work."

Behind her, Porter was very obviously rearranging chairs that didn't need rearranging, while Westley stood nearby, pretending to check "mic levels" on a walkie-talkie that wasn't even switched on. Their act was ridiculous, and deliberate.

"We were all talking last night," I said carefully, keeping my tone even. "Decided the last thing anyone needs today is drama. I guess Porter and Westley took it to heart."

Her gaze narrowed. "So what, you're all just suddenly my personal support team?"

I shrugged, keeping it light. "We just want things to go smoothly. You've got a lot riding on today. We all do."

For a moment, she didn't answer. Just stood there with her arms crossed, one manicured finger tapping against her elbow like a ticking clock.

I let the silence stretch before finally adding, "So... I'm proposing a truce."

She sneered. "Seriously? After everything you've put me through, you think I'm just going to play nice?"

She scoffed, flipped her hair, and spun on her heel like she was about to storm out.

And maybe she would have.

But then the door opened.

Sidney stepped into the greenroom.

Her eyes met mine for a brief second before she flicked them away.

And judging by the slow smiled, spreading across Gwen's face, she saw it too.

"Trouble in paradise?" She purred, her eyes gleaming with satisfaction.

She was like a shark circling. She could sense the weakness like blood in the water.

She closed the space between us until there were mere centimeters between us. "You know, Cameron," she said, her voice dropping into a soft purr that churned my stomach, "I think a truce sounds like a great idea."

Her fingers trailed down my arm.

My eyes dropped to her manicured fingers trailing down my arm.

Then a soft gasp came from beside us. I swiveled my gaze just in time to see Sidney's face crumple.

"S-Sidney," I tried to say her name, but my throat was suddenly dry.

She gave me a small shake of her head and stumbled back a step.

"Not again," she whispered.

"Sidney," I said, stepping out of Gwen's grasp and taking a step toward her.

"No," she said with a defiant lift of her chin. "Don't bother. You two deserve each other."

She took off down the hall toward the bathroom.

I took a step forward. I couldn't let her go without explaining, but before I could take another step, Gwen's fingers snaked around my wrist.

"What a drama queen," Gwen said with a laugh.

I ran a hand through my hair. "Yeah."

"Cameron," she cooed, syrup-sweet, her nails digging in just enough to make her point. "Why waste your time with little girls? Let a real woman show you how it's done."

I turned to face her and forced a smile.

"You know what?" I said. "Why the hell not? I'm tired of Sidney and her games."

Gwen's eyes lit up, victory blooming across her face like she'd just been handed a spotlight *and* a standing ovation.

I wrapped an arm around her waist and pulled her closer to me. "Is this okay?"

"More than okay," she cooed.

"Sidney's not a big fan of PDA," I said, my voice tinged with uncertainty.

Gwen laughed and batted her lashes. "Good thing I'm not Sidney."

"Right," I murmured, pulling her a fraction closer.

"What's this?" a voice piped up behind me. "Porter, get over here. Group hug!"

Before Gwen had time to react, she was ambushed.

Porter lunged from the left, Westley from the right, and suddenly she was trapped in the most aggressively affectionate three-way cuddle pile I'd ever seen.

Her eyes went wide as Westley's arm clamped around hers, while Porter practically wrestled her into a headlock of love.

"Ew!" Gwen shrieked. "Get off me! What is wrong with you people?!"

Westley only grinned. "You're the best Primrose we've ever had."

"Yeah," Porter said, nodding, deadpan. "The best."

Westley let go first, hands raised like he'd just defused a bomb. "Seriously. We mean it. Real shame about Renee, though."

"Total shame," Porter echoed, solemn as a priest at a funeral. "Our girl's just a little clumsy, right?"

Gwen staggered back, tiara askew, fingers trembling as she jerked it straight again.

"I don't know what kind of game this is," she hissed, arms snapping tight across her chest. "But you'd better back off before I have you all scrubbing toilets."

Porter clutched his chest with a dramatic gasp. "Do I still get to wear the sash?"

Westley's grin widened. "So... how long before Renee's back as Primrose?"

That landed. Gwen's head whipped toward him. "What are you talking about?"

He tilted his head, grin softening just enough to pass for genuine. "She is coming back, right?"

"Yeah," Porter jumped in quickly, eyes wide. "It was just an accident. Once things cool down, Chris'll give her spot back."

Gwen's arms tightened, rigid armor now.

"Not if I have anything to say about it," she snapped.

Westley kept his voice light. "Oh, come on, Gwen. You know it wasn't her fault. Renee's great at her job."

"Please." Gwen tossed her hair with a sharp flick, her tone laced with venom. "She got what she deserved. That'll teach her to hog the spotlight."

The air shifted. Porter stilled, blinking.

"Wait... what?" His voice rose, then he burst into laughter. "Silly, Gwen. For a minute it sounded like you were happy about what happened to her."

Gwen rolled her eyes, exhaling like the room itself was exhausting. "Oh, come on. Like it wasn't obvious? I made sure that dress would fall apart."

"You did what?" Westley asked, confusion creeping into his voice.

Gwen stepped right up to him. "Don't mess with me. You see what I'm capable of. I got rid of Renee, and I can get rid of you too. Don't test me."

Silence. A half-beat where no one moved, the weight of her words hanging heavy.

I spotted Chris before Gwen did, storming across the greenroom floor. His face was red, his jaw clenched, and the death grip on his clipboard screamed *moment of no return.*

"Gwen," he barked.

She jumped, spinning around with a nervous laugh. "Oh. Hi, Chris."

Chris didn't bother responding. He just stepped forward, reached behind her, and yanked the mic pack off her costume in one swift, practiced motion. He flipped the switch off with a sharp click.

"Your mic was on," he said through gritted teeth.

Gwen blinked. "My mic? How did that get there? I don't put that on until it's time to go on stage..."

Her gaze darted to Westley, then flicked to Porter. I caught the exact moment realization hit, the flicker in her eyes as her brain pieced it together. During the chaos of the group hug, one of them had quietly clipped the mic pack to the back of her dress.

Chris took another step forward, his stare pinning her in place. "The entire square just heard your little confession. *Including the CEO.*"

For a second, Gwen didn't move.

Her whole body seemed frozen, the color draining from her face as the weight of her words, and what they had just cost her, sank in.

Then, slowly, her gaze snapped up and locked onto something across the room. I turned, following her line of sight. Two figures stood near the far wall, Willow and Sidney.

Sidney's arms were folded across her chest, a knowing gleam in her eyes. Willow stood beside her, lips curved in a small, satisfied smile.

A beat later, Gwen's gaze drifted to the sound booth, where Ridley was stepping casually out.

Sidney met Gwen's stare head-on and gave a small wave.

And in that moment, you could almost hear it, the sharp *click* of realization snapping into place.

Gwen had been outplayed.

And the curtain was coming down on her little act.

Her eyes narrowed into dangerous slits, rage replacing the panic in her expression.

She whirled on us—me, Porter, and Westley—like a striking viper.

"You—" she hissed, taking a step toward me.

But Chris was faster.

"Don't even think about it," he said, stepping in hard and planting himself squarely between us. "You're finished here."

Gwen scoffed, shoulders squaring as if she could still bluff her way out. "You can't possibly mean—"

"You're fired, Gwen." Chris didn't miss a beat, voice cold and final. "Get your stuff. Get out."

"Excuse me?" Gwen spat, her voice rising in disbelief.

"You heard me," Chris snapped, eyes hard. "I don't care if the CEO's still here or if the King of Broadway shows up with a marching band. That kind of behavior? Ends careers. And yours—" he leaned in slightly—"ends now."

For a second, Gwen just stood there, stunned. Her mouth opened, closed. Her face crumpled at the edges, lips trembling as if she might cry.

And for half a second, I almost felt bad for her.

Almost.

But then I thought of Renee humiliated on stage. Sidney, manipulated and targeted.

All the hell Gwen had put them through.

And the sympathy vanished.

"This is sabotage," Gwen muttered, voice shaking, eyes darting around the room as if looking for someone, *anyone*, to back her up. "You're all jealous. You think this place runs without me? You'll be begging me to come back."

No one begged.

No one moved.

The show was over for Gwen, and she knew it.

Chapter Thirty-Nine

Sidney

ALL AROUND THE ROOM, people kept their heads down. No one seemed sure of what to say or do.

Almost without thinking, my eyes drifted to Cameron, standing alone by the stage door. There were only minutes left before he was due on stage.

Drawn by something I couldn't stop, I started toward him.

I knew this was the worst possible moment, with Gwen fired and the whole show hanging by a thread, but still, something in me pushed forward, unwilling to let another chance slip away.

My heart hammered, screaming at me to stop. To save this for later.

But then I reached him. And when his eyes landed on me, that soft, familiar smile breaking across his face, my fear quieted.

"Hey, Carolina."

I smiled back at him.

A hundred words pressed at my throat. Apologies. Explanations. A thousand ways to say I was sorry. That I didn't want to lose him. That I didn't want to just be his friend.

Say it. Just say it.

But as soon as I opened my mouth, the words refused to come.

"Good job," was all I managed.

A faint smile tugged at his lips. "You too. We make a pretty good team."

"Yeah," I breathed. A beat of silence stretched between us, thin and fragile.

Then, gathering what little courage I had left, I pushed forward. "Cameron, about the other night—"

"Please, Sid." His eyes fluttered shut, his voice low, edged with quiet resignation. "If you're about to say what I think you are... don't."

His words hit me hard, knocking the breath from my chest. My heart sank.

Cameron's face was tight with something close to pain. "I'm not going to be another Zack."

I went still. "What?"

His gaze held mine. He didn't look angry...just resigned.

"I'm not going to chase you," he said gently. "I'm not going to keep reaching for something you're not ready to give."

My heart sank.

He was giving up on us. Letting go before we'd even had the chance to begin.

And I was helpless to stop it.

I drew in a shaky breath, desperate to find something that might change his mind. But my throat felt raw, the words trapped somewhere I couldn't reach.

"Showtime," Chris called from across the room.

Cameron gave a small nod in acknowledgment, then turned back to me.

"I get it now." His voice was calm, but a raw edge bled through. "You're not ready. And I'm done standing here, hoping you'll change your mind."

Then he turned and stepped onto the stage. He might as well have been stepping onto a plane, leaving me behind.

I stood frozen, heart shattering too fast to catch the pieces.

The emptiness hit hard, hollowing me out. I felt sick. Like I'd ruined everything.

For one helpless second, I wished I could rewind it all. Go back to Scoops, say what I should've said.

But I couldn't.

I blinked hard, fighting tears.

It was too late.

He was already gone.

"Sidney?" A careful voice sounded from somewhere behind me.

I turned.

Porter stood a few feet away. Normally, there'd be a grin lurking there, a joke ready to break the tension. But not now. Now, he looked serious. More serious than I'd ever seen him.

"Hey, Porter." I forced a smile, but it felt foreign.

He rubbed the back of his neck. "I, uh... kinda overheard that."

I nodded, words tangled somewhere I couldn't reach.

He studied me, eyes steady. "You okay?"

I opened my mouth to lie, but the words wouldn't come.

A quiet moment of understanding passed between us.

My eyes burned. I wanted to run from here. Far away. Away from the castle, away from Fantasy World, away from Florida. Away from *him*.

The words slipped out before I could stop them. "I ruined everything."

"You didn't ruin everything," Porter said softly, shaking his head. "Cameron cares about you."

"He wouldn't even listen to me." My voice cracked on the whisper.

Porter exhaled, folding his arms across his chest. "He's just hurt right now. He'll come around."

I nodded, but doubt curled sharply inside me. Maybe Porter was right. Maybe Cameron would forgive me. But summer was already slipping away. There were only a few weeks left before I had to go home. I didn't want to waste them aching for forgiveness I didn't know how to ask for.

"I think he just needs the truth, Sidney," Porter said gently. "Not excuses, not a half-apology. Tell him how you feel. Show him you're in this as much as he is. Right now, all he sees is that you're too scared to take a real chance."

Frustration bubbled in my chest. I crossed my arms tight. "I tried showing him. And he threw it back in my face. What more can I do?"

"You don't have to fix everything tonight," he said evenly. "But you do have to try. If he doesn't want to see it, then you make him see."

His words hit harder than I expected.

And they actually made sense.

Before I could answer Porter, movement caught my eye.

Renee was heading straight for us, her skirts brushing against the floor as she closed the distance.

"What's going on, Sid?" she asked, her gaze flicking between me and Porter.

The words spilled out before I could stop them. I told her about Cameron, about trying to talk to him, about how he wouldn't listen.

Then, before I could stop it, a tear slipped free and rolled down my cheek.

"Oh, honey," Renee murmured, reaching me in an instant and pulling me into her arms.

"No," I protested weakly, trying to push back. "You're about to go onstage. I'll ruin your dress."

"Screw the dress," she said without hesitation, tightening her hold. "You're more important."

A shaky breath escaped me, and I gave in, arms looping around her, my face pressed into her shoulder.

Porter shifted a few feet away, rubbing the back of his neck. "Uh... should I, like... grab ice cream or something? I mean, maybe a whole gallon?"

A shaky laugh broke free from my chest.

Renee pulled back just enough to smirk at him over her shoulder. "What, Porter? You don't love having a front-row seat to all this raw emotional drama?"

Porter wrinkled his nose. "Yeah, no thanks. Hard pass. But I'll bring snacks if you promise to stop leaking emotions everywhere."

Then, way louder than necessary, he announced, "Oh, wow, look at the time! That's my cue!" and bolted before either of us could say a word.

We watched him retreat across the room.

"What about you?" I asked softly, shifting my gaze to Renee. "Are you okay?"

She hesitated, then leaned closer, her voice dropping. "Sid... can we talk for a minute?"

I nodded and followed her into the dressing room.

The second she turned to face me, my stomach sank. I had been too caught up in my own emotions to notice Renee was battling something herself.

Her hands trembled.

Her makeup, usually sharp and flawless, was smudged under her eyes, like she'd already cried her way through half the show. She didn't look like the girl who had commanded that stage a hundred times before.

"I know I'm about to sound like the world's worst friend right now," she began, voice unsteady. "I know you've got your own stuff going on."

"No, it's fine, Renee." I stepped in. "Tell me. What's going on?"

"I can't do this," she whispered, voice frayed and raw. "Not after everything that happened. I can't go back out there."

"Renee..."

But she shook her head fast, eyes wide. "No. I'm serious. I thought I could do it. But my head's not there. I'm going to mess it up. I'll freeze, and then it'll be another disaster... and this time, it'll be my fault."

"You're just nervous," I said softly, trying to steady her. "You've done this show in your sleep. Believe me, I've heard you. You'll be fine."

"It won't be fine." Her voice cracked, and the sound of it broke something in me. "Sid, I'm telling you. I can't. I can do any show after this, but not with the CEO out there. The last time he saw me, I made a complete fool of myself."

She grabbed my hands, clutching them like they were the only thing keeping her from falling apart.

"I know it's a big ask, Sid," she pleaded, her voice trembling. "But I need you to go on in my place."

I opened my mouth to protest, but she cut me off.

She held my gaze, panic and hope flickering in her eyes. "Please," she whispered. "Go out there."

I hesitated.

And before I could think better of it, I nodded.

"Okay, Renee. Whatever you need," I said quietly. "I'll do it."

The second the words left my mouth, the world blurred into motion.

We didn't walk, we sprinted down the hallway toward the stage entrance, where Chris was barking orders into his mic like a general mid-battle.

"Chris!" Renee called, breathless. "We need to make a change."

He spun mid-command, froze the second he spotted me trailing after her, and threw up both hands. "No. Whatever this is—absolutely not."

"It's me," I blurted before I could lose my nerve. "I'm going on as Primrose."

Chris stared like I'd just announced I was about to juggle flaming torches mid-scene.

"Please, Chris," Renee whispered.

He looked between us, jaw tight, then let out a sigh so heavy I thought it might shake the set. "Fine. I don't have time to ask why you're pulling this stunt, but we are talking later." He pressed two fingers to his temple, already recalculating the entire cue sheet in his head. "Don't make me regret this, Webber."

I nodded, trying to channel confidence I didn't feel. "You won't."

He waved me off. "Costume. Now. You're on in three."

We bolted for the dressing room. Renee stripped out of the Primrose gown while I stepped into it. No time for full makeup. Renee swiped blush across my cheeks and gloss on my lips. That would have to do.

Less than two minutes later, I was standing in front of the mirror, costumed, breathless, heart racing.

Moments later, I found myself frozen outside the stage door. Renee's hand slipped into mine, giving a quick, grounding squeeze.

"Go get him, Sid."

I arched a brow. "Him?"

Her smile was soft, almost wistful, like she could see right through me. And in that second, I heard everything she wasn't saying.

This wasn't only about her nerves. This was about Cameron. About proving I was still here, still fighting for something real.

My throat tightened. "What if he doesn't want me anymore?"

"He's in love with you, Sid."

Those were the last words I heard before she pushed me forward. The stage door swung shut behind me.

Applause crashed like a wave, but it all blurred, distant and hollow beneath the thunder of my pulse. My chest rose and fell too fast, air barely making it in.

Westley swept out from the shadows, his dark wizard costume pooling around him. His hand clamped around my arm. He didn't look at all surprised to see me instead of Renee.

"I have your princess, Peter," he thundered, a wicked laugh echoing through the speakers.

And then Cameron turned.

His eyes widened when they landed on me, recognition flaring bright.

For the briefest moment, I swore it wasn't Prince Peter standing there, it was just Cameron. My Cameron. And the way he looked at me made my stomach twist, like every wall he'd tried to build between us had cracked wide open.

Then, in an instant, the mask slid back into place. His shoulders squared, his voice came sharp and steady, and Peter stepped forward, flawless as ever.

But when the cue came, when he was meant to reach for me, he faltered.

It was the smallest pause, no longer than a breath. But I felt it.

It was like he didn't want to cross a line he had redrawn. Even for the show.

His hand hovered, fingers flexing.

His gaze was sharper than I'd ever seen, something fierce and unspoken warring inside him. Then, just as quickly, it broke. His features softened, and for a heartbeat, it wasn't Prince Peter standing there. It was Cameron.

"Come with me, Princess."

The word hit me like a spark. My eyes snapped to his.

He'd gotten the line wrong. He'd *missed a word*.

The line was supposed to be *my princess*. But that wasn't what he said.

He said *Princess*. The name he liked to tease me with.

For a second, I wondered, had it been a slip, or was it deliberate?

Then something flickered in his eyes. A shift. The faintest crinkle at the corner, like he knew exactly what he'd done.

The corner of his mouth curved slightly upward.

And the whole world disappeared.

Cameron was asking me to choose him, and I was answering.

And maybe I didn't have the right to take his hand after what I had done. Maybe I wasn't worthy of the prince standing in front of me. But I was going to reach for him, anyway.

I slid my hand into his, my fingers tightening around his.

A hint of satisfaction flickered in his eyes as he pulled me toward him.

I drew in a shaky breath, forcing my voice steady.

"I was scared," I admitted, the words trembling out of me. "I thought it was safer to run. But I can't anymore." My throat tightened, raw with truth. "I don't want to run from you, Peter. Thank you... for saving me."

The line should have been simple.

But it wasn't.

It burned on the way out because it wasn't just part of the show.

I meant it.

Every word.

I held his gaze, willing him to understand, to feel what I was really saying beneath the performance.

His fingers tightened around mine. Just slightly. Just enough for me to feel the shift.

He let go, stepping back as the show shifted into its final scene.

Cameron crossed the stage in long strides until he hit his mark and turned back to me.

"Then come with me, Princess."

This time, I didn't hesitate.

I couldn't.

I was already his.

I broke into a sprint, my pulse thrumming in rhythm with the music, each step carrying me closer, not to the stage cue, but to him. When I reached him, Cameron's arms closed around me with a surety that stole my breath. He didn't just catch me, he held me, as if he'd been waiting, as if he'd never let me fall.

He lifted me effortlessly, and the world fell away. The park, the music, the crowd, all of it blurred as he spun me through the air. His hands burned against my waist, steady and strong, and something in the way he held me said more than words ever could.

And in that dizzy, breathless twirl, I felt it. The moment of no return.

When he set me down, neither of us moved.

Our faces lingered inches apart, the heat of his breath brushing my lips, his hands still firm at my waist as if he couldn't make himself let go.

The crowd blurred into silence. The music, the stage, all of it fell away until there was only him.

Cameron's eyes burned into mine, raw and unguarded. "If you don't want to run anymore, Princess... then don't."

The words struck through me like lightning, cutting past the script, past the performance, right into the truth we'd been circling around.

My throat tightened, my pulse thundering so hard I thought it might shake me apart. I swallowed, my voice breaking free before I could stop it. "I'm done running."

Something shattered between us, every wall, every hesitation.

And then he moved.

His lips crashed against mine, stealing the breath from my lungs as though he'd been holding back for far too long.

I melted into him, my hands resting against his shoulders. He pulled me closer like he could anchor me there forever.

The audience erupted, cheers and applause crashing over us like a tidal wave.

When we finally broke apart, Cameron didn't let me go right away. He pressed his forehead to mine.

Then he straightened, slipped his hand into mine, and with a flourish, dipped into a bow.

I followed suit and dipped into a curtsy.

That's when I saw him. The CEO. Standing among the crowd, lips curved in the faintest grin.

The moment we stepped offstage, the world blurred into chaos. Crew members surged toward us, voices colliding into a storm of congratulations. Stagehands clapped us on the back, laughter and cheers surrounding us in dizzying waves. Someone high-fived Cameron. Someone else squeezed my shoulders.

Even Chris looked almost... proud.

The rest blurred past in a rush of laughter and hugs, adrenaline sparking through my veins like lightning. Then Cameron's hand found mine, steady and warm, his fingers threading through with a sureness that made the chaos fall away. Without a word, he tugged me toward the far corner of the greenroom, out of the crush of bodies and noise.

"That," he murmured, breath still uneven, "was one hell of a confession, Carolina."

A shaky laugh slipped out of me, my chest still heaving. "You went off script."

"And I don't regret a second of it." His voice dropped lower, teasing at the edges, but there was something raw beneath it too. He leaned in just slightly, close enough that the air between us seemed to hum. "So... did you mean it? Or are you just a really good actress?"

Heat rushed to my cheeks before I could stop it, the smile breaking free anyway. "I'm not that good of an actress," I whispered.

Something shifted in his eyes, like tension unwinding, like a question finally answered. His mouth curved into that slow, devastating grin that always managed to undo me. And then, without hesitation, he kissed me.

Soft. Certain. A promise sealed in the quiet aftermath of chaos.

I pulled back just slightly, breath catching, eyes flicking toward the chaos still swirling backstage.

"Everyone's watching," I whispered.

Cameron didn't even blink. "Then let them."

A laugh slipped out of me, light, breathless, and I kissed him again.

This time, I didn't hold anything back.

The cast erupted around us, cheering like we'd just won the championship.

Chris made his way over, arms crossed, fighting a smile.

"All right, break it up, you two," he said.

I laughed and took a step back as Cameron slid an arm casually around my waist, like he had no intention of letting go.

"Sidney," Chris said, his tone shifting, more serious now. "Can I see you in my office for a minute?"

I nodded and started to follow, but he paused, glancing back with a smirk.

"For the record," he added, "I'm glad you two finally figured it out. Tell me you're officially together."

I froze, glancing up at Cameron.

He smiled that easy, familiar smile. "Your call, Carolina. You already know what I want."

A grin broke across my face. I turned to Chris. "Yes. We're together."

He gave me a small nod, and I followed him into his office, the door clicking closed behind me.

A wave of panic surged within me.

Before I could stop myself, the words tumbled out. "Is this because we went off script?"

Chris chuckled, hopefully a good sign. "Yes, actually."

My heart lurched.

But then he leaned back, looking far too amused.

"The CEO loved it. Thought we planned the whole thing, the kiss, the big dramatic finish, just for him. Some grand last-minute flourish to impress the boss."

But then Chris's expression shifted, turning serious.

"But that's not the only reason I called you in."

He rested his elbows on the desk, then slid a piece of paper toward me.

"I want to offer you a full-time position in entertainment once your internship ends."

I blinked. "Wait—what?"

"You wouldn't necessarily stay on as Princess Primrose," he added. "Renee's got that locked down. But you could pick another role. Personally, I think you'd make a great assistant stage manager." He lifted a brow. "You're already doing half the work, anyway."

I stared at the contract. My name printed in bold, official letters, stared back at me.

This wasn't what I expected.

Full-time. A real job.

Not just a summer adventure.

I didn't have to leave.

I could stay.

Stay with Cameron—

But this wasn't the plan.

It was supposed to be temporary. One chapter before I went back to my real life in North Carolina.

If I stayed, it wouldn't just be an internship extension.

It would be choosing an entirely new life.

I bit my lip, fingers digging into the armrests.

"But I have a life back home," I said quietly. "I have—"

But the words caught in my throat.

What did I really have? My mom—yes. But beyond that?

I'd built my whole life around the idea of going back. Of moving forward along the path I'd planned so carefully.

But now... here were new possibilities. New doors opening where I hadn't even thought to look.

There were colleges here. Opportunities. A life I hadn't imagined for myself.

It wasn't like I'd be giving up everything.

But if I stayed... I'd be choosing something else. Something entirely unknown.

Still, it was a big decision. Bigger than anything I'd faced before. One I couldn't make in a single breath.

Chris's voice broke through the spiral in my head. "It's your choice, Sidney."

I swallowed hard. "Can I think about it?"

"Of course. But we'll need an answer soon." His tone softened. "Just know we'd love to have you."

I stood slowly, every movement deliberate, fighting the urge to snatch the contract and cling to it.

And just like that, the five-year plan I'd clung to so tightly over the past few years crumbled beneath my feet.

For the first time in a long time, I had no plan at all.

Chapter Forty

Cameron

EVERY SUMMER ENDED THE same way at Fantasy World. With the Farewell Ball.

It was tradition. A night where interns traded polos and name tags for tuxedos and gowns, where the castle courtyard became a dreamscape strung with lights and music, a celebration of everything we'd survived together.

The castle courtyard looked like something out of a dream.

Twinkling lights draped from the turrets like stars had fallen and decided to stay. Music floated through the air, soft and slow, curling around the stone arches and ivy-covered walls. Somewhere inside, laughter echoed, a chorus of crew members arriving in gowns and tailored suits, their real selves transformed into royalty for just one night.

I stood just inside the entrance, fiddling with the sleeve of my suit jacket. I'd never been nervous about seeing a girl before, not like this. But tonight felt like something more. Something special. And the last thing I wanted was to mess it up.

I looked up and scanned the courtyard. No Sidney. Not yet.

Porter and Westley were already inside, no doubt wreaking havoc on poor unsuspecting party guests.

I couldn't stop thinking about how much this summer had changed me. When summer started, I'd been burned out, jaded, and on the verge of calling it quits here at Fantasy World. I'd been running on autopilot.

Then she showed up, and suddenly, everything was different.

Because of her, I started feeling again. Laughing again. Wanting *more* again.

She didn't just change my summer.

She changed *me*.

I'd even called my mom back. *Three* times since that dinner. We were slowly starting to repair our relationship, though it would still take more time. But we were both willing to work at it and that was enough for now.

It was hard to believe that in just a couple short weeks, Sidney would be gone. Goodbye was coming and there was nothing I could do to stop it.

The thought had been creeping up on me for days, refusing to be ignored. And now, as I stood in the middle of a fairytale waiting for the girl who'd ruined me for reality, it hit me fully: *I don't want this to end. I want her.*

Whatever it took to keep her, I'd do it.

For a brief second, I wondered if she might consider staying here, in Florida.

And if not... maybe I could move there, to North Carolina.

I let the thought drift through my mind.

A new job. A new city. A whole different kind of life.

Her life.

It was crazy. It was huge.

But for the first time... it didn't feel impossible.

Not if it meant being with her.

A light tap on my shoulder pulled me out of the spiral of thoughts.

I turned and forgot how to breathe.

Sidney stood there, framed in the glow of the courtyard lights like she'd stepped straight out of a fantasy, *my fantasies*.

Her dress was made of light blue fabric.. Her hair fell in loose waves around her shoulders, a few delicate pieces tucked back with something sparkly that probably wasn't real diamonds but absolutely looked like it.

And her eyes, were locked on mine.

I swallowed hard.

"Wow," I said, barely getting the word out. "You— You look... beautiful."

She smiled, small and shy. "Thanks. And you look very handsome."

I smiled and stepped forward. I held out my arm to her. "Ready to go inside?"

But instead of taking it, she glanced down, then looked back up with something quieter in her expression. Something heavier.

"Can we take a walk first?" she asked. "I need to talk to you."

My heart skipped. Then dropped.

But I nodded.

Because if Sidney wanted to talk, I was going to listen. Even if she was about to say what my heart dreaded.

We walked in silence.

The path curved gently around the castle gardens, the sounds of music and laughter fading behind us as we stepped farther from the party.

The night was cool but comfortable, unusual for a summer night in Florida.

We passed the rose trellis, then the courtyard fountain. All of it washed in golden light, as if the entire park had been repainted just for tonight.

A bridge arched over the narrow stream that ran beneath the castle, its surface shimmering with the reflection of string lights from above. The water shone like liquid starlight.

Sidney stopped halfway across the bridge and leaned against the railing, her hands resting lightly on the stone.

Her expression softened as I stepped beside her.

"There's something I need to tell you," she said, her voice low.

I turned toward her, giving her the space she needed.

"I wanted to tell you earlier," she said, staring out over the water. "But I didn't know how."

I nodded once.

"Whatever it is... I'm listening."

And I meant it.

Even if part of me was already bracing for what might come next.

"Chris offered me a full-time job," she said.

For a second, one blissfully naïve second, my heart soared.

A job. Here. With me.

But then the rest of it hit me, the part she hadn't said.

She hadn't said *yes*.

I swallowed hard, forcing down the surge of emotion clawing at my throat. My heart was hammering, but I kept my voice steady. "That's... amazing."

She didn't answer right away.

The silence stretched.

"Is that... a good thing?"

She turned, her gaze drifting out toward the water. The lights along the shore shimmered and danced across the surface, stars scattered above like a thousand quiet witnesses.

Then, after a beat that felt like an eternity, she nodded. Just once. Firm.

"Yeah," she whispered. "I think it is."

The world seemed to hold its breath with her words, the breeze stalling midair as if waiting too.

Sidney turned toward me and drew in a slow, shaky breath.

I'm not ready to say goodbye," she whispered. "Not to this place. Not to you."

I smiled and turned to her. "Good. Because I'm not ready to say goodbye to you."

And then—

"Cameron... I love you."

Everything froze.

The lights, the music, the ripple of water nearby, it all blurred into the background.

She loved me.

She loved me.

What remained of the walls I'd spent so long building crumbled, piece by piece, from those three little words.

I closed the distance between us in two quick strides.

My hands found her waist as I pulled her in. I held her eyes for a moment before I lowered my lips to hers.

She melted against me, and the world slipped away.

There were no timelines. No doubts.

No future waiting to tear us apart.

There was just us and a sky full of stars.

When we finally pulled apart, her eyes were still closed.

"I was supposed to say it first," I let out a breath and spoke, my voice barely above a whisper, "I've loved you for longer than you think."

Her eyes fluttered open. A smile tugged at the corners of her lips. "When?"

My lips curved into a smirk as I remembered the first time I saw her. "Orientation day, of course."

She scoffed. "You couldn't have known then."

"Okay, fine," I smirked. "The day I took your picture in front of the castle."

She rolled her eyes and shook her head, still grinning. "Still too soon."

I laughed, wrapping my arms a little tighter around her. "You're right. It wasn't just one moment."

She lifted an eyebrow at me like she wasn't convinced, so I continued on.

"There were thousands. Thousands of little things that led to this. The way you talk with your hands when you're nervous. The way you always try to fix things that aren't even your fault. The way you light up when you get an idea and then immediately forget what you were doing."

"Cameron..."

"And now?" I said, my voice thick with everything I felt. "Now I'm hopelessly, madly, crazy in love with you."

I kissed her, slow and sweet, and repeated the words one at a time.

"Hopelessly."

Another kiss.

"Madly."

One more, a little deeper.

"Crazy."

And then the last one.

"In love with you."

I drew back just enough to look into her eyes. There was a light in them, something so bright, so alive, it could have outshone any storybook princess.

And I knew in my heart, if I ever met one, she wouldn't hold a candle to Sidney Webber.

I held out a hand to her.

"Now..." I said, my voice light but threaded with everything I felt, "Come with me, Princess. All I want is to dance with my girl at the ball."

She smacked me playfully. "Wow, you really are a fairytale prince. Did you steal that line from Prince Peter?"

"Nope," I said with a grin. "That's all me. So what do you say, Carolina? Want to make tonight our fairytale?"

Without a second of hesitation, she slipped her hand into mine.

"Lead the way."

Chapter Forty-One

Sidney

THE CASTLE BALLROOM LOOKED like it had been pulled straight from the pages of a fairytale.

Fairy lights shimmered along the rafters like tiny stars scattered across a velvet sky. A soft, familiar melody floated through the air, the kind of instrumental music only Fantasy World could perfect. On the dance floor, employees became the heroes of their own stories, spinning in gowns and sweeping across the floor in sharp suits, until the whole room felt like a storybook come to life.

Near the entrance, a welcome table sparkled with party favors and name cards tied with satin ribbons.

Soft projections of floating lanterns drifted across the walls, as if the whole room had been lightly enchanted.

It was pure magic.

Cameron's hand stayed warm in mine as we wandered deeper inside. We paused for a picture in front of a castle backdrop, the fabric shimmering under the lights.

When they showed us the proof, Cameron turned to me with a grin.

"Told you we'd fit right into a fairytale."

I laughed. "You never said that."

"Sure I did, Carolina," he said, flashing that maddeningly confident smile. "You just weren't paying attention."

I rolled my eyes. "You know you're going to have to stop calling me that, right? I'm officially a Florida girl now."

He shook his head, unbothered. "Nope. You'll always be Carolina to me."

And deep down, I didn't want him to stop.

North Carolina would always be a part of me, where I came from, the place that shaped me.

But Florida was something different.

Florida was where I chose to be.

The music slowed, shifting into a romantic song. Cameron held out his hand, and I slipped mine into his.

He spun me out in an arc before bringing me back in and holding me close to his chest.

I let out a breath of laughter. "Has anyone ever told you that you're a really good dancer?"

He smirked. "I'm literally just doing the stage routine."

"Well, it's impressive," I said, smiling up at him.

His hand never once left my waist. It felt like the rest of the room simply fell away until it was just us, two people suspended in a moment too perfect to be anything but magic.

And then it hit me, every twist of fate, every choice, every dream, it had all led to this.

All because a five-year-old girl once sat in front of a TV and fell in love with a commercial.

Every step, every stumble, had led me to him. To *us*.

It hadn't been perfect. We'd made mistakes. Said things we shouldn't have. Pushed each other away when we were scared.

But somehow, we'd still found our way back. Every wrong turn had led to this moment, and I wouldn't trade a single one of them.

Because here, in his arms, was the best place I'd ever been.

I let my eyes drift closed and rested my head against his chest, the steady rhythm of his heartbeat grounding me.

The music carried us, and I tried to memorize everything: the feel of his arms around me, the warmth of the room, the way the night seemed to sparkle with magic.

This dance. This man. This summer.

I didn't want to forget a single second of it.

We stayed wrapped up in that moment for a while, but by the third slow song, Cameron leaned down and murmured something about raiding the dessert cart and who was I to object?

Across the room, Westley and Porter had fully commandeered the refreshment table, acting like self-appointed kings of carbs and sparkling juice.

Somehow, and honestly, I didn't even want to know how, they'd convinced the bartender to ditch the punch cups and serve their sparkling juice in fancy crystal goblets.

Every few minutes, they clinked them together with grand, sweeping toasts to things like "artistic vision" and "theatrical integrity," drawing amused looks from everyone around them.

Between their dramatic toasts, they were racing through cupcakes like it was a competition to see who could hit frosting-induced regret first.

Porter had also been offered a permanent job at Fantasy World. At least that was another friend we wouldn't have to say goodbye to.

Meanwhile, Willow had danced with at least three different guys, each one more awkward and hopelessly starry-eyed than the last.

She moved like she was made for nights like this, graceful, golden, and absolutely untouchable.

I caught Westley watching her more than once.

He tried to play it cool, leaning against the punch table, tossing out sarcastic comments about the playlist, sipping from his goblet like he couldn't be less impressed. But every time Willow laughed a little too brightly at someone else's joke, he would glare in their direction. I almost expected him to go over there and stake his claim.

Porter drifted away from his dessert kingdom now and then just long enough to argue with Ridley.

They were currently locked in argument number three over by the gift table.

The first had been about how many napkins a single person was entitled to.

The second had involved the "proper Feng Shui" of cupcake arrangements.

This one had escalated into a full-on debate about whether marshmallows counted as a legitimate dessert topping or a criminal offense against buffet standards.

I didn't catch who won. Probably no one, though both likely claimed victory.

And in the quietest corner of the ballroom, I spotted Renee.

She was curled into the soft glow of fairy lights, sitting close to Beckett, the sweet, shy maintenance guy who I'd seen around the green room from time to time. They were laughing over something on his phone, heads nearly touching.

I smiled.

This night wasn't just for Cameron and me.

It was for *all* of us.

A final bow. A last dance. A celebration of how far we'd come, and the strange, beautiful little family we'd built along the way.

All these people I never expected to love, somehow, they had become my home. They taught me that family isn't always the one you're born into. That magic is real if you're willing to believe in it. And that sometimes, the most extraordinary things find you when you're not even looking.

I still didn't have every answer about the future.

Not yet.

Maybe not ever.

But there was one thing I knew for sure, I wanted *this*.

Him.

Them.

Whatever life we built together, whatever it ended up looking like...

I wanted it.

The music shifted to something soft and dreamy, as if even the playlist understood this was the last dance.

Cameron drew me close, his hands settling lightly at my waist, mine finding their way to his shoulders without a second thought.

He leaned in until his forehead rested against mine.

"I still can't believe you're finally mine," he whispered.

I smiled, tracing my thumb along the edge of his collar.

"I was always yours," I said. "You just had to wait for me to catch up."

His smile deepened, and then he kissed me.

It wasn't like the first time, full of uncertainty. It wasn't like the second, full of relief.

This kiss was something entirely.

This wasn't the perfect fairytale.

It was something better.

It was ours.

Epilogue

BEFORE THE GATES OPENED, before the music started and the crowds spilled in with their maps and wide-eyed wonder, Fantasy World belonged to us.

The crew members.

To the ones who kept the magic alive.

Morning was quiet, steeped in soft gold. The castle glowed in the early light, as if dipped in sunrise. Its reflection shimmered across the still moat. The scent of churros already hung in the air, warm cinnamon curling through the lingering morning breeze.

This was my favorite part.

Before the shows. Before the noise. Before everything spun into motion.

Just me, my coffee, and this stolen moment of stillness.

This had become my ritual. My rhythm. My place.

A little moment of peace before the fairytale began again.

I paused at the base of the castle steps, lifting my cup in a lazy toast to the glowing spires above.

I still couldn't believe this was real.

That I was here. That *this,* a place I'd only meant to pass through, had become home.

A year ago, I was just an intern.

Unsure.

Still second-guessing every step I took, wondering if I was good enough to be here, or good enough *anywhere.*

I'd come to Fantasy World hoping to escape the mess I left behind, only to walk straight into another one, just with more glitter and stage cues.

And yet... somehow, in the middle of all the chaos and costume changes, I found something I didn't know I was looking for.

A place where I fit.

A place where I *belonged.*

I'm not just a fill in anymore. Not just a backup plan or an understudy waiting in the wings.

I'm a full-time crew member now. A trainer. A leader on the entertainment team. I help shape the stories we tell here, help cast new heroes and teach them how to find their light. I walk people through their first steps on stage, their first mic checks, their first moments of believing maybe they were meant for magic, too.

And yeah, I still throw on the Primrose dress when someone calls out.

It wasn't just my life that had changed this past year.

Cameron and his mom were closer than I ever expected they could be. It started with one dinner—nervous, quiet, a little stiff. But now? They talk every week. She visits often, usually with a suitcase full of baked goods and aggressively embroidered "Bless This Mess" dish towels.

Sometimes I go with him when he joins her for dinner on Saturday nights. She always sets a second place at the table, always pretends not to tear up when she hugs me goodbye. They're rebuilding something they both thought they'd lost, and I get to watch it happen in real time, one heart-softening conversation at a time.

And my mom?

She's visited three times. Four if you count the surprise visit that ended with her falling in love with churro-flavored popcorn and buying an entire Princess Primrose gift set.

She told me the last time she was here that she finally understood what I saw in this place.

She's even flirting with the idea of moving closer, though I think the idea is less about the magic of Fantasy World and more about a certain someone in Entertainment.

Chris.

Yes, *that* Chris.

The one who once barked show cues like they were battle commands now turns red anytime my mom walks into a room. The last time she visited, I caught them sharing a funnel cake and laughing about making rehearsal blooper reels.

I didn't say anything.

But I might've snapped a picture.

Just in case they ever needed a fairytale origin story of their own.

I turned the corner near the east archway, coffee in hand, mind already running through the show schedule and costume checks—

And ran straight into Cameron.

Like, *straight* into him.

He caught me with the same ease he always did, steadying my coffee with one hand and sliding the other to my waist like it was second nature.

"Well, well," he said, flashing that ridiculous grin. "You trying to run me over, Carolina?"

I narrowed my eyes over the rim of my cup. "If I were, you wouldn't have seen it coming."

"Bold words from someone wielding a travel mug as a weapon."

I took a sip, smirking. "Some would say walking blindly around a corner is a workplace hazard."

He gave me a dramatic sigh. "You've been hanging out with Porter too much. You're getting *spicy.*"

Before I could fire back, he pulled me into a lazy side hug, the kind that wasn't about grand gestures or big endings.

I leaned in, my head resting against his shoulder.

Then he threaded his fingers through mine, and we walked hand in hand toward the castle.

We reached the castle stage just as the new cast was starting their morning rehearsal.

He bumped my shoulder gently. "Proud of yourself yet?"

I didn't answer right away.

I just watched one of the new girls, wide-eyed and fumbling through a monologue, laugh off her mistake and try again.

And I felt it.

That slow, warm swell in my chest.

"I think I am."

Cameron turned to me, a familiar sparkle in his eyes.

Then, without a word, he caught my hand and spun me right there in Kingdom Square. Just like our first dance.

I laughed, the sound tumbling out as I twirled. It made me dizzy in the best way.

I landed against his chest, his arms steady around me.

"Guess this is our real fairytale ending, huh?" he said, voice low and smiling.

I leaned in, resting my forehead against his. "Nope."

He gasped, dramatically, pulling back. "No? What do you mean *no?*"

Before I could answer, his hands darted to my waist, fingers finding the exact spot that always made me yelp.

"Take it back," he teased, tickling mercilessly.

I shrieked and twisted away, laughing too hard to form a sentence.

"Cameron, stop!" I gasped between giggles, trying to squirm out of his grasp.

But he only grinned wider. "Not until you admit it's the perfect ending."

Still laughing, I ducked out of his reach and spun around, catching him off guard.

Then, I looped my arms around his neck, breathless and smiling.

"This isn't our ending," I whispered. "It's only the beginning."

His smirk softened, gaze locking on mine.

"Fine. You win."

For a beat, neither of us moved. The world seemed to slow around us, Kingdom Square glowing in the early light, the faint sounds of the park waking up in the distance.

Cameron brushed a loose strand of hair behind my ear, his touch gentle, lingering. "Ready to see where this story goes, Carolina?" he asked, voice low, full of promise.

I smiled, heart full, certain. "With you? Always."

Hand in hand, we turned toward the castle.

It was the first page of something new.

And the best stories?

They were the ones still waiting to be told.

Acknowledgements

Writing a book is a winding road. One filled with moments of joy, doubt, discovery, and more coffee than I care to admit. I wouldn't have reached the finish line without the people who walked this path with me.

To my husband, thank you for being my greatest supporter and my steady place to land. You believed in me through every late-night writing sprint, every moment of self-doubt, and every chapter I wondered if I could finish. I'm endlessly grateful for your love, patience, and encouragement.

To my three amazing kids, thank you for the joy and inspiration you bring to my life every single day. You remind me to dream big, laugh often, and never take myself too seriously. I hope you always chase your dreams and believe in magic.

To my family, your patience, kindness, and unwavering support gave me the space to dream and the courage to chase it. I'm so thankful for each of you.

To my fellow writers, you inspire me daily with your creativity and perseverance. I'm honored to be part of this community.

And finally, to you, the reader. Thank you for opening this book and stepping into this world with me. Stories live because of readers like you, and I'm endlessly thankful for every page you turn.

www.ingramcontent.com/pod-product-compliance
Lightning Source LLC
Chambersburg PA
CBHW021501110726
47899CB00001BA/240